CAMBALACHE

a novel by

MIKE MITCHELL

This work is completely fictional, but the premise could be just around the corner. The nation-state is a recent human invention. As an institution, it is showing some wear & tear, like the battle flags that so many have carried into conflict on the nation-state's behalf. It is quite possible that one of these tattered nation-states could become the next world power-broker if they were to be the first to harness the secrets of fusion energy. This novel considers these topics and the ensuing challenges. The human infatuation with power, in the form of energy and governance, are as real and accurate as the science and history offered in this novel.

Byblos Press
Newark, Delaware

ISBN13: 978-0-9990111-0-2

Printed in the United States of America
First Edition
Cover artwork by Raul Alonso, design and layout by Kent Bingham
More by this author at *www.mike-mitchell.com*

BYBLOS
p r e s s

PROLOGUE

THERE IS A COUNTRY AT the extreme end of the world that is a mystery to most, even to those fortunate enough to have visited this enigmatic place. Words like Pampas, Patagonia, Gaucho, Iguazu, and Tierra del Fuego stimulate romantic and adventurous imaginations. Ushuaia, located on Tierra del Fuego, nicknamed the "End of the World," is the southernmost town on the globe. Leaving whales, penguins, and glaciers to the south, Buenos Aires, 3,000 kilometers to the north, is still the southernmost capital city on earth with over 10 million inhabitants. Traveling another 2,000 kilometers farther north, passing the tropical borders of Uruguay, Brazil, and Paraguay, we can ride the highest railroad in the world, ending in the Andean Altiplano at 14,000 feet near the Bolivian border. Argentina, with the highest and lowest points and the hottest and coldest temperatures in South America, is a country of contrast; of startling human progress and tragic reversals. A country of extremes, Argentina has also been the beginning for the world in many ways, the obverse of what we think we know. And when it leads out, it does so with the flair and energy of a tango.

Argentina is full of surprises, unsolved mysteries, and rivaled by only a handful of countries in its firsts. Did you know that a large area of Spanish California was once part of Argentina? In 1818, the Argentine corsair Hippolyte Bouchard attacked Monterey, California. After an hour of combat, Bouchard raised his nation's flag over the city and claimed the peninsula for Argentina. He also claimed what is now part of Southern California when his forces subdued San Juan Capistrano. This book of heroes and villains includes a fictitious Hippolyte Bouchard of modern times. He does not claim California, but like a true Argentine, audaciously attacks traditional mindsets and plants his flag, changing the entire world with an Argentine invention that was once one of the world's favorite examples of extreme failure.

CHAPTER 1

Saltar la Ficha
Literal Translation: Jump the Token

Marisa's Explanation: Many Porteños use public transportation to get around Buenos Aires. Bypassing payment by jumping the turnstile is said to highlight poor character. My father suggested the saying was not always negative, but only meant to describe an event or action that revealed true intentions and came from chess or checkers—**Revealing Your Next Move or Your Strategy for Winning the Game.** You be the judge.

H E STOOD AS A SHIP's captain, the first winds of the coming storm only lightly tussling his well-groomed black hair like a father passing by his son offering a masculine show of affection. President Ernesto Starhemberg brushed his hair back in place with his right hand as a confident acknowledgment, almost a salute, to the bellicose clouds. Beneath his feet, Habsburg Rock resolutely provided the foundation and heraldry for the message that he would share with his fellow Argentine citizens. The metaphor was not missed by anyone in the crowd of fifty people gathered around the President. They were all wrong, however, even those closest to him. Just beyond the Rock, the postcard town of San Carlos de Bariloche and the lapis lazuli colored Nahuel Huapi Lake, complete with fine strips of gold created by the wind and sun, filled the Alpine-esque valley nearly a thousand feet below. Marisa had told James that the last time an Argentine president had visited here in the company of a North American was when President Dwight D. Eisenhower visited in 1960 as a guest of President Arturo Frondizi. James chuckled to himself that the President's sister would so easily place him and Eisenhower in the same basket as just two North Americans.

James watched the camera crew complete their final tests and marveled that he was even here at this moment in history. His deepening relationship with Marisa Starhemberg, the majestic backdrop of the Andes Mountain Range, the crisp air smelling slightly of pine and expectation, even the visionary leadership of President Starhemberg and his lieutenants that had taken Argentina from a debt-burdened country to once again one of the wealthiest countries in the world, did not compare with the message that would soon be echoed in every corner of the planet. A ray of light pulled his gaze from the scurrying crew skyward to the billowing cumulonimbus clouds that threatened rain within the hour. Would the President's message bring destructive dark clouds as Marisa predicted, or would his words pierce the fear, doubt, and status quo security like this sword of sunshine?

James felt Marisa move close to his side as her brother turned to the cameras with a casual confidence and authenticity that had propelled him from Governor of Rio Negro Provence to national prominence in Buenos Aires. He wore a tailor-made dark blue suit, but his six-foot lean frame and soft smile made him look like an everyman—fitting in a board room with leaders of industry, or in the local Peronista union building. Having completed three years and three months of his first four-year term, President Starhemberg had allowed even his staff to believe this speech would mark the official launch of his reelection campaign. Little did most of the people gathered here, let alone the Argentine people or the world and its leaders, know the real subject of his speech.

"The sun is shining, but I am shivering," Marisa whispered in James's ear.

James took his cue and put his left arm around her. He could feel the tenseness of her body as she moved closer to him. "He was born for this moment, Marisa, and you know that better than anyone else," James said, not caring who heard his general statement.

"Yes, but, you know what I mean. I know him better because he is the only family I have. I'm already sharing him with thirty million people in Argentina. Now I'm going to have to share him with the world. They won't care the least about Ernesto, just what he represents. Others are going to try to eat him for lunch," Marisa said as she attempted to suppress another shiver.

"Who knows, maybe no one will believe him, and you can continue to live in relative peace and quiet without the rest of the world demanding his attention," James said.

"Right, and that will last about a month until everything becomes very real and Argentina becomes the center of the universe. How did we get here, James? I don't like it. We have worked so hard, but now that we've opened the door and peeked inside, I don't want to move into this new house," Marisa said moving her eyes from James to Ernesto.

On cue, Ernesto turned to his baby sister and winked at her, looking like he didn't have a care in the world. "He is actually enjoying this, isn't he," Marisa noted.

"And why not?" James asked. "He is about to change the world, Marisa. Few people have ever stood at an intersection of history and could play traffic cop with such aplomb. This is about fantastic facts, not farcical fiction. This is like inventing the wheel or discovering fire. It's like my first visit to the Via Flaminia ice cream shop on Avenida del Libertador."

"Because that was our second official date?" Marisa teased.

"Well, that and the inspiring Dulce de Leche ice cream bañado de chocolate," James teased back.

As Marisa turned to punch James in the arm, a member of the camera crew called for silence and announced, "Thirty seconds and we're live, Mr. President!"

Suddenly James wished he were back on that date with Marisa at a quieter and simpler moment. For the hundredth time, James wondered how President Starhemberg handled all this. A president who didn't like to be the center of attention, fascinating. James suspected if the President took a Myers-Briggs test it would peg him as a borderline introvert. He was a person of whom pride had yet to find a chink in his armor. He was without pretense or guile. He was not a politician, but he was a leader. Something the world needed more than what Ernesto was about to unveil to the world. James had kept telling himself he was just a bystander watching all this happen. Not until he walked hand-in-hand with Marisa to this vista did he admit to himself he was involved up to his eyebrows in all this. He was falling in love with the sister of the guy that was about to stop the world's fibrillating heart beat and start it again. Only two months ago a short-term consulting gig had taken him to Argentina, and now here he was, watching the hinges of time open a new era. He suppressed his own shiver and hoped Marisa hadn't felt him quake.

"Five, four, three, two, one!" the camera crew director called. There was a collective intake of breath, and James heard some chirping birds and his heartbeat.

"Good afternoon, my fellow Argentinos," President Ernesto Starhemberg began. "I am talking to you from one of the jewels of our nation, San Carlos de Bariloche, in the beautiful Provence of Rio Negro where I was born and began my service in government."

James knew this was the point in his speech where the country and most gathered here expected him to announce his run for a second term. He held his breath.

"Argentina has long been known in the world as the prodigal son of nations," President Starhemberg continued. James could see the President's strong square jaw flex and his dark brown eyes flash with, what? Anger? Frustration? A dare to anyone who wanted to disagree with him? Instantly his face transformed into a broad smile. "Following World War Two we had nearly $2 billion in foreign capital reserves and possibly the largest domestic gold reserves in the world. Between 1948 and 1952 Argentina beat the United States to become the World Basketball Champions, Mario Fangio was the world's top Grand Prix driver, and Enrique Morea won the Wimbledon Tennis Championships, the first Latin American to do so. Pedro Leopoldo Carrera won the World Billiard Championships. Pascual Perez won the World Boxing Title in Tokyo. Bernardo Houssay won the Noble Prize for Science in Medicine, again the first Latin American to win this prize. Delfo Cabrara won the Gold at the London Olympics in the Marathon. In 1947 the Argentine Air Force was flying the Pulqui, meaning arrow in the Araucana language. This jet aircraft flew at 720 km/hr. It had a service ceiling of 45,000 feet and a range of 900km. With four 20mm cannons, it boasted excellent firepower for the day. In comparison, the United States fielded the F-80 a year later in 1948 and was about equal in capabilities. In June of 1950 the Pulqui II flew. This jet aircraft had a swept wing design, could fly at 1050 km/hr., with a flight duration of 2.2 hours and had four improved 20mm cannons. It was the first true fighter jet from Latin America and only the fifth in the entire world. The Pulqui II was so impressive the Dutch sent a contingency to buy it because they considered it a better option than the British and U.S. designs of the day. This was only the third swept-wing aircraft in the world after the F-86 and the MiG-15 which would have been no match for the Pulqui II."

President Starhemberg took a breath and offered a pained smile to the camera. "So what happened? Why didn't Argentina take its seat at the table of world powers? Why has the world jokingly called us 'the country of the future…and always will be?' It's simple. There is something much more important than resources and riches. It is will. Like the prodigal son, we spent our inheritance in the era of the *Plata Dulce* (sweet money), which was also called *Los Años Locos* (Those Crazy Years). President Juan Peron spent over $600 million to buy the Argentine railroad from the British when it was worth half that. But the money was there, so why manage things too efficiently? When economic times started getting tough, we instituted several austerity packages, but we could never get a handle on our internal government—there was no national will to do so. The first time we could not make our balance of payments was in 1952. We have come to the brink many times since and even tried to pretend we didn't have to pay our debts." President Starhemberg paused, no smile on his face now.

James noticed that the crowd around him was wondering where the President was going with this uncomfortable presentation of their historical dirty laundry. Some were looking around with their mouths open. Others were biting their lips. A few were nodding in agreement.

"It's almost as if we made decisions so we wouldn't have to become a developed nation with the responsibilities this would entail. It is as if we wanted to stay a 'developing nation.' When I began my presidency in 2019, the country was undergoing severe struggles, and for the first time since the Spanish floated up the La Plata River, people were starving. Argentina has been blessed with incredible bounty, raw materials, self-sufficiency in oil, the best and deepest topsoil in the world, brilliant engineers, scientist, writers like Borges, artists like Raul Alonso, musicians like Carlos Gardel, agricultural prowess—we are one of the largest wheat producers in the world, the largest sunflower oil producer in the world, but we just couldn't get our collective act together. So the Pulqui II now sits on a pedestal at the Air Force Museum. Ahead of its time. A beautiful machine and a point of past pride for the prodigal nation. To borrow a term from our countrymen of another era that bravely brought to a close the terrible mal-intentions of the Dirty War of the 1970s and 80s, *Nunca Jamas!* Never again will we turn our back on our destiny. I am here today to announce that six years ago, during my Governorship of this Provence, I directed a reopening of the Huemul Project. As President of Argentina, I accelerated this project."

People were now whispering to each other and ignoring the waving hands of the broadcast director to keep the noise down. It appeared no one remembered their Argentine history lessons. James wondered if the schools even taught any of this. Marisa had told him of the many rumors and incriminating surprises about Argentina, and this area of the country, in particular, going back to World War Two. Ernesto and Marisa were living examples of the reality that some of those rumors were true. Only a quarter century ago, in 1995, when Marisa was one-year-old and Ernesto was nine, Bariloche became the center of shame when several Nazi war criminals were discovered. One was former SS Hauptsturmführer Erich Priebke. Priebke had been the Director of the German School of Bariloche for many years, and Marisa's parents knew him and had no idea of his nefarious background. There were also many rumors that Adolf Hitler and Eva Braun had escaped Germany and had lived a quiet life at one of the estancias near Bariloche, although this last rumor was ridiculous to Marisa. Maybe Elvis, but not a megalomaniac like Hitler, could have lived here undetected. Yet, she could understand the efforts to keep some of the post-war era in the closet of the national psyche.

"Not far from here," President Starhemberg was saying, "on the small island of Huemul in Lake Nahuel Huapi a project began in 1950 to create the world's first fusion reactor. With the help of Austrian Ronald Richter, the project made some headway, but $300 million into the project, it was shut down. I will spare you the details, but I announce today that the Nation of Argentina has successfully harnessed nuclear fusion. What is more, it is essentially a cold fusion process."

James noticed it was dead silent again. He heard the same birds chirping, but his heart was not as noisy. Without looking, he reached down for Marisa's hand and squeezed it.

"I chose this place for this auspicious announcement not only because of its proximity to Huemul Island but also because of the rock I stand upon, the Habsburg Rock. The Habsburgs ruled much of Europe and the new world and then lost their throne. It was almost as if the Viennese decided that they had had enough and would now live more in the moment and enjoy the good life. My family, as you know, had served the Habsburgs for centuries and my grandparents left their homeland of Austria partly in rebellion to that sad transition and partly to escape the German Anschluss which they vehemently opposed. Argentina in some ways has followed that same path—they never ruled an empire, but they lived the good life without the responsibility and little accountability. Now it is our choice to not repeat their history with what has been placed in our hands, but to take on the reins and join the yoke of world leadership. We seek not to replace any present world leaders, but we will take our place at the table that we have avoided in the past."

Many in the small audience were recovering from the shock of the unexpected direction of this speech. These were people who were used to knowing and not being surprised. Yet they spontaneously erupted in genuine and legitimate applause. This group had thought they understood that they were here to add a flavor of support for the President's announcement to run for a second term. They were to be the applause track when that was required and the laugh track when the President told a joke. The President had offered neither. The applause now was unscripted and visceral, having risen from the heart and souls of each person, not from the political animals they thought they were. James looked around and joined in the applause while wondering how the rest of the world was reacting.

President Starhemberg raised his hands for quiet. The audience eventually complied. "You may or may not be aware that Argentina is the world's largest producer and exporter of heavy water, at our production facility at Arroyito in Neuquén Province next door. We produce over 200 tons of heavy water per year, most of it exported to Canada, Germany, and the United States. What you may not know is, the scientific name for heavy water is deuterium oxide, and it is the fuel used in fusion. The only by-products are helium and," he paused then continued, "unlimited clean energy. Why is this so important to Argentina and the world? First for Argentina: our fusion system, which we call with some tongue-in-cheek humor *Cambalache*, is not only at least a decade in front of any other system we are aware of, but it is the only "cold fusion" system in the world. We sit alone at that table and understand the responsibility that brings. And for the world? The global energy market spends about $14 trillion a year. In our system, the deuterium extracted from 10 gallons of water would weigh about one-tenth of an ounce and could supply enough electricity to last a high-energy consumer about 15 years at a fraction of the dollar cost and without the harmful effects to our environment. This, of course, changes the global energy system and economy. We are well aware this announcement, far from being applauded in all corners of the world, is already causing market tremors, and the ripple effect of the potential changes could take decades to overcome. To that end, we will work with global leaders, nations, and energy multinationals, to mitigate the baggage and unintended consequences of this miraculous opportunity for the world. I have assigned a trusted associate, someone whose family my family has worked with for over half a millennium, Otto von Habsburg, to oversee the gradual adjustment of the global markets and in particular the energy sector. At this time we have no plans to simply post our capabilities on the Internet for everyone to copy. That might solve some immediate problems, but it would be disastrous both in the short-term and mid-term to millions of innocents across the globe. As I said earlier, we are not looking to cash in on yet another blessing without the responsibility. We will stand tall, even if that makes us a short-term target as well as a long-term benefactor. This is our destiny, and mark my word, it will be our legacy. The prodigal son has returned, and in this case, we have brought our own fatted calf, direct from the Argentine Pampas. And in this the world must agree, we raise the best beef in the world!"

For a brief moment, the crowd stood spellbound, still digesting what their president had just shared with the world. James and Marisa looked around, unsure what was happening. Slowly, a few began to cry. Some began to sing the Himno Nacional:

Hear, mortals, the sacred cry:
"Freedom! Freedom! Freedom!"
Hear the sound of broken chains
See noble equality enthroned…

As Marisa added her voice to the singing, James held his smile while his mind was wondering what was now happening at 1600 Pennsylvania Avenue, 10 Downing Street, 24 Sussex Drive, Qasr Malik Abdullah bin Abdulaziz, Schloss Bellevue,

Zavidovo, and boardrooms from New York City, Houston and Dallas to The Hague and Dhahran.

Without James realizing it, President Ernesto Starhemberg had escaped the center of attention and was standing in front of him, smiling. "You are the only person here who is not here. A peso for your pensamientos, your thoughts," the President said. He was guiding James with his left arm away from the television camera and the crowd who was still singing. Marisa didn't attempt to follow them. When they were a few meters away from the noise, he asked again, "Well?"

"Outstanding speech, sir," James said trying to gather his thoughts.

"Right, thanks. What are you really thinking?" he asked, his eyes boring into James, the smile nearly gone.

"It really was a great speech," James repeated. "I had no idea about most of the things you listed concerning Argentina's glorious past. But what was going through my mind was the bee's nest you just disturbed."

"Disturbed? I think I covered myself in honey and then took a bat to the hive. It might be wise to not stand too close," President Starhemberg said. He was smiling again.

"If there is anything I can do, let me know, Mr. President. I knew more or less what you were going to say and I think the work Marisa and I have done takes you safely a few steps down the road, but hearing it pronounced out loud was an entirely different thing. Everyone here is thinking about free energy and national pride. I am thinking about bankruptcies, shifts in the regional and the global balance of power, broken alliances, new alliances with strange bedfellows, possible wars, and honestly, your safety," James said finally finding the words to express his thoughts.

"And there's more. That's why I wanted to talk to you, James. There is something I need you to do."

JOAB stood in the small crowd, singing the Himno Nacional, but thinking of another, higher loyalty. It was starting all over again as predicted. This would have to be reported, immediately, but, of course, now the whole world knew. Procrastinating was no longer an option, now that their fears were fully confirmed. It was time for brutal and lasting action.

CHAPTER 2

Ponerse la Camiseta
Literal Translation: Put on the T-shirt

Marisa's Explanation: In sports-obsessed Argentina, fútbol, basketball, polo are often defined by the team jerseys. Wearing a Boca Juniors soccer jersey tells the world whose team you are on. Suggesting a person put on a jersey is a way of saying **Be a Team Player.**

THE RAINS DID COME TO Bariloche and the presidential party decided to stay the night. Unlike what James expected of the president of many countries, Argentina was not a slave to its schedule. Whether or not that was symbolic of some chasm Argentina still had to cross to meet the high bar demanded of a world leader would be for others to decide. President Starhemberg's secretary had warned the presidential party they might spend the night, so James wasn't surprised. He had only once visited Patagonia. "Had that been only two weeks ago?" he asked himself. That visit had lasted only a few hours, and he saw almost nothing of what the President had called a national gem, Bariloche. The main group, including the President and his sister, were transported away from the town to the Llao Llao Hotel and Resort. James was driven to another location, high up the hill from the lake and town. His driver, dispatched from the President's cadre, explained that he would spend the night at a little known Argentine Air Force resort that provided comfortable but not ostentatious cabañas. These cabins were modern, and each one appeared to have a perfect view of the lake. There were no restaurants or any buildings for social gatherings that James could see. "A very private place inhabited by vacationing military officers who knew how to keep secrets," James told himself. "The perfect location for the errand President Starhemberg asked me to take on."

"Familia Weiss, a local restaurant, will cater your dinner," the driver explained as he dropped James' small bag in the living room. "It's not the trendiest restaurant in town, but it is excellent and one of the oldest. It was selected because President Starhemberg knows the family and their wild boar is a favorite of your dinner guest." The driver turned to leave and then stopped at the door. "I am going to get our friend now, but I won't return with him until nine this evening. A small merienda will be delivered to you in about an hour. I will return after dinner, about midnight, to take your guest back to his hotel. I will then pick you up at seven tomorrow morning to take you to the President's aircraft for the return to Buenos Aires. If you have any questions or concerns, here is my number." He handed James a white business card with a number on it. No name, no title. Just a number. James took it and thanked him.

After walking around the cabin and admiring the view, James stretched out on the couch and started to read an old copy of *Apertura*, one of the only Argentine magazines on the coffee table that he recognized.

"James, James," the voice said in soft tones. James felt a nudge and then he smelled an intoxicating aroma of…-cheese and burnt cinnamon? He opened his eyes and nearly drown in the aqua blue eyes of Marisa Starhemberg that were only inches away.

"Nice dream I'm having," James said scooting his lower torso over to make room for Marisa to sit.

"I personally delivered your merienda," Marisa said. "No more napping. Our snack is on the veranda. Let's eat before it gets cold."

James pulled himself up to a sitting position, stifled a yawn and said, "The mountain air is so relaxing. I can't believe I fell asleep."

"We are only at about a thousand meters," Marisa said. "We are at the foot of the mountains, but not up in the mountains. You fell asleep because you are either a lazy North American or you are finally becoming acclimated to the bio-cycle God intended his children—and exemplified to perfection by my countrymen—to live." James watched Marisa walk to the deck and wondered if the combination of blue eyes and black hair was common. Marisa was anything but common. She had the same slender frame as her brother, but that is where their similarities stopped. Marisa had thick eyebrows and Ernesto had thinner eyebrows. Ernesto had an almost square face and a strong jaw. Marisa had a rounder face and a larger mouth framed by fuller cheeks. She wore her hair short which seemed to highlight her slender neck that balanced perfectly with her slender nose. She was also about five inches shorter than her brother. And that was just the physical characteristics. Marisa worried. Ernesto was confident. Marisa smoldered when she was upset and was a Chinese fireworks display when she was really angry. James had never seen Ernesto angry. Marisa was passionate about life and every little thing she encountered but didn't always see the details. Ernesto noticed all the details and was so even-keeled that an outsider could legitimately wonder if anything excited him. He almost always looked happy, but never effervescent. Ernesto had used the word *pispirante* to describe Marisa. James wasn't sure of the exact English definition, but the onomato-poeia fit her.

James joined Marisa outside and saw a fondue pot with six or seven plates of fruit, vegetables, bread, and meats. Next to a bottle of sparkling water was a box of Fenoglio chocolates. "So this is an afternoon snack?" James asked. "Maybe merienda really means feast."

"I thought you deserved something more filling since lunch was just finger foods after the speech. You probably won't get to dinner until ten, so let's enjoy. Then maybe we can take a walk before I need to get back to Llao Llao."

"How did you get here anyway?" James asked just now realiz-ing she was staying about 25 kilometers away. He wanted to ask why she made the effort, but wasn't sure it was the right time to talk about their relationship, or even if this was a relationship.

"I borrowed a car and drove here," Marisa said. "Ernesto thought it best I go with him to the hotel since all eyes would be on him now. Since I am his only living relative, people seeing me leave with you would get mouths flapping and you would not have the privacy you need and deserve. If I drove here with some official entourage, that would be noticed too. So I came solo, much to the complaints of Ernesto's security people. Vangelina almost demanded she come with me."

"Thanks for going to so much trouble to make sure I get fed," James said. Perhaps it was just that simple. Someone had assigned her as his keeper. Maybe they had become friends. All he was certain of was he got hired for a short-term Cultural Risk consulting assignment for KPMG here in Argentina. He began helping the Argentine petroleum industry in building some new bridges with the United States market. The costs of petroleum skyrocketing and the new Argentine oil and gas discoveries left Argentina sorting out the best new markets. Through some curious circumstances, he met President Starhemberg and then the President's sister, Marisa. His KPMG contract only lasted a month when President Starhemberg tagged him to work on a small team preparing Cambalache for global public consumption. He had a two-week vacation plan to visit Iguazu Falls and Mendoza that he canceled, but what he got in return was irreplaceable. He never ventured out of Buenos Aires, except for one brief day trip. His monthly salary was for nearly the same amount of money as the original six-month contract. At first, James thought the big prize was working on such a historical project as Cambalache. Now he was beginning to believe that the truly irreplaceable experience of the past month was getting to know Marisa.

"Do you think that is why I came here, to feed you?" Marisa asked. "James, you and I are a team, the last line of defense to protect my brother. We have worked together for what, three weeks? You should know by now you are considered a trusted member of our inside squad."

"Inside squad?" James asked.

"The private club, the fifth rib," Marisa said.

"Now you have me curious," James said as he placed a small cube of bread drenched in cheese in his mouth.

"Curious, about what? Being on the team?" Marisa asked.

"I think I know the team, but what is this fifth rib thing?" James asked. "Sounds like dinner."

"When God took a rib from Adam to create woman, he took the fifth rib, the one closest to Adam's heart. It is also the rib that protects the heart. Ernesto has quite a few close advisors and most are very trustworthy. They are still skin-deep counselors. They are willing to protect him from the cold and the odd political virus, maybe even take a flesh wound for him because they believe in what he is doing and in his broader vision, but they are soft flesh," Marisa said with a swish of her hand. "They are not solid bone. They do not believe *in* Ernesto, and they would never stand between him and a sharp spear."

"I can see that you would take your place, err, at the fifth rib," James said, "but why do you put me in that intimate place? As you said, we have only known each other for about a month."

"Ernesto and I just know. Admittedly, Ernesto knew before I did," Marisa said with a blushed smile. "You may need some time to discover that for yourself, but it is your fate, accept it, my clueless and sleepy gringo."

James did not attempt to pursue that subject any further. He set that topic right next to his relationship with Marisa on a shelf in the closet marked "Too Hard/Too Scary." They enjoyed the afternoon and never did make it on a walk. Marisa left as the sun approached the horizon. James had several hours yet before his next visitor. He took his clothes off and did calisthenics for about an hour, showered and changed into the other pants and shirt he brought with him and waited, unsure what the evening would bring.

Fifteen minutes before he expected his dinner guest, he heard a knock at the door. There was no peephole, and he couldn't see anything from the only side window. He opened the door and found himself face to face with an heir to the Habsburg throne. James hadn't been sure what to expect, but the man in front of him looked pretty much like just another human being. He was taller than James, maybe a little over six feet. With narrow eyes, a broad forehead and a dimpled chin. Mr. Habsburg—'is that what I call him?' James wondered—looked exotic. His large frame held ample flesh, but he wasn't pudgy. Wearing a double-breasted suit, but no tie, he looked like a million bucks.

"Welcome, sir," James said. "Please come in." As James stepped aside to let his guest enter, the driver who James had met earlier in the day escorted two young ladies up the walkway with the food for the evening. The women looked at no one and were gone in less than two minutes. The driver watched them closely, and when they were done he made eye contact with Mr. Habsburg, bowed slightly and departed without a word.

Not sure what to do next, James said, "I am at your service, sir," and waited.

Either Mr. Habsburg wasn't sure what to do, which seemed doubtful, or he was studying James. Silence didn't bother James, so he walked to the couch, sat down, and waited. As soon as Mr. Habsburg saw that he did not intimidate James he smiled and sat in the overstuffed chair facing the couch.

"Tell me, Mr. Nathaniels," Habsburg began, "do you know why we are here?"

"Something about a fifth rib," James said.

"I'm sorry?" Habsburg asked, surprised at the nonsensical answer.

"Something Marisa Starhemberg said," James explained. "I am here because President Starhemberg invited me to meet with you. I am on contract to the President to support cultural and political risk issues in the rollout of Cambalache, to the world. He said you would explain the particulars of why we are having this meeting."

"So, you are on contract to the President," Habsburg said. "I see. I was led to believe you were more than an employee. Did he explain who I am and how I fit into the, the Cambalache equation?"

"Yes, he explained that you are Mr. Otto von Habsburg. Your grandfather was also named Otto von Habsburg, the last Crown Prince of the Austro-Hungarian Empire. President Ernesto Starhemberg's grandfather was Ernst Rüdiger Camillo Starhemberg, Austrian nationalist and monarchist who believed only the Habsburgs could save Austria from the German Anschluss just prior to World War Two."

"Excellent, Mr. Nathaniels," Habsburg said. "The Starhembergs and the Habsburgs have been working in tandem for the better good of a large part of Europe for nearly 700 years. Ernst Rüdiger Starhemberg, the President's grandfather, was also a prince and the Vice-Chancellor of Austria, by the way. The tables are somewhat turned in this case, with a Habsburg in the supporting role to the Starhembergs. I am honored and humbled to be involved at all, frankly. We decided it best that I not attend the President's speech in person, but I watched it from my hotel room here in town. Yes, I have been asked to oversee the gradual adjustment of the global markets, and in particular, the energy sector as Cambalache takes center stage in the global energy sector, but I have another stewardship as well."

When Mr. Habsburg did not continue, James said, "I am sorry you were led to believe I was more than who I am. That being said, what can I do to help with your various duties?"

"Let's enjoy the dinner before it gets cold," Habsburg said. "I do hope they ordered the wild boar." The quiet young ladies that had been supervised by the driver had set two plates, and James and Otto von Habsburg served themselves from several selections of food in the center of the table. Habsburg served himself ample portions. James selected much smaller amounts because he still felt full from the late lunch. James waited to be spoken to and focused on the wild boar, spätzle, warm spinach salad with a bacon vinaigrette dressing, and warm dark bread with a unique tart jam. "It's gooseberry jam," Habsburg said. "It's another favorite of mine. This isn't Vienna, but it has its amenities."

"You are from Vienna?" James asked, trying to engage in some conversation.

"After World War One there was a sort of Habsburg diaspora," Habsburg answered between bites. "Our family is scattered across Europe and America. I have a small flat in Vienna, but I live in Budapest. I am considering establishing a residence here in Argentina as well. What are your thoughts, um, may I call you James?"

"Please, sir, call me James," he said, surprised at the request for his views. "I apologize for not being more knowledgeable in these matters, but is there an appropriate title I should use to address you?" James asked to buy time to consider the more important question.

"My grandfather was the last royal, James," Habsburg said with a smile. His abdication in 1961 closed some doors and opened many others. I am just a simple businessman. You can call me Otto, or if you prefer, I have some American friends that call me Oats for some unexplained reason. I promise to come when called, whichever you use."

"Americans feel some odd freedom to rename just about everything, often in an irreverent way. It is sometimes an embarrassing practice. I remember once being in Madrid, Spain with a Spanish Army client, as part of an International Monetary Fund issue. We were walking to his office in the Palacio de Buenavista, the Spanish Army Headquarters," James said, wondering if he was wandering too far off topic. "There appeared to be some excitement nearby, and my client called out to someone asking what was going on. The person was from the United States and answered in English, "the Real Madrid soccer team is having a rally at 'Dottie on the Potty.' My Spanish friend was mystified what that meant, so we followed the crowd to what was the Plaza de Cibeles. There is a statue there of Cybele, the Greek goddess of fertility sitting in a small chariot. Fortunately, my friend had a sense of humor and laughed it off."

"That irreverence for stilted tradition that you Americans have is also liberating. No other nation in history has been able to live in the present, unshackled by the past, even your own nation's past. Besides being the world's undisputed superpower, you also play the part of Court Jester on the world stage—saying those things no one else can say. The world laughs and points its unsure finger at America the fool, not realizing all their other fingers are pointing back at them."

"That is a profound subject for an informal dinner meeting, Otto," James said apologetically. "There is much I could say in reply, but thank you for your kind insight. I am sorry I got us off tangent. What is it I can do for you this evening that needed to take place outside of the spotlight?"

"Exactly!" Otto said. "You prove my point. If I were sitting in Budapest, Vienna, Paris, or Prague, we would talk on tangential or irrelevant subjects for most of the night and then approach the main topic of the meeting with caution and probably not do it justice. But we would have beaten the dead horse thoroughly and felt we had accomplished an important work."

"There is something to be said, and gained, from preamble and a healthy respect for history," James said. "Give America another 300 years, when we tire of repeating past mistakes, and we may approach the practices of our elders in Europe."

"Foreplay has its merits, to be sure, James," Otto said, suddenly serious. "But there is a reason it is called foreplay. Yes, it is time to get down to business."

Otto stared at James, but his eyes appeared far away as James tried to match his stare. Otto began again with a soft calmness in his voice, but James could also hear something else—a wistfulness like he was relating a fond memory.

"James, the Cold War that followed World War Two was, in reality, a boiling peace. No one can attest to that new harsh reality more than my family," Otto said with a thin smile. "Then, following the fall of the Berlin Wall and the dissolution of the Soviet Union, a new world order, not the conspiracy theory that suggests the possibility of a takeover by a totalitarian world government, but a hope of a new peace and stability began to take shape. We have seen the removal of a continent of dictators in Latin America, the further opening of China and most other Asian countries, and more recently the Arab Spring and Russia's attempt at rebuilding its sphere of influence from the Balkans to the Baltic. Some good has come, but the immense suffering and tragedies of this chaos completely overshadow those few points of progress. We have jumped from the pot of boiling peace right into the fire. The zeitgeist finds many asking the question: Is stability better than freedom? Is the dehumanizing of man in the interests of the world community? There were terrible and unjustified deaths in Syria a decade ago, but nothing like we have seen over the past eight years, not to mention the refugee crisis that terrible war spawned. Remember, I live in Hungary, one of the gateways to the West that these lost souls have traversed."

Otto paused, again appearing to get lost in his thoughts. James said, "One of the reasons I became a cultural and political risk analyst was to try to make sense of what you are describing. My profession has taken me to many of these hot spots."

"What the collective we, humankind, has created is an unbearable reality for much of the world. Many live in fear, others die in fear, and those who can self-medicate with meaningless entertainments of every kind do so with shameful bravado as they race to the unacknowledged abyss. Not discounting the real suffering of millions, to me the greatest tragedy is we have become only spectators, sacrificing our will and action for a false peace. The world has only one hope."

"And I suspect you don't see the Court Jester, the United States, as that hope?" James asked.

"No," Otto said. "The world is crying out for leadership. The question is, what kind of leadership will the New World Disorder select and accept in its quest for a measure of predictability and security? Will that be someone who offers stability over freedom—a sort of Putinesque solution, or freedom over stability—the United States solution?"

"You paint a very black and white world, Otto," James surmised. "Does it have to be either-or?"

"I am beginning to see what President Starhemberg suggested I meet with you," Otto said with a genuine smile. "There is a third option, and that is why we are meeting tonight. We are the third option and we need you on our team."

James was unsure what that meant. He had thought he was already on the team.

Outside the Argentine Air Force installation, JOAB sat in a nondescript car, listening to the rain and the conversation thanks to an earlier placed listening device. A second report in a single day. It had been so quiet, so peaceful, but the storm had come. It could not be avoided.

CHAPTER 3

Poner la Mesa
Literal Translation: To Set the Table

Marisa's Explanation: Meals are more than eating in Argentina. They are events. Family gatherings, even restaurant visits are taken very seriously. In an Argentine restaurant, the table is set with the expectation of only a single person or group will sit there for that evening. There is no pressure to leave the table for another guest. In fact, the restaurant might be hurt if one eats and leaves. To us, preparing the table is a way we say **To Get Everything Ready,** no matter the actual situation.

"CAMBALACHE IS THE THIRD OPTION?" James asked.

"No, but Cambalache is a means to the third option, a new solution that will change the course of humankind," Otto said. "There have been many third options proposed throughout history. The League of Nations and then the United Nations have provided a global podium, but that has been its principle *raison d'opérer*—to give speeches. It has no power to progress except that loaned to it by the unified approval of its members. And a select few members have the power to say no, so very little happens. More recently there has been the Non-Aligned Movement that began in 1961 in my backyard, in Belgrade. It still exists, but it is a committee of nations that still fight over tiny issues and will never get to the big issues we face. There are economic factions, and there is BRIC, Brazil, Russia, India and China, which encompasses forty percent of the world's population and twenty-five percent of the earth's landmass. They can hardly agree on where to meet, let alone what to do. Several BRIC copycats like MINTS, Mexico, Indonesia, Nigeria, Turkey and South Korea, also provide the appearance of global leadership forums. They make nice acronyms but are hardly in a position to provide global influence, let alone superintendence. So what do all these enterprises have in common, James?"

"Ramen Success?" James asked, not sure what Otto was driving at.

"That's an unexpected answer," Otto said. "Please explain."

"Well, they achieve just enough to give hope of continuing," James said. "They provide just enough nourishment, hope, that no one involved wants to shut them down, but they are slowly starving the world of the nutrients it needs for long-term survival."

"Outstanding," Otto said standing up from the table with enthusiasm. "I have never been able to put that thought in such a concise statement. You are on the right path to what I am driving at. Why are they only 'ramen' successful?"

"I suppose you gave me your answer when you said the word 'committee'," James said. "How was is it Sir Barnett Cocks said it? 'A committee is a cul-de-sac down which ideas are lured and then quietly strangled.'"

"And why is that?" Otto asked.

"Competing interests," James answered.

"Exactly!" Otto said turning from looking out the window at nothing but darkness. "National interests in our scenario. All the third options we have considered, as well as any other options humankind has considered since the Renaissance, include national interests. The nation-state was a byproduct of 15th-century intellectual concepts and processes in politics economy, capitalism, mercantilism, political geography, and technology. Before that, the world knew only small local units of common identity or multi-ethnic empires ruled by a king, emperor, or sultan."

"Like your family business prior to World War One," James interjected.

"Yes," Otto said. "That 'not black, not white,' but gray world had its blemishes and cancers, but it also allowed disparate cultures, interests, and pathways forward to flourish. Do you know what my grandfather's full name was?"

Surprised at the question, James said, "Otto von Habsburg."

"Not even close," Otto said with a chuckle. "I remember having this pounded into me as a boy. His name was Franz Joseph Otto Robert Maria Anton Karl Max Heinrich Sixtus Xavier Felix Renatus Ludwig Gaetan Pius Ignatius von Habsburg, Crown Prince of Austria, Hungary and Bohemia, of Dalmatia, Croatia, Slavonia, Galizia, Lodomeria and Illyria. That is a committee of one representing an incredibly diverse corner of the world."

"So, are you suggesting what I think you are saying?" James asked, now standing himself.

"What is it you think I'm saying?" Otto asked.

"You want to bring back the Habsburg Empire—on a global basis?" James said. "That is the New World Order of conspiracy theories!"

"Heavens no," Otto said. "I can't tell you how grateful I am that my grandfather turned his back on that antiquated throne and all its intrigue, complications, and inherent weaknesses of that empire, past, or future."

"Then I don't know where you are going with this," James said, sitting back down on the couch.

"I think you do," Otto said grabbing his coat. "The night is far spent and I must leave you, but there is time yet to clarify your own thoughts. I have very much enjoyed this evening and getting to know you, as that was the principle purpose of our time together. I hope you have enjoyed getting to know me. If I am correct, and I really hope I am, we will have the opportunity to get to know each other much better in the months to come. I leave you with these questions—which are always much better and more powerful than simple answers. Why does a nation-state exist? What is its purpose and what does it deliver that other inventions of man do not? How does a nation-state achieve its ends?"

"Since you are leaving me with questions," James said, trying to suppress his surprise at the abrupt termination of the conversation, "allow me a few questions for you. And yes, I do hope we have the opportunity soon to continue this stroll through the um, bazaar, the junkshop of humanities search for leadership," James said with a sudden insight. "Why is the energy project that President Starhemberg announced today called Cambalache, the Spanish word for bazaar?"

"That is a question I was prepared to ask you, James, but wasn't sure that would have been a helpful question," Otto said nodding. "I can see I may have underestimated you, once again. My Spanish is not very good, and I appreciate we can converse in English. But I understand you are fluent in the language as well as in the nuances of internationalism."

"A second question since you brought up the nation-state," James said. "Does a nation have a heart, a soul? And finally, President Starhemberg mentioned earlier today that there is something more important than resources and riches. He suggested it was will. Is there something more important than will? Just so you know, I believe there is."

"Interesting questions we have both posed," Otto said. "A final one then, are our questions dancing around the same campfire and we don't dare answer them because we are afraid we will get burned?"

"Nicely asked," James said, reaching out to shake Otto's hand.

As Otto grasped James's hand, he added, "You know, I think Marisa has taken a liking to you. I have been a family friend most of her life. Treat her with kindness and respect, James. As much as with the important matters we have talked about tonight, you will be held accountable for the choices you make in your relationship with her. Life may get very busy, very complicated for both of you. Norisa is a unique spirit, endowed with more passion and spark than most of us. That is a power, and like most great powers, it is also a weakness."

"The proverbial Achilles heel, as the Greeks suggested," James said, opening the door to the cabin for Otto. "Norisa?"

"Ah, her secret nickname known only by family and very close friends. Sort of a Latin diminutive of her grandmother's name Nora and her name, Marisa. You know, there are no new stories, James," Otto said. "There are old plots with new endings and old endings with new plots. The names change, but what is a name but a placeholder. Identity comes from the intellect; purpose comes from the heart. Every name must choose its mind and heart and that is what makes the person and how they play their role and achieve their ending. Again, thank you for a most enjoyable evening. We will see each other again soon. Until then, my friend." Otto turned and walked to the waiting sedan.

James shut the door, wondering what these last words meant. This entire night had been surreal. He sat down at the dinner table absently surveying the plates of partially eaten food. The whole night felt like a partially eaten meal. So much left on the plates, not bitten nor chewed, not consumed. What was he getting into? Were these people nut jobs with a powerful means to their end? Could all these questions be answered as easily as this table cleared? Tired of questions, James grabbed his little moleskin notebook he always carried with him and started writing answers. An hour later he went to bed with a new measure of understanding and peace.

* * *

The next morning he was sitting on the grass outside the cabin watching the sunrise over the lake below him when his ride to the airport arrived. Out jumped Marisa who walked over to him as he stood up.

"Sit back down, Santi," Marisa said as she plopped herself on the grass. "I love grass like this," she said as she ran her hands across the surface of the soft green blades. "I don't get to lay on a lawn like this very often. It's heaven. So, how was your dinner?"

Enjoying watching Marisa bond with Mother Nature's carpet, James was jolted back to reality with her question. "The food was great, the conversation perplexing. How was your evening?"

"Ah, the same old stuff, informal meetings for Ernesto and me as some decoration—there, but not there. You know, seen, but not heard."

"I can't imagine you not being heard," James said as he sat down next to her, but not close enough to touch arms.

Turning to him, she said, "Are you saying I am loud, or that I am not noticeable?"

"Let me face that double-edged sword after you tell me who Santi is," James said.

"My new nickname for you, of course," Marisa said lightly punching his arm that was stretched out to his side propping him up. "Wow, very firm muscles, Santi," she said grabbing his bicep with her soft hand. She didn't let go as she explained, "Your name is James, but that sounds too stuffy, too British, or American. I am Argentine and thus you require a proper name. Santiago is the name for James in Castellano. Santi might be short for Santiago, but it means more in our Italian influenced

Spanish here. Santi can also mean saint, canonized for special qualities, a very good person."

"Wow, that is a lot to live up to, Norisa," James said, taking a leap in using her family nickname. He felt her hand on his arm tense up and then relax.

"No stranger has ever called me that," Marisa said.

"I'm a saint, but a stranger?" James asked.

"Not like that, *estupido*," Marisa said. "No one but my family, and that is only Ernesto now, and a few close family friends that I have known all my life, have called me that. Certainly, no man that I, that is," Marisa began to explain, stumbling on her words.

"A man that is a canonized Saint in the Church of Marisa Starhemberg?" James said with a light laugh.

"That sounds sacrilegious, even if you are a santi," Marisa said, punching his arm again. "Now answer my question, how was your evening with Otto?"

"The Damoclean Sword has fallen. Okay, it was, indisputably curious and disputably certain," James said, glad he hadn't blown up a bridge using her nickname.

"Now you sound like Otto," Marisa said. "You two must have spent the evening singing two different songs and thinking your disharmony made beautiful music."

"If you mean harmony as in clarity, then yes, it was a night of ambiguity," James said, looking off into the distance. "There were times when I was certain we were talking about entirely different things and then I would discover that we weren't that far off in our thoughts. I am used to direct talk and direct answers. I walked away with more questions—some he asked me, some I came up with myself, than I think I have ever had from one conversation. This seems like a big game. You ever play the game *Clue*?"

"I think I have heard of it," Marisa said. "I've never played it. Sounds like a date plan."

"If we can find it somewhere in Buenos Aires," James said. "It's a board game."

"Oh, board games are boring, but never mind," Marisa said. "You can talk me into playing it some other time. Finish telling me about your evening."

"Well, like I said, it felt like we were playing a game, or that he was considering me for a job and that the interview questions had been written by a philosophy major. But…"

"But?" Marisa asked after James didn't continue.

"But dissonance can be emancipating, too. My grandmother was a music teacher, and when I was a young boy, she would teach me lessons. I did take a few years of piano, but not from her. She would talk to me about classical music and opera. 'Do you see, James, how the first movement is an introduction and the third movement emphasizes this theme from the introduction?' I found myself thinking of my grandmother last night after Otto left."

"Your grandmother, music?" Marisa asked as she furrowed her brow. "You are not making any sense, Santi. We need to leave for the airport soon. Can you clarify this mystery with a direct answer in the next five minutes?"

"This is the most direct answer I can give you, Marisa," James said with a smile. "There is an expression in music theory called cadence. More specifically a term called authentic cadence. A piece of music may wander all over the place, but in the end, it comes back to some cords that provide closure or resolution. The cadence is most often a microcosm of the structure of the piece of music and is, as my grandmother used to say, the most direct means to go home, to find the peace that the music offers. Last night, Otto and I were, as you insightfully suggest, singing a song. There was a dissonance because we were singing different notes, most often just a tone off. I was singing an F sharp and he was singing an F natural." James looked at Marisa -and she had a perturbed look and was fidgeting. "It's not important that you understand my musical metaphor, but it was you who brought it up first. Here is the thing, Marisa: harmony is fine and, yes, we did agree on many things, but harmony is something we resolve from the outside of ourselves. It's easy. Disharmony created by a diminished interval—when things are just off enough to not sound terrible—are the most pleasing of cadences because they must be filtered and resolved from inside us. Harmony is pleasing and enjoyable. A cadence with disharmony can sometimes touch us so deeply it moves us to tears."

"So you were moved to tears last night?" Marisa asked.

"No," James said, standing and offering his hand to Marisa to help her up. "I think we are in the middle of the song, but I can see where the song is going. I am certain what notes I am willing to sing, and I am fairly sure what notes Otto, your brother, and you, are going to sing. I think it will be a beautiful piece of music. I hope the world is ready for this song and they take the time to listen and internalize it, and then accept it for what it is, a chance for mankind to finally reach home."

"Thank you for your non-answer, James," Marisa said. "I want to go home."

James walked to the waiting government sedan wondering at the beauty of Bariloche, of Marisa, and the surreal song, if that is what it was, of which he found himself in the middle. 'How had he gotten here? Why him? Where was all this going, for him, and for humanity?' he had asked himself last night and anew this morning as the sun had not yet peeked over the horizon, but its light was beginning to illuminate his little part of the world. The additional spark that Marisa brought with her arrival, combined with the full sunrise was intoxicating. 'Did this abundance of light clarify, or could the light actually obfuscate, or distort reality?'

'We can know more than we can tell,' JOAB thought. The orders were clear, but what was not being said? JOAB's directive said, "Let this progress for now. When the tacit becomes implicit, but not yet explicit, ensure failure. Pile as much rubble on top of this so that it will take another 50 years to uncover the truth. By then there will be a different truth." "Tacit? Implicit?" JOAB asked out loud. 'Those non-specific yet all-encompassing words were meant to distance the Prelate from failed actions, but I will not fail. Habsburg hypocrisy. Of course, he wants to rule.'

CHAPTER 4

A las Chapas

Literal Translation: At the Game, bottle caps or other covering

Marisa's Explanation: as a noun *chapa* can be a badge, insignia, or some type of a covering. As a verb, *chapar* can mean to cover, close, or kiss. You can draw your own conclusions, but it means **To Go Really Fast.** To close up the game, or kiss the girl, requires making it happen now, not later.

THE FLIGHT BACK TO BUENOS Aires was scheduled to take about two hours. Marisa had explained to James that they were landing at Aeroparque Jorge Newbery in Palermo because of its closer proximity to the Quinta de Olivos, instead of the larger Ministro Pistarini International Airport. When James had first traveled to Buenos Aires, his itinerary said he would be met at Ezeiza Airport. He became concerned when the pilot announced their arrival at Ministro Pistarini. He quickly learned that the locals called it Ezeiza, because that is the Partido, or borough, in the greater Buenos Aires area where it is located. 'Not unlike Ronald Reagan Washington National Airport in Arlington, Virginia,' James thought as he settled into his seat in the Fokker F28, call sign Tango 02. He had never heard anyone call that airport anything but National Airport, except pilots announcing their arrival and they called it simply Reagan National. He was more familiar with that airport than any other in the world. He had flown in and out of it hundreds of time in his professional life…

"Your first time flying out of National?" the passenger asked him with a grin.

"Yes, actually," James admitted.

"I guessed that by the white knuckles," the man continued while nodding at James' hands clenched to the arm rests. "Crazy take-off. I used to hate it. Get a lot of altitude fast, with engines not at full power, and then turn to follow the Potomac River north, all in the name of noise abatement. Sounds like a plan Congress came up with, you know? There are times when I feel like we are just asking to fall out of the sky. Add a little ice on the wings in a winter departure, and it amazes me we don't pancake into the Pentagon, or Georgetown University a little further up the river."

James had stopped listening to the man next to him. He had just accepted his first real job in his chosen profession. His family thought he was crazy when he had announced that he was going to become a Cultural and Political Risk Manager. His first job after graduating from the Fletcher School at Tufts University was as an analyst, working for a discreet boutique strategic consulting firm in Washington, D.C. He spent three years there, supporting the firm's asset managers and their private clients (individuals and some private companies) decide where and when to direct their international investments. He left the company with a comfortable savings so he could complete a graduate degree at Johns Hopkins in International Economics. Along the way, he picked up an Actuarial Science Certificate, fluency in German and Russian to diversify his native English and fluent Spanish abilities, and his first girlfriend, who quickly tired of only being a tertiary interest in James' busy schedule. Shortly after graduation, he was toying with the idea of picking up one more language, Arabic or Mandarin, when KPMG approached him with a job offer he couldn't refuse. He would lead a risk management team in support of an International Monetary Fund cultural assessment and improvement process as part of the World Bank Millennium Development Goals. It sounded exciting, governance and risk management were his specialties, the salary was twice what he had ever made before, and he was able to still live in the Washington, DC area while traveling the world…

"What day is it?" James asked the female passenger next to him as they approached at Reagan National Airport.

"Wednesday," the surprised lady answered.

"And this is still March, right?" James asked, oblivious to the incongruous picture of himself in his tailor-made Italian suit, sitting in First Class, and asking questions as if he had just woken up from a drunken stupor in an alley on skid row. The aircraft hit a pocket of unstable air that surprised even the flight attendants. James didn't even notice it. Eighteen months of non-stop international travel and an intense delivery schedule on the ground were culminating with his final report to the Managing Director of the International Monetary Fund in two days. He was done, and he was really done—'burnt to a crisp,' James admitted to himself. KPMG and their client were extremely happy with the analysis and suggested process improvements he proposed. The IMF had offered him a job as their new Culture Czar. KPMG was supporting the move because it would place one of their people in a key position with an important client. He understood this was a significant title and a lot of power, but it had nothing to do with culture and everything to do with implementing a new Data Delivery System that would take the place of the General Data Dissemination System (GDDS) and the Special Data Dissemination Standard (SDDS). This meant breaking down the financial fiefdoms within the IMF while continuing to attempt to bridge the gap between the risk aversion

culture and the IMF vision of fostering global monetary cooperation. Maintaining stability, while facilitating international
trade and economic growth, and reducing poverty around the
world seemed like competing goals that created a dilemma he
wanted no part of.

"Yes, still March," the lady said, glad the flight next to this
odd man was almost over.

"And march I must," James told himself out loud. The lady
next to him made no attempt to clarify his statement or otherwise engage in conversation.

He tendered his resignation one hour after delivering his
report. Much to the disappointment of both KPMG and the
IMF, he did not take the IMF offer. James filled the next two
weeks with sleep, exercise, eating, and more sleep. Traveling to
Jefferson City, Missouri by car, to visit his family, James continued his exercise and sleep regimen, not sure what was next in his
life. He enjoyed his mother's cooking and avoided her questions
about why he wasn't married yet. Not having the time to go on
a single date in the last year had not helped.

One thing his frugal living had provided him was a significant savings. Before heading back to his apartment in the
Washington, D.C. neighborhood of Woodley Park, James paid
cash for thirty-seven acres of farm and woodland between the
towns of New Bloomfield and Fulton, less than twenty miles up
the road from his parents' home. Not fully sure why he bought
this property himself, he told his family it was to remind him
of and anchor him to his home and loved ones. His mother
approved. His father and two younger sisters wondered. Ever
since James had been a small boy he had wanted to travel the
world and live in every capital in the world, every capital that
is other than the capital of the state of Missouri. "Jeff City is
a nice place, great place to raise a family, but I want to see the
world, to know where the best bread shop is in the Fourth

Arrondissement in Paris, where the best view of the Charles Bridge is located in Prague," he would tell his parents when looking at possible universities outside of the state of Missouri.

When pressed by his father about the land purchase, James added that land was a solid long-term investment that took little worry or time tending to, unlike the stock market, rental homes, and other tangibles like artwork, which had become a secret passion that James had discovered and nurtured during his travels. In a weak moment at about the halfway point of the IMF contract, he had purchased a Javier López Barbosa in New York City during a half-hour lunch break, and a Constant Montald in Brussels in commemoration of his last IMF contract trip there. He was not persuaded to rent the land out to local farmers. "I am going to let the land return to its natural state. I will decide what to do with it when the time is right," he explained to his father.

On the drive back to Washington, James decided to try his hand at entrepreneurship and hatched a plan to start JNI, LLC. "When in Rome," James mused over a chicken lunch at the Dirty Bird in Morgantown, West Virginia, "... and the modern Rome, Washington, D.C., is certainly the land of acronyms. It sounds better than James Nathaniels International, his waitress confirmed when he asked her opinion between the two possibilities. Within two weeks of opening his door for business, KPMG had hired him for a job that would eventually take him to Buenos Aires, Argentina. He took the job for the 'ridiculous reason' he told himself, knowing he was jumping back into the rat race, that it would allow him to live in yet another capital he had not yet visited.

Greater Buenos Aires was a large city of over 17 million people, about half of the entire country's population he had read. The *Porteños*, the people of the port, as Latin America called those who lived in Buenos Aires, were mostly of European descent, often only one to three generations removed from Spain, or Italy, with pockets of Germans, Poles, English and French. There were days when he had to remind himself that he wasn't in Europe. The city stretched from the Rioplatense estuary for miles in three directions and encompassed 80 square miles for the Federal Capital and continued well past 100 square miles for the metropolitan area, making it the second largest metro area in Latin America. Exceeding the other two "alpha cities" of Latin America, Sao Paolo and Mexico City, Buenos Aires enjoyed the highest quality of life, highest per capita income, and was second only to Mexico City as the top tourist destination in all of Latin America. Its French architecture made it feel like an arrondissement in Paris. In fact, the house that James had rented in the suburb of Vicente Lopez had been built entirely of building materials and finish work imported from France in the 1920's. And there was a fantastic bread store just around the corner.

"Best night life in all of the Americas," boasted his government contact that first night in the city. They were dining in a parrilla, a steak house, called *-Los Años Locos* on the Costanera Norte across from the river as best as James could tell from the map on his phone. "There is a restaurant on most every block and each one prepares a meal that is better than the last place you ate. Tomorrow night I am going to take you to *La Taurina* right by your house that has tapas that rival the best in Madrid." James had his doubts about the apparent overreaching pride his host had in the food of his city. By the end of his first month, however, James had not eaten a bad meal. In most cases, it was the best beef he had ever had and the Italian and Spanish cuisine were as good as what he had experienced in Europe.

Jogging each morning, James had become accustomed to the weather and the neighborhood. The temperatures were mild and it seemed when the hot, humid weather pushed down from Brazil, a cold front from the South Atlantic would strike back and bring the temperatures back to a pleasant 75 degrees. The Rio de la Plata, the world's widest river, created its own micro-climate that kept a light breeze flowing, even on the most humid of days. He expected temperatures to get into the 50s by July, but so far May had been perfect. By the third week in his rented home, he was regularly greeted by the locals in at least four or five languages. He had become accustomed to the Spanish with a strong Italian accent that the locals called Castellano puro, and recognized the sort of inner-city slang called Lunfardo, along with German, Russian, and what he finally identified as Basque after attempting to write a few words down and asking his host.

"The Jewish community here used to be much bigger, but is now only about a quarter million, which is still the largest in Latin America. I think the majority is still Ashkenazi, but the Sephardic population is growing with new immigration from the Middle East," his host explained.

James was compiling a requested side report from his old boss at KPMG. One of the 'duties as assigned' he thought he had escaped when he left KPMG. "Note to self," James mumbled. "Being a sub-contractor is nearly as bad as being an employee."

Grass root sentiments in Argentina were an interest item in the U.S. government because President Starhemberg had recently announced he would accelerate the previous Argentine efforts of the Kirchner and Macri Presidencies to spearhead the Latin American role in reinvigorating the peace process in the Israeli–Palestinian conflict. Argentina would also take on a negotiation role in the Israeli-Syrian relationship as the Argentine President Carlos Menem had attempted.

"There is still a very tiny minority of anti-Jewish sentiment," his host continued, "but the much bigger issue was our poor security that allowed the Hezbollah to come into the country and bomb the Israeli embassy in 1992 and later in 1994. The government says we have rectified that weakness in our security posture. We are a long-time friend to Israel, a friend to the Arab Middle East, especially Egypt, Saudi Arabia, and Iraq through our joint Space research and ballistic missile programs, and a friend to Iran where we facilitated secret links between that nation, Israel, and the United States. We are in a unique position like no other country to make a difference as a trusted arbitrator."

James was formulating his own private theory that Argentina had long been the Batman of Latin America. Most thought of the country like the playboy Bruce Wayne, while in reality that was a convenient cover for many acts of secret international statecraft and diplomacy. Argentina certainly enjoyed its Bruce Wayne persona, maybe a little too much. Like Batman, the global policing bodies were not always aligned with Argentina's past vigilante actions, but many knew who to call when the chips were down, and they needed a professional and trusted hand.

James' principle function for being in Argentina was to support the Argentine Oil and Gas Industry establish a deeper relationship with U.S. energy companies. By 2014, Argentina was the largest dry gas producer and the fourth largest petroleum and other liquids producer in South America. In 2015 Argentina was confirmed to have the world's second-largest shale gas reserves, with Vaca Muerta, located in the Neuquén Basin, as the world's single largest shale gas field on earth. When Mauricio Macri took office as President, prior to President Starhemberg, he reversed the populist policies of his predecessor, Cristina Kirchner. He adjusted everything from currency controls to export taxes. And although he expanded oil and gas exploration, he did so through Chinese and Russian support. The YPF-Gazprom joint venture of the Argentine and Russian state-owned gas companies followed on the heels of Kirchner's speech at the United Nations where she accused Washington's "Vulture Capitalists" of fanning the flames of instability in Argentina. Chevron, Dow Chemical, and EcoStim Energy

Solutions Inc., a Houston oil-field-services company continued working with YPF, but that was not the same as joint ventures with state-owned companies. There were bridges Starhemberg wanted to rebuild, and he had multiple teams working from different directions to get the bridge construction with the United States underway fast.

"We don't need the United States," the Minister of Energy argued. This was James' first time witnessing a cabinet-level meeting and the first time he would see President Starhemberg in action. He was happy to simply be the proverbial fly on the wall. "We are

running 350-ton drilling rigs that dig 9,000 feet deep in the recovery of our, Argentina's, petroleum. We have over 30 billion barrels of recoverable oil and 802 trillion cubic feet of gas trapped in a layer of shale up to 1,200 feet thick. That is more than Canada and the U.S. have combined!"

The Minister of Federal Planning, Public Investment, and Services cleared his throat in preamble. "And our ministry through ENARGAS regulates the natural gas transportation and distribution activities. It is critical that we establish better relations with the United States, as they ensure our safe passage in delivery around the world. You are looking at this from your small parochial perspective."

"Small perspective?" the Energy Minister shot back. "It is this tiny perspective that is going to save this country and make it wealthy again."

Starhemberg had been quiet, listening to the heated discussion. A few times James thought he caught the beginnings of a smile, but he hid it quickly. "You both make important points, and I thank you for your open honesty. I would like to hear from the only U.S. citizen in the room. Mr. Nathaniels, what are your thoughts?"

James was not only caught off guard, he had no idea that the Argentine President even knew he existed. The entire room looked around in surprise that a North American was even allowed in the room. The few that knew James stared at him with not so hidden smiles. James stood, to give himself a few more seconds to think. "Mr. President, I would not presume to speak on behalf of the United States, nor step into a family discussion as an outsider."

"So you don't have any thoughts to offer, or are you unsure this is the place to offer them?" President Starhemberg asked. "If you had been tasked to write a paper on this and forward it through channels, would you not do so?"

"Yes, sir," James stammered. "Yes, I do have some thoughts on this, and yes, I would feel more comfortable putting them on paper rather than offering a half-baked answer now."

"I am interested in your half-baked answer now," President Starhemberg said with a broad smile. "Half-baked thoughts are often richer inputs to a conversation searching for a direction than the perfectly crafted answer. Take a risk and tell us honestly what you think."

"Sir, the Minster of Energy is right," James began thinking this had been a memorable visit to Argentina but it would now end sooner than he had planned, "you don't need the United States if all you are concerned with is producing petroleum products for your domestic markets. And the Minister of Federal Planning is wrong; the United States would never let a country go into harm's way in the areas of the world where it patrols the lines of commerce, whether they perceived that country as a friend or foe."

James had heard quiet voices whispering to others when he first stood. Now it sounded like a beehive. "However," he continued, "the Minister of Federal Planning brings up a crucial point. This is an opportunity to consider a much bigger picture than your country's energy sector. This is really about more than only one of your national interests." James stopped and looked directly at the President, gauging whether he should continue.

"Go on, Mr. Nathaniels," the President said, his eyes showing kindness and interest.

James was surprised the President was allowing him to read his feelings so clearly. James offered a wan smile back and said, "The world has become so interdependent that it is impossible to speak of something like the global energy sector in isolation. The world operates like a dynamic anarchical system, even if countries like the United States, China, or even combinations like the European Union would prefer to consider it as a hierarchical system where they can call the shots. That world died in the twentieth century."

"We don't need a lesson in international relations from a young man who hadn't even been born when I began my professional career." The Energy Minister interrupted. "Internal actions of states can cause external actions. We are all aware of that young man."

"With all respect, Minister," James said, "I would suggest it is the reverse. Internal causes react with external actions. Long ago nation-states began exchanging their sovereignty for affluence. China and the United States certainly have their disagreements, but the United States wants Chinese goods, and China must continue to produce to keep growing—the tenuous strand on which the present Chinese government's legitimacy hangs."

"So we live in an interdependent world," the Minister said impatiently, flipping his hand as if to shew away an annoying fly. "We watch out for and react to the unintended consequences as we secure our national interests."

"Or," James said, "you wisely manage your national interest proactively from an abundance mentality instead of a zero-sum mentality. Even if you lose a few skirmishes, in the long-run, you will not only secure your basic national interests but possibly achieve your aspirational interests as well."

"You have now progressed from, um, whatever your function here is, to *estafador*, a snake oil salesman," the Energy Minister said with a laugh. He was joined by many in the room. James noticed the President was still smiling, but not laughing.

"Tell me, Mr. Nathaniels," the President said, quieting the room once again, "would you be willing to share an example we might employ proactively?"

"Sir, I am here to help you build bridges with the United States' energy sector. But now I will speak as an unsolicited consultant to your amazing country. One thing I knew academically that has been reinforced since I have been here is there are few things that fully unite your country. One is the World Cup; another is the Falkland Islands, Las Islas Malvinas. I can't help you with your World Cup bid, but I think you could not only win over world opinion to your claim but have the British offering the islands to you within a year."

The room exploded with disbelief, laugher, and general pandemonium. James knew he had just sealed his fate and would have to close up his efforts in Argentina by the end of the week. Then he looked at the President who was still smiling at him, but otherwise unmoved. He stood and walked to James.

"Sorry to put you in the spotlight, Mr. Nathaniels," Starhemberg said as if no one else were in the room. "It is about time our country started acting like a world leader with a vision. You will help us find that vision. Your idea is something I would like to see in a formal paper." He patted James on the shoulder and partially turned to survey the room. "Oh, and by the way, your contract with the Argentine Energy sector is completed."

James gulped, then grimaced and said, "Sorry if I overstepped my bounds. I will pack up and be out of my office by the end of the day."

"Perfect," the President said, seeming to enjoy this sacking more than James would have guessed. "Your new office at the Casa Rosada will be ready by morning. We can discuss the particulars of your new contract tomorrow also."

"Sir, what?" James stammered. "I, um..."

"Just say you will see me in the morning," President Starhemberg said. "I will alert security of your expected arrival around nine in the morning if that will work for you. You will be working with my most trusted confidant. More on that tomorrow."

"I will see you in the morning, President Starhemberg," James said in a daze.

Status Report: "President Ernesto Starhemberg remains teachable and tractable when I need him to bend. His rise to power at the national level has only strengthened our bonds. He was a strong governor and continues his success at the national level. I see no obstacles in our long-term plans. The higher they rise, the more terminal the fall." JOAB

BAJO Chapter 1

"Like father, like son, David," the Guardian of the Dauphin said. "The nation-state is the offspring of royal dynasties. What had been loosely tribal was provided with additional structure, culture, history, loyalties, and often a common language—all required in order to rule. Those very same ingredients, when baked over time, grew into nation-states. The child overthrew the parent."

David knew to hold his tongue when the BAJO Guardian was speaking. The full name of the organization to which he had dedicated the better part of his 57 years was called the Bourbon Ascendency, Justice, and Order. BAJO was pronounced with a soft *a* and an *h* sound for the *j,* following the Spanish in which the organization was first conceived. This word in Spanish meant low, as in under, or in this case, out of plain view. David was a prelate, although this was not a religious order, but an ancient association dedicated to ensuring the continued presence and eventual rise to power of the House of Bourbon in world leadership. His territorial prelature was Latin America, from the Rio Grande River to the tip of Tierra del Fuego. Along with five other prelates a global prelacy was formed, governed by the Guardian of the Dauphin. The Dauphin was the heir apparent to the throne. When BAJO was established in the year 1501, the throne was France, but had become more generic in the Twentieth Century. The Dauphin had also become less specific, as there were multiple thrones and multiple Bourbon family members in potential ascendancy to those thrones.

"Soon, tomorrow perhaps, or the day after," the Guardian said, continuing the lesson David had learned as a boy, "the first shall be the last. The child has outlived its time. It has matured and crumbles under the pressures of the interconnected world. Indeed, our planet has become a little place. Middle management is no longer needed," the Guardian added with a sweep of his hand. "The House of Bourbon must be found standing just off stage, ready to take its place when the curtain rises. What does your JOAB report and what are you doing to ensure the House of Habsburg has no part in this play?"

These personal reports took place three times a year. David always enjoyed his trips to Paris but was also glad to leave. "As you know, JOAB is well positioned and is in the confidence of President Starhemberg," David began. JOAB was the generic name for the key operatives of BAJO. An anagram of BAJO, JOAB also took its name from the Israelite General in King David's army and the kingmaker of men, the point of the spear. To maintain extreme anonymity, only each prelate knew the identity of the JOAB operatives in that prelature. Each only communicated with the moniker JOAB. "We are ready to strike either at your command or as events dictate. Starhemberg speaks of abundance mentalities and has never spoken of Habsburg interest as his grandfather did. JOAB reports that there is little to worry about at this time."

"There are many obstacles and threats on the road to eventual Bourbon ascendency as you know, David. Extreme anti-royalists tend to place us in the same basket with other royal households. A common enemy does not make us allies with those other families. The two households have tried joining forces in the past with disastrous results. Our prime concern has always been the Habsburgs. Political historians say the Bourbon-Habsburg rivalry began in 1500 and ended in 1918, with the destruction of the Habsburg's Austro-Hungarian Empire. That is, of course, far from the reality we face today. There are nominal Bourbons on the thrones of Spain and Luxembourg. We have several clear claims to thrones elsewhere. That the world sees any royal asser-tion as an antiquated and even laughable declaration is to our advantage at present. 1500 is as good a milestone as any from which to mark the start of the rivalry, but not for a minute since 1918 has BAJO taken its eyes off of the Habsburgs and their potential ascendency."

The Guardian looked as ancient as the history of BAJO David thought. The man had been the Prelate of Europe through the height of the Cold War when he became Guardian. He was much thinner than at their last meeting. The Prelates knew that the sitting Guardian always named his successor. In fact, the first duty of the Guardian was to put the name of his successor in a safe kept in this very office where David sat. The Guardian was free to change the name at any time thereafter. David seriously doubted his name was in the safe, but that was all right with him. This mansion, situated along the Seine River where it turns North after leaving Paris, nearly equidistant between Versailles and the First Arrondissement, was the historical seat of BAJO. 'A comfortable life in a beautiful location,' David thought, 'but I prefer Latin America over the Latin Quarter.'

The meeting over, David said his goodbyes to the Guardian and walked from the Maison Decazes with a light heart. Élie-Louis Decazes, the French statesman and Minister of Police, who was also a BAJO Guardian in the 19th Century, had purchased this house and gardens. After the fall of Napoleon, Decazes publicly declared himself a Royalist, and amidst great danger remained faithful to the Bourbons throughout the chaotic Hundred Days during Napoleon's attempted return to power. King Louis XVIII knew of his plan to once again royalize French government and to nationalize the monarchy. This viewpoint being in the minority, Decazes persuaded Louis XVIII to dissolve Parliament. With new elections, the Royalists gained the majority where Decazes had a pivotal role in the French government. David wondered if the time came that he was placed in the intersection of history if he could perform to the level of this able predecessor.

CHAPTER 5

Caliente la pava pero no ceba los mates

Literal Translation: Warm the Turkey but not Kill it

Marisa's Explanation: Cooking a turkey without killing it is not something any Argentine would do. Cooked turkey gets the mouth salivating and the mind thinking about the great meal to come. Only pretending, because you haven't even killed the bird yet is **To Be a Tease.** This is a national pastime, especially for porteñas, the women of Buenos Aires.

"MY NAME IS," JAMES BEGAN.

"Yes, welcome, Mr. Nathaniels. We were expecting you," the gate guard said. "I will still need some photo identification that has been issued by a government."

James offered his passport and his Washington, DC driver's license and was escorted through the metal detector and ceremonial guards, directly to a small office on the second floor. It had a desk and chair with two guest chairs and a window looking out to a park. It wasn't the Plaza de Mayo he saw, so he deduced he must be looking at the Parque Colón. Walking closer to the window, he could see the Columbus Monument and the River beyond.

"You know this is the 100-year anniversary of the Monumento a Cristóbal Colón," a voice said behind him. James turned around and saw a beautiful young lady standing in the doorway. She wore a tight black skirt and a loose fitting floral print blouse. Her hair and eyes matched her skirt. The sparkle in her eyes matched her long dangling earrings and a necklace of large glass beads that made her petite frame seem even smaller, more delicate. "When you get a chance, take a close look at that monument. It still has marks on it from the 1955 bombing of the Plaza de Mayo and the surrounding area. The bombs weren't from terrorists, but from Argentine Navy planes that were part of an attempt to oust President Peron from office."

"Do we expect a bombing?" James asked.

"Not anytime soon, but it is a great reminder of the delicate position of President and the fickle nature of those who brought him to this building." She crossed her arms and studied James. Her bright red lips appeared to pout. James wasn't sure what he had already done to upset someone.

"Sorry I didn't mean to sound flippant," James said in apology. "You caught me by surprise. I say dumb things when caught off guard."

"Dumb things like you can get the British to offer the Malvinas to us after we have battled them in the courts of world opinion since the mid-1800s and fought a bloody war over them, all to no success?" she asked.

"I was surprised the President knew who I was and that I was in the meeting," James said. "But I had thought through the things I shared. They weren't poorly thought out spontaneous responses. You already know who I am," James said offering his hand. "May I ask you name?"

"Yes, you may," she said. She continued to stand there and very slowly a smile developed, overtaking her formal then pouty stance. James was startled to realize that he had witnessed three distinct moods of this person in less than 60 seconds. "I said you may ask, so ask."

"Hi, my name is James Nathaniels," James said. "What is your name?"

"Hello, James Nathaniels. That is much too formal. Do you have a nickname?" this nameless and capricious goddess asked.

"Sorry, just James."

"Just James," she said chewing on the name. "Maybe I could call you JJ. No, that might work in English, but too hard in Spanish. Where did you learn your Spanish? You don't have a proper accent, but you speak with the native fluency of a Colombian, clean, precise, but boring."

"I picked it up in high school," James said matter of factly.

"Now it is you who are manufacturing mystery," she said. "Very well mystery man, we have a meeting in fifteen minutes in the conference room just down the hallway." She turned and left.

James walked to the hallway and watched her walk away. "I can feel you looking at me, James," she said without turning around. "Fifteen minutes. Hasta pronto."

James blushed even though no one was around. He had been gazing her. She was magnificent, an exquisite enigma. For the first time, he also noticed the incredible architecture of the building. The white walls and ornate gold leaf trim. Museum quality artwork and stained glass. Each detail took on a common hue as she marched past it. "Please let her be my co-worker or assigned host while I am here," he mumbled as he stepped back into his new office.

The first to arrive, he hoped. "If not I am at the wrong conference room," James said under his breath. He decided to stand at the door and wait in case anyone was sent looking for the lost *yanqui*. That he was simply left on his own in the Argentine equivalence of the White House was unnerving. No one really knew him. How could they? He had only been in the country for just over a month and even then only working with minor officials in the Energy Ministry. The Energy Minister obviously hadn't known him yesterday at the cabinet meeting. 'Boy, he did now,' James mused. 'For all they know, I could be a terrorist, and they had just let me in the chief executive's offices, the symbol of the country.'

"Mr. Nathaniels?" an older lady asked as she approached him from the bustling larger hallway that connected with the conference room alcove. "Here is your building identification badge. It will not only get you into this building, but you will need it for any government travel or meetings in other government offices. Please guard this carefully, although it will only work with your presence."

James took the ID badge and noticed it had his picture on it. "You already have my picture?" James said.

"We took your picture as you entered the building today. The picture is only for social etiquette, not really for any security purpose. Your badge has an NRFID, a nano radio frequency identification tag that can be scanned from fifty meters. That, along with your brain scan identification, which we also collected as you entered the building is the only biometrics we require."

"Wow, okay," James said, wondering again about how much more advanced the Batman of Latin America really was. "So I'm allowed in the Batcave," he said aloud in English.

"I'm sorry. What did you say?" the lady asked.

"I apologize," James said. "I was just thinking out loud. I do that a lot. Will I be working with you?"

"I am sure we will see each other, but no," she said. "I forgot to introduce myself. I am Vangelina Pereira. I work in the security office. It's good to meet you, Mr. Nathaniels." She began to leave and then turned back. "You can pick up your passport and driver's license at the security office at the main entrance when you leave today. You only need your badge from now on. Welcome to the Casa Rosada."

"Please call me James. Thank you, Vangelina. Do you know if this is the conference room I am supposed to be at? I have a meeting at 9:30 and no one seems to be here."

"I know a lot of things about you, James, but I don't know your schedule," Vangelina said. "Who were you to meet with?"

"I don't know that either," James admitted. "A young lady came to my office a few minutes ago and said I had a meeting in the conference room. I assumed this was the place since it is the closest to my assigned office."

"This building has too many conference rooms if you ask me," Vangelina said. "The young lady, was she in her late twenties, too pretty for her own good, wearing something off a Paris fashion runway?"

"Um, I can't speak for the Paris fashions," James said, "but the late twenties sounds about right, and she was beautiful."

"Well, how nice of you to notice," a voice said from behind James. "Has our guest already caused concerns from security, Vangelina?" the goddess asked.

"No problems so far," Vangelina said with a smile. Turning to James she said, "I think your problem is solved."

"Or just beginning," James said, looking at them both. "Before you go, Vangelina, I do have one more quick question. Who is this person standing next to me?"

"I am not sure you have the security clearance for that," Vangelina said with a serious tone.

"That's right, Mr. Nathaniels," the goddess said. "I am top secret."

"Even the Enigma Machine was solved eventually," James said, knowing he was being played. He saw President Starhemberg approaching with two other men. "If I can't know your name, can I know your job? Are we going to be working together?"

"Would you like that?" the goddess asked, sounding authentically serious.

"Are these two ladies helping or causing problems, James?" President Starhemberg asked as he arrived at the conference room door, apparently the right conference room door.

"Helping, Mr. President," James said, not wanting to throw anyone under a bus, even if this was a joke. 'Was it a joke?' he wondered. The last two days have been nothing but surprises.

"That would be a first," President Starhemberg said. "When these two get together I usually expect the worst."

"We were just explaining security clearances to him, Ernesto," the goddess said with complete innocence.

"I bet you were," President Starhemberg said. "James, let me introduce you to Vangelina Pereira."

"We have met, Mr. President. Thank you."

"She is part of my personal security detail," President Starhemberg explained. "She has been with me on a professional basis since my early days as governor of Rio Negro Province. I thought she would also be adult supervision for my sister, but alas that plan failed miserably."

"I do not need adult supervision!" the goddess, who it appeared was the President's sister, said in the same pouty mood James had seen earlier. "I am an adult as you can see and I am the one who brought Vangelina to our little team if you remember. I am hurt that you would think us," the goddess sister that still remained nameless continued, "two innocent and perfect specimens of the fairer sex, to ever cause any problems."

"Any first impression thoughts?" President Starhemberg asked James, startling him almost as much as he had in yesterday's meeting.

"Those that press to make mischief are usually the first to complain about it," James said with a smile. "I grew up with two sisters, Mr. President. I am used to being outnumbered by the fairer sex."

"Hah! Spoken like a true prophet, James," President Starhemberg said.

"Far from it, sir," James said. "A prophet would have been able to divine the name of your sister."

"I am sorry, James," President Starhemberg said authentically. "I had assumed she had already introduced herself when I asked her to welcome you and invite you to this meeting. All joking aside, let me introduce you to my most trusted confidant, my sister, Marisa Starhemberg."

James shook her hand for the first time, wondering if her other hand had a ring on it. "It is a true pleasure to meet you."

"And you James," Marisa said, finally serious. "I apologize for the less than enthusiastic welcome. I don't like Ernesto bringing on a foreigner who will be working so close with us."

"No offense taken," James said, trying to gain the courage to call her by her first name and failing. "I am wondering what I am doing here myself."

"Let's take this conversation into the conference room, and I will get to that," President Starhemberg said.

They entered, and everyone took a seat. The President opened a bottle of water on the counter and took a drink. "I was going to have this meeting in my office, but too many eyes have their focus there. I want to keep our discussions informal and out of the public eye for a time. Let me also introduce you to Alberto Godoy and Pepe Peralta Monti. Alberto is my Chief of Staff and Pepe is a personal adviser for National and International Security Affairs. It was Pepe actually that first noticed your work with the IMF. I have been getting weekly updates on your work for about six months. It was Pepe's contacts in the Energy Ministry who indirectly brought you to Argentina. You live a boring life, James. But that is good for us, and I hope good for you too. We need your talent, but we didn't want someone with complicated baggage."

"I am honored, Mr. President," James said, stunned. "I am not sure what I can do for you, but I am humbled by the time your staff and you have taken to, um, study me."

"We have a project that we plan to unveil to the world in three weeks and would like to bring you into our confidence and then have you help manage the fallout and rollout," President Starhemberg began. "What I want to know is, are you willing to be a team member of a very small group that will know all the details of a revolutionary idea that is now a reality? I know I am avoiding the particular subject—that is for our protection as well as yours were you to decide to not participate."

"Mr. President," James began, "you have my curiosity, but again I am not sure I have anything unique to offer your team."

"Let me explain a little further," Pepe said. "We are going to announce something to the world in three weeks. If you are willing to keep quiet for those three weeks—and that means you would be under very close watch for that time, we are prepared to explain this announcement is general detail with you right now. If you are not willing, we will let you leave with a month's severance pay, and this will have been a very interesting day. Once the announcement is made, we will not invite you back to this inner circle, but you may find a role to play in the broader project. The three-week informal house detention should not suggest that we don't trust you, but we simply don't know you that well. We believe within that three weeks you will know us better and us you."

"And if after that three weeks if you or I find I am not a fit on the team?" James asked.

"Then we will kill you," Marisa said.

"What?" James asked, not sure he had understood.

"Marisa is not happy with my decision to ask you to our little team," President Starhemberg said with a chuckle. "She is joking of course, but in the case that this arrangement doesn't work out, then…"

"Then we kill you," Marisa repeated.

President Starhemberg frowned at Marisa and continued, "Then we find another job for you here in Argentina where we can keep a close eye on you for six months. At that time the information you would have accumulated over the next three weeks would be mostly public knowledge. You would not be free to travel abroad, and your communications would be monitored. This may not sound like much of an inconvenience, but once imposed you would most likely feel like a prisoner. A much-desired prison, to be sure, but a prison nonetheless."

"I like your proposal better than your sister's," James said. "May I ask a few questions before we decide immediate directions?"

"Please, ask anything," President Starhemberg said.

"First," James began, "you presumably have a rough idea of my values. Does this proposal interfere in any way with what I would consider moral, ethical, and just?"

"You are right, we have made a rough judgment call on your morals, Mr. Nathaniels," Alberto said, speaking for the first time. "We have vetted you as best we can from a distance. You are honest, have integrity, and you are transparent, no criminal record, wise with your money, you aren't married and have no relationship encumbrances, and, he paused then continued, "we believe you have an abundance mentality." This last item seemed to slightly irritate the Chief of Staff.

"You know me better than my mother," James said. "But I am not a perfect person."

"There will be a time—starting tomorrow if you choose to join us, for you to be more specific with your imperfections," President Starhemberg said smiling. "But I must say it was telling that after your previous project you went to visit your family, not party to let off steam from the 18-month pressure cooker you had been in. We thought we had lost you when you left KPMG until you resurfaced professionally with even a better situation running your own private one-man company."

"I apologize Mr. Godoy," James said, looking at Alberto. "You told me what you think of me, but not about whether this project would demand any deviations from my values."

"The answer is no," the President said. "Not only will you not encounter any moral challenges, I personally believe you will be able to celebrate what you believe through this project."

"I don't want to take up so much of your time, but since you are asking for a quick decision, I have two more questions." James looked for approval to proceed. He took the President's relaxed demeanor to say 'take all the time you need.' "The obvious question—can you tell me why me? As you say, much of that explanation will come once the project is explained, but still, I must ask, why me?"

"We have to manage world opinion while keeping perspective of national interests of Argentina, the United States as the only real superpower, and of every other country on the globe, not to mention that of the international monetary system, industry, and technology. You fit plus as we described, you have the requisite values, and you are fluent in Spanish—which simplifies our communications immensely."

"Okay, so my last question," James began. "You mentioned yesterday that I would be working with your most trusted adviser. You introduced your sister as your most trusted adviser today. How will I be working with Marisa who would rather have me killed than be in the same room with me?"

"That, James, is why we are prepared to pay you a princely salary," President Starhemberg said. "It would be part of your duties to win her over."

The four people were staring at James expectantly. James was surprised that Marisa had said nothing when he asked about working with her. He knew what he wanted to do, but he was unsure of his own motives. "I'm in," he simply said.

"You have made my day," President Starhemberg said standing. "We will leave you in the very capable, and I hope non-lethal, hands of Marisa. She will brief you in and be your principle point of contact. We will all get together again next Tuesday at my home. Thank you, James. You are in for an amazing year." The President and his advisers departed after shaking hands and left the room. James was left to face Marisa. He thought it best to let her start the conversation.

"You know I could kill you and my brother would forgive me," Marisa began.

"Just send my month's severance pay to my parents," James said, believing she meant every word. "Listen, I am sorry I am not your first choice or even last choice, but I hope I can gain your trust. We are starting out with the same perspective if that is any consolation. I am still struggling to see my worth in this, but maybe that will become clearer once you explain things to me."

"It's not you personally," she began. "I am very uncomfortable bringing in a total stranger to something that can, will, change the world for the better, but it is so disruptive that it will also put a target on my brother's forehead, my only living family member. He and I have been nurturing each other since our parents died sixteen years ago in a small plane crash when we were both young. Ernesto was 19. I was only 12."

"I am sorry for your loss," James said. "At that age, it must have been terrifying on top of the personal tragedy to you both."

"Enough of my personal concerns," Marisa said sitting up straight and focusing on James. "Do you know what nuclear fusion is?"

"JOAB, through other Guardian channels we have received some disconcerting, but unconfirmed information of a secret project that has been under the direction of President Starhemberg since he was governor. Please confirm and report."

"Met with a new member of the Starhemberg inner circle. A North American, James Nathaniels, has been asked to support an unknown project that will be announced within the month. Unaware of the purpose and potential of the project. Will report with more details within the week. JOAB

CHAPTER 6

¿Trucho?

Literal Translation: Trout; Deviously Smart

Marisa's Explanation: Some fish are hard to catch. Some of the best trout streams in the world are in Patagonia. People spend thousands of dollars to travel and fish in places like San Martin de los Andes which is singled out year after year as the best fly fishing location in the world. I hope those who fish our streams don't feel like they have been duped, but the simple word has come to mean **Counterfeit, Fake, a person who lures foreigners into tourist traps**. The word could originate from the Spanish slang _truchamán_, which in turn derives from the Arabic _turjeman_ meaning translator. I like the fish story best.

"NUCLEAR FUSION?" JAMES ASKED. 'KIND of what I would love to have happen with you and me,' he thought as he sat down across the table from Marisa.

"What's the smirk for?" Marisa asked. "Is this a funny topic?"

"No, sorry," James answered. "You change subjects faster than Juan Fangio could turn a corner."

"You know of Fangio?" Marisa asked now a little surprised herself.

"Of course," James said. "Not everything from Argentina is a secret. He was the greatest Formula One driver in the history of the sport. Five world championships I think. But nuclear fusion?

Like in the sun, nuclear bombs, and the hope of free energy in the future?"

"Yes, that's the topic," Marisa confirmed. "Basically, nuclear fusion is essentially the opposite of nuclear fission, the reaction that is the center of all nuclear reactors today. In fission, a heavy nucleus is split into smaller nuclei and there is a release of energy. With fusion, lighter nuclei are fused into a heavier nucleus and there is a much larger release of energy."

"Okay, got it," James said.

"And you are right. The fusion process is what powers the sun. In that environment four isotopes of hydrogen-1 are fused into a helium-4 with the release of a tremendous amount of energy. And as you guessed, the first demonstration of nuclear fusion here on earth was the hydrogen bomb. A hydrogen bomb is approximately 1,000 times as powerful as the old fission atomic bomb."

"So now that I know your name, Marisa," James said, "can I ask, are you a physicist or something like that?"

"Yes, you may ask, but I don't really want to talk about me," Marisa said. "What I want to explain to you is, we have done it."

"You have a nuclear bomb?" James asked, blinking.

"No, you *imbécil*, we have the sun, in all its glory," Marisa said smiling.

"You are right," James said. I am not keeping up. You have the sun? Are you saying you have fusion? There have been some very embarrassing similar claims. If my history lessons were right, one of those happened here in Argentina with some escaped Nazi."

Marisa pursed her lips and James could tell she was holding her breath. "Like most histories of Argentina, they are biased against us. Austrian scientist Ronald Richter was not an escaped Nazi, although he did briefly work with scientists in Nazi Germany. He was not able to prove his theories with the technology of the day. This was before the era of the computer, before the transistor, before modern methods of testing and recording. On February 16, 1951, multiple scientists stated for record that they measured temperatures within the experiment chamber with an unexplained increase in heat. They concluded he had created energy by fusion without creating an uncontrollable explosion. The experiment was not verified and could not be reproduced by others."

"I am not a scientist, Marisa," James said, "but if you can't reproduce it, it doesn't exist. Science is brutal that way."

"I am so tempted to ensure that you never reproduce," Marisa began, but I will say, not only are you not a scientist but it is that attitude that kept the world flat for nearly a thousand years after Pythagoras said it was round in the 6th century BC."

"Wow, I am really pushing the wrong buttons here," James said. "I am in listening and learning mode. Please tell me what you need to explain."

"First let me provide some background," Marisa began. "You might know some or all of this, but assuming I am starting from the basics with you …," she paused then tried to smile and failed. "To achieve fusion, there are three main problems, temperature, time, and containment. With temperature, science has assumed that an extremely high energy level is required and the traditional avenue for that energy is a lot of heat, about 40 million degrees Kelvin. To get to Kelvin you need to add 273 to the Celsius temperature. That is hotter than the sun, James." Marisa paused to see if James was following her so far. James remained quiet. "The second challenge is time. The charged nuclei of helium or hydrogen isotopes must be held together very close for at least a second for the fusion reaction to start. A second is a very long time in this environment. The third issue is containment. Keeping this gas together at 40,000,000 K, has proven impossible. The best materials developed to this point would all vaporize when exposed to this temperature. The only ways conceived to heat something to this temperature and keep it in the same place for the required amount of time is through magnetic fields or lasers. Because the gas plasma has a charge, magnetic fields can be used to contain it, theoretically anyway. But if there is a leak, any leak, the reaction won't take place. And scientists have yet to create a magnetic field that won't allow the plasma to leak. Using lasers to charge the hydrogen isotope cocktail solves, or better said, skips, the containment problem. But no one had figured out how to protect the lasers themselves from the fusion reaction. As soon as the process starts, it stops."

"I think I am with you," James said, trying not to think about how beautiful Marisa's lips were when she talked science. "Continue."

"There is a fourth issue," Marisa continued, "which is really the sum of the first three issues I just explained. No one has ever reached a breakeven energy point, that is, getting out more energy than was put into the process, and without creating a runaway hydrogen bomb explosion."

"The bomb thing would be good to avoid," James said smiling.

Marisa ignored him and stood up and walked over to a white board. She began to write while she talked. This frustrated James as he could no longer see Marisa's lips moving. "There are several ways that have seemed promising. The first is Inertial Confinement Fusion," and Marisa wrote it on the board. "China has focused on this avenue and they have reported creating an environment three times hotter than the sun but for only about 100 seconds. Impressive, but still far from achieving a breakeven energy point. Then there is Magnetic Confinement Fusion. While no one has kept the gas plasma contained as I already explained, a recent new advance by a small fusion company in your country deserves a bit of research. If they've figured out an inexpensive way to increase the density, temperature and confinement time of a plasma to make nuclear fusion they might be a decade away from achieving breakeven." Marisa wrote this down with a question mark beside it. The third option that many have pursued is called Magnetized Target Fusion" She wrote this down and turned to James. "This method takes the best compatible features of magnetic confinement fusion and inertial confinement fusion. Like the magnetic approach, the fusion fuel is contained by magnetic fields while it is heated to the required temperature. The idea here is to initiate fusion by rapidly squeezing the plasma to increase density and temperature. The resulting density is far lower than with other techniques, but the theory is the combination of increased confinement times and longer heat retention will sustain a fusion reaction, while solving the construction challenges of the other techniques."

"Clear as mud," James said. I think I understand the basics of your explanation. I certainly understand the promise of easy fuel, no complicated or harmful garbage, and the potential to meet all of humanity's energy needs for hundreds of millions of years."

"Exactly," Marisa said. "But it isn't that simple of course, and I am not talking about solving the problems I just outlined."

"Which one did you solve?" James asked.

"None of them," Marisa said. "You mentioned the embarrassing claims of the past. None have been more ridiculed than the claims of cold fusion. People say cold fusion has never been replicated, but there's been 17,000 replications worldwide since Pons and Fleischmann made their claim," she said.

"You are saying you have not only solved the fusion mystery, but you did it without all the heat?" James asked. "I guess if someone could do that it would solve all the time and containment issues as well."

"Exactly professor," Marisa said, now smiling, showing her sparkling white teeth.

"You know if you are wrong you have not only committed academic suicide, but you will make Argentina a laughing stock among nations for a century," James said.

"The Bariloche Atomic Center overlooks the island where Richter's experiments took place and was founded by the very scientist, Jose Antonio Balseiro, who told General Peron about Richter's experiments," Marisa explained without commenting on James' concerns. "Even though Richter left Argentina in shame, scientists from the institute have continued experimental research and have developed advanced research nuclear reactors and designed a uranium enrichment plant that places Argentina in an elite community of nine countries with such technology."

"So it is this Institute that developed the fusion break-through?" James asked.

"Not exactly," Marisa said. "The Institute provided the cover and some of the same personnel from the Institute worked on the fusion project first started by Richter. His most closely held notes have never been shared with anyone outside of a small group of Argentine scientists. You know, until about twenty years ago, Argentina's nuclear program was considered dangerous by arms control officials in your country and in Europe, since we refused to let the International Atomic Energy Agency inspect our sites. President Carlos Menem finally let inspectors in and they found a very harmless, albeit advanced research and development facility. What the world was unaware of was the reopening of the Huemul Island facilities, sponsored by my brother as the new governor of Rio Negro Provence."

"This isn't some recent breakthrough," James surmised, "but many decades of work."

"And many failures and dead-end streets," Marisa said. "And that brings me to why my brother wants to involve you in this project. As he said, in three weeks he is going to announce this to the world. We have three basic concerns. First, no one is going to believe us. Scientists have two basic roles, first to learn new things, find new information, and prove new theories correct or incorrect. Their second role is to communicate the truth to others. They are going to want to see the science. They are going to want to take it home to replicate it themselves. They will want us to give away, what we want to control. The irony is, our goal is just that, to give it away. But more on that issue later. My brother feels you can help us sort through the risk issues with this announcement."

"I will do my best to add to whatever you have already prepared," James said.

"Well, let me explain our other two concerns," Marisa said. "Secondly, we are concerned about security. Once this goes public, there will be those who have a zero-sum mentality and will want to take it and keep it for themselves. We know security, physical security is not your expertise, but Ernesto seems to think you will have some valuable input there as well. Finally, we know this isn't a fairytale. We can't simply announce that energy will soon be basically free and we all live happily ever after. The world's economic ecosystem could collapse with such good news. Governments could fall, wars could be fought. On this I grudgingly agree, we need someone who might help us walk through this minefield. Nothing personal, but we have many excellent Argentine Cultural and Political Risk analysis experts. I was overruled. Ernesto wants an outsider and he is right, you have recent experience that you might be just that person."

"That you are even thinking about these issues is a credit to your wisdom," James said. "I will do this, but with one small condition that I don't think will upset your brother and the other members of the team, but might be a show stopper for you."

"And that is?" Marisa asked with furrowed eyebrows.

"Two dates," James said. "Two opportunities for us to get to know each other. I call them dates because no business talk would be allowed. If you have a boyfriend or um, a significant other, then let's not call them dates, but "get-to-know -you sessions," or something that doesn't get caught in your throat. The bottom line for me is, we need to learn to work together or I might as well pack my bags, because this won't work."

"Ha, we've got you there," Marisa said. "You already agreed that if we shared our project with you, you would not be going anywhere for quite some time—whether you take the job or not. And the answer is no."

"No, you won't get to know me?" James asked disappointed, but not surprised.

"No, I don't have a serious boyfriend or significant other," Marisa said suddenly on unstable ground. But for the first time today I agree with you. We will not call our outings dates."

"Good," James said. "The sooner the better for our first outing. We need to find some common ground, fast. You can choose the time and place. So what is the next step?"

"I have no idea, you just laid this plan on me," Marisa said, back to her defensive mode.

"No, I mean with the fusion project roll out," James said smiling. I would first like to better understand President Starhemberg's goals and what success for him would look like. From that foundation, we can build some "what if" scenarios and then build some risk mitigation plans."

Marisa stared at James for what felt like several minutes, but was only 30 seconds Marisa knew. This foreign interloper had just stated off the top of his head a plan that Ernesto and his team had struggled to put into words for over two months. Some of what James had just explained was underway, but not in an organized fashion. For the hundredth time this week Marisa wondered if Argentina was ready for the role her brother was thrusting upon the nation.

"You know, they aren't going to believe us," Marisa said.

"The world isn't going to believe you have actually cracked the fusion nut?" James asked.

"No dummy," Marisa said. "My brother is not going to believe that our outings are not really dates."

"Is that going to be a problem?" James asked. "I would be happy to explain if that would help."

"It doesn't matter," Marisa said. "I'm a big girl. Although now that I think of it, you may have to explain to Vangelina. When our parents died, Vangelina became our caretaker. She was an acquaintance of my parents and the closest thing to a godmother I had, so she just stepped in. Ernesto and I were in such shock, we just let her. It was only later she took on a security role. She takes my security very seriously."

"Not to change the subject, but you know there is a very real possibility the world will just laugh in your face when you make your announcement. Are you prepared for that?"

"The name calling and laughter?" Marisa asked.

"That, and some way to prove what you have done is real," James replied. "I am guessing, from what you explained to me the Ministry of Energy is not going to be giving guided tours of your facility."

"The Energy Ministry doesn't even know about this project yet. This has been very, very closely held. You are the Sixth person outside of the core development team themselves that knows about this."

"You mean the President, yourself, Alberto Godoy and Pepe Peralta Monti, is it?" James asked.

"That's it, except for one other adviser that you will meet soon enough and of course the actual engineers and physicists which are 18 people," Marisa said. "There are many others that have played a role, through our regular nuclear research and development efforts, but they have no idea what has been going on under their noses. We thought it best, just in case failure was the final outcome."

"What has been your part in this, Marisa?" James asked. "You seem to be well educated and more than merely the spoiled sister of the President."

"Let's save that for another time," Marisa said. "I prefer you think of me as you said, the spoiled sister of the President. Since we are off topic, I would like to say one other thing that has been bothering me. A major plank of President Fernandez's foreign policy back in 2015 was her failed effort to open talks with Great Britain over the sovereignty of the Malvinas Islands. President Macri dropped it, but my brother wants to resurrect this as an item of international dialogue. Please do not encourage him. He is going to have so much on his plate once Cambalache goes public."

"I wasn't kidding that I think I could help you get your islands back," James said. "But I will not bring it up again, unless your brother brings it up."

"Thank you," Marisa said. "Let's go see your actual office now. You will also have a room at the Quinta de Olivos."

"I've already been to my office," James said. "You met me there."

"That was a temporary parking spot," Marisa explained. "That room and the surrounding hallway offers the feeling of "being on the inside," but it is under constant video surveillance and there are plain clothes guards in some of the adjacent cubicles. We use it for visitors that we want to provide the feeling of being on the inside, when in fact they are still outside. You have an office closer to Ernesto, for his convenience."

"And a room at the Quinta de Olivos?" James asked. "Is that necessary? Also for the President's convenience?"

"That was actually my idea," Marisa said. "I didn't know you were already located so close in Vicente Lopez. I wanted to keep better tabs on you, plus, I tend to work late into the night and it would be easier to have you closer by. Plus, it will be easier to kill you if we need to."

"Project pronouncement probable. Could be announced in San Carlos de Bariloche on 25 May. Not the usual security precautions with this situation. Could be a local project in support of the President's run for a second term, so minor it hasn't hit anyone's radar. Could be something more sensational. Could this portend Ernst Rüdiger Starhemberg's project considering the location of the announcement? Three generations with the same hope the same hex? Yes, it is a possibility." JOAB

CHAPTER 7

Cambalache
Literal Translation: Bazaar or Junkshop

<u>*Marisa's Explanation*</u>: One man's junk is another man's treasure. A second-hand store is a place of discovery, and you never know what great find you may uncover. It's **A World of Opportunities** if you know what you are looking for, or have an open mind toward what's being offered.

THE NEXT THREE WEEKS WENT by as fast as Lionel Messi can change direction with the fútbol at his feet. James had a few nightmares that he was back in his IMF contract, minus the airports. At times he felt like a Messi fútbol; go here, no there, position, react, attack, run, kick! And quite often, a goal.

"Time for a break, James," Marisa said one evening about ten. They were about a week into their scenario building. They had met with the President, Godoy and Peralta Monti twice. James and Marisa had not left the Quinta in all that time. Marisa bent back in her chair and stretched her arms. They were working at the Quinta de Olivos briefing room typically used by the President's Ministers when they visited. "Our first unofficial get-to-know-you session begins now."

"That wasn't the deal, Marisa," James said, ready for a break himself. "It has to be away from business. We can't just sit here where we have been working for days and call this a break."

"We won't just be sitting here," Marisa said. "I am going to take you on a tour of the Quinta." They walked out into the fresh air and listened to the quiet country sounds. A distant siren reminded them that they were actually in the middle of one of the larger cities in the world. Walking past the vegetable garden, Marisa said, "This raised garden was started by President Macri's wife, Juliana. I am sure there have been gardens since President Justo initiated beautification projects in and around the Quinta. The jacaranda trees along the Avenida del Libertador were planted by him. Some say those projects were in preparation for the first North American guest at the residence, U.S. President Franklin Roosevelt."

"Lots of beauty and history here," James said, actually thinking about her.

"And lots of tragedy and strange goings on," Marisa added, unaware of the compliment. You know, Macri's decision to get into politics came after he was kidnapped back in 1991, I think. A gang of corrupt police officers held him for two weeks until his father paid a $6 million ransom. They kept him in a coffin you know. I can't imagine. Sometimes I wonder if the gardens his wife created were for him, you know a place of peace and safety."

"It does feel peaceful here," James said, putting his arm around Marisa's shoulders when he noticed a slight shudder. "Are you cold? We can do this another time if you like. I was just kidding about being away from work,"

"Thank you, James," Marisa said. "No, I'm not cold, but I appreciate your arm around me. You know, this is where Evita Peron died. Then her body was kidnapped, for nearly twenty years. Another kidnapped coffin. At first, the military hid the coffin, then a few years later, in 1957 through the covert support of the Vatican, she was taken to Italy and buried in a Milan cemetery under a fake name. Even then she was not allowed to rest in peace. In 1970 the Monteneros, an Argentine terrorist group, kidnapped and then killed the former president, General Pedro Eugenio Aramburu. They said they targeted him because he had overseen the initial kidnapping of Evita's corpse."

"This is stranger than any fiction I read," James said, both enjoying his arm around Marisa and the crazy story. "I know she is buried in Recoleta. How did she finally come back to Argentina?"

"When the Peronist Party was legalized, those who protected her body decided she should be returned to her widower, Juan Peron, who at that time lived in exile in Spain. Her coffin was once again dug up and driven secretly across Europe and delivered to Peron's home. He took the body out of the coffin and laid it on a table. Evita's body was cleaned by Isabel Peron, the President's wife. Isabel even cleaned Evita's hair and blow dried it. Evita's fingers were missing, probably removed after the military coup of 1955 to verify the body was actually that of Evita. The original embalming work had kept her well preserved. In 1973, when Juan Peron and Isabel returned to Argentina, they left Evita in Madrid. As you know, Peron was elected president with his wife as vice-president in 1974. When he died suddenly the following year, Isabel became president, and it was she that brought Evita's body from Madrid to Argentina. It was right here," Marisa said, pointing to a nondescript building she had stopped in front of, "where Evita's body was, how would you say it, restored? Made presentable? Evita was once again put on display for the public, with her husband's closed coffin next to hers. Both Juan Peron even in his death, and Isabel full of life knew the power was in Evita, alive or dead."

"Are you alright, Marisa?" James asked. "It is a somber story, but you tell it like it is your family."

"I remember my own parents in their coffins. Remember, I was only 12. Trying to make sense of that at my age then was impossible for me. Coming here and learning the stories of this place bring back the nonsense of death and the sometimes nonsense of life. They say Peron sat at the bedside of Evita as she lay dying, holding her hand and crying. Her enemies say he was weeping because, without her charisma, his power, his presidency was doomed." Marisa fell silent, and she and James walked toward a row of garages. "One of Evita's last statements," Marisa began again, "was how she wanted her nails manicured. Those would be the same fingers that would later be taken from her."

James realized this tour was really a personal confession of Marisa's fears and wisely kept quiet. He rubbed her soft shoulder with his hand as he let his arm drop and then he took her hand in his. She accepted his grasp without recognizing it.

"This building used to be a stable for polo horses," Marisa said as she pointed to the garage with her free hand. For a time it was converted into a school, called the Union of Secondary School Students. It was established by President Perón just months after Evita's death in 1952. The school was for athletic young girls. In 1953 a secret tunnel was built giving Perón covert access to the school. When this was found out, it became one of the scandals that led to the military coup in 1955. The coup was led by General Pedro Aramburu, who as I mentioned would be kidnapped and killed for his part in taking Evita's body. He also became the first president to reside habitually at the Quinta de Olivos. You know there are times when I feel like this place is cursed. It was the site of secret negotiations between President Arturo Frondizi and the Argentine-born Cuban revolutionary and Economy Minister, Che Guevara to try to find a solution to the US-Cuban crisis in 1961. Of course, when that became public it led to Frondizi's overthrow a year later. Even the happy times seemed cursed. President Juan Carlos Onganía held a large party here in 1969 that caused a fire to almost burn down the entire Quinta."

"There is much good that has come from this place, Marisa," James said. "I am sure the White House in Washington, D.C. has similar tales of tragedy, but also stories of overcoming the worst parts of our nature."

"That is my hope, James," Marisa said. "I love this place for its potential. I hate this place for the toll it has taken on our nation and on those who have found themselves at the helm of this nation. That is now my brother, and for odd reasons of my brother's past, I am the de facto first lady, since Ernesto is not married. I didn't want any of this, but Ernesto was born to it. For him, I am here."

"You too may have been born to this, Marisa," James ventured. "You are one of the smartest people I have ever met. You are beautiful, certainly, but that only keeps your real talents in the shadows until you are ready to employ them. Argentina is blessed to have both you and your brother at this place in this most defining moment in the history of your country and perhaps the world. Honestly, I can't believe I am standing here with you. I am holding your hand," James said, lifting her hand in his, "partly because I want to hold you closer to the ground where I am at. I fear you could rise in greatness like a helium balloon and escape me."

"Or more likely, pop like a balloon," Marisa said. "I like holding your hand for whatever the reason. Let's keep this simple, though. We have to keep our heads out of the clouds and get through the next months without losing our heads, literally."

"Agreed," James said, squeezing her hand and then letting it go. "One suggestion, though," James added. "On our next non-date, let's do something more light-hearted. I am honored that you have shared your fears, but I also want to know what makes you smile, what makes you laugh, and what you love."

"Oh, that is easy," Marisa said. "Let's finish our scenario building and celebrate with one of my favorite places in the city."

"That sounds like a motivator to nail the scenarios right away," James said with real enthusiasm. They parted company when they reentered the main house at the Quinta. 'To think this place almost entirely burnt down,' James thought as he walked to his room. The workmanship and beauty of the place continued to overwhelm him. He thought of the miniature golf course, the theater, the paved paths through hundred-year-old trees that were all part of this presidential residence, "It's all just surface level junk. A very nice junkyard to be sure, but it is the people and their ghosts that make this place what it is." James knew at that moment that he would do whatever he could, whatever it took, to help and to protect Marisa and her brother. It never occurred to him to ask himself if that was his heart or his head that was expressing this commitment.

Three days later the 'what if scenarios' were outlined and briefed to the President. Starhemberg was happy with what James and Marisa had produced. He suggested they continue their efforts toward getting a rough draft of the follow-through actions of each scenario before bringing in Godoy and Peralta Monti for a review of which direction they should plan for. President Starhemberg pulled James aside and said, "Day after tomorrow you will take a little day trip to see Cambalache. Marisa suggested it is time to let you see the actual project. You have gained Marisa's confidence James, and that is no little feat. Thank you for everything you are doing for us."

James wondered what he had meant when he said 'us.' Did he mean Argentina, the world, the Cambalache team, or did he mean Marisa and him? James didn't ask. He simply said, "It is an honor, sir. I hope my efforts go unnoticed because that will mean they were fruitful and your project is successful."

"Well said, well said," President Starhemberg said with a thoughtful stare. "Marisa's favorite ice cream flavor is Dulce de Leche, and she likes it bañado de chocolate."

"Bathed in chocolate, sir?" James asked. "Why should I need to know her favorite ice cream?"

"You'll see," Starhemberg said. "She had to run her plans past the security detail and of course they came to me. Sorry, but Vangelina will be chaperoning you on your second date with Marisa. Security is an unfortunate part of life for Marisa."

"Our second date?" James asked still completely lost in the conversation.

"That is what Marisa called it," President Starhemberg said. "Be good and don't say out too late."

As Starhemberg walked away, James stood there wondering what all Marisa had told her brother. So, a second date? "Outstanding," James said aloud.

It wasn't until after lunch the next day that Marissa announced that she would be taking James on an outing. She didn't call it a date, but James didn't mind. Marisa and James met Vangelina at the garage, and the three of them got in a black Mercedes sedan, and the driver proceeded through a side gate of the residence onto Hernan Wineberg Street. Turning on Corrientes then again on Avenida del Libertador, they soon arrived at what the sign said was Helado Villa Flaminia. 'Ice cream,' James thought. For the first time in more than two weeks, he felt prepared for something.

While Vangelina paid, even though James had attempted to pay, Marisa began to explain the art and science of Argentine ice cream. "Next to Argentine beef, the ice cream here is the best in the world."

James was mesmerized watching the attendant prepare a cone for another customer. He had scooped out the ice cream but then turned the cone upside down. The ice cream did not fall out but instead started elongating. "The ice cream has a unique viscosity that not only enhances the flavor but slows the melting time and allows for this stretching process," Marisa was explaining. By this time the ice cream was maybe a foot long. James was wondering how it would maintain that shape once the cone was again turned upright. He got his answer. The attendant moved the cone over some sort of pot built into the counter and dipped it in.

"The chocolate is kept at a temperature that doesn't melt the ice cream, but liquid enough that the ice cream can be completely dipped," Marisa explained.

The attendant pulled out the ice cream and dipped it immediately in another canister that appeared to super cool it. He then took it out and turned it right-side-up and handed it to the customer.

"I want one of those," James explained. "Two dulce de leche bañado de chocolate," he told the attendant. "Vangelina, what did you want?"

"Nothing, thank you, James," Vangelina said. "I'm on duty. I don't want to be distracted. I will be out in front, Marisa," Vangelina said and walked out of the shop. It was a relatively quiet part of a very busy street. The neighborhood was mostly residential homes and a few small businesses. It didn't look very dangerous, but he was out on a date with the President's sister. The all–glass front of the shop and the bright pink walls made for clear silhouettes that made Vangelina nervous.

"So, is this our second official date?" James asked. "If it is, you sure know how to show a guy a great time."

"Did Ernesto talk to you?" Marisa asked as she took her cone from the attendant.

"When it comes to you, your brother and I are of one mind," James said watching his cone being prepared.

"Ernesto is never of one mind," Marisa said. "He always has at least two or three going at the same time. As for you, James, …you know I really need to find a nick name for you, but never mind. As for you, I am not sure I have met anyone so single-minded. Few can say they can outwork me, but you can. You exhaust me."

"That's much better than you telling me you are tired of me," James said as he took his first bite. The chocolate was just soft enough not to shatter and hard enough to hold the slowly melting ice cream inside. "Oh my, that is good! *Helado* heaven. Forget anything else. This could change the course of humanity right here."

Marisa smiled and leaned into James's ear and whispered, "This is another kind of cold fusion, here with you."

"I love it," James said and he leaned into Marisa's ear, "The other thing can't be any better than this, here with you."

"We will find out tomorrow," Marisa said. "I want your honest opinion, promise?"

"Promise," James said, even though he wasn't quite sure what he was promising.

They enjoyed the afternoon hour eating ice cream, laughing at childhood memories, and coming up with reasons to whisper in each other's ears. Before either was ready, they found themselves back in the car on the way back to work. By the time they arrived at the Quinta, they were back in Cambalache mode. They worked late into the evening and were up early the next morning to take Tango 02 to San Carlos de Bariloche.

The airport at Bariloche was just a few miles from town. They drove through the center directly to the lake front. A sleek hydrofoil was waiting for them along with Pepe Peralta Monti. They took the boat farther to the North West and were on Huemul Island less than ten minutes later. James noticed several large brick and concrete buildings that had fallen into disrepair."

"That bunker-looking building was the original building Richter constructed to house his experiments," Marisa explained. "The building to the right was living quarters and storage. The other buildings in the original operation were blown up when the world believed the project was closed down."

"Much of the actual project," Pepe Peralta-Monti continued from Marisa's introduction, "was underground. No one considered that option in the day because of the relatively small size of Huemul Island. The other nuclear research facilities spawned from the Huemul Project also help deflect focus on the ruins here at Huemul. Some of Richter's lab machinery went on to form the core of the technological structure of both the Centro Atómico Bariloche and the Instituto Balseiro. For nearly thirty years, the Richter particle accelerator he purchased from Philips in the Netherlands was the only one in use in South America. Although none of this was created as a smoke screen, once the Huemul Project got its second start, no one even noticed."

Pepe escorted James and Marisa beyond the old buildings to a gate in a chain-link fence. Danger signs were posted, and there was a roll of barbwire at the top of the fence, but otherwise there was no obvious security. Pepe opened the gate with an electronic key and the three entered. They walked about ten yards down a path where the group was hidden from the fence area. Two men in camouflage stepped out from a hidden guard post and greeted them, not friendly, but not confrontationally.

"We have been on closed circuit T.V. since we landed on the Island," Pepe explained. "We decided long ago that it was better to keep security low key so as not to lure unwanted attention. That has worked well for years, but as we move to a new phase with the announcement, we have needed to rethink our entire security arrangement."

The two guards checked all three individuals, identification and then allowed them to continue on down the path. They came to a metal maintenance shed, a posted sign announced. Pepe produced another electronic card that he touched to the maintenance sign. His face was scanned by a hidden camera whose lens was disguised as one of the screws of the sign. The shed door clicked, and Pepe opened it. Inside it appeared to be an actual maintenance shed. Several older vehicles were parked to the right; a jeep and a large four track. To the left was a snowmobile. They walked past the vehicles to a wall where tools were hung. To their left was a set of stairs that led down to a small trench below an oil change rack. They went down the stairs and through yet another door in the trench. They entered a small elevator and when the door closed a fine mist blew past all three people.

"That was a final security measure, a collection of our DNA to confirm all three of us are expected," Pepe explained. "If there is any doubt, this elevator becomes our temporary jail. We have not installed the newer bran scan technology here."

The elevator began to descend and opened far below the lake water level. The doors opened onto a catwalk above a large open area.

"There is another entrance where we can bring in large items, but we try to use that as little as possible," Marisa said. "This is the central assembly area and as you see it is mostly empty now. The machine, C1, is in the accelerator room next door."

They walked above the assembly area and through a glass door into the accelerator room. What James saw defied simple description. Below him was a huge metal doughnut, maybe twenty meters in diameter. Three people dressed in white head to foot were standing near the doughnut. They recognized Marisa and waved. She blew a kiss back.

"The most common approach to fusion efforts are with Tomamak machines," Marisa said. They look distantly similar to this and cage ionized gasses called plasmas in magnetic fields while heating them to the outlandish temperatures needed for hydrogen nuclei to fuse. I explained that type of machine on day one with you. Then there is the Stellarator, the largest of which is a third smaller than Cambalache and is at the Max Planck Institute in Germany. It employs super-cooled coiled copper to create a magnetic field to hold the plasma. Do you remember the fusion lesson I gave you?"

"Yes, as long as I won't be tested," James said.

"Both the Tomamak and the Stellarator must battle the tremendous temperatures. With Cambalache, the shell is to contain the resultant energy, not the near room temperature energy required to produce it."

"Maybe a silly question, but we are safe just walking in here with street clothes?" James asked. "I mean, is there a radiation danger?"

"Cold fusion does not use any radioactive materials, nor does it produce any radioactive bi-products," Marisa explained. "We generate heat nearly compatible to fission reactors, but without burning nuclear fuel. We aren't breaking anything apart, we are simply putting things together. Hot fusion does this with high heat. We accomplish this through the consumption of hydrogen in a non-radioactive nuclear process. All other cold fusion experiments are built on table tops and create tiny bursts of energy in the twenty-watt range. None are sustainable. They all are so unstable and built on guess work that they appear to be wrong measurements or quack science. Richter's original tests were categorized as quack science because no one could duplicate his tests. Hans Thirring, the Director of the Institute for Theoretical Physics in Vienna, reported something like, "it is a 50 per cent probability that Perón is giving credit to the ravings of a fantasist; a 40 per cent probability that the president has been the victim of a massive scam; and a nine per cent chance that Richter is telling the truth." It was a tragedy for the world that this technology was so quickly rejected. Perón set up an analysis board that after several months of reviews of Richter's work reported that Richter didn't even attain nuclear fission. Well, of course, he didn't. Neither have we with Cambalache. He did create a power burst that cracked the concrete structure you saw when we landed on the island. The analysis board explained it away as a hydrogen burn. Richter died in Buenos Aires in 1991 not realizing he actually did establish fusion, he was just decades ahead of his time and didn't have the right equipment to control and measure his process."

Pepe Peralta-Monte chuckled and added, "James, your country's patent office stopped accepting patents around the cold fusion topic in 2004. They reject all patents in this area with the Luddite argument that they don't work."

"So, how does it work?" James asked. "I mean, the basic idea—I'm not looking for the full scientific explanation."

"The technology centers around the ratio of hydrogen to palladium atoms," Marisa explained. "When that exceeds 90 percent, cold fusion results. Of course, it isn't that simple. Electrical current density must be carefully managed, and that takes some supercomputing—something not available to Richter nor his naysayers."

"So why does this reactor look like a pile of junk?" James asked. "No disrespect on what you have created, but it has so many warts and bumps."

"That is partly for collection of data input, and partly for output, that is for fusion control and for the resultant power from the fusion reaction," Marisa explained. One of the problems of present table top fusion experiments is the small size. Most want to believe that one of the incredible benefits of fusion is the lack of need for energy distribution because they can be provided anywhere and everywhere. This is only partly true. In order to create the exact environment and control of the reaction for sustainability, it requires size and supercomputing that so far Moore's Law has not reduced to that level of miniaturization."

"Thus, the name Cambalache?" James asked.

"I am guessing you have researched the word?" Marisa asked. "As you know then, Cambalache means bazaar or junkshop and this machine resembles that. But in Argentine slang, it means much more. As defined by the tango song of the same name, written in 1934 by Enrique Santos Discépolo, it attacks 20th-century corruption. This Cambalache," Marisa said pointing to the machine below, "is the 21st-century bazaar, the optimistic, the hopeful, the Argentine answer to the Argentine problems, the Argentine answer to humanity's failures."

"We would love to show you Cambalache in operation, but is down for scheduled maintenance," Pepe said. "In a perfect world, we would have two already running, so constant energy is always available, but we are limited to C1, and so far secrecy has been paramount. C2 and C3 are still in development and testing. Let me just say that six of these machines will be able to provide for the energy needs of the entire country of Argentina, or about 20 Megacities, at our present rate of consumption for over one hundred years at an amortized cost of about one million U.S. dollars per year. That is mostly for the cost of the machine, maintenance, personnel, and distribution. That is pennies per person per year. Of course, the fuel itself is almost free. The cost of containment and delivery far outweighs the fuel itself."

"Come, we must go," Marisa said, looking at her watch. "We need to make a necessary side-trip. I will explain once we are on the boat again."

"Research requested on subject James Nathaniels. Possible connection to Ernst Rüdiger Starhemberg project? Very close, very fast, to President Starhemberg. He is also making inroads with President's normally recalcitrant sister Marisa Starhemberg. Appears he is connected to the 25 May announcement. No one knows who he is or what his role may be. Spending most of the day, every day, with M. Starhemberg. Nathaniels could be a keystone to project. Remove him and project buried in rubble as directed?" JOAB

CHAPTER 8

¡Ojo!
Literal Translation: Eye

Marisa's Explanation: The Eye of Providence, the all-seeing eye of God, knows and sees all. It warns of danger: **Caution, Be careful!** Argentines love to warn of trouble as if they are all seeing. Oftentimes we are you know. Argentines struggle to communicate without hand gestures, thus we touch the skin below our eye and give it a little tug. A vociferous people, Argentines amplify the caution by just uttering in an ominous tone the single word. After all the threats my parents gave me as a child, I knew I had hit the limit of their patience with me when my father finally looked at me and said ¡Ojo!

"**N**ORTH OF US, ABOUT 25 miles," Marisa was explaining to James, "is the National Park Bosque de Arrayanes. This is the only place in the entire world where the Luma Apicuata trees are found in a natural habitat. Many of these trees are over 300 years old and some over 600 years old. This forest can only be reached by boat via the port of Villa La Angostura, our next destination. There is a path there that some walk, but we will take by mountain bike."

"We are going mountain biking in an ancient forest?" James asked. "Is this date number three?" he asked hopefully.

"This, dear James, is a diversion," Marisa said smiling. "You may call it what you wish, but in order to look the tourist, we have added this additional leg to our day. If we only visited

Huemul Island and not anything else in the area, not even the town of Bariloche, well, someone would begin to wonder what might be going on at Huemul."

"Okay, I can play tourist," James said. "Can you tell me a little more about this forest we are going to visit?"

"Los Arrayanes, the park, was created in 1971 to protect the rare arrayán trees as I said. At first, there was a dirt path that visitors used to see these trees, but that was causing significant damage to the soil around the trees. A wooden path is now the only way to walk through the forest. As a girl, I used to visit and would see pudú and huemul deer, guanacos, monitos de monte and small foxes, and lots of birds; condors, eagles, hawks, and woodpeckers. With so many people visiting now, I am not sure what we might see."

"May I ask a question while we are on the boat about Cambalache?" James asked, wondering if this was a safe place to talk.

"No not now," Marisa said. "The boat pilot and two crewmen are of course cleared through security, but not for anything related to Cambalache. Please play the tourist for now and if you can, be my, um, be my friend, you know my friend trying to become my boyfriend. It provides a much more convincing picture. Remember, I am the spoiled and capricious sister of the President, so I might not respond to your advances, just so you know."

"I hope I am your friend, Marisa," James said. "No play acting, I really hope you have gotten to know me enough that we don't have to pretend. As for the pursuing boyfriend, I don't remember that being in the contract discussions. That is asking a lot don't' you think?"

"Is it?" Marisa asked, looking away toward the approaching dock. "You don't have to, of course. I just thought it might help deflect a focus on, well, you know maybe you are right. Let's just be friends or even just work associates, and I am showing off the beauty of Argentina to a poorly educated North American."

"Ha, ha," James said as he put an arm around Marisa. She stiffened but did not move away. "You are indeed showing me the beauty of Argentina. You did that the day you turned up to greet me, or kill me, at the Casa Rosada."

Marisa turned to look at James and displayed her pouty face.

"I love it when you make that face," James said. "Your lips puff out and demand, kiss me, kiss me! Your eyes, however, say don't you dare. One of these days I hope I can figure out which to obey."

"Ojo, James," Marisa said as she touched the skin just below her right eye and pulled it down slightly. "Be careful and obey the eyes."

"You've got to help translate some of the Argentine dichos, sayings that I hear so much," James said trying to lighten the mood. He could see that her eyes were filling with tears, but none were spilling over. Marisa was no longer pouting, but she wasn't happy either. Melancholy perhaps? Vulnerability, but with a thin veneer of distrust or maybe anger. He decided to follow her wishes and obey the eyes, for now.

The hovercraft landed, and the boat pilot told Marisa, "Two hours Señorita Starhemberg. I need to get you back to the town by four. Your plane departs at five."

"I have arranged for bikes for three," Pepe Peralta Monti added, "but I don't think I am up for the ride today. I will grab my lunch and do some reading while I enjoy the sunshine and peace here at the dock. A security team came here earlier today and are strategically stationed at points along the trail. Enjoy your ride, but the captain is right, be back in an hour so we can get back to Buenos Aires by eight. President Starhemberg would like you both to join him for dinner at nine."

James and Marisa put a bag lunch that had been prepared back in Buenos Aires, along with water bottles in their small backpacks and set off on the bikes. They road through the bright orange and cinnamon colored trees. Most had irregular white spots and smooth, cool bark and were twisted in odd directions, but all reached skyward with the highest ones reaching 40 or 50 feet. Their trunks were slender, maybe 20 inches in diameter and there was little vegetation on the ground. A few miles down the path James noted more vegetation; emerald ferns and lime green grasses, and a few park visitors. He hadn't seen any security personnel.

"These trees were the inspiration for the forest in the Walt Disney movie, Bambi," Marisa explained. "We can stop just up the path at a tea house called Bambi, and eat our lunch if you like."

"Sounds perfect," James said. "This is certainly a magical place. Why am I not surprised there is a Bambi tea house in the middle of it all?"

"The Cordillera, the Andes Mountain range is a magical place," Marisa replied as she dismounted her bike by the tea house. "I wish we had time to see some of my favorite places not that far from here. The Perito Moreno glacier about 50 miles west of the quaint little town of Calafate, for example. That glacier field is the world's third largest reserve of fresh water. Not far from Calafate is also Mount Fitz Roy. It is one of the most challenging mountains to climb on earth. Its sharp granite peaks are only accessible a few days a year, and although not as high as Mount Everest, many more conquer Everest than Fitz Roy."

"You ought to be a tour guide," James said.

"When I was younger that was my plan," Marisa said. "I spent hours memorizing places and facts. I never wanted to leave Patagonia. I had plans for a cabin in Bariloche and a summer flat in Ushuaia. There are places in Tierra del Fuego that defy description."

"So why did you leave?" James asked.

"School," Marisa said.

"Where?" James asked.

Marisa stared at James trying to make up her mind if she wanted to share her past with him. She took another bite of her bocadillo sandwich and chewed on her thoughts. She said, "I completed my undergraduate degree at the Autonomous University of Madrid, in Spain and then did some post-graduate studies first at the University of Vienna, but transferred to the University of Innsbruck, and finally landed at Cambridge in England."

"Impressive," James said.

"My education?" Marisa asked.

"No, I just noticed we have Havana alfajores for desert," James said with a broad smile. Of course, I mean your education. What did you study?"

"Science, physics mostly, but also fashion and parties and getting into trouble," Marisa said.

"Ah ha," James proclaimed. "I knew you were more than the spoiled sister of the President."

"No in those days, I was pretty much the spoiled daughter of deceased parents who left Ernesto and me with a sizeable inheritance. I was lost and looking. I just didn't know what I was looking for. Ernesto, on the other hand, was much more stable. He studied at the University of Buenos Aires and then at the National Autonomous University of Mexico, in Mexico City. You have never asked me why neither of us is married. You might be able to find some small piece of information about Ernesto's love life past, but mostly the news focuses on him as one of the world's most eligible bachelors. In truth, he was married once. He fell in love with a classmate in Mexico. She was from the DF, the Distrito Federal, the center of Mexico City. When Ernesto decided to return to Rio Negro Provence and go into local politics, she traveled with him to Viedma. She had something else in mind, as some years ago President Alfonsin had talked about moving the capital of Argentina to Viedma. It's not a small town, but it hasn't changed much since Ferdinand Magellan visited in 1520. She left him and never looked back. Ernesto has never looked back either and has not given himself the time to be in a serious relationship since."

"And you?" James asked. "Why isn't the most eligible bachelorette in Argentina not married, or at least seriously dating?"

"Because I need to take care of my brother," Marisa said. "He spent his young life taking care of me when I was bouncing around Europe. Friends there tried to keep me from anything really idiotic, but more than once he had to drop his life and come rescue me. Since he became president, there just hasn't been time."

"Well, we are on our third date, so thank you for your time," James said. "I really want to continue this conversation, but we better get back on the trail, or we will miss the boat."

"Wouldn't that be great," Marisa said. "Just miss the boat. Spend a week or a month here. We could see Ernesto when he comes here on the Día de la Revolución de Mayo, May 25th, for the announcement."

"Sounds like a great plan and I can think of nothing I would rather do for the next month," James said, "but I think the security people would find us first and then you might get your wish, and they would shoot at your kidnapper first and ask questions later. You know, it is powerful poetry that Ernesto chose May 25th for the announcement. The day that marks the Argentine Republic's first step towards independence will always be remembered in Argentina and the world as humanity's first step towards independence, if we do our job right." He looked at Marisa, and she had a pained look on her face.

"Don't joke about kidnapping, James," Marisa said. "I told you those stories back at the Quinta, on our first date," she added with a thin smile, "because I live in fear of kidnapping. I don't know why. This is not then, but it is my irrational fear. Do you have an irrational fear?"

"I don't think so, but then I have lived a pretty simple life. Both of my parents are still alive and welcome me whenever I show up on their doorstep. I have two wonderful sisters who I would love to introduce you to. I attended the schools of my choice and was only jilted in love once, but she was wise, and I knew it, because I wasn't really interested in romance at the time, just learning. Vulnerability isn't something that I have ever thought about, let alone lived, but I see it in you, and it is one of the things I really like about you. It is one of your strongest and most powerful attributes, but it carries with it those irrational fears."

"You think I am vulnerable?" Marisa asked as she got on her bike.

"No," James said, pedaling after her. "Vulnerability and being vulnerable are two different things, I think. At least they are when I think of you. You ask that question in a way where I am guessing you are replacing Vulnerable with weak. If you are asking, do I think you are weak—then my answer is absolutely not. You are the strongest woman I have ever met and let me tell you, my mom is one tough lady."

Marisa began to pedal harder. She rode her bike with fury and aggression, and James struggled to keep up. At one point she tried to navigate a turn in the wooden path and a corner in the shade was moist and her bike tire slid. She corrected and crashed into one of the few tourists also on the path. It was an older man who was thankfully built strong and was able to absorb much of the momentum but found himself on the ground with Marisa and her bike on top of him. James was able to stop before smashing into the pile-up. He lifted Marisa's bike and set it aside, noting that the front wheel was bent.

"Are you alright, Marisa?" James asked not sure whether he should try to move her. She moved her arms but didn't say anything.

"Get her off of me," the man pinned underneath her said. "Be careful, though, I think she is injured."

"And how are you doing, sir?" James asked. "Any injuries?"

"I don't think so," he said. "It wasn't that hard of a crash, but I couldn't keep us both upright on this wet wood."

As James reached for Marisa, he could hear her quietly sobbing. He tenderly rubbed her back with his hand to let he know he was there and then gently turned her to the side so she could sit and the man under her could stand. A quick visual scan and James guessed she was alright except for a sore knee where her jeans had been scraped and slightly torn.

"I think you are going to be okay, Marisa," James said. "Do you feel hurt anywhere?"

"I'm fine," Marisa said. "Thanks to this kind gentleman who so graciously volunteered to be my landing pad."

"For such a beautiful woman, I would gladly do so anytime," the man said as he slowly stood and brushed himself off. "You need to be more careful, young lady. You were going at quite a clip."

"You are right, sir," Marisa said. "I let my emotions get the better of me, and I was racing my boyfriend and well, you know better than my words can say what happened next. Are you sure you are alright?"

"Are you kidding, wait until I tell my wife, no better yet, my 18-year-old son that I spent part of my day with Marisa

Starhemberg. If they are unbelieving, I will also mention that you wrestled me to the ground."

"So you know who I am?" Marisa said. "I guess I lived up to the silly rumors that I am a reckless and wanton woman. I am so very sorry."

"I have not heard any of those stories, and it was just a silly accident," the man said. "Of course, I am from Peru, so I don't bother with rumors from other countries. We have enough of our own with Keiko Fujimori, who I expect is just trying to live her life as well. My name is David, David Rosado. It is a pleasure to meet you, and your boyfriend."

"It's good to meet you Mr. Rosado," Marisa said. "Do you have a camera?"

"Yes, on my phone, why?" David asked.

"James, can you take our picture, that might prove he is really telling the truth," Marisa said.

James took David's cell phone a clicked a picture as Marisa stood next to him.

"One more," Marisa said. When James was about to take another picture, Marisa turned her face and gave David a kiss on the cheek. The kiss would make for a nice picture, but the surprised look on David's face made it priceless. They said their goodbyes, and David went his way and James and Marisa continued on to the dock. They had to walk because Marisa's bike was not rideable.

"That was a sweet thing to do," James said.

"Giving that nice man a kiss on the cheek?" Marisa asked.

"Well yes, that and telling him I was your boyfriend," James said.

"I wanted him to know I wasn't alone, James," Marisa said.

"You could have said I was your friend," James noted. "Anyway, why the sudden burst of speed and why the tears, were you actually hurt and just putting on a brave face?"

"You saw right into me, James," Marisa said. "Not even Ernesto sees in me what you see. I don't want to feel so, so vulnerable, but I know I am, and it scares me. I guess I was running from you like I ran my way through my university years. And like my younger days, I crashed, and kind and caring people were there to pick me up again."

"I am no expert, but you shouldn't be afraid of being vulnerable," James said. "Only courageous people can be vulnerable. You are inspiring precisely because you are vulnerable. Other people may not recognize what they are seeing, but they know there is something there that touches them. David just saw it, and he will remember that crash for the rest of his life. He won't remember it because you are the sister of the President of Argentina. He won't remember it because you are beautiful—although that gives him bragging rights with the public. No, deep down in his own heart, he will remember you because you opened up your own vulnerability to him and that made it meaningful. You showed him your secret identity and that was a human, intimate moment."

"It is starting to sound like it was you who hit his head on something hard, not me," Marisa said. "I made a decision at some point in my time at university to be strong. I stopped running from my parents' death, and that took strength, not giving in to weakness. If I had given into my vulnerability I think I would have crumbled, like an empty plastic water bottle that constricts on an airplane as it descends to land."

"You can be strong and vulnerable, Marisa," James said. "They aren't mutually exclusive. But it is okay to need someone, to open up to the needs you feel. That isn't weakness, it is a kind of faith. Faith in yourself that you can take the possible rejection or denial of that need, belief in the person or people you trust to share that need, and hopefully faith in something bigger than yourself and others, faith in God. I am not a super religious person, but I think it is mostly fear that drives many to reject the idea of deity. Only after that does pride seep in and then other rationales to replace deity. It takes courage for the wise to fly an airplane solo. When I was in high school, I took flying lessons. I never got my pilot's license, but I do remember taxiing out to the runway by myself for the first time. I loved the thrill of it, but as soon as there was no more runway under me, I felt my own vulnerability. I couldn't just pull over to the side of the road and park. I felt the oneness of knowing I must act, not be acted upon."

James stopped and waited for Marisa to say something. She just continued to walk in silence, so James continued. "Vulnerability is a powerful paradox. Growth requires will. Will requires faith. Faith demands hope. Hope springs from struggle. Struggle comes from vulnerability. Don't be afraid of vulnerability, Marisa."

"Ojo, James," Marisa said. "It is starting to sound like you have a Latin soul. In some corners of the world, that can be interpreted as weakness. Art not just science, poetry over tech manuals, slow food over fast food, song and dance over elevator music and commutes, breathing over consuming, living over existing, that is the Argentine way. Once you taste real life, you may not ever return to hospital food."

"Keep your focus on the message of the eyes and don't be enticed by the lure of the lips," James mumbled. "There is much I can learn from you, Marisa."

"What did you say?" Marisa asked.

"There is much I can learn from you, Marisa," James repeated.

"No, the first part," Marisa said, suddenly stopping to face him. Here eyebrows were scrunched, there was fire in her eyes, and her lips were protruded.

"Um, I was just reminding myself to keep my focus," James said.

"Your lips puff out and demand, kiss me, kiss me! Your eyes, however, say don't you dare. One of these days I hope to understand which to obey. That is what you told me earlier today," Marisa reminded him. "I told you to be careful and obey the eyes, right?"

"Yes, and I am doing just that," James said.

"And what do my eyes tell you to do?" Marisa said.

James looked in her eyes and saw Marisa's vulnerability in all its glory. He leaned in and kissed her. She kissed him back. "Yes, much you can learn from Argentina and especially your private porteña tutor," Marisa whispered. James inhaled her words and held them in his lungs until he was sure they had absorbed into every cell in his body.

That night, after a pleasant journey back the Quinta de Olivos, dinner with President Starhemberg, a shower, and about thirty minutes of sleep, James got a quiet knock on his room door. He opened it to Marisa who was still dressed in her scraped jeans and soiled blouse.

"Sorry to wake you, James," Marisa said. "It took me awhile to find this in my university boxes. It is a note from a young man at Cambridge who wanted to be my boyfriend. I was still in *running away* mode. In frustration, he gave up on me, but in an astrophysics lab weeks later he passed this thought to me. I want out of my casket." She handed the note to him and walked away.

James opened the note and read,

To love at all is to be vulnerable. Love anything, and your heart will be wrung and possibly broken. If you want to make sure of keeping it intact you must give it to no one, not even an animal. Wrap it carefully round with hobbies and little luxuries; avoid all entanglements. Lock it up safe in the casket or coffin of your selfishness. But in that casket, safe, dark, motionless, airless, it will change. It will not be broken; it will become unbreakable, impenetrable, irredeemable. To love is to be vulnerable. —C.S. Lewis

"JOAB, Requested research has turned up nothing unique on subject James Nathaniels. Possible connection to Ernst Rüdiger Starhemberg project? Not very likely. He is a cultural risk manager and may be working on bridge building with the United States. He is single with no relationships. Could he be ingratiating himself with the President through the President's sister? He may be useful for leverage into the Starhembergs in the future. Nurture your relationship with him, but keep digging into the 25 May announcement."

JOAB burnt the note and crushed the ashes. "I don't like it. I don't like Nathaniels' growing relationship with Marisa Starhemberg. I need to insert myself between them. And how dare I be admonished to keep my eyes on the 25 May announcement. I have been working this case for longer than my so-called supervisor has been a Prelate."

BAJO Chapter 2

D AVID ROSADO ADMITTED TO HIMSELF that he had enjoyed meeting Marisa Starhemberg. Fortunately, she was not a concern to him or BAJO. JOAB had not reported on Marisa's deep inner character that was shrouded by her beauty and hot-blooded temperament. The archetypal Argentine; so much to give the world, so dedicated to hiding it with emotion and prideful pulchritude. "If they ever discover meekness, they could rule the world," he told his cat as he entered his quiet home in the Barranco neighborhood of Lima, Peru. "It was a joy to be entirely honest in my unexpected encounter with Señorita Starhemberg, but now, on to the project of the day." He would enjoy a relaxing lunch at his favorite café, Bisettis and then begin the pre-training and assessment of a new JOAB candidate, to be placed in Brazil. The house of Bourbon-Brazil still had its supporters, and the chaos of the present elected government suggested that in another decade, the possibility of a constitutional monarchy was not out of the question.

"So, what do you think about the Argentine President's announcement?" The JOAB candidate asked later that day. "That puts Argentina on the map. My father's preparation for my candidacy in BAJO included lessons on the Starhembergs."

This candidate came from a family historically involved with the Bourbon Ascendancy and with accompanying knowledge of BAJO. Most candidates knew nothing of the organization or its history. Those lessons were presented during indoctrination training in Paris with the Guardian, after passing the pre-assessment with the regional prelate.

"You are well-informed young man," David said. "The Starhembergs were themselves listed in the Almanac de Gotha as one of the original royal sovereign houses of Europe. Yet through history, they were more than content to support and serve the Habsburg Ascendancy. Whether President Starhemberg is even interested in any royal ascendancy is always of curious concern. He has dedicated his professional life to public service as an elected official which suggests a certain anathema to royalty. His grandfather was, of course, a well-known supporter of the Habsburgs and even brought that passion to Latin America. Ill-conceived schemes to support the Habsburgs on this continent came to a sad family tragedy. His father Heinrich and Aunt Maria lived quiet lives with no outward signs of support to the Habsburgs. Maria never married and died at a relatively early age and was always distant to her brother and his family. President Ernesto Starhemberg's parents died when he was a teenager and his sister, Marisa, was twelve or thirteen I believe. It is unlikely they were taught or trained to continue the traditional family support to the Habsburgs. Yet," David began, not sure how much to share with this young man who had not been fully vetted.

"Yet, a Habsburg was announced as the pivotal player in President Starhemberg's global energy gambit," the young man completed.

David was aware of the young man studying his face. Interesting that this candidate made him feel uneasy. "Your family and mine have been players in this game of thrones centuries before there was a silly television show of that name. This is a deadly game at times, and I would caution you to hone your discretion and diplomatic skills. And remember what an ancient wise king stated, "He that answereth a matter before he heareth *it*, it *is* folly and shame unto him.""

"Noted Prelate," The young man said, not sounding at all humbled. "And the man James Nathaniels? Are you going to have him executed or possibly turned?"

"Where did you hear that name?" David asked trying hard to extinguish any surprise in his voice.

"The Guardian shared it with me," the young man said with an insolent smile. "He assigned it to me as a case study. I am to report to him my findings when I continue my training in Paris."

"You will stay out of actual operations," David said, losing his patience. "You are what, 27 years old? You do not have the judgment or experience to even ask such delicate questions. This is not a Mafioso organization. I have never had to sanction someone's death. I know it has happened in the past, but the rules and practices of the past are not acceptable today. I am not saying it would never happen, but your impertinence has earned you my disrespect and a formal letter to the Guardian."

"Noted Prelate," The young man said again.

"Preparatory training has been terminated," David said. "I am turning this matter over to the Guardian. Good day." Even though this was David's home, he left the room but waited just outside the door until the young man departed.

As a young man, when his father initiated the BAJO recruiting process on behalf of his only son, David had recoiled during training when the lessons suggested the potential need for extreme measures. He was assured this was for historical context only. The Guardian at that time noted that the last termination, as he called it, was the wife of Ernst Rudiger Starhemberg, in a neighboring country to where he would begin as a JOAB. David

Rosado was dedicated to the cause of Bourbon Ascendency. He was a royalist and saw the future solution to the chaos of the modern world in the hands of single leaders. Committees and bureaucracies were drowning governments. The philosopher king was the government of the future. Getting there through murder, even indirect involvement in such actions was repugnant. He posted a coded letter to the Guardian that very evening.

CHAPTER 9

Che

Literal Translation: Hey Dude

Marisa's Explanation: The word comes from one of the indigenous tribes in Argentina. It means I, me, or man. It is mostly used among friends to mean brother, pal, friend, or generically as man. To anyone inside and outside of Argentina it also means **An Argentine.** This became one of my favorite words in the world after being away from home.

"I DIDN'T WANT TO BRING IT up at dinner last night," James was explaining to Marisa in the board room, "But when you had that crash yesterday, there was—no security that showed up. I didn't see any the entire time in the park. What if that man, David, was someone who wanted to hurt you? What if he were someone even worse?"

"You were there," Marisa said, waving her hand in the air. "No matter, nothing happened."

"What about the next time?" James persisted. Pepe Peralta Monti didn't even ask why we were a few minutes late and why the bike wheel was bent, why you looked a little scuffed up."

"I'm always late, James," Marisa said, somewhat exasperated. "If you have a concern for my safety, bring it up with Vangelina. She wasn't with us yesterday, but she would want to know."

"I will," James said. He couldn't understand that in one moment Marisa could be fearful of kidnapping and the next brush off a potentially dangerous situation. "Once Cambalache goes public your world is going to be very different. I don't want to add to your fears, but you will no longer be the most eligible bachelorette in Argentina, but one of the top targets of those who are looking for a shortcut to becoming Energy Czar of the globe."

"Got you there," Marisa said smiling. "I am no longer most eligible. I have a boyfriend, haven't you heard?"

"Why is the wannabe boyfriend always the last to hear?" James said in mock shock. "Let me guess, you and David. He has left his wife, and you are considering taking up residence in Lima?"

"It was that obvious?" Marisa asked.

"Don't forget, I was the only witness to your first kiss with David," James said.

"And if I remember correctly," Marisa said, standing and approaching him, "you were also the only witness to our first kiss."

"Exactly, there should have been security around," James said.

Marisa socked him in the arm. "That is what you get, James," Marisa said. "You were going to get your second kiss, but not this morning."

"What is not happening this morning?" President Starhemberg asked as he walked into the room.

"You tell him," Marisa said to James.

"I, um, I was just telling Marisa I was concerned about her safety. I didn't see any security yesterday while at the National Park."

"Really?" President Starhemberg said. "I will speak with Vangelina about that." He stared at James and then at Marisa. "Why do I get the sense that I am not getting the full story? I feel like I just walked into my election team headquarters and they had been arguing about who will have to tell me we are down by twenty points. So what is going on?"

"If you must know, sir," James began again, "Marisa is a home-wrecker, and she is thinking about eloping with a man twice her age and moving to Lima, Peru." Marisa socked James in the arm again.

"Has this been going on for a long time?" President Starhemberg asked, playing along.

"I can't say, sir," James quickly answered, "but I would have to admit under oath that I have seen Marisa on top of said Peruvian."

Marisa gave James yet another sock in the arm.

"Marisa, am I detecting a pattern of co-worker abuse here?" Starhemberg asked.

"You men," Marisa growled.

"Che, que me acusa?" Starhemberg asked. "Hey, what are you accusing me of?"

"Che! I am accusing you of being Che," Marisa retorted. "We've got important work to do, and you two are playing around like the 25th of May is months away. You *Chenesto* have a country to run on top of that."

"So tell me what you are trying so hard to obfuscate, and I will get back to running the country, and you can get back to preparing us for the Cambalache announcement," President Starhemberg said, staring them both down.

James looked at Marisa. Maria shrugged her shoulders and said, "If you must know in order to govern 42 million people, then I will explain as simply as I can." She turned to James and gave him a passionate kiss. "Better?" she asked them both as she stomped to the door. "And I may just move to Peru," she added as she left the room.

"I'm good," James said.

"I'm good," Ernesto Starhemberg said. He left the room without a further word.

James returned to his work. Marisa did not return until lunchtime. "Let's get some lunch, James, then we can finish tackling the scenario five action plan."

"I finished a draft of it," James said. "We can review it after a couple empanadas from the kitchen." He knew better than to bring up the morning that had started out so well and ended in another storm. He realized he was partly to blame. He had a long way to go to know when to back off the games with Marisa.

They ate in silence. When Marisa pulled out two flan desserts and added a dab of dulce de leche to them, James said, "Now that is quintessential Argentine." After a couple bites he hesitantly said, "Which reminds me, if you are not still mad at me, could you explain your uses of the word Che earlier today? I was totally lost."

"I am still mad at you, and I am glad you admit you are totally lost," Marisa answered. "I don't remember exactly what I said."

"There were multiple uses of Che," James explained. "I thought I understood its use, but now I am not so sure."

"It's a word that is mostly used in Buenos Aires," Marisa said. We didn't use it much growing up on the other side of the country. My dad used to call Ernesto Che-Ernesto that just became Chenesto because he has always had plans to move to Buenos Aires and make his fortune. Sometimes when he, or very rarely me," Marisa accentuated with a smile, "were bad, mother would threaten us that Che Guevara would come and get us in the night if we didn't mend our rebellious ways. You know, his real name was Ernesto also. Other than that I never heard the term until I visited Buenos Aires. Sometimes it means hey, as in hey you, but usually targeted at a friend, teammate, or associate."

"But you also accused your brother of being Che," James said.

"Oh yes, I remember now," Marisa said with a laugh. "He was being so Che. Like Che Guevara, Che means 'you are Argentine.' He was being so Argentine this morning acting all innocent and naïve when he was so guilty and so aware of what was going on. He just wanted me to say it."

"And say it you did," James said with a bright smile. "Say it again anytime."

"In your dreams, Che," Marisa said matching his smile.

"You have already visited me there Norisa," James said. Marisa just smiled. "So that is something I have been thinking about in regards to our scenario building."

"Your dreams of me?" Marisa asked.

"Plenty of scenarios there also," James said, "but no, the thought about being so Argentine. We are trying to anticipate potential outcomes and how to handle them, right?"

"Right," Marisa agreed.

"So I am struggling with the Argentine psyche. I mean, any generalization has its dangers, so there is not an exact description of the everyman Argentine, although they all probably want to be something close to your brother and you." Marisa was about to speak, but James held up his hand for her to hold her thought for a minute. In many countries, actually most countries, immigrants and minorities tend to try even harder to be more. More American, more Japanese. Catholics were a small minority in the early days of the United States. Only one signer of the Declaration of Independence was Catholic. Yet today their generations in the U.S. fill the ranks of the FBI, the military, firefighters and police forces in large part because they are still working hard to be more American. In Buenos Aires, if you ask people where they are from, they will tell you they are Italian, or French, or Spanish, even though it was their grandparents who migrated from the old country. It's like they all have this dream to return one day, to a place they have never been. They are only Argentine when it comes to certain things."

"Being from Bariloche, Ernesto and I noticed the same thing when we moved to Buenos Aires," Marisa agreed. "Because the porteño mindset makes them temporary guests, they don't feel the responsibilities of full citizens. We think nothing of tossing a piece of trash out the car window, or not cleaning up after our dog while walking him on a public street. That is certainly Che. At least in the past decade or two, we have closed down all the gnocchi attitudes."

"What's that?" James asked.

"It's a good luck tradition to eat gnocchi on the last day of the month," Marisa explained. "There used to be more than a few people who only showed up for a job on the last day of the month to get paid. Other than that, you never saw them. Many had several of these ghost jobs. We called them gnocchis."

"Have we sufficiently created scenarios for the in-country reactions to the Cambalache announcement?" James wondered out loud. "My mind has been focused internationally and with the world's most influential players, but if we don't keep things stable here at home, we won't be able to manage issues abroad. Or if someone from abroad sees a chink in the home armor, you will bet that will be leveraged to their advantage and probably not the President's."

"Good point," Marisa agreed. "I sometimes wonder, with all these scenarios and action plans, can we really prepare for every eventuality?"

"We can't even get close," James admitted. "It's not the plan, though, but the planning that counts most. We'll be ready, and we will have thought this out enough that even the surprises will have answers. I just want to make sure we have the clearest big picture possible. We are going to brief the President's team in three days, and I think we will be ready."

"You know," Marisa said, "we do have those groups that try harder than most to be extra Argentine. Sometimes that's a blessing, sometimes that is a burden. Our history of coups d'état has one of its roots in the military trying, no, believing they know how to be more Argentine. The shortfalls of others' civic loyalties drive some to feel they are obligated to make up the difference. And then there are others who make this country great, despite the lack of patriotic enthusiasm of the majority. That isn't usually the Catholics because we are in the majority, although there are many fine Catholics. We think we must be the most Argentine without having to do anything about it. Even the Pope is Argentine, for heaven's sake—no pun intended. But it's really our Jewish community, the Mormons, the recent Middle Eastern immigrants, and the Bolivians and Chileans who come here for better work opportunities—they do far more than their share."

"Well said," James noted. "I must say, Argentine blemishes when it comes to immigration are not quite so pronounced as they are in my country. Our recent wave of nationalism over patriotism is something that comes and goes in the United States. Except for the Malvinas issue, I have not seen much of that here."

"You mean the Charles de Gaulle thought that patriotism is the love of one's country and nationalist is the hatred of other countries?" Marisa asked. "I don't think the United States fits into that category, at least not like Russia, Iran, or North Korea. No one does as much good in the world as your country."

"I am not sure Russia or Iran would appreciate you placing them in the same category as North Korea, but I get your point," James said.

"Well, we aren't going to solve those problems. Maybe Cambalache is a start, but not a solution," Marisa said. And by the way, I didn't mean to pick on other countries. That would put me in the North Korea category, wouldn't it? It's always been a dream of mine to visit Russia and Iran. Let's see what we can do to finish up the Cambalache plan a day early and let it sit so we are fresh when we meet with the rest of the team."

"My brother, we have completed additional research by extreme means. We still have some concerns over the Prelate's abilities and loyalties, but we appreciate your facilitation of the lapse in security during the Bariloche outing of Marisa Starhemberg and James Nathaniels, that allowed for our information collection. I know you are on the inside of this venture, but yet outside of the day-to-day details. As you are well aware, Ronald Richter, who was nicknamed El Alemán ("the German") was actually born in Czechoslovakia. He was not born in Germany as most of the world would believe. He was raised in Austria. He was not unknown to the Habsburg Empire. In 1948, when Richter was invited to Argentina by Kurt Tank, again the world would assume that Richter's ties were mostly German. Yes, Tank was the lead aeronautical engineer for the aircraft manufacturer Focke-Wulf between 1931 and 1945 ,and he had been appointed to the Aerotechnical Institute in Córdoba under the codename Dr. Pedro Matthies. What the world doesn't realize is it was Ernst Rüdiger Starhemberg who contacted Tank to make introductions between Richter and Perón. Tank went on to usher in the modern era of what is now the Fábrica Militar de Aviones (FMA), the Argentine Air Force factory in Cordoba, and never crossed paths with Richter again. Richter was just a pawn in a bigger game. Ernst Starhemberg had a broader and more dangerous vision than even the achievement of fusion technology, which in and of itself is not our target. Richter and his fusion technology were simply a means to that end. And Starhemberg's end was our beginning—our continued raison d'être, and the reason for our first footprint in Latin America since we chased Maximilian's wife from Mexico 80 years earlier and ended his reign, and life, months later. We thought at the time that our termination of Nora Gregor Starhemberg, Ernst's wife, was the end of this entire affair. Somehow history is about to repeat itself. We have confirmed that the fusion project is very much real, as you have reported.

Just how real and how developed it is, remains a partial unknown. I have entrusted you with the mission and means to find out how real this project is and how it plays into what we assume is Starhemberg's true project. DO NOT FAIL. Our JOAB and the America's Prelate, the hapless Rosado, will be the lightning rods as we planned, but you are approved to begin mission execution immediately." Guardian

CHAPTER 10

Lo Atamos con Alambre
Literal Translation: We tied it with wire

Marisa's Explanation: In my parent's generation, there were high tariffs and import taxes as a way to fight the South American dependency on North America and Europe manufactured goods. Unfortunately, all this accomplished was protected low-quality manufacturing in our country. We had to constantly fix the car or the washing machine and find ways to work around the constant problems. We became world experts to **Jerry-Rig it, MacGyver-it** to keep life going.

"MR. PRESIDENT THERE HAS BEEN an explosion near Bariloche!" Alberto Godoy reported, charging into the President's office unannounced. "No immediate report of casualties or other damage." Godoy could claim direct access to the President as his Chief of Staff, but as both knew he was also the ad-hoc public relations manager of the Cambalache Project. Both knew there were only five days until the official announcement of the Project.

"How did you hear about this?" President Starhemberg asked. "Any chance it was something else? A lightning strike, an unauthorized campfire that just looked like the smoke from an explosion?"

"Witnesses on the Cau Cau, the regularly scheduled boat from Bariloche to Bosque de Arrayanes. They were just passing Huemul Island and nearly everyone on the boat both heard it and saw it," Godoy said. "No one suggested danger or foul play. One tourist got it on her phone as she recorded going past the Island. Several voices are heard on the boat suggesting it must be some demolition work of the very old and dangerous structures there. The Intelligence Fusion Center picked it up when the tourist tried to sell it to *TodoNoticias*. I tried to contact the Project, but there is no answer. Hopefully, just the communications tower was knocked out."

"The Intelligence Fusion Center, how apropos. I never liked that name actually, but it wasn't my watch when it was set up. What does it look like?" President Starhemberg asked.

"A puff of smoke, nothing substantial," he began, looking toward the door to ensure no one else was within listening distance. "But who knows what kind of damage might have occurred below ground."

"Get back to me as soon as you hear anything specific from the Project," President Starhemberg ordered. "Hopefully it wasn't an industrial accident below ground, I mean I worry about the loss of life and that would be the worst-case scenario. That someone might know about the project and could get through both the passive and active security is less likely, but Alberto, this is terrible."

"Sir, I request to travel to the scene, no matter whether we hear from the Project or not," Godoy said. Between you, me, and Peralta Monti, I am the least likely to be noticed."

"What about Marisa?" Starhemberg asked.

"She is on the cover of magazines more than you, sir, plus I can't say that won't be any danger. If she were to travel, she would require a security detail and that makes things complicated."

"You're right," the President said. "We may need Marisa here to discuss next steps for the Project, plus I want her advice on what to do about the May 25th announcement, if it is impacted. Go now and call me as soon as you can. If you hear from the Project, call immediately to my personal cell." Following Godoy out of the office, the President asked his secretary to cancel his 2:30 appointment with the ambassador from Nigeria. "Please tell her that I have a small domestic matter that requires my attention and that I would like to invite her to the Quinta for an assado—the one we have already scheduled, what a week from now? Also, let Archbishop Poli know since this *digno evento* is to honor his work. Hmm, also invite Maria Alcaraz, the Director General of the Teatro Colón. My sources tell me the Nigerian Ambassador is a patron of the arts. A Catholic Archbishop, a Muslim Ambassador, and if I remember correctly, Maria has a degree in Cultural Management and worked in Spain as an Ibero-American-African cultural expert. That should be fertile ground for some fascinating conversations." The President was in the hallway heading for his transportation detail so he could get back to the Quinta. Not for the first time he wished the Casa Rosada and the Quinta were on the same grounds. He turned back to his office and said to his secretary, "And make sure Marisa and my friend, James Nathaniels, are also invited."

"Half an hour," President Starhemberg mumbled as his armored Audi A8s pulled into the Quinta de Olivos. He walked straight to the conference room where Marisa and James had been working for the last two weeks. James was at the white board and Marisa was on her laptop.

"Do you two ever stop working?" the President asked.

"Ernesto," Marisa said surprised. "Checking up on us?"

"Just making sure you haven't had James killed or deported," Ernesto said. "And," he paused, "I have just received a report of a possible bombing on Huemul Island. Our initial efforts to contact the Cambalache team have failed. Godoy is on his way to Ezeiza and will fly to Bariloche tonight. Hopefully, he will be able to get to the Island before dark."

"How, who?" was all Marisa could manage to voice. She had several dear friends on the team and had worked as an assistant to just about everyone there. She knew their families.

"This is a scenario we have considered," James offered. "Of course, our scenario takes place after the announcement, but there are some useful actions we can employ while we sort through what really happened."

Marisa looked at James and nodded. "He's right, Ernesto. Scenario 11 or 12 I think. If I remember right, yes, here is our draft action plan." Maris pulled out the action plan from her stack of files that she had pulled out of the safe earlier that morning. She glanced through it to make sure it was the full draft and then handed it to her brother. "As James said, this plan assumes Cambalache is already public knowledge, but I think if you treated it as merely an incident at a historical site, there might be some useful thoughts here."

"Sir," James said, "In speaking, I think I jumped the gun. None of our plans are at the competency level of something many professional eyes and many more hours would create through your government offices. I am sure your government has its own plans to handle this."

"For the moment," President Starhemberg said, "we will handle this as a simple, isolated incident that will be researched by a select group. Once we get word from Godoy or the Cambalache Team themselves, we will know what direction to take. We may have to announce the project early, and we may need to face the possibility that the project has been destroyed."

"How could this have happened?" Marisa echoed what her brother and James were thinking. "Who could have known and how could they have launched such an attack?"

"First of all, we don't know this was an attack, Marisa," her brother said. "Secondly, the real question is why?"

"If it was an attack," James suggested, "it came from one of the two extremes. Either someone was ill informed, and they thought this was some secret nuclear project that threatened their interests, or it was from someone who knew exactly what this was and that threatened their interests. The center ground does not demand such an aggressive reaction. Let's consider,"

James was interrupted by the President's personal cell phone. He was surprised President Starhemberg even had a personal line that could be directly answered. He doubted the President of the United States had this kind of freedom, and then he wondered if this would be something that would soon disappear from President Starhemberg's tool box.

"Thank you, Alberto. Call me when you get there," the President said, clicking off his phone. "Alberto Godoy," the President said to Marisa and James. "He has heard from the Cambalache project. Two members of the security team are dead. There may be others injured. They were still battling a fire in the underground facility, but it hasn't reached the operational reactor. At present, it appears the project and the engineers are safe. There is a concern that further explosions and additional damage would require a full evacuation and abandonment of the project. The temporary living quarters were filled with smoke, and so the team will eventually have to leave and return to their homes in the Bariloche area. That could slow down any clean-up before May 25th."

President Starhemberg went back to his schedule for the day, at least those things he could take care of from the Quinta. Marisa and James were left to discuss probabilities and follow-up possibilities. Just after merienda, the President returned to James's and Marisa's habitat. "Just got an update from the Project. Alberto arrived about twenty minutes ago. The fire is out, and the C1 reactor is safe. The security team's best guess at this point is, there was an attempt to enter the project via the personnel entrance, the same way you came the other day, James," the President explained. "Failing to enter, an incendiary bomb was placed at the entrance. Whether that was placed there in a further attempt to gain access, or just to cause as much damage as possible, is unknown. The bomb would have caused little damage on its own, but the vehicles parked in the garage created a secondary explosion, and that is likely what the tourists saw from the boat. The explosions damaged traditional communications lines, and the attackers left behind a cell phone blocking device. Apparently, that device didn't last long, and cell service was returned. The security team discovered the blocking device after the fact. This was a deliberate attack, and they knew about the entrance."

"I suppose no clues on who or what executed this attack?" James asked.

"Not yet," President Starhemberg said. Turning to Marisa, he said, "I need you at the Cambalache Project. I need your talents to get this project back online, and I need your eyes and ears there to tell me the reality of the situation. Alberto is a good man, but he has never been directly involved with the inner workings of the project like you, and he can only report what the engineers tell him. I trust them, but their opinions have a tendency to become skewed. Can you leave in the morning?"

"I almost suggested I leave with Godoy when you told me he was going there," Marisa said. "I will be ready to go first thing in the morning."

"Is it still dangerous?" James asked. "I mean, someone knows about this project and will probably also figure out that they didn't shut it completely down. Does that put a target on the Cambalache team and Marisa?"

"This attack immediately followed your visit," President Starhemberg said. "I am afraid you and Marisa are already potential targets. I also thought about sending you, but wanted to get a report first. As far as the Cambalache project, we have upgraded the security team and will publicly report some malicious mischief around an old shed and will be able to upgrade visible presence without raising too many suspicions."

Again President Starhemberg returned to his regularly scheduled duties. Marisa stared at James. James stared back. "So you are some kind of fusion genius?" James finally asked.

"Hardly," Marisa said laughing. "I know enough to get into trouble, but Ernesto is right, I can be his eyes and ears and tell him what is going on. I need to go. It is sweet of you to be concerned about me."

"All the same, be careful," James said. In an attempt to sound light-hearted, he added, "And remember, I need an expert to guide me through all the dichos, the sayings you Argentines use. Your explanation of Che got me thinking. I heard the gardener this morning tell someone, *me tomo el piojo*. That requires some explanation. You are the only person I can turn to."

"How very appropriate," Marisa said. "It means goodbye. Well, of course, it literally means what it says, I am taking the louse. But it really means I am leaving. I am honored to be your DI, your dicho instructor. I need to get ready to travel, so can I leave you with this mess?" Marisa said pointing to the stacks of paper.

"I can handle it," James said, "But I deserve a prize."

"You deserve nothing," Marisa said. "You should be paying us just to breathe Argentine air, our buenos aires."

"Nice pun, Norisa," James said. "I am going to miss you."

"And me you," Marisa said. She stood and hesitated and then turned toward the door.

"James stood and grabbed her right hand, turned her around and sang in his best Argentine accent, "*Me quisiste… me dejaste. Que te puedo reprochar? Hoy, estamos como antes… volveremos a empezar.* You loved me…then you left me. How can I blame you? Now we're like we were before…back where we started."

Marisa put her left arm on his right shoulder and leaned back and then snapped upright. She could no longer keep a straight face and began to laugh. "Lyrics from a tango. Bravo James!" Marisa said.

"I have been listening to some old tango music. That is from *No Me Extraña, She doesn't miss me.* Boy gets girl, boy loses girl."

"Tangos last longer than two dates, my fearful and faithless yanqui. My father used to sing one to me," Marisa said, looking beyond them both. She said in a quiet voice, "*Una Piba Como Vos*—A Girl Like You. *La vida se hace hermosa y lisonjera, Es eterna primavera si a mi lado oigo tu voz*— Life is beautiful and flattering. It is eternal spring if by my side I hear your voice." James noticed tears welling in Marisa's eyes. He leaned in and kissed her. She kissed him in return, placed her head on his shoulder, held him, and started dancing to a tune he could not hear. When the silent song ended, she strengthened her embrace and then turned and walked out the door. He walked to the door. Marisa said, "I can feel you looking at me, James," she said without turning around. "Just a few days. Hasta pronto."

James did not blush or hide inside the door. He continued to watch her as she disappeared around the corner of the central garden. He made a note to listen to *Una Piba Como Vos.*

Vangelina Pereira watched Marisa leave the briefing room that was off limits to everyone in the Quinta. That was not so rare, but the amount of time it had been off limits was odd. She turned her attention to James. From where she stood on the second floor of the residence she could not see his face, but even from that distance away, she could feel the electricity. Was she glad for Marisa? She had to admit she was still untrusting of this North American who had just appeared one day out of nowhere and somehow gained the trust of Ernesto and Marisa Starhemberg. She knew she was a little jealous, but was that all that concerned her? She would keep a close eye on Mr. James Nathaniels of Jefferson City, Missouri.

Marisa left for Bariloche early the next morning before James was even awake. She would ensure Cambalache had sufficient duct tape and bubble gum repairs to prove to the most adamant naysayer it was not only real but online and capable of changing the world. She succeeded in bringing the system to minimal operational standards with a plan to be fully functional within a month. She explained that the problems were mostly cosmetic. The Cambalache engineering team knew they had just witnessed once again the rare genius that was Marisa Starhemberg.

JOAB was wide awake. The Huemul Island attack had been a surprise and yet failed to provide any new information about what was happening in Bariloche. The world had not converged on that tiny island, which put into doubt that a major project was located there. Yet, this morning Marisa Starhemberg left Buenos Aires and JOAB had just confirmed that the airplane she was on was traveling to Bariloche. 'Coincidence?' JOAB wondered.

JOAB had already reported the attack as both a failure and potentially a success as it put the Starhemberg Presidency on notice that someone was watching, someone knows something, and that the someone is invisible, so far invisible to JOAB as well. Minimizing loss of life has always been a value of JOAB's superiors, but the loss of life was not a hindrance to the organization's long-term goals. Long before JOAB was even born, in fact, hundreds of years ago, an earlier JOAB had arranged for the death of Marie Antoinette. Count Georg Adam von Starhemberg had successfully negotiated the marriage between the Habsburg Archduchess Maria Antonia and the Duke of Berry, the future King Louis XVI of France. In 1770 Starhemberg accompanied the archduchess to the first encounter with her future husband. Starhemberg had been threatened by JOAB in the same month as that visit, but he did not listen. The results were known to history. Certainly, they were known to Ernst Rüdiger Camillo Starhemberg just prior to World War Two when a JOAB approached him with the threat of losing his wife if he did not end his efforts to put a Habsburg on the throne in Austria again. Starhemberg and his wife escaped to South America where he resurrected a plan, through impressive means, to put a Habsburg at the center of the modern world. Soon thereafter his dear wife, Nora Gregor was reported dead from suicide in Viña del Mar, Chile. Not reported were the whereabouts of the children of this couple, Heinrich and Maria (named after Marie Antionette) Starhemberg. Heinrich became the father of Ernesto and Marisa who now served as the President and de facto First Lady of Argentina, and these two had become the principle threat on the watch of this JOAB.

CHAPTER 11

El que se va sin que lo echen vuelve sin que lo llamen
Literal Translation: He who goes without being
thrown out returns without being called

<u>*Marisa's Explanation*</u>: This is a warning to do as the dicho says, leave on good terms so you can always feel free to return. Argentines have long memories. In my case, I almost destroyed those bridges (and almost destroyed myself on a bridge), but I was welcomed with open arms on my return. **I'm the Prodigal Daughter.**

MARISA SAT IN THE EMPTY 12-passenger jet with the tune of the tango she had shared with James still in her mind. She missed her father. She missed James. She also missed her old life when there were no encumbering romance or complicating emotions. She was exhausted. She had completed packing within twenty minutes of returning to her room. She went to bed early because she had to leave for Ezeiza Airport by 4 A.M., but got little sleep. As Buenos Aires got smaller out the window of the aircraft, she remembered leaving Buenos Aires on another plane, bound for Madrid, Spain. She was 19 years old and not sure she was running from her past life or running to a new one.

"Welcome to Madrid, Norisa," Otto von Habsburg said as she exited the customs area at Adolfo Suárez Madrid Airport. With the same concern James had experienced landing in Buenos Aires, Marisa had experienced a moment of anxiety when the flight attendant had welcomed the passengers to Barajas Airport. She glanced at the signs as she entered the terminal and saw the Adolfo Suárez name she was expecting. All was well. When she saw Uncle Otto waiting for her she completely relaxed. It wasn't until she ventured to ask her roommate at *la Autónoma*, the Autonomous University of Madrid that she found out the airport was called Barajas for the local area in which it was located. "Kind of like you, my *porteña*," her roommate said. "Your Argentine accent certainly places you." From that day forward and throughout her university experience she was known as *la porteña*. Initially, it irritated her. She wasn't from Buenos Aires. She gradually began to identify with the name and wear it as a badge of pride. In a particularly contemplative mood some years later at Cambridge, she realized she at first had been running from her old life, and that was the real reason the nickname had irritated her.

"Your classwork is excellent, when you complete it," her curriculum counselor explained. "In fact, I am not sure you are even being challenged with derivative equations or thermodynamics. You are very smart, Marisa, but you aren't applying yourself."

Marisa knew this all too well. She had almost missed this last opportunity appointment to salvage her academic standing because she had been out all night tapa hopping and dancing. "I know my attendance and efforts have been below standard," Marisa began. "I promise that from now on,"

"No, I am sorry, Marisa," her counselor interrupted. "You have made that promise too many times for it to hold any hope for a course adjustment. May I make a point and then a suggestion?"

"Whatever," Marisa replied not caring now. 'Have I ever really cared since I got here?' she wondered to herself.

"This university is consistently in the top 50 universities in the world, the top 15 in Europe and the best university in Spain. We have high standards, and those standards have been flexible for a Starhemberg, but you have surpassed our breaking point. It is time for you to find your way somewhere else. On a more personal note, I know you are facing some challenging opposition in your life. This may be one of those defining moments you will look back on in your life where your failure was your greatest success. Take a close look at your values—not those virtues you say you hold in high esteem, but what your actions echo. How closely are they aligned to the principles in life that determine long-term success? You are smart enough to take a physics test without preparation and do well enough to be the top half of the class, but you only take a test when it fits in your schedule. That is random and rare and those short-term wins, if indeed they are wins, highlight potential, not performance. You know what changes you need to make. Stop running from them. Discard the burdens that are breaking you down and pick up the loads that will make you stronger. You have the means to self-destruct or succeed. It is the direction you choose to travel that will tell you what you really value.

"You've got all the answers," Marisa said. "Thanks for fixing me as you drop kick me out the door." Marisa got up to leave. She didn't want to hear any more of this guidance wisdom. "You are starting to sound like my brother. He has all the answers too."

"Selfishness, indifference, and irresponsibility are the usual culprits of failure," her counselor continued without acknowledging the sharp barbs. "They spring from anger, pride; I don't know. Rarely are they because of a fear of success, which I have come to believe is your burden. The day will come when I am able to say, I knew that woman and I always knew she would take on the world in her own way and win."

Marisa left the school without a clue what to do next. She had only two people in the world she could turn to—her brother and Uncle Otto. She could not contact either one. Her brother was far away and was trying to get his own life in order. Who was she kidding? Ernesto's life was always in order. She didn't want to contact him precisely because his life was in order, and hers was not. As for Uncle Otto, well, she had disappointed him already by choosing to live in Madrid instead of Budapest or Vienna—his first choices for her.

For the next month, she worked as hard as she had ever worked in her life, to see how fast she could prove her physics professor wrong. He had said, "There is no such thing as centrifugal force. We call it a fictitious force." Marisa knew that he was talking about that feeling on the merry-go-round that seems to pull you off as it spins faster and faster. That is what Marisa wanted to do, spin faster and faster until she was flung off. Mass × Acceleration = Force. She was the mass and her life was in acceleration.

"Marisa, you don't have to do this," a boy whose name at that moment she could not remember. "They never even measured the height of the bridge." She was pretty sure she had spent the entire night drinking and dancing and thought she had agreed to a sunrise trip to Segovia. Instead, here she was, standing on a bridge over the Lozoya Valley in the Sierra Madrileña. The sun had crested the horizon as she stared straight into its light, looking for answers. Someone had wrapped a harness around her upper body and about twelve people were taunting her to jump. The small river and rocks were 130 feet below her. Life had come to this, a bungee cord and centrifugal force. Was it fictitious? She was about to find out. Eyes wide open she let herself fall. Was she flying or falling? She wasn't sure until she saw the rocks rushing to meet her. She felt the bungee cord tighten.

Which would win, centrifugal outward force or a centripetal inward force she had doubted since her parents' death?

The light water spray from the river hitting the rocks moistened Marisa's face as the bungee cord stretched to its limit. Marisa reached out at that instant and touched the cold water. A spark traveled up her arm and filled her chest almost to bursting. As the cord pulled her up and away from the rocks and water, she thought of her brother Ernesto and his sad face as she glanced back one last time before she had entered the plane in Buenos Aires. He had been bright and optimistic through her preparation to leave and their drive to the airport. She had caught him off-guard with her last second glimpse. She knew what she had always known, but had tried to forget; the force is directed toward the center of the circle. Dangling on her lifeline, her physics professor's lecture again surfaced in her consciousness. "The Latin roots of centripetal means 'seeking the center.' Centrifugal, a word that means 'fleeing the center,' only proves that there is such a thing as centrifugal motion; but centrifugal force is a different matter. The difference between centripetal force and a mere centrifugal tendency—a result of inertia rather than of force."

"Inertia is a value, a choice, but force is a principle, a governing law," a voice within her proclaimed as the bungee jump concluded and she felt those above her pulling her to them. The group greeted Marisa with cheers and a comradery that she could now identify as mostly hollow. These were the same people that were cheering her on to her potential death just minutes earlier. She couldn't find the person who cautioned her. As soon as she got back to her Moncloa apartment in Madrid, she called her Uncle Otto. She was on a plane to Vienna the next day.

Two months of waiting tables at the El Gaucho restaurant just off the Leopoldstadt on the banks of the Donaukanal had toughened Marisa's courage and character. She re-entered academic life the next term at the University of Vienna, thanks to Uncle Otto pulling some strings. Marisa had known Otto von Habsburg since she was a child when he visited her parents. As an adult, Marisa came to know a very different person. He was supportive, to the point of spoiling her, as he had been to her as a child—always with candy in his pocket for her.

Uncle Otto's support now was introducing her to an impressive crowd of leaders, thinkers, and doers. "Makers," he called them. "We don't always get to choose how our lives will go, Marisa, but we can choose to make a difference, to create, to lead by example," he told her the day she approached him about transferring to the University in Innsbruck. Marisa missed her mountains in Argentina and the relative flatlands of Madrid and Vienna had made her homesick for real peaks and valleys, plus the physics program in Innsbruck was more demanding and offered a nuclear studies major that intrigued her. She excelled there and still found time to visit Garmisch-Partenkirchen, Oberammergau, and the Italian Tyrol that reminded her most of home.

She completed her undergraduate studies in two years, and Uncle Otto celebrated by arranging a private tour of the Starhemberg Castle in Eferding. Two years in Austria, three in Europe and this was her first visit to her ancestral home. Otto said she had earned it and her family would be very proud of her. Her biggest surprise awaited her in the elongated cobblestone courtyard where the tour was to begin. Her brother Ernesto was waiting for her. Life had never felt better than his embrace. She was home. She loved the tour of the tan stuccoed castle, the lead glass windows, and pictures of people she had only heard about from her father's stories. The best part was just being close to her brother.

"What are your plans now Norisa?" Ernesto asked.

"I don't know," Marisa admitted. "How is the money situation? I mean, can I continue my studies or should I get a job?"

"Marisa, the money is not a problem," Ernesto said. "That you asked tells me a lot about your growth that Otto has been singing about in his notes to me. Our trust fund does not make us part of the rich and famous, but you certainly have the resources to live comfortably for the rest of your life. If you want to continue your education, then do it."

"I was considering Cambridge, England," Marisa said. "They have a great nuclear physics program there, and I would like to get my Master's degree before I start my job hunt."

"I always knew you loved math and science, Marisa, but I would never have pegged you for a nuclear engineer," Ernesto said. "I am thinking about entering politics, which is about the last thing I ever considered for myself, so we are a family of surprises."

"Speaking of surprises," Otto said, "There is a little program that your father was involved with before you were even born that might interest the both of you. He had asked me to stay apprised of its potential before he passed. It sits dormant in the mountains by your home in Bariloche. Actually, dormant is not the right word. The facilities have been dormant, but the project has been plodding along since 1947. Some real progress has been made, and it is about time to make it tangible. You could be a big part of this effort, Marisa, so study with a purpose and you too will be a maker one day."

The family gathering was short-lived. Ernesto had completed his studies and was excited about the prospects of local politics in Bariloche and the governor's race in a few years. He left the next day for a Mexico City stopover on his way back to Argentina. Marisa returned to Innsbruck three days later and was situated in her own apartment in Cambridge three months later. Her enrollment application had been accepted, and she began her postgraduate studies on 3 October.

Graduating with honors, Marisa excelled in her two-year study program. During her last Lent term, she had a lab partner from Italy named Giacomel. Marisa knew he was interested in her, but didn't realize he had fallen in love with her. She was still running from her old life, and a serious relationship was still not part of her vision. When he passed a note to her like a love-sick grade schooler in their final lab class together, the shock caused her to start thinking forward, not just back. She was running to Bariloche and this mysterious project Otto had mentioned. Ernesto was seriously considering running for governor of Rio Negro Provence, and he needed her more than ever. Three days after graduation, Marisa was departing Heathrow Airport for Buenos Aires. "At least the British are sensible enough to simply name the airport after the place where is it located," Marisa said as her taxi pulled up to the British Airways terminal curb.

"It was called London Airport for nearly twenty years miss," the taxi driver said. "Even us Brits come to common sense slowly. Mind the curb now."

"We all come to common sense much slower than we realize, that is until we get there," Marisa replied. She landed in Buenos Aires 17 hours after leaving the taxi and its driver's common sense. She hadn't realized how long she had been away. On the aircraft, during departure, everyone was orderly and mindful of what the flight attendants requested. Fasten your seat belts, watch the emergency video, turn off your overhead light if those around you are sleeping, etc. Somewhere on the runway after touching down on Argentine soil, the rules were obviously different. People got up during taxi to get a bag from the over-head. All around her, she could hear the click of seatbelts coming off. People talked right through the flight attendant's remarks. At first, she was the shocked European, but as the outside air gradually mixed with the recycled cabin air from Europe, she began to smile. She was home. It was a cold, rainy day, but she could smell the Pampas. She could see the Cordillera beyond the horizon. She could hear the chaotic traffic that she would avoid on this transit. "*Life is beautiful and flattering. It is eternal spring if by my side I hear your voice,*" she began to sing the tango song under her breath.

An older man in the row behind her smiled and said, "The great Argentine writer Julio Cortázar noted during his travels abroad, "Whistling old tangos about the melancholic destinies of coming and going is one of my many ways of feeling like I'm still in Buenos Aires." Welcome home, señorita."

"I have had lots of comings and goings," Marisa said. "It is good to be home." Of course, she had a connecting flight to Bariloche before her journey's coming was completed. When she finally did arrive home, Vangelina Pereira met her at the door. Vangelina had been a friend of her parents and the adolescent Marisa's surrogate mother. Marisa had not left in the best of terms with this person who had sacrificed so much for Marisa and Ernesto. Marisa was going to do everything she could to make up for those hard years.

"Ernesto is in Viedma," Vangelina said. "He wanted to be here more than anything, but could not get a flight. He made me promise to say that to you before I even gave you a hug. So, the message is delivered. I need a hug from my little girl."

Marisa held on to Vangelina without words until the stress and time zones threatened to knock her unconscious. Marisa let go and said, "Thank you for being here to meet me, Vangelina. It means the world to me. It really wouldn't be home without you here. And thank you for your open arms. I left here the spoiled brat, and I hope I have returned with a pinch more maturity, and appreciation for all my blessings."

"Oh, Norisa, it is just so wonderful to have you home. It is a blessing to me, but it is a necessity of life for your brother. He has still not overcome the break-up with Gabriela. A wife for only six months. She visited Viedma and got right back on an airplane and returned to Mexico City. Such a tragedy. But enough of that. Tell me everything."

Vangelina got out the yerba mate tea, and they shared a bombilla straw as Marisa told her story. Two hours later Vangelina was holding Marisa in her arms while the prodigal daughter slept like the ancient mountain boulders outside the Starhemberg home.

The next three weeks were busy with reacquaintances and new introductions. The biggest surprise was her meeting with an eclectic team of engineers and scientists that Ernesto had set up in the greatest of secrecy at the old Huemul Island buildings. As a child, Marisa and her family had picnicked and camped here many times. That Marisa and Ernesto went there for a visit was of no surprise or concern to Vangelina or anyone else in the local community. A week later Marisa began work at the site on a full-time basis under the guise that she was an intern at the Bariloche Atomic Center, which was not far from the truth. She quickly became a valued member of the development team. She knew from day one that the team had been working on the historical cold fusion project from the Richter days. What she hadn't realized until she got deeper into the work was how far the team had come and that they were ready to actually build a device. The next surprise was the size and scope of the planned system. No table-top proof of concept plan here, but a massive operational system capable of powering Buenos Aires and much more.

"So, does this system have a name?" Marisa asked after three months of just calling it 'The Project.' Ernesto, who had taken on a leadership role at the urging of Uncle Otto, and for the first time providing a coalescing function agreed it was time to give this vision a proper name. "Why not call it Cambalache?" Marisa suggested.

"You see this as a junkshop?" one of the engineers asked in shock.

"Well, the planned reactor does kind of look like a junkshop with all its attachments and appendages," she said with a disarming smile. The name, if ever leaked would also be disinformation, because this is anything but a junkshop. A deeper meaning though tells a story. Cambalache means an exchange of something of low value. Our input fuel is one of the most abundant resources on the planet. Certainly, hydrogen is of relatively low value in today's energy market. We exchange this low value hydrogen for nearly limitless energy. As the tango lyrics to Cambalache tell us, *it's all the same! Now up is down! No one's ahead, no one's behind.* I know the context I am suggesting is different than the original song but isn't that the beauty of this? We can change who and what Argentina is. Up will be down in this new energy age. And as far as energy goes, it will be the first time of true abundance, when no is ahead, and no one is behind." The team loved it and the name stuck. The Cambalache project was born.

Through Ernesto's rise to power in Rio Negro Provence and then to the Casa Rosada, the Cambalache project was the secret that succeeded in remaining a secret. Great leaps and little failures kept the project moving forward. When it became apparent that Cambalache was ready to be unveiled to the world, both Ernesto and Marisa got cold feet. Ernesto saw the disruptive nature of this breakthrough. Marisa saw life, and most assuredly Ernesto's life changing. She feared for her only family member most of all. Ernesto wanted to bring on this whiz kid from the United States of all places to help them through the minefield of a successful international launch.

"Why not just turn this over to the United Nations?" Marisa asked. "Let's just give it away and let a bigger, more mature organization handle this."

"And watch the United Nations Security Council or the rich and powerful either strangle it to death or keep it for themselves as an instrument to ensure they stay in the global driver's seat?" Ernesto asked in rebuttal. Like it or not, this is an Argentine call, and it has happened on my watch."

"So this is about you and Argentina?" Marisa asked as the duel of questions started drawing blood.

"Yes, this is about Argentina, Marisa," Ernesto answered, ending the duel before someone suffered a mortal wound. "And there is more, Marisa, much more. You are right, I have a role to play, but ultimately this is not about me, but about a promise I made to our father. I will explain that when the time is right. For now, I need to know you are by my side. I can't do this alone."

"Are you kidding me big brother?" Marisa joked. "You could do this in your sleep. I worry about you, but I won't let that get in the way of what this could mean for the world. Now about this North American..."

I have had Pepe Peralta Monti on the lookout throughout the world for just the right person. Someone trustworthy, no baggage, experience and a track record on the international stage, and smart, really smart. It just so happens our guy is from the United States. I want you to meet him and give me your honest opinion. Be emotional and difficult if you must, but dig deep and tell what you really think."

Marisa met with James Nathaniels as her brother requested and what made her mad was, he was the perfect person to help them through the launch. She told her brother he was right and James quickly became a trusted and valued member of the Cambalache team. It didn't take long for her to start feeling an additional connection to James. He was handsome, strong, more wholesome than any man she had met during her university years, and he respected her. She had a feeling he understood her better than her brother did. She could also feel his presence and when he looked at her. It was its own kind of fusion, but it was certainly not cold fusion.

"I like James," Marisa told her brother one evening.

"I am glad he is working out so well," Ernesto said, never being one to say I told you so.

"No, I mean I have romantic feelings for him," Marisa said. "I am only admitting this because I don't want it to influence my judgment when things get more stressful and complicated with Cambalache."

"If, no, when things get more complicated," Ernesto said, "it will be your blessing to have James by your side. What are his feelings for you?"

"He likes me," Marisa said, blushing. "I worry that this whole project, mind blowing that it is, may cloud his feelings for me. I might just be part of the excitement, the obligatory girl that sits by the guy as he cruises Main Street, like in the North American movies."

I don't know James that well," Ernesto admitted, "but he is clearheaded and is not the guy cruising Main Street. He was probably the person at home working on his Latin verb conjugations so he could get into medical school. In many ways, he is like you," Ernesto paused and then said, "and like me. In the romance department, we really stink."

"Ernesto, I have simply been too busy," Marisa said. "You have had a run of bad luck and I am sure that will change once you make time in your life for it. As for James, we shall see. I am taking him on our first official date tomorrow night—a tour of the Quinta."

"Oh boy, that's a great date," Ernesto said raising his eyebrows. "This is where my brother and I live. Here is the kitchen, the guest bathroom. Want to watch TV? Do you want me to crash in on you, to play the part of the parents? Wait Vangelina has already claimed that role. I will be the big brother and threaten to beat him up if he tries to kiss you."

"I may initiate the kissing," Marisa said. "You just stay out of it. He still calls you Mr. President and sir. He respects you greatly. I am not sure he has fully digested the fact that his new girlfriend is the President's sister. Let's allow that part to sink in slowly, so it doesn't cause indigestion."

As Marisa hoped, their relationship did progress gradually. Their trip to Huemul went well as did their two official dates. By the time of the bombing of the Cambalache Project, they were both considering each other as boyfriend and girlfriend. In some quarters that would seem almost sophomoric to want and need to go through this adolescent relationship phase, but neither had ever really experienced teenage dating, and they reveled in it. The official Cambalache announcement arrived a month into their courtship. They depended on each other, and even the casual observer could see that they were in love, or approaching it. Of course, they didn't realize this. They stood at the rudder of the Good Ship Cambalache; making wise course corrections when approved by the ship's captain, yet they had no ability to describe or explain the waters into which their relationship was sailing. Full speed ahead was their only thought.

It was important for Marisa and Ernesto that James meet with Otto von Habsburg. Their reasons were worlds apart. Both were pleased with James's description of the meeting and thrilled that Uncle Otto was impressed and pleased with him. Their flight back to Buenos Aires had Marisa wondering what would happen next, for them, for Cambalache, for Ernesto, and for Uncle Otto.

JOAB also wondered what would happen next. The outside attack, attempting to close down the Cambalache Project, had not succeeded.

"It was time to disrupt, derail, and destroy key relationships. The greatest danger is always from inside. Alter the vision; the direction changes on its own; disruption takes over. And there are the pretenders. There are always pretenders. How to find them and exploit them?"

CHAPTER 12

Arrimar el Ascua a su Sardine

Literal Translation: To Bring Coals or Embers to One's Sardine

<u>Marisa's Explanation</u>: Argentina is famous for its beef and lamb, but remember, my country has over 3,000 miles of coastline and some of the best deep-sea fishing in the world. Sardines and deep fried squid are typical appetizers at large gatherings. Only worrying about your own appetizer is a selfish act. **Putting one's interests first and working things to one's advantage** is, however, a trait of more than some Porteños.

"IT HAS BEGUN, MR. PRESIDENT," Alberto Godoy, his Chief of Staff reported. "You win the bet."

"So it's the Russians on day two," President Starhemberg said with a smile. "Just luck. It could have been the United States, or who knows who. That there was a day of silence, digestion I think you called it, Alberto, is the interesting thing."

"The Russian Ambassador would like a meeting today at your earliest convenience," Godoy continued.

"Tomorrow night is the party at the Quinta for Archbishop Poli correct?" President Starhemberg asked, knowing the answer. "Could you get him on the line for me?"

Without explanation, Godoy gave President Starhemberg a twenty peso note. Godoy was confident the North Americans would be the first to contact the President and on the very evening of the announcement. Once again Ernesto Starhemberg called it accurately. Within minutes, Archbishop Poli was on the phone.

"Thank you for taking my call Archbishop," President Starhemberg began. "I am calling for two reasons. First, I hope your schedule still allows for me to host you at the Quinta de Olivos tomorrow night?"

"Of course," the Archbishop replied. "I would much rather avoid the pomp and circumstance on my account, but I am honored you would think to invite me."

"Wonderful," President Starhemberg said. "I have a thought to reduce the focus on your presence. You would still be the guest of honor. That you cannot escape. Due to the announcement of our new energy program, there has been some interest by other nations to visit with me. I don't want to create the appearance of favoring one nation over another at this point, so I was considering adding a few names to our guest list. As you know, we already have the Ambassador from Nigeria attending. I would like to add the Ambassadors of the United States, Russia, China, and the Mayor of Buenos Aires."

"But of course, Mr. President," the Archbishop said. "It is your party, I am just another guest, and from what it sounds like, the least important. You are very kind to speak with me, and I look forward to the diversity of the guest list."

"We will have a variety represented by the original guest list your office should already have, but I don't want to dilute the original reason for our celebration." President Starhemberg said. "You are still my primary interest Archbishop. Not only has your work touched many lives, but specifically your service in Villa Lugano has lowered the crime rate by 60 percent. That is a model for the world."

"You are very kind, Mr. President," the Archbishop replied, "but let's allow the pastoral work itself be the center of attention."

"That we will do Archbishop," President Starhemberg said. "I do have an additional minor request."

"Of course, Mr. President," the Archbishop said.

"Could you offer a brief homily on the topic of abundance? President Starhemberg asked. "I apologize for the very late request."

"Mr. President, homilies are usually reserved for the Mass celebration," the Archbishop replied.

"Yes, but isn't a homily a commentary, without formal introduction, division, or conclusion, on some part of Sacred Scripture, that can be offered and is indeed necessary for the nurturing of the Christian life?" President Starhemberg asked.

"In honor of learning and remembering your catechism my son," the Archbishop said with a chuckle, "I would be delighted to say a few words. I fear to ask if you have a scriptural reference in mind."

"I was thinking that perhaps a brief commentary on Philippians 2:13-15?" President Starhemberg suggested.

"I will see what I can do for you, Mr. President," the Archbishop said. "God's energy? Very good."

"Until tomorrow then Monsignor." President Starhemberg hung up the phone and called for Godoy. They huddled briefly on the President's ideas for the next evening's asado and Godoy took notes on seating arrangements and discussion topics for a few cabinet members. Ten minutes later Starhemberg was back at his desk for a conference call with his Minister of Agriculture on a looming sunflower oil trade deal with Turkey, followed by a briefing from the Commander of the Air Force on the potential acquisition of the F-35 from the United States.

James was enjoying the sunshine mixed with the light breeze off the river. A light rain the evening before had cleaned the air, and he could smell the Jasmine in bloom along Haedo Street in Barrio Vicente Lopez. He had moved back to his rented home in the neighborhood not far from the Quinta de Olivos. He felt strange as the President's house guest without Marisa in town. It felt good to decompress from the last month of work and the increasing complications of his life and his relationship with the sister of the President of Argentina—who claims to have harnessed the power of cold fusion.

He had just rounded the corner onto Jose Penna and was about to cross the cobblestoned street to reach the café where he had planned to eat lunch. He looked right for cars, and he noticed a familiar face walking along the platform at the rail station.

'Wasn't that Vangelina?' James asked himself. He was going to wave, but she looked preoccupied, and he wasn't fully certain it was her. 'If it was, what would she be doing here in Vincente Lopez?' he asked himself. He shrugged and refocused on the salad and fresh baked bread that was calling his name.

James thought no more about the potential sighting until the next day. He stepped outside for a jog, and he thought he again saw Vangelia on the corner, only three houses away. She was walking away from him, so he wasn't sure. After a very brief stretch, he jogged to the corner, but the cool damp morning fog had consumed her. She had disappeared. He completed a four-mile circuit and didn't notice her partially hidden by a large Bougainvillea across the street as he entered his home.

The event at the Quinta de Olivos was to start early, at 7 P.M. James arrived at 6:30 to go over some notes before the festivities. He wasn't sure why he had been invited, but he looked forward to seeing Marisa who was scheduled to have arrived home from Bariloche earlier that afternoon. James used his pass card to enter the Quinta conference room where he and Marisa had worked for the past month. He heard voices just down the hall. He thought about leaving but wanted to grab some notes first. He couldn't help but listen a man almost yelling.

"The Peronistas demand a share in the spoils of this discovery paid for by the Argentine people for all of Argentina. The Desicamisados want more than salchichas, Mr. President!" the menacing voice said. "Remember the Carapintadas, the Painted Faces Group of military men who made feeble uprisings during the presidencies of Raúl Alfonsín and Carlos Menem? Of course, you do. They supported your run for the president and now you owe payback. They voted for you against their own Peronista leanings because they thought you were the right course for the country. It is payday, Mr. President," the voice said. "The other option is international embarrassment as we shut down the country."

James couldn't hear the President and was glad to get out of the building unheard and unnoticed. He wondered, not for the first time if this could have ever happened at the White House. 'Even his own countrymen were standing in the way of success— all for short-term selfish gains. Could President Starhemberg stare them down?' James wondered. That was a scenario he and Marisa had worked on and playing chicken was the game.

"Do you think the President can deliver to the world before he is eaten alive by political foes at home?" a voice behind James asked.

James turned to see Pepe Peralta Monti standing in the shade of the pergola just outside the conference room door. "You startled me, sir," James said.

"As the President's National and International Security Advisor I have my own thoughts on the matter, but I was wondering what fresh eyes are thinking," Peralta-Monty said.

"Domestic political dynamics are more unpredictable than international actions," James said. "The most unexpected things happen in families."

"I counseled the President to appease the Peronistas with generic promises to hold them at bay for now," Peralta Monti said.

"They say they would shut down the country, but I don't think they will. This isn't like when President Bush visited from the United States in 1990 and the Carapintadas staged their uprising. That took nothing from their own pockets. They thought they could embarrass Menem into giving in to their demands. They were forced to take off their shoes before being carted off to jail as I remember reading, embarrassing themselves at the command of President Menem. This time around they would be shut down with more than just a visiting head of state watching, and they would suffer more than an embarrassment."

"Thirteen people died in the uprising you cite, Mr. Nathaniels," Peralta Monti said. "That was much more serious than an embarrassment. That the Peronistas and the Carapintadas are joining forces is not surprising in this scenario, but that makes this all the more volatile."

"Is it true some wealthy businessmen footed the bill for the rebellion in 1990?" James asked.

"I believe there is some evidence to support that," Peralta Monti replied, but no one can pay enough to a professional army to ask them to mutiny and die for a cause they only partly believe in."

"Exactly," James said. "I don't think they believe in the short-term benefits over what could become a much larger long-term benefit almost as fast. They will take valuable time away from the President, but they won't derail his vision."

"Whose vision?" President Starhemberg asked as he walked out the same door James had recently exited.

"Oh, hello, sir," James said. "Is it time for the asado? Where should I be?"

"You should be wherever you want to be," President Starhemberg said with a smile as if nothing the least bit unpleasant had happened all day. "This is an informal gathering. No assigned seating, no assigned tasks. Just enjoy the great food and wonderfully diverse company."

"I will do that, sir," James said. "Have you seen Marisa? Is she back in town yet?"

"I long ago gave up trying to keep track of my sister, James," Starhemberg said. "She is back, but probably freshening up, so she doesn't look like the overworked scientist. I am sure she will be out soon."

"Thank you. If you will excuse me then, I will go check out the asado preparations," James said. As he walked away, he could hear President Starhemberg begin a quiet conversation, probably about the Peronista demands.

"You know, Ernesto," Peralta Monti said, "most people want to hang on you like tics on a dog. That fellow treats you with respect, but could take you or leave you."

"It is one of his endearing qualities," Ernesto said. "He is free to see things as they are, not as they should be and even rarer, not as the world wants it to be."

"I am not sure that is the case when it comes to Marisa," Peralta Monti said. "He says the Peronistas and the Carapintadas are more bark than bite."

"Let's hope so," Ernesto said. "The good Mayor of Buenos Aires and his *helpful* threats may not stay too long tonight, so let's follow James's lead and get this party started."

The guests arrived over the next half hour, some early and some fashionably late, as if they had more important things to do this evening. The Archbishop showed up exactly on time; no pretense and no guile, just like his host.

The Russian Ambassador had tied up the Nigerian Ambassador much of the first half-hour of the gathering James had noted. He watched as President Starhemberg introduced Maria Alcaraz, the Director General of the Teatro Colón to the Nigerian Ambassador and walked the Russian over to the Mayor of Buenos Aires. The U.S. Ambassador had been talking with the Chinese Ambassador and the Archbishop, but abruptly exited that conversation and walked over to James who had been standing with several government functionaries he recognized from the Casa Rosada. Like himself, they were there mostly to fill up the space like the trees and flowering bushes, which was fine with James.

"Mr. Nathaniels?" the U.S. Ambassador asked.

"Yes, sir," James said. "Good to meet you, Ambassador Todman."

"President Starhemberg speaks highly of you," the Ambassador said as the Argentine government functionaries quietly retreated to another group of people. James watched them retreat just as Marisa made her entrance to the party. Both the Ambassador and James watched her add measurable spark to the otherwise quiet feast. "Beautiful young lady," the Ambassador noted.

"Yes, she is," James agreed as he felt his heartbeat increase. It was as if a particularly beautiful song had just reached his ears. If anything, the party had quieted to another level at her entrance, but the silence hummed a Julieta Venegas tune that touched everyone's ears with a joyful melancholy that made the asado taste better, the air smell better, and their own words sound more meaningful. Marisa wore a green dress that flowed with her slightest movements. Her delicate face carried a smile that told each person there that they were valued and that they were the reason for her joy. James smiled at the thought that she could fill some pretty big egos with just a simple smile.

"A friend of yours I understand," the Ambassador was saying.

"We have had the opportunity to work together, sir," James said. "You are well informed."

"Not nearly as informed as I would like to be James," Todman said. "What can you tell me as one American to another about this Cambalache Project?"

"It's the real deal, sir," James said. "I have seen it, but I am no expert."

"The President has authorized you to tell me that, that you have been there and seen the actual system?" the ambassador asked.

"He hasn't given me any directions whatsoever, sir," James admitted. "Just so we understand each other, sir, I am a patriotic citizen, but I am not telling you anything I wouldn't tell any other guest here."

"You know," the Ambassador said, "my father was the Ambassador here in the late 1980s. He used to tell me that the more he listened, the smarter he became to those doing the talking. I am listening if you ever have anything to say. And as you said so eloquently, just so we understand each other, I am not asking you to share anything outside of what your employer would approve."

"I appreciate that, sir," James said. "I know President Starhemberg is counting on the United States to be a stabilizing force as the rollout of Cambalache takes shape." James knew this because he and Marisa had mapped that out in their scenario planning. He also knew tonight was not the time to get into details with the Ambassador. Tonight was, as Starhemberg had explained to him, 'a billiard table. The balls will bump into each other. Some will group together on the table, while a few balls will repel each other, and a few will fall into pockets out of site of the table. Tonight is more about figuring out what the game is to be, 8-Ball Pool, Snooker, or Carom Billiards. Each game has a slightly different table, different rules, and goals, and what we need to first understand is who plans to be the cue, who thinks Argentina is only a feckless cue ball.'

"Good evening Mr. Ambassador," Marisa said as she approached James and Todman. "I hope I am not interrupting anything."

"Nothing but our prayers that you would join us," Ambassador Todman said.

Before Marisa or James could say another word, President Starhemberg interrupted the conversations and possibly additional prayers with an announcement.

"It is such an honor to have each of you here tonight to honor the work of Archbishop Poli. He made me promise to focus on the work, not the person, but as my favorite US. President, John Quincy Adams said, "If your actions inspire others to dream more, learn more, do more and become more, you are a leader." Archbishop Poli is a true leader and one I attempt to emulate on a daily basis. His work in the poorest parts of this great city have significantly lowered crime rates, increased secondary education graduation rates, and most importantly, touched the lives of countless desicamisados," President Starhemberg said as he stared at the Mayor of Buenos Aires. Instead of listening to me, however, I have asked the Monsignor to say a few brief words."

Everyone politely turned the Archbishop even though their hope and interests were to perhaps hear a few more words for this select group about Cambalache.

As if reading everyone's minds the Archbishop began, "I know there are many important thoughts swirling in the Quinta breezes this evening that you would rather hear than the long-winded thoughts from the mind of an old man. You will not. You will hear brief feelings from the heart of a humble servant of God. When Paul visited Philippi, it was in response to a dream that called him there, and it became the first European city evangelized by the new Christian religion. In chapter two are the words of an idiomatic translation of the original languages of the Bible offer this interesting passage: *That energy is God's energy, an energy deep within you, God himself willing and working at what will give him the most pleasure. Do everything readily and cheerfully–no bickering, no second-guessing allowed! Go out into the world uncorrupted, a breath of fresh air in this squalid and polluted society. Provide people with a glimpse of good living and of the living God. Carry the light-giving Message into the night."*

The Archbishop had everyone's rapt attention. The theme was not what they had expected and the use of the word energy, *God's energy* he had said, seemed to have a message about the ownership of Cambalache for this group. He continued, "Paul commanded no bickering, no second-guessing, no corruption. He spoke of a polluted society in need of fresh air and hope for good living. President Starhemberg's message to the world of nearly free energy just a few days ago could be as disruptive as the new Christian religion was to the people of Philippi. Christianity is eternal and not just of this world of course, but the metaphor is a useful one. Bickering, corruption, and pollution are synonymous with the world we live in. I am here tonight to remind you that everything on this earth is God's, not ours, including the energy created by the Cambalache contraption. This new invention provides the people of the world with a glimpse of good living. It is up to this group and the countries and governments you represent, to carry the light-giving message into the night. And what is the message of Cambalache? The promise of cheap, clean, and limitless energy suggests an abundance perspective. Energy is no longer a single pie with limited slices where in order to win, others must lose. No, scarcity, along with its jealousies, tragedies, and short-sightedness, are not what Cambalache demands. My message tonight, and I believe the message of President Starhemberg, is we must be prepared to shed the old ways and start considering cheerfully the long-term and start reaping the win-win opportunities at humanity's doorstep. The Cambalache tide is raising all our boats together, the rich and the poor, the small and the large, the old and the young. No bickering, no second-guessing allowed! God bless you my sons and daughters that you use wisdom in supporting President Starhemberg global vision."

James saw that Maria Alcaraz had tears in her eyes. Others were moved, some had forced smiles on their faces. The Russian Ambassador was frowning.

"The Apostle Paul also said," Starhemberg added before the moment was lost, "Do not be deceived: Bad company ruins good morals. Let us choose to work together in an ethical manner that blesses all of humankind. No under the table, behind closed doors, secret collusions that create false competitions and needless tragedies. I will be traveling to the United Nations next week to speak to the world body. I will outline my plans for Cambalache and for risk mitigation of the global energy sector and peripheral economies. In a symbolic gesture, I am now offering to provide the electrical power to five cities via the existing energy grid during my trip. Those cities are Buenos Aires, Brasilia, Bogota, Mexico City, and New York City."

Everyone was still quiet, speechless. This was very fast becoming real and those used to sitting in the driver's seat were unaccustomed to the back seat.

President Starhemberg completed his words as if he had just announced the opening of a hydro-electric dam in some forgotten corner of his country with the incongruous words, "Now let's enjoy this nourishing meal and don't forget to thank Archbishop Poli for his life-saving work."

"I am at the door and will soon be invited inside," JOAB reported. "Starhemberg is a complex mix of street-smart and school boy naiveté— neither of which inoculate his vison from real world brutality. He believes in people, both individually and en masse. He believes in paradox; power

from vulnerability, holiness from the humdrum and habitual, change from harmony. He believes Machiavelli was satire. Here is a paradox for him: trust and reliance is not reality."

BAJO Chapter 3

"WHAT IS TO BE LEARNED from the example of the Maid of Orléans, the one the world calls Joan of Arc? Was she mad, schizophrenic from the voices she heard or was it really the voice of God that led her to her victories and her final defeat?" David Rosado laid down his pen and closed his journal. He rubbed his weary eyes and looked at the clock on the wall in his den. Nearly midnight. He hadn't bothered with dinner.

'The ghosts of doubt always visited in the dark. Was he, BAJO Prelate of the Americas, the oldest son of a former prelate, and whose great grandfather was a confidant to Bourbon kings, entertaining these ghosts or fighting them?' He was afraid to raise those thoughts out loud. He lived alone. His wife had died ten years ago at the age of 45. An aneurysm the doctors had told him. He didn't think his house was bugged and his cat kept secrets very well. He simply didn't want to disturb the air by making sound waves of his thoughts. "Pondering is one thing, but voicing those thoughts sets one's feet into the tar pit of treason, a place difficult from which to retreat," he voiced to remind and reprimand himself.

David poured himself a lemonade from his refrigerator and returned to his den. He opened his journal and chuckled. "I can't say it out loud for fear of offense, but I have no inhibition to writing even my deepest thoughts on paper, which is more substantial and lasting than the spoken word." He turned to the words he had begun earlier in the day when he had received several communications from the Guardian. The JOAB candidate he had ejected from his home two weeks ago had been accepted into BAJO and would serve as a JOAB under David's supervision after completing his training. Training usually took several months, but David girded himself to once again have this impertinent young man in his home within six weeks. The Guardian also commended David for his excellent work in shaking up the Cambalache Project and putting "that Starhemberg upstart" as the Guardian had termed the Argentine President, on notice that someone knew and someone could impact or shut down his bigger goals at will." What the Guardian didn't realize was, David had only authorized reconnaissance which had never taken place to his knowledge, not actual damage to the system that neither JOAB nor he really understood. His JOAB reported that the damage could have been far worse and the mercenaries employed had not cared about the dangers to human life or what nuclear power unleashed could potentially do. "Stupid," he grumbled out loud. Yet he also knew he shouldn't second guess perhaps the most experienced and well placed JOAB in the entire BAJO system. He hadn't been there—well not that close to the actual action.

His word had poured out as he had begun writing. With his dear Perla gone for so many years, he only had his journal and his cat with which to converse. He began reading his words from earlier in the day. "There is no doubt Joan of Arc's swift victories in the last phase of the Hundred Years War—a war of succession between the Houses of Valois and Plantagenet, inspired the French to their final victories. Their conquests ensured the Capetian Ascendancy from which the House of Bourbon was a cadet family and rose to prominence in France. Again we are back to the Habsburgs, cousins to the Plantagenets through the Merovingian bloodline. Without Joan of Arc's victories and ensuring the coronation of Charles VII, there might never have been a Bourbon Ascendancy. Am I like the dithering Jean, Duke of Alençon, a kinsman to the King of France, Charles VII? He was unsure and halting in his willingness to take risks and get the job done. The king needed Joan, but also feared the nationalism she was inspiring among his subjects. Eventually, Joan of Arc was captured by the Burgundians when King Charles VII had his back conveniently turned. The Burgundians were Habsburg cousins, and they burnt Joan at the stake. Am I afraid of being burned at the metaphorical stake?" David skipped the next two paragraphs where he considered and rejected fear of failure or death for his cautiousness.

"The Hundred Years War was one of the bloodiest campaigns in human history," he read on the next page as if he had never seen these words before. They were a horrific surprise. "Over three and a half million deaths, at a time when there were only 75 million people in all of greater Europe! France lost half its population during the Hundred Year War—although some of that was probably due to the Bubonic Plague. Yet England only lost twenty percent of its population due to the Plague, so I think it is safe to say warfare caused most of the deaths in France— warfare over a right to rule by this family or that."

"Nationalism had its rise during this terrible time, however. The disparate tribes of what is now modern day France united to become the French people, not merely subjects to a king that had little loyalty to them or the concept of a country. The English began thinking of themselves as an island people and different than the Continentals. Rather than focusing only on Europe, they became the great explorers and built a global empire from which the sun never set. Even the seeds of the nation-state were planted during this time. The war gave new life to the Magna Carta in England and quickened the death of feudalism on the continent.

"I was raised to believe that Joan of Arc was the model JOAB, although she died seventy years before BAJO was born. I remember as a young man thinking JOAB and JOAN are nearly the same word. Why didn't the founders of BAJO call their operatives JOANs? Then I realized, the only difference was the "B," and that stood for the whole reason for the organization—the Bourbons. I never raised that thought again for fear of being seen as a traitor to the cause. Yet what is the cause—that one family should rise above another? Really? Is that what my life has been about? Have I just served as a vassal to the idea of a feudal lord, rather than a knight to an ideal? BAJO told me from the beginning the answer to that question. I just chose to see it differently. As was the custom in the feudal system, the lord would make someone a vassal through a commendation ceremony. This ceremony had two parts, an act of homage and an oath of loyalty. The homage included a contract that in turn for land or another benefit such as a title, the vassal-to-be would promise to fight for the lord at his or her command. I took a similar oath when I was inducted into BAJO. The royal houses of Europe claim their legitimacy to rule through their royal bloodline traced back to King Solomon who God placed on the throne. I know history well enough to know that many were king because of their strength in battle or their wisdom and cunning. Are all men really created equal, or are some more equal than others?"

David stopped reading and yawned. "So many questions! Young men have few and sleep contentedly after counting a few sheep. Old men are kept up counting their questions and sheepishly admit they have few answers." He closed his journal and walked slowly to his bed.

CHAPTER 13

Mejor solo que mal acompañado
Literal Translation: It's better to be alone
than to be with bad company

<u>Marisa's Explanation</u>: This dicho is universal. **It's hard to be alone,** no one knows that better than me, but I learned a very hard lesson **it is better than looking for love in the wrong places.**

"**C**AMCON," OTTO VON HABSBURG REPEATED. "Short for the Cambalache Confederation. I prefer Confederation over Consortia or Coalition because a confederation presupposes a central government in a union of sovereigns."

"There must be hundreds of organizations that use the shortened version of that name," Alberto Godoy said.

"Yes, there are a few, including a petroleum consortia, a research technology enterprise, and a female modeling organization, but this will eclipse those enterprises on day one," Habsburg explained.

"We certainly don't need to worry about buying the dot com domain name to ensure our success. How would this system work?" James asked, completely enthralled. "Each country would be a part of an energy cooperative called CamCon?"

"We can get deeper into the workings of this ecosystem later, James," Otto von Habsburg said. "We can also answer each other's questions we posed during our visit in Bariloche. Here is the brief outline of what President Starhemberg and I have been working on for several years. We have kept this between just the two of us because honestly, it was more of an intellectual exercise than something real—at least until Cambalache proved itself. In short, this global confederation would mostly ignore the nation-states and include select mega-cities as its principle members. Since the energy is mostly free, instead of a capitalist model, we would employ a syndicate model, with the cities as the owner/members. Those that want the free energy would need to agree to the organizational structure. We wouldn't demand political agendas or determine membership by some rigid rubric, but there would be some membership expectations. Over time we would expand to smaller cities and rural areas, but that would be a CamCon decision of where, when, and how fast."

"Excuse me, sir," a secretary interrupted over the intercom. "The King of Saudi Arabia is on line two." President Starhemberg left the conference room to attend to the call in his office.

"It was the Russians this morning," Peralta Monti said. "A very tenacious president who can't stand to not be calling the shots. He cordially called to make us a promise that he would include us in the new world order with him at the helm—or death and destruction if he were left out."

"A nice carrot and stick approach," Godoy said only half joking. "Nice of them to consider including us in their plan."

"Getting back to the subject at hand," James said, "You propose to simply ignore the sovereignty of countries and their propensity to use their power—like Russia, and work with mega-cities and President Starhemberg is going to outline this in his speech at the United Nations day after tomorrow? My mind is churning with the possibilities, but also the potentials for cataclysmic failure. I mean, Cambalache is delivered to select cities and then the countries they reside in take the money they were spending on energy and build weapons to attack their neighbor. Or certain cities become so dependent on Cambalache and then the have nots somehow shut down Cambalache—say a nuclear bomb is dropped on us by oil rich Russia and entire mega-cities enter the dark ages and have to come begging at Russia's doorstep for help. The negative consequences are as limitless as the promise of free energy."

"Yes, yes," Habsburg said. "The dangers are real, and that is why President Starhemberg is standing tall as the Cambalache focal point, target, and single spokesperson of the new reality for now. I prefer to think of his speech at the UN as another catalyst for this new reality that is already in progress. Key leaders will begin to see what is right in front of them and join ranks. It will also be my coming out party. He will announce my role as the Confederation Administrator, and then there will be two targets. That will probably cause some fireworks. In short, his speech at the United Nations will outline the outdated model of the nation, and ironically the U N itself."

"Saudi Arabia promises Argentina a special rate on oil and a place at the OPEC table," President Starhemberg said as he re-entered the room.

"No one has been able to make the paradigm shift yet," Marisa said. "They all think they are driving the only car. They all believe the old rules still apply."

"It's those old rules that we need to consider most carefully," James said. "We can only do the least damage by softening the blow to the traditional systems of rules because in most cases they reflect the values that people will fight and die to protect. I am certain they know their economic world has suffered a tectonic shift. Oil prices are down to $45 a barrel, and you haven't even delivered a single kilowatt-hour yet. They just don't know what to say, because there really isn't anything to say. Now the death of the nation-state, that is another matter. You are definitely a couple standard deviations away from the mainstream paradigm."

"Crossing the chasm, that is what I am afraid of," Peralta Monti said. "There will be some early adopters of our perspective, but they will likely be the have-nots. This puts us in the crosshairs of some of the most powerful nations on earth. I believe actions are already in motion to shut us down. They won't wait for your speech at the UN."

"You know we even got a direct threat from Greenpeace this morning," Godoy said shaking his head. "They are complaining that our energy initiative prolongs the use of fossil fuels in vehicles, aircraft, water-borne shipping, and trains because petroleum will now be more plentiful than ever because it is no longer needed in any form for the energy grid. Like it's our fault we didn't solve all the world's challenges in one pass over the problem. No "thank you," no offer to help with a rollout, just a "how dare you breathe new life into the internal combustion engine.""

"We just shook their raison d'être as well," James said. "They will get over it long before any country will. They also will not feel threatened with our circumvention of sovereignty."

"Have you read Ayn Rand, James?" President Starhemberg asked James.

"Yes, of course," James answered. "Required reading for any undergraduate student from Political Science to Sociology."

"Then you will remember that she suggests that your country's greatness is in the insight that government is the servant of the people." The President continued, standing up to pace around the room. "We can argue all night about the origins of nationalism, but your nation was the first to recognize its demise, even though at the same time it has been a powerful example of nationalism. Rand said something like, 'All previous systems had held that man's life belongs to society and it can dispose of him when and how it pleases. The freedoms offered that men are at the permission of capricious society. The United States, on the other hand, held that man's life is his by birthright.' That concept was a nail in the nationalism coffin. Totalitarianism leveraged nationalism against the freedom of the individual. Communism claimed a hollow leap forward with the term social republicanism that claimed nationalism was not dead, but that it would expand to a new hegemony where individual freedoms were forfeited to society."

President Starhemberg let those thoughts take their course with the small group and wondered, 'If I can't explain it to these people who trust me, how am I ever going to face the world at the UN and expect anyone to see past their own emotions and fears?' He continued, "Totalitarianism only survives in North Korea. Communism died first of its own weight and then the coffin was nailed shut with the invisible hand of capitalism. Only the republic has survived, and that has weakened nationalism over time."

"But the republic is a thing, and nationalism is a feeling, a value," James said.

"The embodiment of nationalism, the nation-state, is also a thing. Both nationalism and republicanism come down to practices," President Starhemberg said. "Republics live and die by the rule of law. Nationalism lives and dies by the values of that nation's people. Both revolve around right and wrong, winning and losing, ups and downs. Both serve something bigger than self, both are absolutely certain of destiny."

"Nationalism has long been the dominant political ideology, but it is a relatively modern invention." Otto von Habsburg said. "I don't want to get too philosophical, but the nation-state is assumed to be an a priori fact—that is, independent of all particular experiences. It simply is. In reality, the nation-state is a posteriori knowledge; something derived from experience.

Humankind has organized, by family, tribe, by city-state, by kingdom and empire, and only recently by nation-state. The rule of law that is republicanism, champions pluralism. Pluralism breaks the 'magnetic force, the glue,'" Habsburg said making air quotes with his hands, "that hold a body of people together. To your point, James, nationalism also seeks to eliminate any perceived viruses that might infect the common-held values, norms and expressive symbols of that society. I suggest that pluralism is already doing that, but people have not yet recognized that fact. Without the obligational legitimacy of positive or negative nationalism, the state in a republic form of governance will eventually disintegrate into communities of practice. That is in large part why we see the growing interests of groups to leave the European Union, or Scotland and Wales to leave Great Britain, or Catalonia to leave Spain, and so on."

"I believe we have a presently unwitting partner in supporting our vision," President Starhemberg interjected. "Isn't it interesting, that other than a quiet approach by the U.S. ambassador, the American voice has been deafeningly silent?"

"Don't take American silence as tacit approval, sir," James said. "The house is not yet on fire, and they are willing to let the smoke rise for a time. And I will bet the CIA, NSA, and other organizations are already looking for the source of the smoke. That has simply not come to our attention yet."

"We can't do this alone," President Starhemberg said solemnly. "We can joke about Russian threats, but there are many who would rather live in the Stone Age and be the king, than in a free energy world and be on equal footing with everyone else. There is some comfort in a scarcity mentality for the shortsighted independent actor and the fearful dependent actors of this world. Argentina cannot fulfill its destiny without the help of the United States."

It became clear at that moment, to both James and Marisa, why the President had insisted on James, an American, to be a part of this team. He had proven himself as an outstanding Political and Cultural Risk analyst, but he was also American. He would be a bridge that Argentina desperately needed.

"But, we will also need to keep the U.S. at arm's length," Otto von Habsburg added. "If we appear too much in the American pocket, some areas of the world will not trust us. Indeed, if we do find ourselves marching to the American's drum beat, Argentina will again be shrinking from its responsibilities and destiny."

"You can't have it both ways," James said. "If the nation-state is on its death bed, why are you so concerned about the destiny of a nation-state, such as Argentina?"

"Yes, Uncle Otto," Marisa added, breaking her uncharacteristic quiet, "Ernesto's speech in Bariloche berated us for our failures and celebrated our new-found place at the table of world leaders. Where does the future of Argentina fit into this post-nation-state vision?"

"That is the conversation James and I will have later, perhaps this evening," Otto said. "In short, the nation-state took millennia to mature into the governing form we have today. It will take perhaps a hundred or more years to morph or disappear altogether. Part of the CamCon plan is for the nation-state to sacrifice itself on the altar of a new abundance mentality. Argentina, like Abraham being commanded to sacrifice his son on the altar, has found itself in the ultimate sacrifice situation of offering its future for the future of humankind."

"Who is commanding us and who said my brother, an elected official, as great a person as he is, can decide for Argentina and its millions of citizens that we must sacrifice our nation to a world that really couldn't care less about us?" Marisa asked with a flaming sword in her eyes.

"Marisa," her brother said, "I am not deciding for anyone anything. My job, as I see it, is to provide as much time between stimulus and response as possible so the people of Argentina and the world can make up their own minds. There is no compelling reason to run from the nation-state. It has served us humans well overall. Certainly better than chaos and anarchy would have anyway. We, mankind, must want to run toward something better, something that isn't just enticing, but overwhelmingly compelling so that we are willing to change our present nature. You love Argentina. You are willing to die for your country. Are you ready to die for a course of action that includes the death of your nation-state? Not yet. Cambalache is not, by itself, a sufficient enough rallying point for such a sacrifice. I am betting my life that CamCon will become that castle on the hill."

"There is an engineering point in all this philosophical talk that we haven't broached," Pepe Peralta Monti interjected, to lower the emotions in the room. "You mentioned, Mr. President, at the Archbishop Poli event, that Cambalache would offer free power to five cities for the week you would be in the United States to address the UN. That you could promise that, and no one would ask how is another nail in the nation-state coffin. Only five years ago, in 2015 that promise would have been impossible to deliver, no matter how much power Cambalache could produce. There was no global power grid. Just like the slow death of using AC, alternating current, to provide electricity long distances, the nation-state's importance to deliver large society glue is diminishing. In shifting to a high-voltage direct-current (HVDC) transmission system, the world has significantly lowered the cost of delivery. Without getting into the scientific details, the new system reduces the transmission line size, while losing almost no actual electricity to transmission. Plus HVDC allows for the easy transfer of power between regional grids that are operated at different frequencies. The bottom line is, it isn't just pluralism, roads, commerce, and mega-cities that cross borders. The world is, save a few places, physically a single power grid. Many will begin to see the high cost, low delivery abilities of the nation-state system."

"The parallel movement towards microgrids provides an excellent metaphor for national fractionalization," James added, happy to move away from what was usually one of his favorite topics, the nation-state system. "I understand storage is less efficient than transmission, so a super grid really does make sense. As global society also breaks into smaller pieces, it is priming the pump for global connectivity."

"E Pluribus Unum," Otto von Habsburg said. "Out of many, one," is the motto of the United States. Unum Pluribus might be a start to a CamCon motto. One manys. A confederation of the many."

"I don't want to jump back into the esoteric," Marisa said, "but fission—the old model of nuclear energy, is about breaking things apart. Fusion, the Cambalache energy model, is about bringing things together. Both require energy and fission has a lot of negative baggage in radioactive waste, meltdown potential, and contamination dangers. Only with Cambalache does fusion deliver much more energy than it requires to power the system. Only with Cambalache is there hope for a post-nation-state world. I am not sure I am ready for that, however. I love my country. I love what it means to be Argentine."

"Fusion, as you just described it, Marisa," Godoy said, "does not mean losing, but gaining and combining. Fusion music might combine jazz and rock for example. You don't need to lose what you love about being Argentine, except eventually the state side of the nation-state."

"Whatever the final outcome," President Starhemberg said, "in the short-term, we will be going it alone with the hope that the U.S. will join us as at least our security partner, and at most a quiet evangelist of the Cambalache system."

"That's it isn't it," James said with a sudden insight that had eluded him until this moment. "The Cambalache Project is not just named *bazaar* because of how the actual machine looks, but because the world becomes a single second-hand shop of slightly used treasures, nations without the baggage, Brazil without the *jeitinho,* Iran without the *bakhshesh,* Argentina without the *gnocchis*—and I am talking about the workers who only show up on the last day of the month to get paid, not the wonderful pasta, Marisa. It sounds like a perfect world, but of course, it won't be exactly that. Even still, Cambalache is a significant step forward."

"JOAB, hold off on any disruptive actions prior to the newly announced visit to the United Nations by Starhemberg. The world's eyes are on this man your reports mark as misguided. Further attempts to damage the machine will only add to its potential credibility. At worst he will outline his plans, and we will better understand how to derail him. And hopefully, the world will laugh him out of town. At best, some other country or threatened commercial enterprise will shut him down. He might not even make it to New York with plans intact. Continue to build trust with him and his trained monkey Habsburg. If you are able to travel with his team to the UN, that would be helpful. Much can happen in a week in New York City."

"I have been confirmed as part of the travel team to accompany Starhemberg to New York. I am ready for action at your command. I can terminate this Habsburg ascendency in a New York minute as well. Just say the word." JOAB

CHAPTER 14

Quien no comprende una mirada tampoco comprenderá una larga explicación

Literal Translation: He who does not understand a look will neither understand a long explanation.

Marisa's Explanation: **Keep It Simple,** something I struggle mightily to accomplish. I fear to say more.

66 J EFF KAY?" MARISA ASKED. "I thought we were landing at Kennedy? Are we in New York?"

"Don't get me started with airport names," James said. "The pilot said J.F.K. We are at the right place, thank goodness. I don't know if my body could handle another hour in this seat."

Marisa had insisted on traveling commercial, instead of arriving with her brother and the official party from Argentina. Of course, this was highly irregular, and presidential security fought it, but finally realized they had met their match. Vangelina and one other security person known only to Vangelina, traveled with James and Marisa. Marisa was right, no one on the American Airlines flight from Florianópolis, Brazil, where they were discretely dropped off by Tango 02, seemed to know who she was or didn't care enough to make a big deal about it.

"Traveling with the official party will mark me as your sister, Ernesto," Marisa explained. "I want just one more day of anonymity. James and Vangelina will make sure I am a good girl. I only want to arrive one day before you, and once you get to New York, I will rejoin the official delegation." Her brother was the only person who could have told her, no, but he was as much a pushover as James had become. "And since James will disappear while we are in New York, it will be the only time he will have to show me the sights."

President Starhemberg had decided it best to keep James out of the public eye for the time being. A U.S. advisor might not go over well with many at the UN and the U.S. themselves might get the wrong idea. "I want them in our corner, but not assuming they are already in the driver's seat." James agreed completely. And Marisa got her way.

Although IMF Headquarters offices were in Washington, DC, the Fund Office was in Dag Hammarksjöld Plaza between 47th and 48th Streets in New York City. James didn't consider himself an expert on the city, but he had visited enough in his previous employment that he knew it sufficiently for a day of sightseeing. Neither Marisa, nor Vangelina had ever visited here, and he wasn't sure who was more excited, the ladies or himself. James had helped craft President Starhemberg's address to the UN and was really starting to feel ownership of the Cambalache launch, the full launch as he now understood it. It seemed Marisa was less interested the UN speech, except it would spell the end of her anonymity. Vangelina was always hard to read, but she had mentioned three times her hope to visit the Statue of Liberty.

"We could take the Staten Island Ferry and see the Statue as the ferry passes it, or we can take a tour." James had explained while sitting in the airport in Brazil. If we can't get a reserved ticket for the Crown or Pedestal, we could be there all day. Also, the tour includes a visit to Ellis Island. I think it will take us about five hours for the tour or two hours for the Staten Island Ferry. Of course, we could also tell them who you are and we could probably bypass all this."

"No way, Santi," Marisa said. "We are just tourists like everyone else. And we have only one day of anonymity. Vangelina, could we do the statue tour the day after the speech?"

"Oh, it's not that important," Vangelina said. "We can drop that from the plans altogether."

"Right," Marisa said rolling her eyes in mock frustration. "Santi, let's do the statue after the speech. The more I think about it, we really would get the best tour after we are outed. I hate the idea of taking advantage of the celebrity status, but for Vangelina, both Ernesto and I would love to do this."

James noted that Vangelina had blushed and her eyes teared up. 'So she does have some emotions after all,' James noted. "So it's decided then. We land at 6:20 in the morning. We drop our bags off at the Hyatt on Union Square." James would continue to stay there after Marisa and Vangelina joined the rest of the Argentine delegation at the William Beaver House for the remainder of their five-day stay in the other Big Apple. "Breakfast at City Bakery not far from the hotel, then a short visit to the Strand Bookstore, taxi to the 9/11 monument, then a slow drive through China Town, Washington Park, the Empire State Building, Bryant Park, and at Times Square we can walk to Rockefeller Center. We buy lunch items at the Amish Market and enjoy it in Central Park. Depending on our energy level, we spend an hour or two at the Metropolitan Museum of Art. We will drive by the Lincoln Center, but you will attend a performance there with your brother later in the week so we won't stop. Same with Broadway. We get a gelato while we walk Highline Park and return to the hotel to freshen up and relax. Maybe an afternoon walk down St. Marks in the East Village and then take the subway over to Brooklyn to Juliana's for pizza and walk the Brooklyn Bridge across to Manhattan. We catch a cab back to the hotel. I guarantee you, you will be ready for bed, having only seen a tiny fraction of the city."

"But I will be seeing it as a regular tourist!" Marisa said.

They arrived at their hotel as planned and the day went mostly as planned, except a short rain shower kept them from walking the Highline Park. Marisa seemed to get more and more energy as Vangelina and James depleted theirs. Soon the day was nearly over. They found themselves sharing a large Margherita pizza and enjoying the view out the large bay windows.

"I don't want this day to end," Marisa said. "Ernesto probably just landed, or they are on their way to the hotel. I am so afraid for him. I have been saying I don't want the celebrity that will come with his speech, but honestly I don't care about that. I am really just afraid for him."

"He knows what he is getting into and what might come unsuspectedly will be a delightful surprise for him," James said. "We have gone through his speech, the scenarios, the probable meetings, and he's ready. I've never thought anyone was really born for this. I've come to believe that your brother was born to lead and serve. He's rare, and the world needs him."

"This pizza is heaven," Vangelina said. "Thanks for the day, James. And I am glad President Starhemberg trusts you. I am beginning to myself. We talk of everyone but you. What are your plans now?"

"I don't know," James said, looking over at Marisa. "I hope I still have a part in all this, but that is the President's call."

"No contact from your country yet?" Vangelina probed.

"Nope, nothing. I don't think the right hand knows what the left hand is doing," James said. "I mean, someone in the government knows I am in Argentina, and the U.S Ambassador certainly knows I am connected indirectly to Cambalache, but until tomorrow's speech, they have no idea what is actually involved with Cambalache."

"Surely they have to be interested in the possibility of free energy," Vangelina said.

"I'm sure they are, but they know I am not an engineer and hardly understand the difference between fission and fusion," James said. "Tomorrow they will see there is more to President Starhemberg's vision than energy."

"Is that something I am allowed to know about?" Vangelina asked, looking at Marisa.

"You and the rest of the world will know tomorrow," Marisa said, smiling at Vangelina. "Ernesto has sworn us to secrecy. You won't miss his speech, though. You will be sitting next to me in the gallery. Poor James will be watching the UN web TV from his computer in the hotel."

The walk over the Brooklyn Bridge was the perfect end to an exciting day. Marisa took James hand and squeezed it. Vangelina, ever vigilant and aware of the other security team member who had just walked the bridge in front of them, dropped back to give the couple some space. She put a tiny speaker in her ear.

"So what do you want to do after the speech tomorrow?" Marisa asked.

"The impossible," James said. "I want to spend another day with you, watching you laugh, smile, close your eyes in a park, and breathe like you don't have a care in the world."

"I like that answer, Santi," Marisa said. "But I was asking about the long-term. This is getting real, and you will sooner or later be a known part in all this. Governments might want to own you, or failing that, put you on their hit list. You might be the fall guy for some in Argentina even—the Norte Americano who blinded the President with crazy ideas about the death of the great nation of Argentina."

"All I know is, I believe in what you and your brother are doing, and," he paused and took a breath, "I am the guy who is falling for you."

They walked in silence for a while pretending to be lost in the view of the lights of Manhattan. They didn't notice the older gentleman standing to the side of the walkway who nodded to Vangelina as she passed. He walked the other way after they were nearly over the bridge. Had they seen him, they might have recognized him as David Rosado, the man from Peru that rescued Marisa from her fall at the National Park Bosque de Arrayanes.

"I hope you sleep well tonight, Marisa," James said as he turned from escorting Marisa to her hotel room door.

"Santi, I need some help figuring out my TV. The cable connection does not seem to be working. Could you check it out before I call the front desk and make a fool of myself?"

James stepped into Marisa's room and as soon as the door was shut Marisa grabbed his arm and pulled him to her. She put her finger to his lips to quiet him and then replaced her finger with her lips. She held him tight and ran her hand through his hair. As suddenly as this began it was over. Marisa turned him to the door, opened it, and with her foot, she pushed him playfully out into the hallway and shut the door.

The United Nations General Assembly Hall was bigger than Marisa had expected. She and Vangelina had met the Argentine delegation once they entered the building. Security escorted them to some reserved seats where they sat next to Alberto Godoy, Pepe Peralta Monti, and the Argentine Ambassador to the United States. The smell in the room was exotic with its many colognes and perfumes, but Marisa could also smell tension. "Maybe that is me I'm smelling,' she thought. Some UN official took care of some General Assembly administrative details and then the same person offered a brief introduction of President Ernesto Starhemberg. All of a sudden it seemed to

Marisa, there was her brother who had just picked her out of the crowd and smiled at her like a little boy. She almost expected him to say out loud, "Can you believe I am standing here? It's all because of you, little sister." She pushed away that thought she almost never allowed to surface in her mind and said a little prayer.

"Mr. President, Mr. Secretary General, fellow heads of state, delegates, and diplomats, technical officials, and the curious listener, it is an honor to be with you in this remarkable edifice today," President Starhemberg began. "Many have come here through the nearly 75 years of this organization's history to express its nation's concerns, ideas and issues often more for domestic consumption than for international interest. Assembling this body for parochial petitions is not a misuse of this podium —for where else can a nation be truly heard? Others have also used this as a pulpit, such as Pope Francis who only a few years ago expressed his appreciation for the work of this organization. With all the rhetoric, nationalistic passions, and agendas, there has also been an irrefutable human connection. Connection is the energy that creates the spark that is humankind. Conversely, it is energy that connects humanity. It was Pope Francis who standing here said, "[Our] achievements are lights which help to dispel the darkness of the disorder caused by unrestrained ambitions and collective forms of selfishness." That is the theme of my brief comments here today—to dispel the darkness with light, literally and figuratively. I am not here as simply the Argentine President, but as a citizen of this globe— still the only home we know." He scanned the vast audience and seemed to take new energy from the view.

"The paradox of connection, electrical and human, suggests, the broader its reach, the less efficient it becomes. Soon everything expressed here becomes exclusive in some way to someone on earth. Diversity Connection, also called transculturation by a fellow Latin American, the DC current of humanity has turned this paradox on its head, just as high-voltage DC electric power grids are enabling a cold fusion reactor in Argentina to deliver power to this great city at this moment. Literally, lights are dispelling the darkness, and my amplified voice is piercing the silence. As much as the grid is a marvel, the power that flows through its veins is a miracle. I am here today to tell you that the same system God established to power the Sun and in-turn brings life to our world, also powers Cambalache, our fusion reactor. The sun is a free gift from God. Cambalache is a free gift from the scientists, engineers, and people of Argentina, who in-turn acknowledge the master craftsman of the universe in their offering." He said these last words staring directly at Marisa.

"Mankind has had many millennia, indeed our entire existence, to adjust and evolve to live with the blessings and brutal realities of the sun. Cambalache offers only days, weeks, and months to adapt to the benefits of nearly free energy and the short-term brutal realities for some industries and nations. To that end, I offer a plan to minimize disruption and mitigate the risk of any unintended consequences to our innovations."

"I speak now as an individual, a brother of all who will hear my voice or read my words. Perhaps more importantly, I speak on behalf of the billions of people who will never know my words. I speak not as the head of a nation state to other nation states, but as simply an observant voice of mankind. Nations, and more recently in the course of human organization, nation-states, have both "mothering" and "othering" tendencies. *Mothering* endears its citizens to itself—a defensive self-preservation modus. *Othering* grows from poor or skewed mothering—an exclusionary practice. Of course, there is inclusionary othering that observes and celebrates diversity and differences. But there are few examples in the history of nationalism that has successfully continued inclusionary othering when the core nation-state was threatened. Altruism has its limits in the nation-state model." He paused and could hear the rustling of bodies that were trying to stay still and quietly whispered words in over one hundred languages.

"It is not my intention, nor is it self-proclaimed authority I assert because I happen to hold the keys to Cambalache, that I dictate to other nations, states, or industries. I am here to offer a way forward, a path of autonomy from the weaknesses and impedances that the modern nation-state model imposes upon us. Some so invested in the present model may feel threatened by my words. I pose no threat, except to the shackles of a decrepit system that is dying, dying so slowly we don't see it. I won't take your valuable time today to press that point except to say, the *mothering* and *othering* of nations is an unintended consequence perhaps, disagreeable baggage, or all too often, a tool of rationalization in support of national interests. The nation-state and its circular arguments I have always felt uncomfortable with as a politician, the system we have fashioned, is evolving and often in chronically debilitating ways. For example, carbon exchanges, such as the European Climate Exchange, allow nations to claim a higher ground while they keep indigenous peoples—nations in their own right, from their traditional lands because it is now a valuable carbon credit. Nationalistic walls are going up all over the world to both keep people out and keep people in when at the same time those nations espouse rights and freedoms for themselves, but not others. The nation-state's good intentions of categorizing people to ensure minorities are provided fair and measurable benefits of a nation often take away the individual freedoms of the person by type casting them within defining ethnic rubrics—after all, all Latin Americans only eat tacos and speak Spanish, right?" President Starhemberg stared directory at the Brazilian Ambassador. He took a drink of water and smiled at the audience, then continued.

"Let us set the past, with its successes and failures, on the shelf of wisdom, where it can inform, but not dictate. Our future will be decided by the present, the present we will allow to bloom with authentic progress, not choked by the weeds of pettiness and short-sighted self-interest." He again paused, and his body language invited the listener into his living room.

"My great-grandfather was present the seminal day Ernest Renan, French humanist, and philosopher offered his treatise Qu'est-*ce qu'une nation?* What is a Nation? at the Sorbonne in 1882. I often wonder if my grandfather's first name and my name have their roots in that day. In that speech he defined the nation-state system in all its glory, but also predicted its demise. In his words, "Let me sum up, Gentlemen. Man is a slave neither of his race nor his language, nor of his religion, nor of the course of rivers nor of the direction taken by mountain chains.... You can be French, English, German, yet Catholic, Protestant, Jewish, or practicing no religion. Mutuality of interests is fine for corporations and their affiliates, but nationality is based on sentiment. Geography merely leads us astray, and often to violence: Mountains don't know how to carve out countries... They had a beginning, they will have an end. A European confederation will probably take their place." Starhemberg paused once again to let these words settle on the audience. Then he changed course.

"When Renan shared his thoughts less than ten percent of the world's population lived in urban settings. By 1900 only 12 cities in the world had one million or more inhabitants. Only half a century later nearly a third of the world's population lived in urban environments, and there were over 80 cities with over a million people. The year I graduated from university, there were more than 400 cities over 1 million and 20 over 10 million in population. In just a few years in 2025, 30 cities will have populations greater than 10 million and more than 600 cities will have populations greater than one million. Studies suggest that by the end of this century 80 percent of the world's population will live in urban centers. I am from Argentina where half of our entire population lives in one urban center. São Paulo, to our north, produces 60 percent of Brazil's industrial GNP. We find ourselves today in the center of the Boston–Washington Corridor. This Northeast megalopolis crosses state lines with impunity and is home to over 50 million people, nearly 20% of the U.S. population on less than 2% of the nation's land area. This city, New York, has over 8 million people, the same population of the cross-border corridor between the cities of Oslo in Norway, Goteborg in Sweden, and Copenhagen in Denmark. Megacity leaders typically have more credibility and more power to shape the quality of life of its inhabitants than national leaders. Urban-to-urban cross-border migration is the prevalent form of global people movement. I could go on with statistics that press the point that the reality of global life is centered in urban environments and megacities are the new city-states."

"Today I announce the establishment of the Cambalache Confederation. CamCon members will be the first recipients of Cambalache electrical power. I also announce that the CamCon Administrator will be the internationalist Otto von Habsburg. In the coming days, Mr. Habsburg will issue clarifying statements of the planned structure of both the energy delivery plan that will take several years to complete, as well as how CamCon itself will operate. It was the request of Mr. Habsburg that I conclude with the words of Archbishop Desmond Tutu who said, "Peace, in its most fundamental form, is the connection of one human spirit to another." I pray that you have felt the peace of my message and the peace I have to offer through CamCon. God bless our path forward."

It was done. Ernesto looked relaxed and confident as he departed the world stage. Inside he was on fire. He was excited about the future and that no matter what would happen, he had been there to open the door. He was also feeling weak from the effort it took to look so calm and confident. Minutes after stepping off the stage he was escorted into a private office overlooking the river below. He was informed that it was the office of the United States Ambassador to the United Nations and the President of the United States had requested a brief private meeting with him. "So it begins," Ernesto told himself and the probable listening devices in the room.

"Much can happen in New York City in a week you said. We have let it happen. Continued procrastination on our part has made him the talk of the new global village he describes. If it were just Starhemberg, perhaps there would be no real danger, but he has slipped von Habsburg into the driver's seat while keeping the attention on himself. Far from laughing him out of town, he has become the global mega-city maven, the most magnetic mahatma since Princess Dianna. You must decide. Does he escape New York City alive? How far do we let this charade of energy go before it is too late to stop a Habsburg Ascendency and his actual plans?" JOAB

CHAPTER 15

Arrastar al Ala
Literal Translation: Drag the Wing

Marisa's Explanation: I think a better literal translation would be to sweep one off their feet. To me a clear definition would be to **Make a Romantic Advance,** to bring down to earth, that of the heavens. That's how I feel and that is hard to put into words. Pulling at wings is as close as anything else when words will not do.

THE PRESIDENT OF THE UNITED States walked into the room less than a minute later and shook hands with the President of Argentina. Ernesto was slightly taller and significantly younger. There was no smile on the American President's face.

"President Starhemberg," the North American President began.

"Please, call me Ernesto," President Starhemberg said.

"Thank you, Ernesto," the American President said. "I represent citizens of a country that have revolted over the past decade at what they see as the decaying power of a great country. They would love nothing more than to get out of the United Nations completely. These people, and I am one of them, not just their elected voice, prize their independence. The liberal economists and far left political theorists who call for the over-throw of the nation-state system are not just crackpots, they are the enemy. We spent the last half century fighting a Cold War against a communist world order that wanted to dissolve the nation-state world and the nation-states won. You come to this country and try to hold us over a barrel and tell us to just quit who we are?"

"Of course I know I was going to cause some significant turmoil, Mr. President," Ernesto said. "Better a war of words to get the emotions on the table, than to hold those emotions and eventually find ourselves in a new global war." He waited to see if the North American President would offer a reciprocal first name basis. James had predicted he would not when they role-played this very meeting. He didn't, so Ernesto continued. As a child I played a game we called diplomatic tug of war. That is a misleading name for a brutal game. Four teams were assembled and pulled ropes from a center. Four quadrants fighting against each other. Do you know this game?"

"No, I don't believe I ever played that," the American President said, barely holding is impatience in check.

Ernesto continued, "Sooner or later two teams would join together before the other two realized it. In a clever version the second strongest team would join with the weakest team to take on and beat the strongest. Eventually the now strongest, defeats the weakest easily. That simple children's' game teaches a nation-state attitude and springs from a zero-sum mentality."

"Is that a threat, Ernesto?" the American President asked, his brows now furrowed. He reminded Ernesto of a bull who just discovered the Matador's red cape and not thinking about whether it was the harmless capote de brega or the more dangerous muleta that hides a sword.

Ernesto offered disarming smile and said, "The center of the four ropes is the scarcity—be that the winning of a children's' game, or ideology, natural resources, technology, wealth, energy... What if there was no center? The tug of war evaporates because there is nothing to pull, nothing to connive to obtain. Of course, power over others is always a temptation for some. Short-term success trumps long-term success for the impatient or chronic zero-sum gamers. My question today is, how do we neutralize those scarcity mentality outliers in a world of abundance? Is neutralizing them just another form of enlightened zero-sum math? Heavy handed abundance?"

The furrowed brow was gone, replaced by an unreadable stare. "I have no idea what you are talking about, Ernesto. I am wondering if I am talking to a nut or a visionary," the American President said.

"Thank you for the honesty, sir," Ernesto said. "Let me finish my thought and then you can decide for yourself. A crazy man usually thinks he is a visionary and a visionary may harbor doubts of his own sanity at times, so that person is the least credible to answer. "

"Excellent," the American President said. "Continue."

"The biggest challenge that humankind faces today is not how to successfully rollout free energy, or some other breakthrough technology. Those are harbingers, even catalysts for change, but they aren't the change itself. In a perfect world the change actually precedes these great advances, but usually change happens in the trough of despair or challenge, not at the peak of success and easy going. The change that must come, either proactively or as the surprise tsunami to the unprepared, is to the institutions of society that must evolve to handle the new landscape."

"Change within those institutions is always a challenge. Bureaucracy is very adept at survival," the American President interjected.

"I'm not talking about change within, sir," James said. "I am talking about changing the actual institutions. That doesn't just mean understanding the new technology, nor the institutions themselves, but the deeper human interrelationships.

The physics of cities with 20 million people, connecting with similar urban centers across the globe, creating first ad hoc and then formal interdependencies has been happening for a decade now. We are moving into a world of billions within this forming interdependent system. The nation-state system is all about internal interdependencies and the external independence you mentioned you prize. This new system, whatever it is, is about external interdependencies and internal independence—which includes independence from the nation-state that gave it birth, but now blocks its greater access to the flow of resources in this new ecosystem. The complexity of this new system is beyond the control or understanding of the nation-state system that has treated us well and has transported mankind to this intersection. Loyalty to an antiquated system, however, is not a sufficient reason to keep it. Gradual modification keeps the steam in the pressure cooker under control for a time, but at some point, the heat overcomes this gradualness. Societal evolution at times obstructs the growing demands and involuntarily gives way to revolution."

"So you think we are on the brink of revolution?" the American President asked.

"No, I believe we are already in the early battles of that revolution," Ernesto said. "Your day-to-day reality as the strongest nation on earth is filled with brinksmanship, so you may be so close to it you can't, how do you Americans say it, you can't see the forest for the trees?"

"Point taken," the American President said. "If the world only knew what I hear each day in my morning briefings...it's hard to remember sometimes there are good, even great things happening. Every head of state knows or soon discovers that they can't control everything and that we are always on thin ice. We collectively hold our breath and we convince ourselves that we can direct our course, that we have the power, but mostly we don't and we can only nudge in a direction."

"And you more than any other nation that has ever existed on the earth has that power, but even you are not big enough, or strong enough to hold back the tide. However, your nation may be just the visionary to help the world see our way forward, "Ernesto said leaning forward now with his own intensity. "We must find a new system that can operate with flexibility and efficiency in our new reality. We need structures that define rules of conduct, with appropriate incentives and punishments that align with natural flows of resources, ideas, and global psychosocial mentalities. Mountain ranges, oceans, rivers, or even traditional mindsets are no longer boundaries. Those rigid frontiers," Ernesto said, sweeping his hands in front of him as if he were wiping them away, "which once defined our political and economic systems are now only quaint vistas inside a bigger, self-organizing system. That new system is going to take form with us or without us. Without us, it will make change with violence only nature accepts. With us, I believe we can mitigate much of the potential damage."

"Yep," the American President said with a half-smile, "you're a nut alright."

With his own genuine smile, Ernesto said, "I am not a prophet. I am not even a visionary political leader. But I was handed a catalyst for change and I won't step down from that responsibility. I will not abdicate to another. What exactly the new world will look like is not something you or I can clearly see. I have surrounded myself with a few very smart people and we have considered everything from derivatives of the present nation-state system to holonics and complex collectives. It is my feeling that we can design CamCon with enough structure to avoid chaos and sufficient flexibility to mine and leverage our diversity and complexity for lasting success. I am not saying we stop being nation-states, but we have to start thinking there is more that we are. We have to stop thinking of this as our challenge—it is our greatest strength and our only real hope. People, collectively and individually, much smarter than us will find the best answers. We just need to provide the transitional leadership to keep this pot from blowing up."

"A certifiable nut," the American President said. "The thing about smart people, Ernesto, is that they seem like crazy people to dumb people. The world is brilliant, as you said, but we can have some extremely dangerous flashes of dumb. And that makes you a target of a very dangerous enemy."

"Just one enemy, sir?" Ernesto asked with a laugh. "Every pressure cooker has its weak points, Mr. President. Those dumb points might be where some steam can exit. Great. I don't want to be a target, but better me and Cambalache energy production, then the Cambalache Confederation." Ernesto wanted to ask for help and some protection that only the United States could offer, but he held his tongue and waited.

"Crazy people also appear to be courageous," the American President said. "But you have to have fear and overcome it to be brave. Absence of fear is neither rational nor wise."

"Faith and fear cannot coexist," Ernesto said. "I believe in the brilliance of mankind and in God who is the author of that brilliance. Don't get me wrong," Ernesto added seeing the President was going to interrupt. "Faith is not a substitute for rational thought, but faith can be that freeing element that allows us to think beyond the traditional, the comfortable and familiar."

"Almost thou persuadest me," the American President said as he stood and looked out the window at the southern tip of Roosevelt Island in the East River. "President Franklin D. Roosevelt, in his 1941 State of the Union address suggested there are four freedoms everyone in the world should have, Freedom of speech, freedom of worship, freedom from want, and freedom from fear. The context of his words focused on the U.S. national security. Less than a year later we were at war with Japan and Germany and those words became a summary of the values of democracy, not any one nation-state." He turned back to Ernesto and said, "You play a good game of poker, Ernesto. You haven't asked and I haven't offered. I'm offering now. You need protection and so does your Cambalache compound. We'll see about the CamCon organization. Perhaps Argentina needs a little extra help. Now you have me thinking it—I need to protect a nation-state so it can arrive healthy at its own funeral. Let's keep this quiet, both for my own domestic political reasons, but also because that makes a more powerful tool. I will publicly announce the United States' interest in studying your proposals and applaud your energy breakthrough. We will also publicly offer our help in replicating Cambalache. To the world that will sound like our own soft power grab, but it will enable me to appropriate funds to allow you to accelerate production—no strings attached except priority energy delivery when available."

"Thank you, Mr. President," Ernesto said also standing and reaching out his hand.

"So enough with the 'Mr. President,'" the American President said. "I have come to really dislike that title. It was once a humble title to replace old titles like Your Excellency. Now it sounds just as royal and full of its own pomp and pride. Even the acronym, POTUS, for President of the United States of America sounds like and is accepted by many as a royal title. I honor the office— that should be revered, but the person in that office is just a person. A person with a first name. Call me Tony."

The remainder of the day was filled with meetings with various nations, all at the Argentine Consulate Offices on West 56th Street. It was a lovely building but also appropriately humble for the occasion. Several countries offered to meet at more ornate and power play locations, but all were politely declined.

A mixture of placations, guarded threats, and legitimate interests filled the Argentine note taker's journal. By nine that evening Ernesto and his staff were exhausted. Marisa was bored, but didn't want to admit it. James was sitting in a local pub near Union Square listening to the banter to get a feeling what the average American thought of the speech. As he expected, most didn't care or have much interest, compared to topics such as the Knicks chance to get in the playoffs, or whether the new mayor was going to finally solve the trash pickup problems.

"So tomorrow we visit the Statue of Liberty?" Ernesto asked Marisa over a light dinner.

"It's for Vangelina," Marisa said.

"I was told the Mayor of New York will accompany us in a police boat," Ernesto said. "He is trying to be a good host, but also keep me alive while we are still in New York City."

"Quit joking, Ernesto," Marisa said. "The world is crazy. You would think you just threatened humanity with a nuclear bomb."

"In a way I have," Ernesto said with a soft smile. "I have also been briefed that you have already catapulted to most eligible bachelorette in the world. Congratulations. When's the *People Magazine* photo shoot?"

"Don't be silly, Ernesto," Marisa said and paused. "I signed a contract with *Hola*."

Ernesto glanced up, for a moment taking her seriously and then realizing he had been duped said, "So I can meet with world leaders, all practiced negotiators, gifted scam artists, and some extortionists, and I get tricked by my own sister."

"There are the gifted and then there is genius," Marisa said. "We are also scheduled to attend the Lincoln Center, the opera Le Corsaire. Mom and dad would have loved that."

I don't know that opera—any political overtones—you know, offering a headline like, "The Argentine President and his beautiful sister chose to attend the opera where a dangerous despot pillages his unsuspecting subjects."

"It's a love story. More dance than song I believe. It's a story of sensational rescues and a dashing pirate's love for a harem girl according to the flyer."

"Oh, a James and Marisa story," Ernesto said.

"And a death by high heel of the unfeeling brother," Marisa said as she threw one of her shoes at her brother.

"Pay dirt!" Ernesto said laughing. "Honestly, I am glad you and James have hit it off. How is he weathering this storm?"

"I have no idea," Marisa said. "You told us he should keep his distance from you and me while we are in town. I think he is scheduled to fly out tomorrow to visit his family for a couple days and then on to Buenos Aires about the time we get home."

"I hope his time at home is rejuvenating, because things are going to get really busy from here on out and we am going to need his one hundred percent focus."

"Does that mean I can't pursue our, um, friendship?" Marisa asked.

"Would you follow my request if I gave it?" Ernesto asked.

"No, but I wondered what you would say," Marisa answered.

"As I thought," Ernesto said. "Pursue your um friendship as you will. Just be kind if he does not reciprocate."

"Boy you are either nuts or dumb," Marisa said shaking her head.

"So I have been told," Ernesto said. "I'm going to bed. We have packed a week into one day Norisa. Thanks for being there, at the UN today. Your face got me through that speech."

"You loved it and did it like it was an informal staff meeting back at the Casa, Marisa said. "And by the way, I heard from Pepe that you are now the most eligible bachelor on the planet."

"You are either nuts or dumb yourself," Ernesto said. "I was falling apart inside and who would want to date the pariah of the nation-state and all humanity?"

"Do you ever wish things would have worked out with Gabriela?" Marisa asked. "I mean do you think you would have even gotten into national politics or found yourself here at this moment had she gotten her way?"

"I miss the idea of Gabriela," Ernesto said. "I don't miss Gabriela. She was full of herself and self-sacrifice was not part of her nature. She was smarter than me when she saw that and left."

"So will there ever be another?" Marisa asked.

"Yeah, I will schedule that into the free half hour I have next month," Ernesto said.

"When it happens, let it happen," Ernesto. "Don't be afraid of something repeating itself. It will be just what you need when that time comes."

* * *

James busied himself with an art purchase, a Julia Dickens painting, that reminded him of Nahuel Huapi Lake in Bariloche. The artist's use of blue and gold leaf seemed to capture the lake the day of President Starhemberg's speech. The brush strokes suggested an impending storm and somehow the overall work offered hope and suggested all would be well after the storm. He mailed the artwork to the company in Washington, DC he had entrusted with his other valuables.

He traveled home, this time by plane and surprised his family with a visit. He hadn't called in advance because he wasn't sure how the New York trip would go. He hadn't explained any of this to his family and for all they knew he was on some boring contract in a city far away, not unlike he previous jobs. It was easiest to just let them think that.

After a few hours at home he took his two baby sisters for a drive to see his land. "So what do you think I ought to do with this?" he asked his sisters.

Jessica looked at her younger sister Jacey and said, "You are asking us?"

"Yes, I'm asking," James said.

"Why did you buy it?" Jacey, who was 19 asked.

"I had the money and I guess I needed an anchor," James said.

Jessica, at 21 and a junior in college had taken the lead in the family. She had been a delightful surprise to the family after trying to have another child for so many years after James's birth. Because he was eight and a half years older than his sister, their parents wanted another child and had Jacey a couple years later. They were almost twins in most respects and interests. They respected their brother, but he had always been so much older and then gone out of their lives for the last five years that this big brother asking advice was a new experience for them.

Jessica nodded at her sister and said, "Mom and Dad have been pretty worried about you, James. You disappear and then show up without notice. You spend a fortune on some land and yet have no idea what to do with it. You don't allow any farmers to rent it for cash crops, in short you have no plans. They worry you aren't doing anything with your life. Have you even been on a date in the last year?"

"I've been on a few dates in the past couple months," James said a little defensively.

"Tell us everything!" Jacey said with a broad smile. She was lighter complexioned than her older sister and had more freckles. Both had strawberry blond hair and brown eyes, from the Welsh side of the Nathaniel's line their father had proclaimed. Both were athletic, energetic, and very content to spend the rest of their lives in central Missouri.

"Just a girl I met and just a few dates, a walk around her house, er, neighborhood, ice cream, a little sightseeing," James said. "So seriously, what should I do with this land?"

"Put a little house on that hill overlooking the pond and the hardwood forest beyond it," Jessica said. "If you ever find a girl who will put up with you, she could be no happier than to live right there. I got to hand it to you, big brother, you bought a beautiful piece of property."

"Would you two be willing to earn a little cash by overseeing the construction?" James asked, touched by his sister's inspiration.

"You mean, we would be in charge?" Jacey asked.

"I mean, if I put $200,000 in the bank and you earned $15 hour overseeing the design and construction, maybe with a little guidance from mom and dad where you think you might be getting in over your heads, would you be willing to do it?" James asked again. "I could put another $25,000 into the building fund in a month or two."

"So you're not like a drug lord or something are you?" Jacey asked only half joking. "That's more money in cash than I thought ever I would see in my life."

"It's my life savings Jacey," James said. "I have been working my tail off and like you and mom have all pointed out, I haven't had many other reasons to spend it. I don't know about bringing a girl here someday. Like you said, who would want to put up with me? But I want to make a wise investment and this seems like the best plan. I wish I could drop in more often, but Argentina is a long way away."

"That's right, you are in Argentina," Jessica said. "There have been some pieces on the news about it, after that President of theirs made that speech. Seems like a nice enough guy, but he's got a lot of people excited and a lot of people upset."

"He's cute too," Jacey said.

"Well, I will keep my eye out for him Jacey and let him know he has one fan anyway," James said. "If I see him."

"Yeah, if you see him," Jacey laughed. "Maybe you will find an Argentine beauty to date James."

Yeah, maybe," James said.

"JOAB, the Prelature's decision is to focus on the head of the snake. As Guardian, I most certainly agree that Otto von Habsburg must capitulate. As you noted, he is not the present focus and thus easier to remove without world attention. Let Starhemberg play his games, as long as it leads you to the illusive Otto. Begin aggressive plans immediately to accomplish this task. Forward plans and schedule as soon as formulated. We have another operative, perhaps two at your disposal. You have trained and worked your entire professional life for this potential. The Habsburg ascendency is upon us and we must not fail. You must not fail. Accomplish the task within the week, two weeks at the outside. If you use our other assets, ensure the Prelate is kept out of the loop. Continue to report to him, but keep these operations from him until further notice."

CHAPTER 16

Taca Taca said while slapping the back of the hand into the palm of the other hand
Literal Translation: Hard Clam

<u>Marisa's Explanation</u>: Put the clam in my hand, **Put Your Money Where Your Mouth Is.**

JAMES WAS HAPPY TO BE back in Buenos Aires, but missed his family more than he had in a long time. The hours spent with his sisters were fun and light-hearted. He actually started getting excited about the house project. His professional side told him he was crazy to turn over such a huge project to his younger sisters. His big brother side thrilled at their excitement and the awe that he would trust them with such an important undertaking. "If Argentina can take on the world, why can't my sisters take on this building task?" he reassured himself on the plane ride south. "Besides, now we have something to talk about, that I can talk about."

The day after James's return he went to the Casa Rosada, not sure if he should just assume he still had a place at the informal arrangement at the Quinta de Olivos. He had considered just staying at his rented home and wait for a call, but his proactive nature wouldn't allow it.

"Welcome back, Mr. Nathaniels," the guard, who he wasn't sure he had ever met, said.

"Thanks, good to be back," James replied. He walked to his previous office, wondering if it was still assigned to him. The office was just as he had left it. Sitting down he stood right back up as a young man leaned his head in and said, "Mr. Nathaniels? You have a call on line 1."

The man waited until he saw the surprised James pick up the receiver, then disappeared. "James Nathaniels," James said, wondering who would have guessed he was here.

"James, I know you would be there," President Starhemberg said. "Do you have a minute? I would like your advice."

"Of course, sir," James said.

"So the Peoples Republic of China has just announced they have also created a cold fusion reactor and that they had kept this secret for many of the same concerns I outlined. Any thoughts on what I should say?"

"Tell the press that is great. What a fantastic turn of events. Words to that effect," James said.

"Why?" President Starhemberg asked. "Godoy is telling me to say something more like, "we look forward to Chinese proof as we demonstrated ourselves earlier this week."

"Well, both tactics are nice enough, but if they really have it, they will show it soon enough. Let the rest of the world tell them to prove it. Argentina should take the highest road possible and welcome it at face value. Yes, that might sound a little naïve and that might be Alberto Godoy's concern, but Argentina is the driver's seat. You already have it and have proved it. If it's real, we might have a partner instead of a competitor. If it's not the real deal, we will start to look like the calm and confident world leader, the abundance mentality leader you really are."

"That was my intuition, James, but I couldn't have said it so well," President Starhemberg said.

"I am sure you could have said it even better, sir," James said. "But thank you all the same."

"It was Marisa who said I should call you," the President said. "The team here said you would be taking it easy your first day back. The lady who wanted to knee cap you or whatever her initial threats were is now your biggest fan."

"I think she threatened certain death, sir," James said. "To be honest I wasn't sure what I could accomplish today, but thought I should be here. Anything more I can do?

"With the largest concentration of mega-cities in a single country, it's no doubt China might feel threatened by the CamCon idea," President Starhemberg began. "Start thinking about how to build some bridges with them and what we might do to work together, whether they have fusion or not. We wish you were here with us, but I am glad we have kept you from the center of attention. Marisa is going through the motions like a trooper, handling the paparazzi like a pro, but I can tell her heart is someplace else."

"I am sure she wants to get home, sir," James said.

"Yes, something like that," the President said. "Did you have a good trip home? Your family doing well?"

"Very well, sir," James replied, wondering why the busiest guy on the planet at the moment was having this conversation with him. "It was great to spend some quality time with my sisters."

"I would love to meet your family someday," the President said. "Unfortunately my time is not my own at this moment."

"My youngest sister Jacey is a big fan of yours, sir," James said. "If you were a rock star she would have your poster up in her room. But don't worry, sir, I haven't even brought your name up, nor suggested I am at all involved in any of this."

"Really?" President Starhemberg said surprised. "Over the past few days I have met so many people who either hate me and everything I stand for, or they are *chupa mangas*, sleeve suckers. It's good to have at least one authentic fan."

"You have at least two fans in the Nathaniels family, sir," James said.

"Oh, both your sisters?" the President asked.

"Something like that, sir," James said chuckling. "Actually my other sister, Jessica is still on the fence. She tells me you are too cute to trust."

"Yes, my curse," the President said also laughing. "I will dedicate time in the near future to win over Jessica and all in her camp. Thank you for the conversation, James. I hope I am not taking up your day, but I needed to get my feet back on the ground. Marisa is out on a last minute visit to the top of the Empire State Building before we start preparing to head home. I am causing so many security issues for the city that, like me, I think they will celebrate when I get out of their hair. *Me tomo el piojo.*"

"I guess I still don't understand that one, sir," James said. "Marisa explained it to me, but it doesn't sound like something you would say."

"I'm not sure what she told you, but it's just a way to say I am leaving, a saying of the young people in Buenos Aires," the President explained. "You're right, it's not something I would typically say, but seems to have more meaning in my present context. I sort of feel like I have lice and the sooner I'm gone the better. See you soon. Oh, before you hang up, you might have a chance to meet with Otto this evening if that works for you, that is, if Otto can make a plane connection." The line went dead.

"James sat back in his chair grateful he had chosen to come in this morning, but surprised Marisa could read him so clearly, better than he could read himself. He opened his desk and retrieved paper and a pen and started writing thoughts about the Chinese government. Two hours later he sat his work aside and opened up his notebook where he had recorded the questions he and Otto von Habsburg had exchanged only a few weeks ago in Bariloche. 'An eternity ago,' James thought.

"Taking work home with you?" the guard asked, nodding to the papers in James's hands as he exited the building later that day.

"Well, yes, I am. I am still struggling with jet lag and I, well, you probably don't need to know all that," James stammered. "Is that okay?"

"Any government documents?" the guard asked.

"No, just my thoughts on a couple projects," James answered. "What if I was just carrying my laptop in a backpack?"

"I see your point, Mr. Nathaniels, but you basically have permission to come and go with just about anything, so my questions are just routine. You have a good night, Mr. Nathaniels." The guard turned his attention to the next person leaving the building.

James was amazed at the trust placed in him and realized how complacent he had become with that trust. He couldn't imagine what would happen if anyone got their hands on his notes. He returned to his office and left the papers in his office safe. He walked out of the Casa Rosada empty handed, confident he could continue his thoughts at home without them. He took the subway to Retiro and then the train to Vicente Lopez. This mode of travel was much slower and not as convenient as a taxi, or government vehicle with driver, which he had been authorized. He wanted to hear what, if anything, people were saying about the President's speech at the United Nations and that wouldn't happen in a protective bubble. He heard snippets of conversations here or there, but nothing of note. 'Maybe most of the world really doesn't care that much,' he thought. 'It's not like it has impacted life at the man-on-the-street level yet.'

James was trying to decide whether to cook something to eat or wait for the illusive Otto von Habsburg when his cell phone rang. It wasn't a number he recognized. "Hello," James said.

"Oh, splendid, I caught you," Otto said on the other end of the line. "I just landed and can meet you wherever you choose, if that will work with you."

"Yes, that works perfect for me," James said. "President Starhemberg gave me a heads up you might call."

"Our matchmaker Ernesto," Otto said with a smile James could feel in his voice. "It's what, 7 PM local time? Where would you like to meet? I am not much of an expert on localities in Buenos Aires I am afraid. I really only know the Quinta de Olivos and my Spanish is not a good as yours."

"I assume you would like to get something to eat. There are restaurants in which to be seen and restaurants where in you are not seen," James said. "You would love Chila I think, Argentine cuisine with a French flair. It is in the *to be seen* category. Oviedo for seafood, Nectarine to stay with the French flair, and Casa Cruz for modern Argentine cuisine are in the quiet-confidential category. Do any of those sound interesting?"

"There is a time to be seen, but that isn't tonight," Otto said. "I will meet you at Casa Cruz say at 9?"

"I will take care of the reservation," James said. "The restaurant has an unmarked entrance but any taxi can find the address." James passed on the address and a description of the restaurant front. "See you soon. Anything I should bring with me?"

"Just your mind, my friend," Otto replied.

James called the restaurant and fortunately he was able to make a reservation without having to ask someone from Alberto Godoy's office to intervene, but he let Godoy's office know just the same, since it involved Otto. He refreshed his memory of the notes he had taken the night after his first meeting with Otto and walked to the Vicente Lopez train station where he caught a taxi to Palermo. He got out of the taxi a few blocks from the restaurant, not that he was concerned anyone was following him, but he needed the walk to sharpen the mind that Otto wanted him to bring. The gold and white façade and brass doors were easy to find. James had been here once before and was happy he found it in the dimming twilight. He had decided to wait inside, but as he reached to doors, a taxi drove up and Otto disembarked.

"Perfect timing," James said, opening the door for Otto.

"I have been running since yesterday," Otto said as they entered the restaurant. "Funny how we make plans and then life does what it wants anyway."

They were guided to a table for two in a corner of the wood and mirrored room. The tables in the center of the room were mostly full, but the noise was subdued by the alcoves, partitions, pillars, and plus gold carpet.

"Excellent choice," Otto said. "How have you been?"

"Good," James said. "And you?"

"Better than poor Ernesto," Otto said. "He is still the center of attention, and I know how he detests that. Marisa has taken a little of the focus off of him as the beautiful sister. If they only knew."

"If Marisa and the President only knew? What?" James asked.

"No," Otto said while studying the menu. "If the world only knew Marisa."

"She is an amazing woman," James said.

"Genius," Otto said continuing his half thought sentences. James knew his brain would hurt by the end of the night.

"The President said he was being bombarded by chupa mangas," James said.

"Chupa mangas?" Otto asked looking up from the menu.

"Sleeve suckers, groveling groupies," James explained. "Instead of kissing the Bishop's ring, the person is said to start sucking his sleeve."

"Yes, something else Ernesto detests," Otto said. "Against my practice, I must jump right to business, James," Otto added abruptly. "The Chinese do not have a fusion reactor."

"Oh?" James said. "I haven't seen that in the news yet. Is this from some other source?" James had been kept out of any Argentine intelligence discussions or circles and was happy for that. He assumed Otto was tied into that world through Starhemberg.

"I have my sources, my circle of friends that have their circle of friends that eventually leads to power centers here and there." Otto said obliquely. "Chinese leadership legitimacy has been teetering on a precipice for some time. They are anything but communist and so what do they claim as their right to rule? It has been stability and prosperity. They have delivered on both since Deng Xiao Ping spoke of building socialism with Chinese characteristics—translated, capitalism, in 1983. Growth has declined due to international market declines and not sufficient growth in their domestic market. The CamCon plan to support megacities first in its rollout and its loose confederation has got the Chinese scared. They have the largest number of mega-cities in the world, James. Where does that put the Chinese Communist Party?"

"They have published several clever metaphors that allow the Party to take opportunities as they arise," James began. One such saying is "Mozhe shitou guo he" or "Crossing the river by feeling for stones." In this case, those stones have left them in the middle of the river. If they allow CamCon to connect their mega-cities with low cost electricity, they give up some of their control. On the other hand, if they keep CamCon at arm's length, the relative cost of electricity sky rockets and they become one of the most expensive places for manufacturing and to live."

"And so?" Otto asked "Where does that put the Chinese leadership? Are they going to join CamCon, or not?"

"They have another saying," James said. "It doesn't matter if a cat is black or white, so long as it catches mice. They are the consummate realists. They will eventually join the game, but it will be years, maybe decades, before they adjust to an abundance mentality. They are also consummate scarcity mentality practitioners. They have over a billion people and scarcity is always knocking on their door."

"You don't seem that worried about that billion people and their leadership's million plus army and nuclear weapons," Otto said. They stopped their conversation to order and Otto waited from James to reply.

"There are too many variables in this entire plan to get too excited," James said. "That doesn't mean we should ignore threats. But we need to learn to work with them by what we do best, not by what the opposition does best. Like the ancient Greek parable of the hedgehog and the fox. The fox knows many things, but the hedgehog knows one pivotal thing. It's the fox who runs around sniffing here and there and ends up with hedgehog quills on its nose. We know how to produce virtually free energy. We are offering a way to mitigate most of the risks of delivering that energy through a confederation. We need to focus on what we do best and let them choose. They aren't going to send their million man army to Bariloche and they aren't going to send nuclear weapons. They are going to try to steal the Cambalache technology. We need to defend ourselves, and hopefully President Starhemberg and the U.S. President came to some agreement on that, but honestly, I believe the Chinese will come to the table."

"And their announcement that they have their own cold fusion technology?" Otto asked.

"I am not a technical expert," James said. "Could they have it? Maybe. As you say, they probably don't. If so, they will make a face-saving announcement that is something like, "A government official spoke out of turn and all energy research issues are classified. We might have it, but that announcement was premature. We look forward to speaking with Mr. Otto von Habsburg and perhaps we can be of help where they fall short in their delivery efforts to the world."

Otto stared at James and was shaken out of his stupor with the arrival of the food. "Maybe you should be running CamCon instead of me," Otto said.

"I am not a leader, just an analyst," James said. "I can see this as clear as I see you, but I can't see the people behind me. You somehow can. You know the trees and the forest. I can hardly get the forest in focus."

"So you are a hedgehog," Otto said. "Am I a fox?"

"In an abundance mentality, there are more animals than just those two," James said. "I see you as an owl. Above the fray, not the natural predator of either."

"Chupa manga," Otto said, laughing.

"I hope not," James said. "I'm not a hedgehog, just a lowly field mouse that both the fox and the owl can eat up at will."

"We are all just field mice, I am afraid, James," Otto said. "I hope Ernesto is the survivor hedgehog in all this. Another subject; small but important countries that presently have no mega-cities."

"Someone is already feeling left out of the CamCon?" James asked.

"Israel," Otto said. "An associate in the Rothschild's organization contacted me with a curious question. Can nation-states or smaller cities pay to play? I told them we aren't offering our product or services to the highest bidder. I used your net neutrality metaphor that you and Marisa developed and passed on to me. I told him, the reason the Internet has flourished is because the service is provided across all ports, without favoring or blocking particular products or websites by who can pay more or who can't."

"That's only half the metaphor," James said. "We are initially still leaving out large rural areas and small urban centers, which in effect is not a neutral stance. We aren't globally ubiquitous and may never be. That was the guidance from President Starhemberg and I assume you and he had already discussed this."

"Oh, we have, in great detail," Otto said. "Like I said, there are plans and then life takes over. Cambalache can create energy, but we must rely on global HVDC grids for delivery. Those grids do not yet exist in most rural areas and many third world countries. Yet, there are first world outliers that," Otto paused, focusing on something or someone outside of James' view. James turned and saw a large man in jeans and a brown jacket marching toward their table. James stood, not sure what was happening. The man pulled out a gun and pointed it at Otto von Habsburg. Three steps away and the man cocked the pistol.

To Guardian: *"The Habsburg Ascendency will come to a halt tomorrow night. Starhemberg provided the perfect provocation. The world will witness a predictable reflexive rejoinder. JOAB Buenos Aires"*

The Guardian wondered what JOAB had meant with the statement, "...come to a halt tomorrow night." The prelate had not forwarded any plans or even an earlier communiqué suggesting any actions. The Guardian smiled. This would be piled on the doorstep of the Prelate. All was going as planned.

"It's time I take some immediate actions," David told himself. He had felt for several weeks that JOAB Buenos Aires was out of control and misconstruing directives or accomplishing actions without directives. He would be in Buenos Aires tonight. First stop, James Nathaniels. Should he take a chance of directly contacting him?

CHAPTER 17

Dar en el clavo
Literal Translation: To give on the nail

Marisa's Explanation: **Hit the Target, Spot On**. The challenge with this for an Argentine, given to enthusiasm and a willingness to give it our all, sometimes a hammer is more than is called for.

Otto Habsburg jumped up, realizing he was the assassin's target. James wanted to shout, 'Otto you just made a bigger target of yourself,' and his impulse was to pull Otto back down, but there was no time. A scream by another diner broke the silence and for a heartbeat, the concentration of the charging man. James filled that same fraction of a second by grabbing his chair as he shifted his weight to his feet and swinging it with all his might at the man. It found the shins of the attacker. The gun recoiled. James could see and smell the burnt gunpowder before he heard the sound of the discharge.

Another scream added to the cacophony. It was Otto's voice. Fighting the impulse to look back at Otto, James, still in a crouch, tackled the gunman, who still held his weapon. The gunman stunk of stale tobacco and cheap cologne. "Call the police and get a doctor," James yelled as he tried to wrestle away the gun from the attacker's hand. The man was powerfully built, and

James wasn't sure how long he could keep him pinned on the floor. He immediately found out. The attacker pushed with his open hand and freed it from James's grip. The man smiled at James with his yellow stained teeth. James immediately dedicated both his hands to the gun, and it dropped to the floor almost as if the gunman let go of it. Both of the attacker's hands reached up and grabbed James's head and pulled him down quickly to meet the man's upcoming head. James was dazed and easily pushed aside by the gunman. As the man stood, he savagely kicked James in the stomach and then the groin. James doubled into a fetal position, unable to breathe or move.

Bracing himself for another blow, James felt a soft hand on his shoulder. "Are you alright?" a female voice asked him.

"I'll live," James grunted, not sure at all if that were the truth. He struggled to stand but couldn't get control of his limbs. As he fell back to the floor, he thought he saw the vaguely familiar face of a man he had seen before. Then Marisa's face came to his mind, and he blacked out.

"They tell me you saved my life," James heard as he struggled to open his eyes. He was lying in a bed, 'in a hospital gown?' he thought to himself. Slowly turning his head toward the voice, he felt vertigo set in and turned back to look at the ceiling, concentrating on a blemish in one of the tiles.

"I'm the one who got shot," Otto said, "but you seem to have gotten the worst of the attacker's wrath."

"Are you okay?" James asked.

"I'll be all right the doctors tell me," Otto replied. "Thanks to your quick move the single bullet fired passed through the flesh of my right arm. It's painful, but a much better outcome than what could have been. You, on the other hand, received a concussion and some internal bruising."

"Did someone stop the gunman?" James asked, concentrating on keeping the ceiling tile he was focusing on from spinning.

"He got away," Otto said. "Can you believe in this age of cell phone cameras not a single person even got a picture of the guy."

"I can believe it," James said. "I felt like I was frozen, just watching it all happen."

"You were the only person that did anything," Otto said. "Well, except for me who obliged the gunman with an easier target. It was partly you telling me that, and partly you hitting him with the chair that saved me. I started to turn just as you hit him and I think surprised him into firing early."

"I said you made a better target?" James asked. "I could have sworn I only thought that."

"Maybe you did only think it," Otto said. "I don't know. I do know that I heard it. Your order for the police and doctor brought a few people out of their stupor, and we had transport to the hospital within minutes. You have been out for about an hour. The doctor told me that he expected you to wake up soon and that if you did, you would be fine by tomorrow. I called Ernesto and told him about the event. The police have a guard stationed outside our room."

"So do you have many enemies, or do you think this was related to CamCon?" James asked.

"Oh, I have a few enemies, and there are always a few crazies who want to shoot the heir to a non-existent thrown," Otto said, "But I think this is CamCon related. I have no proof of that, however."

"I thought I saw someone else in the room I recognized," James added. "Of course I also saw Marisa's face before I lost consciousness."

"The police will want to hear what you remember," Otto said. Hopefully, there will be some fingerprints and some security camera footage of the guy. Pity we never got to finish our meal. I'm starving."

"We never finished our conversation either," James said, not wanting to think about food.

"I can picture the food on the table, the color of the table cloth, even the placement of the silverware, but I can't remember what we were talking about," Otto said.

"You were telling me about the *have-nots* in the Cambalache plans," James said.

"The have-nots?" Otto asked. "Oh, those outside the global HVDC grid. Yes, we are decades away from connecting the entire world to Cambalache. That is the hard reality."

"And that is the justification for keeping those outliers from CamCon as well?" James asked.

"CamCon is not a final solution, James," Otto said. "It is another strand in the eventual grid, just like the lines that will deliver electricity."

"There are times when I really tire of this constant peeling of the onion," James said. "I have put my entire focus into what I think is the big picture, only to find the picture is just a pixel of a bigger picture."

"Oh, come on," Otto said. "You know more than you are allowing yourself to consider consciously. So we connect mega-cities with a loosely structured governing system. Assuming this would even overcome the inertia and reticence of the present nation-state system, CamCon would continue to morph into something more structured and useful. As much as less structured organizations are the flavor de jour, like holonics for example, my belief is we are naturally order seeking animals. In that holonics gets it right—there are certain recurring patterns of self-organization among interdependent systems. From atomic levels and physics principles that make Cambalache energy and delivery a reality to biology and, I believe, to the governing systems at both the micro and macro levels. CamCon is just an additional nudge in the direction things are already moving."

"So, can I use my present mental state as an excuse and you tell me what you think I already know?" James asked.

"What is better dependence or independence?" Otto asked.

"For a country or an individual?" James asked.

"Either, James," Otto said. "You're stalling."

"I suppose that depends on how you define the terms," James said. "Yeah, yeah, I'm stalling. Dependence has more baggage than independence. Choices are more limited, and decisions are based on some flawed inputs. Decision-making in a dependent environment is contingent on something or someone else. Individual responsibility is at a minimum and reliance on an external actor is at a maximum—which may include over-influence and control."

"And between independence and interdependence?" Otto asked.

"Independence suggests that the actor—a person, a nation-state, is free from influence, guidance, or control. They are self-reliant. Individual responsibility is at its maximum and reliance on external actors is at a minimum. The importance is put on autonomy, self-governance, and being free from the influence and control of others. This is making my head hurt Otto," James said.

"So what about interdependence?" Otto continued.

"Some freedoms are sacrificed," James began. "Mutual dependence replaces that singular freedom to choose and act. Value is placed on differences, that is, we are not the same, but we are equal. In a perfect interdependent system, we build on each other's strengths and compensate for each other's weaknesses."

"You once accused me of painting everything black or white," Otto said. "The topic was stability vs. freedom, one or the other. I shared with you the full name of my grandfather? Remember?"

"Yes, the night of questions and few answers," James said. "Perhaps the seed of my present vertigo," James added trying to smile.

"That system, my family business as you termed it, was a volatile environment of dependents and independents. There was a small amount of interdependence when it came to security and some commerce, but mostly it was illegitimate and broken from the start. The weak and questionable legitimacy of a royal title is all that held it together. Today's nation-state system is the same, minus the royal titles. Dependents and independents under a de facto umbrella called Earth. The nation-state system foments, nurtures, and protects this flawed system. So I ask you, why does the nation-state exist?"

"To protect and propagate a common identity of ethnicity and culture," James said. "I have pondered the concept of the nation being an extended and somewhat dysfunctional family, so there would also be, long-term, a biological component due to intermarriage within that broad family."

"And sometimes the state encompasses multiple nations, such as the old Yugoslavia, the United Kingdom, many of the countries of post-colonial Africa, as well as the Sykes-Pico states of the Middle East."

"The United States could be added to that list," James said. "At the time of the American Revolution, the U.S. was about 60 percent English, 80 percent British, and 98 percent Protestant. With that common identity as a nation, we became a state. Then the nation became diverse through immigration, including sadly through the forced immigration of slavery. In the countries you listed, there were many forced, pushed, and pulled migrations, but changes took place over centuries. In the U.S. it could be measured in decades or years. That has created its own instabilities and at the same time a huge part of the creations and innovations of the modern world."

"And where there was once a workable interdependence in the United States, there is a significant independence," Otto added. "Coal from Appalachia for the steel mills in the Northeast is gone, volume agriculture in the Midwest and later California is now supplanted by products from China, Mexico, and Chile. The U.S. is now a service economy with a large mobile workforce. Politics are stove-piped. The conservative listens only to the sensationalism of Fox News, and the liberal prefers MSNBC and their own flavor of reality. Neither can sit down and talk to the other. And there are extreme dependencies where once there was vital interdependence. Those who cannot work and survive on the social security net are higher than every country in Europe. That cost, about one-third of the U.S. GDP has created a dependency that is over double most socialist countries in the world."

"So your argument," James surmised, "is that the nation-state has created independents and dependents where interdependencies have existed?"

"No," Otto answered. "New interdependencies have supplanted independencies, and the nation-state is in a defensive posture to protect that costly environment. Dependencies grow out of that defense. Like I said earlier, we are not trying to create a new reality, just give the already developing ecosystem an extra nudge. When a child of extreme socialism, Alexander Solzhenitsyn formerly of the Soviet Union, accepted his Nobel Prize, he said something like "The disappearance of nations would impoverish us no less than if all peoples were made alike, with one character, one face. Nations are the wealth of mankind; they are its generalized personalities the smallest of them has its own particular colors and embodies a particular facet of God's design." I am not talking about the disappearance of nations, but of the nation-state model. States will fight this, but nations will eventually see the benefits."

"Wow," James said with new insight. "The flip side of Marxist-Leninism. Communism wanted to rid the world of its diverse nations and become one state. You are saying rid the world of its diverse states and become a nation of interdependent nations. How will that work?"

"For another day my convalescing friend," Otto said. "I am ready to chew on my own arm I am so hungry. I am going to ring the nurse and see if I can order some wonderful hospital food. I am betting the Argentines, like the French, take their dining very seriously, even in their hospitals."

"Uncle Otto!" James heard as he stirred from his sleep. It was Marisa's voice and James was not sure if he was dreaming again of if she was really in the room. He caught a whiff of her perfume and smiled. "Are you going to be alright? I knew this whole thing was going to blow up in our faces. It's all my fault," Marisa said. James could tell she was crying.

"I am going to be fine, Norisa," Otto said. "None of this is your fault child. If anything it was my carelessness that put me in this bed."

"I am so afraid," Marisa said. "For you and for Ernesto. You joke like it's nothing, but your wound tells me this was inches from everything."

"Take care of yourself and the world will continue to be a better place for it," Otto said. "You traveled home fast, what time is it?"

"As soon as you contacted Ernesto I went straight to the airport and got a flight home. I had to stomp my feet a little, but I am here. Ernesto will return this evening. I didn't want to wait that long."

James was wondering if Marisa even knew or cared that he was in the room. He understood that Otto was practically family and the closest thing Marisa had to a father, but what was he, just a contractor that could be replaced? He was about to say something when he felt a hand on his brow. A soft hand that was warm and caressing him with a tenderness that reminded him of his mother's touch when he was sick with the flu that had kept him from competing in the state track championships. Yet, this was not the touch of a mother he realized. This was the touch that would make Aphrodite blush.

"And how is my hero?" Marisa asked.

James opened his eyes and looked into the smiling face of the most beautiful person he had ever met. Her eyes were glistening with tears, probably for Otto, but James pretended a few were for him. "I am doing great doctor," James said. "Your healing touch has saved me."

"That is just to take away the pain," Marisa said. She bent down and kissed him gently on the forehead where her hand had been and then on his lips. He could feel her lips quivering. "That is the cure the doctor ordered," she said as her face lingered inches from his.

"Would you like to take a little walk?" James asked. "I need to get out of this bed. All I got was a tiny bump on the head, and I am feeling fine now. Otto is the one who needs to rest."

"Yes," Otto said with a false grumpy voice. "I need some peace and quiet! Can't an old man be alone to nurse his wounds."

"Instead of telling us to get a room," Marisa said as she stood, "he is telling us to get out of the room."

"Right," James said as he sat up, the vertigo happily gone. "Otto has a way of turning the expected and traditional upside-down." James took Marisa's hand, and they walked to the door. It was only then that James realized he was still in a hospital gown. "Oh, I think we won't go too far if that is alright with you."

"Did you mean that in distance, or something else?" Marisa asked innocently.

"Um, in every sense of the word," James said.

"Now look who's blushing," Marisa said. "The nurse told me before I came in that you are being released as soon as the doctor makes his rounds. I will stay until then. Ernesto also said he hoped to see you and thank you for everything you have done, both in preparation for the New York trip and with Otto. So I hoped to take you back to the Quinta de Olivos for dinner and a meeting."

"Dinner and a meeting," James repeated. "Now you're talking the language of love."

"That tiny bump on our head might have caused more damage than the doctors thought," Marisa said with a laugh. More seriously she continued, "How are you really, Santi?"

"I'm good, really," James said. "I had a little vertigo, and I was out for about an hour the tell me. No internal injuries. I'll live. Thanks for asking. How are you? Was your New York stay as fun as the first day?"

"It was just okay," Marisa said. "No internal injuries. I'll live. The Mayor was kind. Most everyone else wanted to skewer Ernesto and me. Some people burnt Argentine flags outside of our hotel. Ernesto told me the American President is in our court, near the exit door, but willing to help. I am sure he will explain more tonight."

They walked in silence down the corridor. James wanted to tell Marisa her face was the last thing he saw when he blacked out but decided against it. "I thought I saw someone else I recognized just before passing out at the restaurant. I didn't tell the police. I am not sure what I would even say. If it was the same guy, it could have been a simple coincidence. It was the guy we met in Bariloche, in that forest. He helped you up when you crashed on your bike," James explained.

"First of all I did not crash on my bike," Marisa said. "The path was wet, and I slipped. Secondly, the forest was the National

Park Bosque de Arrayanes. Finally, I think the guy you are talking about is David Rosado."

"He said he was from Peru, right?" James asked. "I suppose it is the realm of possibility that he could have been in Buenos Aires. It was just odd for some reason. The picture of his face in my mind appeared frustrated, not in shock, not surprised, not worried or afraid."

"So you had his face in your thoughts as you faced possible death?" Marisa asked in a huff. "I was right to have you killed from the start." She crossed her arms, and her lower lip protruded in her copyrighted pout.

"I was talking about something possibly important here," James stammered. "I mean, the same guy in two odd places when we were without security."

"So I am not important?" Marisa asked with her eyes wide. "Listen, Mr. Nathaniels, you are really close to having to find your own ride to the meeting tonight, and there may be no dinner for you."

"Wow, I've dropped from Santi all the way to Mr. Nathaniels, not even a pause at James." He took a breath and began with his recollection of the entire event, including her face as the last thing he saw before he blacked out. "Really, I am not making that up, Marisa. I wanted to tell you, but I was afraid it would make you uncomfortable."

"You face a gunman with a chair, and you are scared of me?" Marisa asked, still on fire.

"Oh yeah," was all James said as he shrugged his shoulders.

"JOAB, The Habsburg Ascendency appears intact and perhaps even stronger than ever thanks to your non-authorized and ill-conceived actions, if these were, in fact, the result of your actions. You are relieved of your present involvement in this operation until we have a face-to-face meeting. Death is such an ugly solution if a solution at all. If you had anything to do with this attempted termination, you will be relieved permanently. This is

not the 18th or even the 19th century, but I am hopeful, as you should be, that this will entice Habsburg and his dedicated lieutenants into a quiet retreat." Americas Prelate

JOAB Chapter 4

DAVID WAS IN NEAR APOPLEXY. He had been present at the shooting merely by accident. He had followed Otto von Habsburg and James Nathaniels over concerns of what JOAB would attempt to do, not expecting such an extreme event. It had all happened so fast that he hadn't even been able to ascertain if there were actual JOAB operatives in the room. He had departed in the pandemonium with most of the other restaurant patrons as soon as the police arrived.

"It could possibly have been an individual or group outside of BAJO that had attempted this shooting," He told himself. "Habsburg was now a target for many frustrated with the Starhemberg project." David had tried to contact the BAJO Guardian, but so far the Guardian had not returned his call. Since he was already in Buenos Aires, it was not that difficult to schedule a meeting with JOAB. That call was returned and he did not go into details and did his best to keep his tone normal. He demanded they meet sometime the very next day.

Here he was, waiting for JOAB to arrive at the Plaza General Lavalle. It was a small park, but easy to find, being located just behind the Teatro Colon in the center of the city. It was lunch time, so there were quite a few people out walking and office workers taking a lunch break. They would be inconspicuous as just two other people of many. It was also far enough away from the Casa Rosada that JOAB wouldn't be recognized by co-workers or others from the President's office.

"Nice day for a walk," JOAB said approaching David.

"Excellent choice of locations," David said. They didn't shake hands but began to walk. "I appreciate you being able to make time for me on such short notice. The event with Otto von Habsburg has got me on edge."

"How so?" JOAB asked.

"I didn't know about it," David replied. He had decided not to mention yet that he had been a witness to the shooting. He didn't want JOAB to know of his concerns until it was fully apparent there was a control problem. "Did you have anything to do with the shooting, or was that some issue outside of our doing?"

"Habsburg has enemies and now with the Cambalache announcement, I am sure he picked up a few more. I didn't have anything to do with this, but not a bad idea," JOAB replied a little too nonchalantly. "Do we have other assets on this operation?" JOAB knew there were others, as the Guardian had said, but was still unsure whether the Prelate know this.

"You are our only asset," David explained. What David didn't say was he feared there were other BAJO forces at play here, but didn't want to share that with this untrustworthy JOAB. "We are not as all-seeing and all-knowing as we once were. I don't like surprises, and I don't like violence except as a last resort. I just want to make ensure we are still on the same page."

"Same page boss," JOAB replied. "Events are moving fast, however, and I need to understand my role and our goal here."

"For right now I need you to also be an information collector," David said. "The vision, Bourbon ascendancy. The mission, to facilitate that ascendancy by appropriate means at our disposal.

I don't need to add, but I will, that we have values that inform our execution of that mission. This is not the 1800's. Life is held to a higher value than it must have been in the old days."

"Or," JOAB replied, "we are getting soft because we aren't protecting a presiding potentate, just nudging here or there, biding our time, until the world comes knocking at our door. Do you think that will ever happen in our lifetime?"

"Patience, patience," David counseled, although he too wondered about that *if and when.* "It will happen, but world events will have to be more chaotic than they are now. Trust of present governing bodies is still high, and the need for a single focus strong hand has been diluted with the crazy despots that still exist. We must be entirely trustworthy. Nothing, including our actions, should ever tarnish the good name of the House of Bourbon."

"Sewing a few seeds of discord, as well as tarnishing the name of the House of Habsburg could speed things along," JOAB said.

"Caution JOAB," David said. "To many, one royal family is the same as another. We play a very delicate game. We must dilute the credibility of the Habsburgs, while not diluting the idea of monarchy nor the royal ability to govern."

"When the world comes, and they will, it will be because they mistrust and are out of options, not because of trust." JOAB was struggling to maintain composure. "I am done babysitting ideas, Prelate. I didn't have anything to do with the attempted hit on Otto von Habsburg, but like I said, it was a good idea. Starhemberg and his cronies, including that North American upstart Nathaniels, need to be removed before they are either successful and provide the leadership that will push our cause even further away, or they are successful in putting a Habsburg on a thrown, even though the title is CamCon Administrator and not CamCon Czar."

David wanted to ask if the sacrifice of great leadership like a President Starhemberg was worth only the potential of Bourbon leadership, but he didn't. He found it ironic that the person working closely with Starhemberg was willing to do just that, while he from a distant was more hesitant. "So Starhemberg is less than he appears? I mean, he is not the leader that his public persona portrays?"

"With him, what you see is what you get," JOAB said. "He is authentic, but he is temporary. There cannot be a dynasty with elected officials. I am in this for the long-term. A year from now we could have a nut in the President's office and then what tune would you be singing?"

"Maybe that is a partial answer," David said, more just thinking out loud.

"You mean, wait until the election is over?" JOAB asked. "With this Cambalache thing that much farther down the road and if entirely successful—at least the energy part, that will ensure his reelection. Better to do something now."

"Then let's put plans in place to discredit Cambalache," David said, things suddenly more clear to him. "Better to slow down free energy than take the life of one of the few decent leaders the world has. That outside foray into the Cambalache lab didn't slow things down long enough."

"End it or steal it?" JOAB asked, also seeing things more clearly.

"If we could gather enough information to replicate Cambalache, we could put the Bourbon Ascendancy on the fast track—play the Starhemberg/Habsburg game as it were."

"Consider it done," JOAB said. "I've got to get back to work, so I have to end our visit."

"Be safe," David said. As JOAB walked back to 9 de Julio Avenue to catch a cab, David worried anew about JOAB. "Impatience, spring loaded to action, and overly confident—a volatile mixture. Sooner or later someone's hands are going to get burnt."

CHAPTER 18

Tal Palo Tal Estilo
Literal Translation: Such a stick such a style

Marisa's Explanation: **Like Father Like Son** is certainly something that runs in the Starhemberg family. Though the saying suggests some genetic disposition, I think it is more from training, education, and experience. And expectation.

THE SOUND OF THE AIRCRAFT wheels, going from zero to 193 kilometers per hour jolted President Ernesto Starhemberg out of his half-sleep. The landing at Ezeiza Airport marked the end of his trip to New York and his United Nations debut. 'A scream of complaint from tires that have no job while in the air, and a little distress smoke, marked the demand placed on resting wheels which will now have to carry the weight of the aircraft once again. Safe arrivals, happy transitions, always seem to be inaugurated with a jolt of pain. "Change is always hard, even if it is desired change," Ernesto remembered his father telling him. "We tear out and leave a little piece of ourselves with the discarded." 'Like the rubber marks on a runway,' Ernesto thought.

"I miss you so much, dad," Ernesto said under his breath, exhaling with a stretch of his arms. He sat alone in the President's chair. His staff were either still asleep or gathering their paperwork they had toiled over during the long flight. 'Argentina really was a long way from most everywhere. Now it is the center of everywhere,' Ernesto thought. 'My father would be so proud of his children and his adopted country.'

The plane continued taxiing down the runway to the last turnoff, heading for the guarded presidential hangar. No customs, no lines, no baggage claim, no fight for a taxi or waiting for a spouse who was going to be late because of the traffic on the Ricchieri Expressway. 'Did that mean life was good?' Ernesto wondered. 'Is that how the good life is measured, by the absence of some inconveniences? What I wouldn't give for a spouse that was late in traffic, in a car that had a baby seat in the back and crusted old cereal on the seat upholstery from her older brother who had tried to feed her while mom and dad in the front seats discussed how they were going to afford a vacation to Mar del Plata this year.' Ernesto's thoughts drifted to the black rubber marks on a life-landing nearly eight years ago.

"This is the capital city?" Gabriela asked as she looked out the window of the car taking them to their apartment. "How could President Alfonsin have considered this a suitable replacement for Buenos Aires? There is not a single city in Mexico that is this, um, windswept. I am sure it has its charms, but Ernesto, I don't understand why we have to live here. Why not Bariloche part of the year and Buenos Aires part of the year?"

"This is the capital of the province, Gabriela," Ernesto explained. "This is where my public service begins. You will learn to love it here, I promise."

"How oblivious I was to reality back then," Ernesto said as the President's plane pulled up to the hangar. Realizing he had said that out loud, he retreated to his thoughts. 'Was I oblivious to the *windswept* qualities of Viedma, my career, my wife, myself?'

"The reality is," Ernesto's father Heinrich told him on his twelfth birthday, "our family has a calling, and it requires sacrifices. Your grandfather sacrificed his family. I have sacrificed my career and desires to do more than live a quiet life here in the Andes mountains at the southern tip of the Americas. You will be called upon to sacrifice as well. I have come to understand that our sacrifices are very personalized and will lead to blessings that would not otherwise be ours."

"Isn't a sacrifice giving up something, for something you want more father?" Ernesto had said, trying to understand what his father was telling him.

"Or to help someone else," his father had added. "The Starhembergs are of royal lineage, but our calling is to support and defend the royal Habsburg House in leading the citizens of the crown. We have been at this for a very, very long time. Remember when I told you that the House of Bourbon began in 1268? Well, our family had already been standing at the side of the royal Habsburgs for nearly 300 years. The Bourbons ruled France from 1555 to 1792 and then briefly again for less than twenty years in the 1800s. The Habsburgs ruled the Holy Roman Empire from 1438, that's more than half a century before this continent was discovered, to 1740. After that, they ruled in many places, from Bohemia, England, Germany, France, Russia, Spain, Portugal, Mexico, to the Astro-Hungarian Empire until 1921."

"So much history father," the young Ernesto said in awe. "Almost a thousand years…"

"Yes my son, and it is our duty to put a Habsburg on the throne of leadership once again if that mantle is handed to us. Will you accept this charge?"

"Yes father, I will do my best," Ernesto had replied with the fervor of a naive youth. "Extreme zeal and little understanding," an older and wiser Ernesto had realized while pursuing his post graduate education in Mexico City. His father had introduced him to several Habsburgs in his teenage years. Otto von Habsburg became a dear friend and mentor to Ernesto and

Marisa with the loss of their parents when Ernesto was 19. With his added understanding, Ernesto had decided to go into politics himself. Otto had helped him map out a plan, for education and stepping stones to the Presidency of Argentina. And then Ernesto met Gabriela González.

"Frijolito saltón!" Ernesto exclaimed to a friend as they left their Politics of National and Global Economic Relations class his second day at the National Autonomous University of Mexico, in Mexico City, "who was that?" Gabriela had walked by with a group of women deep in a noisy conversation. Everything had gone totally silent for Ernesto as his eyes met Gabriela's. She had smiled timidly but didn't blink or turn her eyes away.

It took Ernesto a whole week to find her again, and this time he did more than stare. Their first date, thanks to a little help from Otto von Habsburgs connections, was a private tour of Chapultepec Castle, the home of Maximilian I, Emperor of Mexico and younger brother of the Austrian emperor Francis Joseph I, of the House of Habsburg.

"My family's friends were on the losing side of the battle that is commemorated by your Cinco de Mayo holiday," Ernesto explained. "My great-great grandfather was tied up with the Austro-Prussian war at the time," Ernesto explained with pride, "but the stories of the beauty and wonders of Latin America became lore and a lure. When my grandfather had to escape the Nazis on the eve of World War II, he turned to Latin America."

"My family fought on the side of a free Mexico, Ernesto," Gabriela said. "We are enemies."

"And it's time we make peace, don't you think," Ernesto said as he reached for her hand.

"Romeo and Juliet?" Gabriela replied. "That didn't end so well," but she didn't pull her hand away.

"I was thinking more like Ferdinand and Isabella," Ernesto said. "They stopped fighting, and their union elevated the new nation as a dominant world power, including discovering the New World."

"So you already have us married," Gabriela laughed. "I'm not even sure there will be a second date."

There was a second date, and a third in quick succession. They quickly became inseparable. With only a few months left until Gabriela's graduation and Ernesto's completion of his post graduate degree, they were married. It was a quiet ceremony with just Gabriela's family and Otto von Habsburg representing Ernesto's side of the union. Marisa was not able to attend. Looking back at dates, Marisa was able to confirm that the day before she had faced her life on a bridge in Spain.

Immediately after graduation, Ernesto and Gabriela planned a month in celebration of graduation and as a delayed honeymoon in Bariloche. The first two weeks were wonderful, and they explored the mountains, lakes and each other. Gabriela didn't realize it, but Ernesto could see that Gabriela was getting bored. He entertained traveling to Europe to see Marisa, who had reached out, and Otto but he knew he couldn't afford it. Instead, they spent a few days in Buenos Aires and then returned to Mexico City and enjoyed the last of their break with Gabriela's family and the city they both loved. Ernesto had to return to Argentina for a job he had secured in the office of the Mayor of Viedma. He planned to run for governor within the next year, and the clock was ticking.

They flew from Mexico City to Buenos Aires and then on to Viedma all in the same day. To say Gabriela was in shock with the rustic beauty of Viedma was an understatement. Ernesto could still remember the minutes Gabriela's suitcase actually touched the floor of their new apartment. Two. That is how long it took her to silently walk through the rooms, look out the windows, kiss him on the cheek, pick her suitcase back up and walk out the door.

Gabriela returned to the airport in time to catch the very same plane that carried them to Viedma back to Buenos Aires. She did not trust herself and did not answer any of Ernesto's calls. Ernesto had traveled to Buenos Aires, but could not find Gabriela. He traveled to Mexico City, but she had not returned home. Her family said they did not know where she was, but Ernesto knew that they knew. He returned to Viedma and threw himself into his work, hoping she would return. The only thing that came to Viedma was an annulment document. Ernesto found out you do not need your spouse's consent for an annulment in Mexico and legally this action was equivalent to never having been married.

"Never been married?" Ernesto had yelled to heaven. "How could a court take away the last six months, the happiest time in my life since my parents had died?" He wanted to lash out at Gabriela, at his own blindness, at his pridefulness of possibly creating bigger expectations than the reality of his humble situation. He knew he was losing his self-control, self-medicating with wine and then hard liquor, but when he tried to check himself, he found he didn't care. Then Marisa reentered his life. Or he reentered hers. Marisa had just completed her studies in Europe and returned a different person. She was a grown woman to be sure, but mature in ways that strengthened Ernesto. Only twelve when their parents had died, he had tried to be the big brother and parents for her, but knew he had failed. Somehow she had pulled through that vacuum and became the nurturing mother to him. She motivated him to run for governor. She quietly opened up the fusion project and was by his side as he ran for President. Somewhere along the way, their paths crossed and he became the courageous leader, and she retreated to the quiet and secure world of science. She changed her role from advocate and instigator of higher achievements to cautious advisor and risk mitigator.

Ernesto had never heard from Gabriela again. He sent her letters and even tried to call her, but all her contact information had changed. He thought he might get at least a congratulatory card from her when he won the Presidency of Argentina. When nothing came, he made the only personal request he would ever make of his new powers as President. He had his intelligence agency research her status and whereabouts. She had not married again, briefly lived in Mexico City working for a fashion design house and then she again disappeared. He thought about reaching out to her but didn't want to become a stalker. He never dated seriously. Inside he still felt married.

Marisa and Otto were his only family. He would do anything for either one of them. He also greatly appreciated Vangelina Pereira who had become a good friend and adult mentor to Marisa, but there was a space that only Marisa and Otto were allowed in Marisa's life. Ernesto had confided in Archbishop Poli about his concern. The Archbishop had sent him to Psalms 142 verse 4, which he had shared with Marisa. "I looked on my right hand, and behold, but there was no man that would know me: refuge failed me; no man cared for my soul." He hoped that mental and emotional place where Marisa escaped would not become a cave, like the cave King David had escaped to in those Bible verses, only to discover it was more a prison than a safe place. Marisa had faced her Goliath but was retreating more and more.

Not for the first time, Ernesto wondered if he was creating his own caves, and then discarded that concern for whatever he could do for Marisa. She was so much more than the world knew; brilliant at the Einstein level Ernesto guessed, wise, and strong. The world saw her beauty and emotions, both of which obfuscated her real gifts. How grateful he was that Marisa had found a new friend in James Nathaniels. James was another amazing human being who had no idea of his actual abilities and destiny.

Ernesto's thoughts were interrupted by a flight attendant that told him his car was waiting and asked if he needed more time.

'More time to sort out my emotions?' he asked himself. "No, thank you." He recognized the attendant, but couldn't place her name. "How do you think I am doing?" he asked her.

"Sir?" she replied.

"I am your President unless something changed over the week I was in New York. How am I doing, really, your honest answer?"

"Honest answer, Mr. President," she said and paused. "It is a great day to be Argentine. It's like winning the world cup once a week. Even better."

"Do you think you are in the minority or majority?" he asked.

"I think I am pretty smart and I think most of my fellow Argentines are pretty smart too. We've got your back, Mr. President."

"You're right, it is a great day to be Argentine," President Ernesto Starhemberg said smiling. "Thank you for being the first to welcome me home."

As Ernesto slipped into the back seat of his limousine, he thanked God for his ability to see the best and demand the best of people. The success of his leadership as Governor and President were directly linked to his talent of surrounding himself with amazing people. The first time he considered himself the smartest or best in the room would be the day he would fail. He hoped that day would never come and he smiled as he knew it never had to come.

"It's a great day to be Argentine," he told his driver. He made a phone call. Pepe," he said to his National and International Secret Advisor, "I just landed. I will be in the office shortly. I just wanted to remind you that it is a great day to be Argentine. Spread the word."

"Will do, sir," Pepe Peralta Monti said. "I will brief you when you get in, sir, but Iran, Iraq, and Kuwait have started a Mêlée à Trois. It will soon be a three-way shooting war. All three are blaming you."

"Rubber on the runway, Pepe," Ernesto said.

"You can explain when you get here, sir."

"President Starhemberg is back in Buenos Aires. Time to harvest the sour seeds I have planted and propagated. We will achieve our goals and deconflict with their destiny. Painful perturbations provide the preparation for positive permutations." JOAB loved alliteration.

CHAPTER 19

Venir Como Anillo al Dedo
Literal Translation: To come like a ring to a finger

Marisa's Explanation: A ring on my finger usually would fit perfectly, or fit like a glove, but when the person adds venir, the verb _to come_, it changes the meaning to closer express when something comes unexpectedly to solve a situation, as a solution, **Come in Handy.** Certainly, the right ring would be the perfect thing to come to my life if the giver was the right guy, hint, hint.

"HOW SOON WILL CAMBALACHE 2 be online, and C3?" President Starhemberg asked Marisa over dinner.

James found it interesting that he asked his sister rather than Godoy or Peralta Monti, or another staff member now that the program was more out in the open. He knew it was still held tightly under wraps due to security concerns, but Marisa was only peripherally involved. Marisa looked beautiful tonight. He had walked with her earlier that day at the hospital, but it seemed like it was a week ago.

"Components were taken off of C2 to get C1 up and running after the attack," Marisa said matter-of-factly. C2 should have been operational by now. It will be another two weeks. C3 is a month behind C2."

"With all three operational," Starhemberg continued, "how much delivery capacity will that provide?"

"Using New York City as a baseline of 11,000-megawatt hours, which includes residential, commercial, electrical based transportation, and industrial needs, we can power twenty New York sized mega-cities. The additional lines to connect to the global grid were completed while we were in New York. We are almost ready, Ernesto."

"Otto will have a list for us within the week," Starhemberg said in between bites of flan con crema batida. "He tells me the cities are lining up, even as their associated nation-states push-back. Speaking of push back, what do you have to report, Pepe?"

"As I briefed you earlier, Kuwait, Iran, and Iraq are experiencing firefights along their borders," Pepe Peralta Monti began. "This started out to be a small conflagration of ship traffic in the Persian Gulf and has quickly escalated. This is mostly emotions driven, not market or security driven. Everyone is trying to get their oil to market, and they are willing to cause an oil glut before Cambalache makes their commodity even less valuable. Saudi Arabia has been quiet, too quiet."

"Please put out a communiqué to those countries and then go global, reminding them that Cambalache will not impact their principle transportation markets and will never touch lubricants nor petrochemicals and bi-product uses. It will take years, even decades to shift all heating over to electric, and defense, technology, and new products from synthetic fibers, chemical fertilizers, pesticides, plastics, and who knows what tomorrow will bring." President Starhemberg finished his flan and added, "Instead of fighting like children, they should be spending money on research and development of new petroleum products. So, why are they blaming us? I mean, I know the excuse, but how are they framing it?"

"Even if we have the capacity, we should have very gradually brought on the power offerings, perhaps phased in over ten to twenty years," Pepe Peralta Monti said.

"James, you built a scenario for that, right?" President Starhemberg asked. "The reasons it was better to bring this online now, for global financial reasons, the environment, economic tradeoffs, and so on."

"Yes, sir," James said. "It is a pretty convincing argument, even for the leading oil producers."

"Great, get that to Pepe for added support." President Starhemberg stood and stretched. It had been a long day. "James, I have another request for you. I need you to travel back to the United States, tomorrow. How are you feeling? The doctors say you are fine, but you need to take it easy for a week or so. Tell me honestly, are you up for another long trip?"

"I'm good, sir, honestly," James answered. He wanted to ask what he would be doing in the U.S. but figured that would come.

"Great," President Starhemberg said sitting down again, more relaxed. "I have run this by Pepe who I wish could travel with you, but I want him to focus on the rest of the world and domestic issues which are getting serious. I have our military working with the American Defense Attaché office here in town, but I need some risk mitigation coordination at a higher level. Cambalache is a sitting duck if someone really wanted to take it out. I am not ruling out any threat or point of attack, from a Russian Spetsnaz team to a Chinese ICBM, from hitting the Cambalache site directly to disrupting power lines. I know most of those possibilities are what you and Marisa worked on for weeks. You are more comfortable in Washington, DC and I really need Marisa here. Bottom line you will be meeting with President Tony Marcasano and his National Security Advisor, maybe the Chairman of his Joint Military Staff, I don't know, but the meeting is day after tomorrow, early morning sometime at his house. I have asked the U.S. Ambassador to meet with me tomorrow for lunch, and I will brief him on your trip. I don't want him to feel completely out of the loop, but Tony, your President, intends to keep this very close hold. You should only be gone a few days, a week max."

"I'll pack tonight, sir," James said, trying not to sound too overwhelmed. "I'm happy to go and I won't keep pushing back, but are you sure I am the right person for this? I am not Argentine, and I am not a physical security expert."

"You won't be representing Argentina," President Starhemberg said. "You are representing Cambalache and CamCon. I trust you, and you know the scenarios package better than anyone." Marisa picked up an olive from a bowl and threw it at her brother, hitting him on the forehead. He smiled and said, "Better than almost anyone. And you speak North American, not just the language."

"Any marching orders?" James asked.

"Yes, do the right thing for the right reasons," President Starhemberg said. "If you have any really tough questions, call Marisa."

"And you better have some tough questions," Marisa said with a syrupy voice. Then she threw an olive at him too.

"One last thing, James," President Starhemberg said. "Like I said, this is very close hold. No contact with family or friends. If you bump into any old associates or acquaintances while in Washington, DC, you are there on contract with the Argentine petroleum industry. You are meeting with principle industry insiders who also have the President's ear. Thus the one White House visit. We will corroborate that story at our end. The President's people will meet you at your hotel room and escort you. They have you booked at the Army Navy Club for the week as the special guest of the U.S. Defense Attaché here. You will be on your own in the security department when not with your new friend President Marcasano. Sorry to throw you to the wolves, and remember, some will be in sheep's clothing."

"So far your association with this entire matter has been kept under the radar," Alberto Godoy said. "All that means is, the press doesn't know. Countries know that you have been involved in something and that you know President Starhemberg and his sister. Once, if," Alberto paused, "you are connected with Cambalache, you will be a different asset. Safer and less safe. Anonymity is your friend right now, but that means we can't offer overt security. In the future, it might be different, but then you won't be able to go anywhere without security."

"Sir, will I get the chance to talk with Mr. Habsburg, Otto?" James asked.

"He thought you might ask," President Starhemberg said. You have his private number. Give him a call en route north using my aircraft's comm scrambler. He is at an undisclosed location himself, and it is better to keep it that way for now after recent events." President Starhemberg stood up and said, "I apologize. I meant to thank you before we even started dinner." He walked to James and gave him a big hug and a slap on the back. Looking into James's eyes, he said, "Thank you, my friend. Otto is more than just a friend and mentor. He is our second father," Starhemberg said as he glanced at his sister.

"Any word on the assailant?" James asked, partly to get the focus off himself.

"No fingerprints on the weapon," Alberto Godoy said. "Still nothing from facial recognition. A complete mystery."

"Not a complete mystery," James said. "He was a thug, not a professional. I am not expert, of course, but I am guessing that a professional would not have tried to kill Otto inside a crowded restaurant and wouldn't have been surprised by my amateur reaction. Someone was sending a message, and they used a contract hire to deliver."

"Whatever the case," Godoy said, "we are taking no chances with Otto's safety from here on out."

"Speaking of safety," Marisa said, "I will need to escort you home tonight."

"Okay," James said blushing.

"I'm not staying," Santi. "Don't get any crazy ideas."

James noticed she was blushing slightly herself. "No ideas, I promise," James said.

"What?" Marisa said throwing a handful of olives at James. "No ideas? Really? I have never been so humiliated in my whole life."

"Except for the time you made a marriage proposal and were turned down," President Starhemberg said. "And you will pick up all those olives dear sister."

"Marriage proposal?" Pepe Peralta Monti said. "I know I would never turn you down, Marisa."

"Your wife might have something to say about that, Pepe," President Starhemberg said. "When Marisa was what, thirteen?"

"Thirteen and a half, going on fourteen," Marisa said.

"Yes, thirteen and a half, a grown woman, practically, I think were the words you used to describe yourself." Turning to the group, President Starhemberg continued. "She proposed marriage to Otto von Habsburg, adding he would have to wait until she was done with high school."

"And I was dead serious," Marisa said. "Don't make fun of me, Ernesto. Otto had just told me the story of how our mother and father met and fell in love," she added to the group. "It was so romantic. I missed my parents so much, and suddenly they were right there, and it was a sad memory. I wanted to be closer to them and thought I could do that by marrying Otto. I think it would have worked."

"What did Otto say?" Pepe asked.

"He told me that I was a princess, a real royal princess and that if there was anything the Habsburgs had learned after centuries of royal intermarriages, it was to stay away from an uncle marrying his niece. I knew he wasn't my real uncle, but it was the nicest turn down I have ever received."

"You have had others turn you down?" James asked.

"Well, no," Marisa said. "But it was still the nicest. I'm afraid I have never asked anyone else. Others have asked me, and I am sorry to say I was not as gentle. Basically, I just gave them the silent treatment. You wouldn't know it, but I was very immature once. I will probably never get married."

"Because you will do the asking, but you never will?" Pepe asked.

"No, dear Pepe, because Otto won't have me and you are already married," Marisa said. Getting serious she added, "And because I need to take care of my brother until he gets married and I don't know if that will ever happen. Now if you will excuse me, I need to powder my nose before I take James home."

Everyone stood as Marisa got up and walked out of the room. Pepe leaned over to James conspiratorially and said loud enough that everyone could hear, "Grab on to that girl and hold on tight. She is one in a billion, even if she does throw food and then leave it on the floor.

James smiled but said nothing. He had just discovered this pain in the depths of his stomach. Marisa had spoken some truth in her banter. 'Would she ever marry? Was there any hope for James beyond being a close friend and even a romantic friend?' he wondered once again.

"You really should consider moving back into the Quinta de Olivos, James," Marisa told him a few minutes later as they both sat in the back seat of one of the President's more nondescript cars. The driver pretended not to hear their conversation.

"I will be fine," James said. "I don't want to be an imposition. It made sense during the scenario building, but I am not family. That is your home."

"When you save the life of a family member that makes you family," Marisa said.

"So I am family now," James said. "Does that mean we can't date?"

"Good point, Santi," Marisa said. "There is only one way to find out if you are a brother or a boyfriend." She leaned over and gave him a very long and tender kiss. "Nope, you're not my brother," Marisa whispered. She kissed him again. They had just pulled up to his house. "Why did you have to rent a place so close to Olivos?"

James put his hands on Marisa's cheeks and looked into her eyes and asked, "I am not saying this would ever happen, but could it ever happen that I became family; more than a boyfriend?"

"Oh, Santi," Marisa said with tears welling up in her eyes. "Don't ask what ifs. Don't make this complicated. My world, our world, is insane. We don't even know from day to day what continent we will be on. You have rescued me from my *no-boyfriend cave*. Isn't that enough for now?"

"Not if this is all it will ever be," James said.

The driver cleared his throat loudly, and both Marisa and James were startled to remember there was someone else in the car. Marisa put her hand to her mouth to stifle a laugh. James looked out the window and decided it was time to get some sleep before his trip in the morning.

"Marisa, I am grateful I can be of service to you and your brother, Otto, and the whole Cambalache group, but maybe this thing between us is getting in the way of what we need to do right now. Let's stop pretending it's more or that it will ever be more. We practically lived together during the scenario building, and that got our heads in the wrong place." He leaned over and kissed her on the cheek, got out of the car and entered his house.

James stood just inside the front door and didn't move. As soon as he heard the car drive off he walked to the bedroom, sat down on the bed and made a call. With that done, he showered and got to bed. A car would pick him up in six hours.

Marisa stifled her tears all the way back to the Quinta. 'How had this evening and their reunion ended so badly? What did he want from her? More than she was willing to give? Commitment?' Vangelina had tried to prepare her for this possibility, seeing something Marisa had refused to see.

"This will never work out Norisa," Vangelina had explained. "He is from a different world and you are destined for greatness. He won't want to be a peripheral part, a beside the point boyfriend."

"Vangelina was right," Marisa told herself. "I am committed to my brother and to my little baby that has grown up and proved itself and is now about to have two babies." Only a handful of people on the Cambalache team knew that it was Marisa that had made the breakthroughs to make the fusion engine work. This whole mess was her fault. Free energy, making the only two people she loved targets—and one who had almost died, riots and shooting wars, unstable markets... "What have I done?" she asked herself and then realized she wasn't talking about Cambalache.

JOAB watched a crying Marisa run to her room like a dejected debutante. "Very sad, very good. Now to play ghost from the past."

CHAPTER 20

A lo Hecho Pecho
Literal Translation: In fact the chest

Marisa's Explanation: In life, the necessity or desirability to face up the consequences of any mistake or failure and not spending too much time fretting about it, is a harsh lesson. We need to hold our head high, stick out our chest and press forward. **What's Done is Done.**

"BE BRAVE, TAKE HEART," MARISA ssaid to herself and an imaginary James. "This is one of my favorite dichos, sayings, dear James, Santi. A lo hecho pecho literally could be translated, "in fact the chest." What's done is done. Water under the bridge. You did it, you can't back down, but you can move forward. Make peace with what's been done." She got into her bed and tried to sleep.

Ernesto had told Marisa the next morning after the aircraft carrying James Nathaniels north to his last assignment for President Starhemberg was off the ground. "James called me last night, after you dropped him off at his house, Marisa," Ernesto began.

"He called you?" Marisa repeated, surprised. "What did he say?" Marisa had tossed and turned most of the night but wasn't going to let on to her brother.

"He will be ending his contract after the visit with President Mancuso. He really didn't want to do this trip, but didn't want to leave me hanging. I appreciate that."

"But his contract states," Marisa began.

"His contract states he will stay quiet for the remainder of his initial six months. He declined pay for that time," Ernesto explained.

"I don't care about that, Ernesto," Marisa snapped. "Of course someone could kidnap him and torture him and get some pretty good information, but it wouldn't change any of our plans."

"Sounds safer than your initial plans to simply kill him," Ernesto said, obviously enjoying this. Marisa could see that, and it made her even madder.

"Just when we need him most, and he abandons us," Marisa said. "See, Ernesto, I was right all along. It was a mistake to hire him."

"Otto doesn't agree with you," Ernesto said.

"You have already talked to Otto?" Marisa asked. "Before talking to me? What did he say?"

"James called him after speaking with me," Ernesto said. "Otto called me. You see, I didn't get much sleep last night either."

"And, what did Otto say?" Marisa repeated trying to keep the focus off her.

"Otto said James had become more than a trusted associate, but a dear friend. He asked if we could get James to reconsider. I told him I didn't think so. He understood and said he would have done the same thing, but he had been the pursued, not the pursuer."

"The same thing?" Marisa said, exasperated. "What are you talking about? This is no time for Otto's metaphysical double-talk."

"Marisa, I love you, and beyond that love, I also know that you are a genius, but you can be so dumb sometimes," Ernesto said shaking his head.

"Me, dumb?" Marisa said. "You are the one talking in circles. Fine, I will give James a call and get a straight answer from the coward himself."

"His plane has already taken off," Ernesto said. "And James is not the coward here."

"Then who is?" Marisa said. "I will talk to him—Otto?"

"Not him, she," Ernesto said. "James told me he was in love with you, but that was not ever going to work out, and so he thought it best he move on. Otto and I happen to agree with him."

"Oh, that is the most ridiculous excuse for jumping ship I have ever heard," Marisa said. "He is just afraid he will become the next target."

"So he voluntarily left, knowing he is dropping any security we might be able to provide?" Ernesto asked. "Suddenly kidnapping and torture are off the table? Marisa, when you sort this out, you will want to contact him. He asked, and I gave him my word. No calls, no emails, no letters, no contact."

"I wouldn't contact him now if he were the last man left in the world," Marisa said. She turned and started her march for the door.

"He did leave a message for you," Ernesto said. "He told me you wouldn't ask if he had, but wanted me to pass this on to you anyway."

Marisa turned, and Ernesto saw his baby sister trying to be emotionless and failing miserably. Tears were brimming in her eyes, but she would not let them fall. She would not blink. "Well, what?" she asked.

Ernesto picked up a piece of paper and said, "Sorry I had to write it down so I could get it right. He said, "Dear Marisa, long ago you entered that safe, dark casket C.S. Lewis described, sure it would provide safety and security. You had been hurt, deeply, and you would not be hurt again. But I have seen your vulnerability, and it is your greatest strength. I know you can open and give your heart. I looked in the casket, and you were not there. I can only conclude that I am not the one for you. Perhaps Otto will reconsider your childhood proposal. You couldn't do any better. Thank you for the part of me that is and will always be Argentine." Ernesto handed her the paper and added, "He knows you even better than I do sis. Sorry it didn't work out."

Marisa grabbed the note, crumpled it in her hand and marched out the door. Ernesto followed her for a few steps and saw Vangelina meet her in the outer office and put her arms around Marisa. Vangelina looked at Ernesto and smiled sadly, then turned her attention back to Marisa. Ernesto retreated back to his office and the demands of his day.

James fell into an exhausted sleep somewhere over the Amazon Rain Forest. No longer just packing a bag for a brief trip north, James had spent the night packing up everything he wanted to take home with him. He could settle most of his affairs by email and online. It wasn't the smartest thing he had ever done, but he went for a jog around his neighborhood at two in the morning. He would miss everything about his experience in Argentina, especially Marisa. Everything else he would miss, he realized, would remind him of her.

He landed at Baltimore-Washington International Airport at three in the afternoon. He had just flown on the President of Argentina's plane as the only passenger. He was about to meet with the President of the United States, to talk about the most impactful change on human society since fire was invented. Why did he feel like he was being sent to the principal's office? He knew why of course and only hoped this feeling would pass with time.

James was met by the Argentine Defense Attaché and a driver who took him to the Army Navy Club, a block from the White House. The Argentine officer made small talk on the drive but didn't ask any questions. 'Argentina truly is the consummate Batman country' James thought and wondered how many times Argentina accomplished complex international tasks in such anonymity. He had a quiet early dinner at McCormick and Schmicks Steakhouse next door. The steak was good, but not in the same universe as the Argentine beef he had grown accustomed to. He walked around the Army Navy Club, reading the historical plaques, enjoying the artwork, and visiting its library on the top floor and promising himself he would try the food here tomorrow night. He fell asleep reading a signed copy of General Colin Powell's book *My American Journey*, that he had borrowed from the library.

He was up at six and enjoyed thirty minutes in the fitness center with some very fit hotel guests. At 8 A.M. exactly, he heard a knock at his door, and a man in a black suit asked to see some identification. Not sure if this was protocol or what was going on, he showed the man his passport. "Thank you, Mr. Nathaniels," the man said. "If you could follow me, I will take you to your meeting." They descended the carpeted stairs and a car waited for them just outside the main doors. The drive to the main entrance of the White House took all of three minutes, and that was due to traffic. James showed his passport again at another gate. The car pulled to the curb on the west side of the main building that James had always thought of as the White House. They entered a small portico with a double white unmarked doorway. Just inside another gentleman met James, and the escort disappeared down the corridor straight ahead. James and the unnamed man walked to the right, past a door marked White House Situation Room. 'I am really here,' James thought to himself. 'What am I doing here?' They went up some stairs, and James saw another room marked Cabinet Room. The door was open, and James guessed the chair that was just a little taller than all the others was the President's chair. They turned left into an office, and his escort said, "Have a good day, Mr. Nathaniels," and left. Two people in the room got up from their desks and shook James's hand. A kind older woman said, "Good morning, Mr. Nathaniels. My name is Gloria, I am the President's personal secretary. He will be with you in just a moment. James sat in a chair and waited.

James noticed that the walls were curved and he assumed that was to conform to the walls of the Oval Office. Surprisingly he wasn't nervous but felt more like a tourist than a personal representative of a President that was about to meet with the most powerful man in the world. James could also see the Rose Garden with the main White House building just beyond it through the office window. James heard a quiet click and turned to see a curved door open and a man in uniform nod to Gloria. Gloria said, "The President will see you now, Mr. Nathaniels."

James stood and walked to the door. He lost the tourist feeling and felt a little wobbly in the knees, but he kept walking. "Mr. Nathaniels, good to meet you. I hope your trip went well. My name is Jim Hutchinson. I work for the National Security Advisor. She is out of town and asked me to sit in on our little pow wow." Jim turned to the President who was standing by a couch and said, "Mr. President, Mr. Nathaniels."

"Good to meet you, the President said. "Did Gloria offer you anything? Would you like some water, juice, anything?"

"No, thank you, Mr. President," James said.

"Well, let's get right down to things," the President said. "You bring word from President Starhemberg? How is he, and how is Otto von Habsburg?"

"Both are well, sir. Mr. Habsburg is still recovering, but fortunately, the assailant's aim was not that good."

"Yes, that isn't what my people tell me," President Marcasano said studying James. "I am glad he is getting better. Colonel Hutchinson and I were just talking about what we could do to help out President Starhemberg. First, I would like to hear from you what you think we ought to do. What has President Starhemberg asked you to convey to us?"

"Sir, my only marching orders were to do the right thing for the right reasons," James began. "I tell you this, so you won't misconstrue my message versus President Starhemberg's wishes. Up until a month ago, anonymity was Cambalache's best security. Of course, that is no longer the case. Two weeks before the announcement the Cambalache facilities were hit by some unknown assailant. It had to be a small group and the damage was minor, but they knew what they were doing and left no trace as to who they were. As far as I know, no one has claimed responsibility and Argentina has not identified any potential actors. If the attempt on Mr. Habsburg's life was part of the same group, the gunman was an unprofessional thug and was probably contracted for the job. Much of the Argentine security forces have been kept in the dark and have not been involved in strengthening security around the Cambalache facility. They have taken a much bigger role in protecting the delivery grid, within Argentina of course."

"So do you think Starhemberg mistrusts his own security people?" Colonel Hutchinson asked.

"There may be some concern with trust issues, although President Starhemberg and his Cambalache staff have never mentioned that in my presence. I believe it is more to keep a distance between Argentina and Cambalache and certainly a distance from CamCon."

"This Cambalache staff you mention," the President said, "who is that?"

"The President of course, and his sister, Marisa, who has been involved on the science side of the project. Otto von Habsburg is a close family friend, even a father figure to the President and his sister. Alberto Godoy, the President's Chief of Staff, and Pepe Peralta Monti, his Advisor for National and International Security are the only other people involved. Of course, there is a group of 18 engineers and scientists at the Cambalache site. They have been employees of the Centro Atómico Bariloche and the Instituto Balseiro."

"Amazing, and this tiny group, with a budget they were able to hide from the world, did something that all of the rest of the world is still trying to accomplish," the President said.

"With the help of the original work of Ronald Richter and the Huemul Project," James added.

"And who is the lead scientist? The one who led this breakthrough?" Colonel Hutchinson asked.

"I don't know, sir," James said. "I think it was a team effort."

"And you have seen Cambalache?" the President asked.

"Yes, sir," James answered. "I am not a scientist and couldn't tell you much. It is a huge donut-shaped machine with hundreds of appendages."

"So how can you be certain that what you saw was not some scam and they are delivering the electricity by some other means, and they are as fake as the original Huemul Project was thought to be?"

"I can't provide any additional proof, sir. I do know two more Cambalache systems are also almost complete. I think the proof will be in their ability to deliver electricity. The plan is, within a month to provide to twenty mega cities at a level of 11,000-megawatt hours twenty-four seven."

"And these cities," the President asked, "have they been identified?"

"More than twenty have been identified," James said, "but those volunteering to enter the CamCon Agreement presently stands at 4 as of last night when I spoke with Mr. Habsburg."

"And only mega-cities will be recipients?" Colonel Hutchinson asked.

"For the present, yes, sir. Mr. Habsburg and I have had discussions around other possibilities in the future."

"Which brings me to a point you left out, Mr. Nathaniels, may I call you James?" the President asked.

"Please do, sir," James said.

"What is your part in all this, James?" the President asked. "How did a United States citizen get tied up in this elite little group, and so rapidly?"

"They approached me, sir," James said. "Marisa Starhemberg was initially very opposed to bringing me on board. This is my last assignment, however. I tendered my resignation yesterday,"

"What?" the President said surprised and a little upset. "Why would you do that? Do you have doubts about this? Are they doing something wrong we should know about?"

No, sir, none of the above," James said. "My value in this project has waned, and it was time for me to move on."

"I don't suppose there is something we can say or do to get you to change your mind?" the President asked. "Can we lean on your patriotic duty to keep your hand in this game? To have a trustworthy American citizen on the inside is important to us."

"Sir there is nothing you will gain from my involvement," James said. "I am free to tell you everything I know, but I promise you President Starhemberg will tell you the same—and he knows a lot more than I do. This is not like anything I have ever been involved in. It is an open book. No hidden side agendas or secrets. They need additional security, and although they are a little reticent to directly ask for it because there are a few things they, President Starhemberg, will not allow to fall into outside hands, they need you. Badly."

"And they want it done quietly," Colonel Hutchinson added.

"Yes, sir," James said. "They trust the United States. That might sound a little naïve in some corners, but they know they can't do this alone, but on the other hand, they feel strongly that they have to take responsibility to do their very best with this rollout, to minimize as much of the unintended consequences as possible. Argentina has few real enemies. They aren't neutral, but they are far from being the United States. If you took this over, the energy creation and delivery, half the world would mistrust you—not because you would cheat them, but because it's you, the only super power in the world."

"And why this crazy scheme to roll out a confederation of mega-cities?" Colonel Hutchinson asked. "If they want to keep things from blowing up, why make every nation-state in the world their enemy?"

"They don't see it that way, sir," James said. "They see the changes already happening, and they are planning on riding that wave. To them, it is a risk mitigation action, not something that is adding to the risk. Sir, one-seventh of the people on the globe will soon sign on board. And that one-seventh represents nearly half of the teachers, doctors, scientists, and leaders that will take our world into tomorrow. And they aren't attacking nations, just the state side of that equation. And even then, they are supportive of those states to take an active role in this evolution of human governance."

"So these so called antiquated states, who hold enough nuclear arsenals to obliterate mankind," Colonel Hutchinson said, agitated, "are being asked to just quietly go away? Talk about naïve. That is not even in the most radical peace activist's playbook."

"Maybe fusion reactors are the harbinger of the final elimination of fusion bombs," James said, knowing he now sounded like the naïve activist.

"There is still a lot for us to sort out," President Marcasano said. "We aren't going to solve everything here and now. My goal is to understand as best I can, what the situation is, if it is in our national interest to support it, and lend a hand if it aligns with our best interests. Thank you for your time, James. I would like you to work with Colonel Hutchinson over the next few days. Can you do that?"

"Yes, of course, sir," James said.

"Great. You can meet in the Eisenhower Executive Office Building—much less conspicuous. There are some who have nothing better to do than pay attention to who comes and goes from the White House. I would like to hear what you two come up with before you leave town. Will you be returning to Missouri?"

Startled at the President's knowledge of his background, James stammered, "I suppose so, sir."

"My advice, always run to something, not just away from something," the President said.

Over the next two days, James and Colonel Hutchinson mapped out ways to establish a nearly invisible security presence in Argentina and along the key electrical grid corridors. The United States also agreed to provide initial contract security for Otto von Habsburg and any staff he brings on at the CamCon headquarters, to be located in London. With Great Briton's exit from the European Union, London provided a more independent and non-aligned location for CamCon. Unannounced to the world, the Mayor of London was the second to sign up for CamCon, after the Mayor of Buenos Aries. James and Colonel Hutchinson briefed President Marcasano and then James briefed President Starhemberg via secure conference call.

James said his goodbyes to President Starhemberg and Otto von Habsburg. Marisa's name never came up, although she was on the mind of everyone during these last communications.

"Nathaniels is out of the picture. The Cambalache team is starting to crumble. Von Habsburg is dangling on a string." JOAB

BAJO INTERLUDE
Death of Guardian

DAVID HAD NOT HEARD FROM the Guardian for nearly a week. It was not like the BAJO leader to go so long without answering a Prelate's questions. Confirming with other prelates that they had not heard from him either, the European Prelate agreed to travel from Madrid to Paris to check on him. The next day David got a phone call. It was a conference call in fact.

The European Prelate began, "I traveled immediately to Paris and visited the Maison Decazes yesterday late morning. I found the Guardian dead in his library. It looks as if he were attempting to open his safe. He had probably passed away only the night before, possibly of a massive heart attack according to the paramedic responders. The day servant was not due back to the Maison until Monday. I then called the Russia and Asia Prelate who was also able to travel immediately to Paris. She arrived today. We are in the Guardian library and will open the safe if each of you can provide your part of the combination."

After authenticating that both prelates were who they said they were, each prelate offered their part of the combination. The safe was opened, and the purple pouch was placed on the table. Together the two prelates read the name of the new Guardian. "It is my express wish that David Rosado accept the leadership of role of BAJO. He is experienced and presently oversees the most dynamic operations within BAJO's sphere of interest. We must not fail to continue our duties to protect and support the Bourbon Ascendancy. This, of course, includes the delicate derailment of any other royal house ascendancy, including our archrival the House of Habsburg. May God be with you in our quest. If you are reading this transcript, be it known that I completed this communique on 27 September, the birth date of King Loui XIII, the Habsburg Humiliator, thanks in part to our fellow BAJO member, Cardinal Richelieu."

"David, are you there?" the Russian Prelate asked. "May I be the first to congratulate you."

David Rosado was speechless. He had never gotten along with the Guardian and thought he would come in last on the Guardian's list of Prelates to follow him. "I am here my friends," David said. "I, I am speechless."

"Please make arrangements to take your place here within the month as is tradition. As you know, the by-laws allow for a three-month transition, but our world travels much faster than it did half a millennium ago when those laws were established. If I can be of help," the European Prelate stated, "please do not hesitate to contact me."

David thought he detected a slight resentment in the voice of the European Prelate, who traditionally became the Guardian. Yet it was also a tradition that no prelate ever turned down the BAJO Guardianship. David would not be the first. "Thank you, my friends. I can be ready to relocate within a week. My situation here in Peru is simple. The dynamics that the Guardian noted here in Latin America however will require some delicate arrangements. I have a JOAB in mind, but recent events have cast doubt on my thoughts. Nevertheless, I will take care of these matters and travel soon. In accordance with the by-laws, I have written the name for my replacement and placed it in my Bible for now. It will stay there until I arrive at the Maison Decazes and establish a new combination for the Guardian safe."

David listened numbly to the congratulatory remarks of the other prelates and the plans for the quiet internment of the previous Guardians body in the crypt on the Maison Decazes's property.

The new Guardian contacted JOAB Buenos Aires before sending out a communique announcing the death of the Guardian and that the new Guardian was in his or her place. Each Prelate would accomplish this for their prelature and only reference the Guardian in general terms, not by name, which again was according to tradition. Of course, it would be less than 24 hours when everyone in BAJO would know of the change and who exactly the new Guardian was, but tradition must be maintained.

"I will be making the announcement of the change of the Guardianship within the hour," the Guardian explained. "Can I count on your continued loyalty and trust?" David had not spelled out that he was now the Guardian, but he knew this JOAB, in particular, would understand. That was one reason he had decided to make this JOAB the Prelate over this region.

"Of course, you know I have always given my all for the organization," JOAB said.

"Wonderful, would you then consider taking on the role of Prelate for the Americas?"

"I am honored," truly," JOAB stated. "There is so much happening, however, and I wonder if this is the best time for a change."

"I am guessing there is another operative working directly for the previous Guardian that may be at your location. I should have that knowledge within the week. It is your call of course, but perhaps that person would be a suitable JOAB to replace you. Of course, you could also continue working operations in your local area as long as they don't impinge on your abilities to administer the prelature."

JOAB hung up the phone, excited but also surprised. Not always seeing eye to eye with the Prelate, selection to take his place was never considered an option. But now a great opportunity presented itself.

CHAPTER 21

Dejar a Alguien en las Astas del Toro
Literal Translation: To Leave Someone
on the Horns of the Bull

Marisa's Explanation: Obviously this dicho has its roots in the bull ring. Bullfighting is not something that came with the Spanish to Argentina. That's surprising because we are one of the largest beef producers in the world and no question every porteño sees himself as a matador. We've all seen the pictures of someone in the ring or while running with the bulls being bounced on the horns of the animal. We can feel the shame and sometimes the helplessness of **Leaving Someone In Their Hour of Need.**

His duty completed, James traveled home to Missouri. He had made more in the last three months than he had earned the previous year, and that had been a banner year. He looked forward to seeing how the house construction had been progressing. His sisters had been slightly miffed at this slow response to their questions, but the project had moved forward, and it was something to take James's mind off of Marisa.

"So you completed you contract in Argentina so quickly?" his mother had asked him at the dinner table the first night he was home.

"Not much of a contract really, and I am glad to be home," James said. "I want to see how and where Jessica and Jacey have spent all my hard earned money."

"You are going to love it, James," Jessica said. "So did your contract with the Petroleum industry end because of President Starhemberg's new energy plans?"

"No," James said nonchalantly, "The contract just ended."

"And you never got a picture for me of Ernesto Starhemberg," James's youngest sister Jacey said.

James just filled his mouth with food as an excuse to responding, not that anyone expected a response to Jacey's joke.

"And I saw a picture of the guy's sister," his dad said. "Now there's a looker."

James mom slapped her napkin at her husband.

"What?" James dad asked surprised. "Probably not a thought in her head. You see those pictures of her in New York City? The world's most eligible bachelorette, but she looked like a lost puppy. Something was bothering her. Beauty is not happiness."

James got up from the table and said, "I think I will go check out the house site. Jessica, Jacey, you want to come?"

"Go ahead, I will try to get over there before dark. I have a regular life on top of your project. You have no idea what busy is really like," Jessica said.

James left the house, hoping these conversation topics would stop once the thought of James having been in Argentina became old news. The drive did him good, and he was actually excited as he turned up the new entrance, which was still a dirt path, to the house. It was a stick frame, but it looked great. Something in his life was going in a positive direction.

Marisa couldn't think of anything else. She knew she was the coward when it came to her relationship with James, but her pride wouldn't allow herself to do anything about it. She wouldn't go against her brother's wishes. She had not contacted James, although she had started to several times.

Two days after James's departure Marisa interrupted her brother in his sleep. "Ernesto, are you asleep?"

"Not anymore, Marisa," Ernesto said. "What can I do for you? A nightmare like when you were little?"

"Sort of," Marisa said. "Not ever seeing James again is kind of like a recurring nightmare. Can I ask you something really personal?"

"I'm your brother, there's nothing you can't ask me," Ernesto said sitting up.

"Do you miss Gabriela?" Marisa asked.

Surprised by the question, Ernesto said, "Like I told you before, I miss the idea of Gabriela. A wife, family, the intimacy of a spouse as your closest friend and confidant. Gabriela the person? No, I guess I am over her."

"So far I am missing James both as the person and the idea," Marisa said. "How long does it take to stop missing the person?"

"Years maybe," Ernesto said. "I still miss mom and dad, and I don't expect that to ever go away. You need to start dating and find someone else to make miserable."

"Is that what I do?" Marisa asked almost in tears.

"No, not really," Ernesto said. "But sooner or later you have to open your heart to someone."

"How do I do that if I only have chards of my heart to offer?" Marisa said.

"I don't know how to put a heart back together," Ernesto said.

"All the President's horses and all the President's men couldn't put Humpty together again," Marisa said, now allowing her tears to succumb to the forces of gravity. "If you were me what would you do?"

"I tried to find Gabriela after she left, but that didn't work," Ernesto said. "I don't have an answer except to take each day as it comes and press forward. Time has a way of changing heartache into sweet memories. You will forget the difficult and painful moments and remember the wonderful events."

"Thanks for talking," Marisa said as she stood back up.

"You will sort this out," Ernesto said. "You are Marisa Starhemberg. She can do anything she puts her mind to."

Before she even got back to her own room, Marisa had figured out what she was going to do. It took her two more days to get her plans together. She got a large glossy picture of her brother from his personal secretary, a read-ahead copy of his next speech to be presented at the opening of the CamCon Headquarters in London in two weeks, and some key ingredients she would need for breakfast the day after tomorrow. The nice thing about being the President's sister, she could take all these things with her in a diplomatic pouch, although in this case it would be the diplomatic ice chest.

"I will not contact James," Marisa told herself, but James's request said nothing about meeting his family."

"Ernesto," Marisa interrupted as she walked in on him and Pepe Peralta Monti. "I am going to the United States, tonight."

"If you do me a favor, you can take the President's aircraft," was Ernesto's reply.

Startled, Maris asked, "What favor?"

"In three days I need you to meet with President Marcasano's National Security Advisor, along with Pepe. Pepe can handle the specific security concerns with Cambalache, but your scientific expertise will also be needed. You know better than anyone what could be said and what should not be said. We need the United States' help, but I don't want to give them Cambalache. Pepe was going to leave a day later than your plans demand. I trust you have a good reason to travel so soon and change Pepe's plans," President Starhemberg said.

"The best of reasons," Marisa said. "I am going to meet my future in-laws if they will have me."

"And your future husband, he has nothing to say in the matter?" Ernesto asked.

"None at all," Marisa announced. "I actually don't have plans to meet with him, and I have not contacted him as you demanded of me."

"I see," Ernesto said. "Are you sure about this? What if he isn't sure about this?"

"Then I will make him sure," Marisa said. "It's even clearer than what needed to be done to make Cambalache work. I have never been more certain of anything in my life."

"You know this is going to completely blow his anonymity," Ernesto said. The Kardashians may sue for taking the celebrity spotlight away from them. You might get rebuffed, on the public stage."

"Vulnerability has its drawbacks," Marisa said resolutely. Being an inmate of the invulnerability prison is no longer an option. Rejection is better than stamping out someone else's emotional license plates for even another month."

"I hope the warden lets you out on good behavior," Ernesto said. "The promise of future good behavior, that is. Your track record up to this point suggests the need for further rehabilitation."

"If you can also talk him into coming back to work with us, that would be great," Peralta Monti added.

"I am going to visit his family, not him," Marisa reminded them. "And if he thought I was pursuing him because we wanted him back on the Cambalache project, I would lose him and then you would lose me."

Marisa, Peralta Monti, and ten gallons of Via Flaminia ice cream departed that evening for Jefferson City, Missouri. President Starhemberg's office coordinated the visit with President Marcasano's office. President Marcasano deduced the situation and offered his assistance if he were needed. It turned out he was quite the romantic. Otto von Habsburg departed London three hours before Marisa.

It was muggy for six in the morning when Marisa's plane landed at the Jefferson City Memorial Airport. They had cleared customs at the Miami International Airport in the middle of the night. Marisa had tried to get some sleep, and she was worried she would look as exhausted as she felt when she visited James's family. Her plan was to wait for Otto to arrive and they would travel together. Otto arrived on the red eye regional flight from Atlanta at seven thirty. Marisa had been able to get another hour of sleep and felt better. Otto traveled ahead of Marisa in a separate vehicle. He arrived at the Nathaniels' home at eight fifteen, hoping everyone had not left the house for work already. It would turn out that everyone was there, except for James, who was getting an early start at this home site, preferring to work in the early hours before it got unbearably hot.

Otto was dressed in a suit and a ceremonial sash. He knocked on the door. It was answered by a young lady, perhaps 19 years old Otto guessed. "Would you be Jacey Nathaniels?" Otto asked.

"Um, yes," the young lady said.

Grateful he had guessed right, Otto continued. "May I have the pleasure of speaking with your family?"

"May I ask who you are and why you want to talk with us?" Jacey asked as she looked beyond Otto to see if there was a candid camera crew or some local friends playing some kind of joke.

"I am Otto von Habsburg, and I have come here from London to speak with the family of James Nathaniels. I can explain more when the family is assembled."

"Please, come in Mr. Habsburg," Jacey said. You are lucky you caught us at home, Oh, James is not here. He left over an hour ago."

"That is quite alright," Otto said. "I have actually come to speak to his family."

"Mom, Dad, Jessica," Jacey called out. "There is someone here to see us all." She turned to Otto and said, "Is James in trouble? He is a good person."

Otto chuckled, "That depends on your perspective, but thank you for the positive reference."

When everyone entered and were seated, Otto said, "As I shared with Jacey, my name is Otto von Habsburg."

"I know who you are," Jessica said in sudden awe. "You are the new Administrator of the Cambalache Confederation. Your grandfather was the crown Prince of the Austro-Hungarian Empire."

"Very good," Otto said. "You must be Jessica. Since you know who I am, I will skip the longer explanation of my presence. One of my ancestors, along with the help of a Starhemberg, negotiated the marriage of Marie Antoinette to King Louie XVI. I have been called into service for a similar action in alignment with another Starhemberg, but hopefully with a happier long-term ending." He paused as they all looked at each other. "I represent a member of the Royal House of Starhemberg who has asked me to negotiate for the betrothal of you son and brother, James."

"Is this some kind of joke?" James's dad asked. "James can speak for himself, and he hasn't mentioned a thing about meeting anyone, let alone being interested in anyone. He has been out of the country, and..."

"Yes, he has been working with me, the President of Argentina, and his sister, Marisa Starhemberg."

"He what?" Jessica asked. He hasn't said a word about this. Are you really who you say you are? I read that you were wounded by an assassin. Nearly died."

"I hope it wouldn't come to this," Otto said. "Very undignified." He took off his sash and his suit coat. He unbuttoned his white shirt and pulled the shirt off his right side. He displayed a very bruised, recovering wound. "I am here today in your living room because your son saved my life. He attacked my attacker without regard for his own life, a gun against a chair. Your son won, and I am alive."

"Why haven't we heard anything about this?" James's mother asked, suddenly concerned for her son.

"President Starhemberg and President Marcasano have asked that he keep his activities as anonymous as possible."

"Wait, President Marcasano, of the United States?" Jessica asked.

"Yes, just before arriving here at home he spent several days in consultation with President Marcasano, who also adds his endorsement to my meeting here today."

"You understand this is all a little hard to believe," James's father said. "Why the formality and beating around the bush. Like I said, James is a big boy; he can handle his own affairs."

"I agree, Mr. Nathaniels. As I have just highlighted, I am living proof of that fact." Otto pulled a phone out of his pocket and pressed one button and put it back in his pocket. "You have a unique son, Mr. Nathaniels. I have worked with some amazing people around the globe, and James is not only refreshing, but his mind is incredibly sharp, and he thinks things out like few anywhere. He can also keep a secret and maintain a meekness that is as uncommon as the story I am telling you. I am also the God Father of Marisa Starhemberg. Her parents were killed when she was twelve, and I have watched out for her interests ever since. In just a minute Marisa will arrive here. Her interest is to meet you and present herself to you."

"You still haven't gotten to the point Mr. Habsburg," James's father said.

"Like father like son," Otto said smiling. "James and Marisa have been working closely together on the Cambalache rollout. Perhaps you heard some of President Starhemberg's speech at the United Nations. Many of those words were from James. I digress again. A European habit. James is in love with Marisa, and as it turns out, she is in love with him. She was not able to express that love for fear of her situation as the Starhemberg sister and her own habits of keeping all men at arm's length. James left our project early for fear of not being able to work in such close quarters with Marisa day in, day out. James asked that we not try to get him back on the Cambalache project or to contact him as it was time for Marisa and James both to move on."

"Now we're talking about my dumb brother that I recognize," Jacey said. "I could punch him."

"At some point that may be required, Jacey," Otto said with a smile. "This is not part of the script," Otto said, leaning in. "Marisa is an amazing young lady. I will leave it to you to discover her many talents and charms. She is brave beyond measure, but she is scared to death to meet you for fear of being rejected. Please treat her kindly. She very well could be rejected today and have to go to Washington DC for further meetings with President Marcasano with that public humiliation. She asked me to offer a few gifts to soften her abrupt injection of her crazy life into yours. For Jacey, I offer a signed photo of President Ernesto Starhemberg and a promise of a dance at any event in which the two of you might attend together. Jessica, this is a draft copy of the speech President Starhemberg will present in just short of two weeks at the official opening of the CamCon headquarters. He welcomes any comments or thoughts you might have. The event will take place in London and you are invited. CamCon will pay for your travel of course, but don't feel obligated if you have other plans. Mr. and Mrs. Nathaniels, I offer you my service if there is anything I can do for you. I would like to invite you to my country estate in Hungary at your convenience. I would be honored to get to know the parents of James Nathaniels. Please don't think of these little gifts as bribes, they absolutely are not. They are bridges to understanding I hope and tokens of gratefulness from myself and the Starhembergs for getting to know your brother and son." Standing, Otto added, "Now I have a reservation to visit Westminster College in Fulton where Sir Winston Churchill gave his famous Iron Curtain speech. He spoke warmly of Fulton to me and of course, the event that he speaks of, the Iron Curtain, significantly altered the lives of many in my family. The Argentine National Security Advisor is waiting for me. Marisa will provide my private contact information. Thank you for your time, and I apologize for barging in on your tranquil morning."

As soon as the dust had settled from Otto's departure, Marisa drove up. She had a single security person with her. He waited outside with the car. The Nathaniels had hardly talked during the interim. Jacey ran to the door and met Marisa before she could knock. "Hi, I'm Jacey, James's baby sister," Jacey said. "You are even more beautiful in person than your pictures. Come on in. She whispered to her dad as she walked by, quite a looker."

"Thank you, Jacey," Marisa said with an accent.

Marisa shook hands with each member of the Nathaniels family, and Jacey gave her a hug. "I am sorry to interrupt your day, but I couldn't wait another minute to set things straight between James and me. I asked Otto to do the introductions as he is as close to a father as I have. I asked him to keep it simple, but knowing Uncle Otto, I am sure he got you as mixed up as he did explaining things. I don't know what the silly celebrity magazines say about me, I don't read them, but I wanted to come and meet you and let you decide for yourself. I can leave and come back at a more convenient time if that would be better for you. I thought about calling ahead but was afraid James would make sure everyone was out of the house on errands or something. None of that would be his fault. I have earned it."

She stood in silence, placing herself on the altar of this family's decisions. They stood in silence for just a moment longer than what was socially comfortable. Marisa was about to turn and run when James's mom reached out and embraced her. Marisa melted in her arms.

By the time James pulled up in the driveway Marisa had told James's family about her growing up years, schooling, her brother, Argentina, and Uncle Otto. They had shared every embarrassing James story they could think of. They were laughing in the living room when James walked in.

"Whose car is in the driveway and why is everybody still home?" he asked. Then he saw Marisa. "Marisa, you're here,"

"I told you he was kind of dumb," Jacey said.

"Santi," Marisa said, switching into rapid-fire Argentine Castellano. "I came because I couldn't stay where I was. I followed your wishes and didn't contact you. But I am trying to be vulnerable and have introduced myself and all my shortcomings to your family. I am not here to get you back to the Cambalache Project, but if it is not too late, I am here to get you back in my life."

"Marisa, you are the only thing I think of, day and night. Even so, if this can't go any further, I am willing to stop things right here, even with you here. If I can't live with you, I have to figure out a way to live without you. I can't live in your shadow."

"Do you love me?" Marisa asked.

"I do," James said. "I always will, no matter how you feel about me."

"Good, you are very wise," Marisa said. "I am worth loving, I hope. I plan to dedicate the rest of my life proving that to you."

"What are you saying, Marisa?" James asked.

"Your sister is right, you are dumb," Marisa said. "I love you, Santi, and I came here, to prove that to you. So did Otto, you just missed him."

"I don't want to marry Otto, Marisa," James said.

"Good," Marisa said. "I already tried that, and it didn't work. We are stuck together."

Switching to English James said to his family who wasn't following the conversation, "Mom, Dad, this is Marisa."

"Well, duh Einstein," Jacey said. "We probably know her better than you do. We are considering adopting her and selling you to the Gypsies."

"They wouldn't take him," Marisa said. "But I will, for pity's sake. I will." With that last statement, there was a sudden bolt of emotional lighting that everyone in the room felt. Marisa stood and walked to James, still not sure what he would do and kissed him passionately on the lips.

It was James's turn to melt, in Marisa's arms. James was beginning to tear up, and Marisa could not stop smiling enough to pucker for another kiss.

"Get a room," Jacey said.

James's mother threw a couch pillow at Jacey. They all stood up and had a big family hug. Although a natural thing for the Nathaniels, Marisa was overwhelmed having never experienced this before. She felt home for the first time since she was twelve.

"Meetings with the North Americans may be a passing of the baton and a weakening of the Starhemberg/Habsburg hold on Cambalache. I will get a full picture when Marisa Starhemberg returns." JOAB/Americas Prelate

With the death of the Guardian, JOAB was unsure of directives and plans status that the previous Guardian had coordinated. As a prelate, the door was wide open because some plans were now initiated at this level. 'What should the next move be?'

CHAPTER 22

Ser Gardel
Literal Translation: To be Gardel, the
World-Famous Tango Singer

Marisa's Explanation: When you become who you want to become and you don't feel the need to become anything more. **You are Gardel when you achieve your most desired goal, when you've attained the supreme level of achievement**. Ernesto says that of me, but I still feel mostly like a theme in one of Gardel's tangos.

"**D**ULCE DE LECHE ICE CREAM! This is a more important Argentine invention than cold fusion," Jacey announced. "This reminds me of our first date," James said as he placed a spoonful in his mouth with his eyes closed.

"That is why I brought it," Marisa said, rolling her eyes for Jessica and Jacey to see. "I thought I might need to bribe you into listening to me. I didn't know what to expect." Suddenly tears welled up in Marisa's eyes, and she turned her head, embarrassed.

"Did Marisa tell you that the first time she met me she wanted to kill me?" James said to lighten the moment. "I mean literally kill me? Her brother saved my life. And now, Marisa, you have saved my life." The lightening moment came and went quickly as everyone in the room felt the emotional surge once again. James took a breath and spoke as he tried to regain control of his voice. "Then she explained the "For Dummies" version of nuclear fusion. It is a miracle that such a beautiful face can house such a smart mind."

"Not a thought in her head is what some have said about you," Jacey stated, glancing with a smile at her dad. "How do you handle all the attention?"

"It's been a local thing in Argentina for years since Ernesto became a Provincial Governor," Marisa said, glad for the shift to another topic. "Since Cambalache, however, it has been ridiculous. I smile at someone, and all of the sudden the magazines are reporting our volatile romance and that it will never last. That James has been kept from that has been a blessing for both of us."

As if on cue, there was a knock at the door. The single man security detail was the first to stand. He had stationed himself by the door and looked to Mr. Nathaniels whether he should answer it. "Thank you, Paco," Mr. Nathaniels said. "I'll get it. Probably an Amazon delivery for Jacey." He opened the door, and a camera took his picture. A camera crew and satellite TV van filled his front yard. Two more cars were pulling up to the house. Their quiet residential neighborhood was being invaded.

"What is going on?" Mr. Nathaniels asked the reporter on the porch.

"We understand Ms. Marisa Starhemberg is visiting. Are you family friends, or are you connected with the family in some other way? You are Mr. Nathaniels I presume? Does your work at the local Farm Credit Bureau connect you with the financial challenges caused by the Starhemberg announcement of free energy?" The questions kept coming faster than a politician offers excuses. Nathaniels had an earful.

"Take a breath young man, or you are going to faint," Mr. Nathaniels said chuckling. "It must be a slow news day. We have nothing to share with you, so you made the drive for nothing."

He was about to close the door when he felt a hand on his shoulder. He turned to see Marisa standing there.

"Let me give them something, and hopefully they will go away," she said. She turned to the door, and the voices outside increased in volume. Paco stepped outside and scanned the crowd, then nodded.

Marisa stepped out onto the porch and smiled and waved. Jacey followed her out with two gallons of dulce de leche ice cream and enough paper bowls and plastic spoons for all the visitors. "You are just in time for some Argentine ice cream," Marisa began. "You came for a news scoop, and you will get a scoop of some of the best refreshment on earth. This is your lucky day." People still called out some questions, but the oddity of the situation put many off guard. Jacey and Marisa were smiling, laughing, scooping, and passing out the bowls. With most everyone taking and then tasting the ice cream they were clamoring less and almost in a listening mode.

"So thanks for welcoming me to Middle America," Marisa said. "I've been to a few great North American cities, but nothing as special as this. I am only here for the day so I would appreciate it I could enjoy it with my friends the Nathaniels. Jacey and I have become good friends after she expressed interest in my brother and his efforts to bring free energy to the world. Not much news here, though. Sorry. If I discover anti-gravity or something newsworthy before I leave, I will be sure to give you a call."

Jacey got into the game and added, "Thanks everyone for taking the time out of your important and busy day to drop by. I hope you enjoyed the ice cream as much as we did. Just set your bowls and spoons on the porch, and I will clean it up later."

Jacey and Marisa waved at everyone, who were nearly silenced by the quick turn of events once again and dutifully began collecting the paper bowls. The mood was quickly broken by reporters who were announcing the impromptu ice cream social with one of the nicest celebrities on the planet. One or two reporters still called out questions, but unexpectedly most everyone felt like they had achieved their goals and were happily packing up their equipment. The local police arrived and accelerated the news teams' departures. Except for a few neighbors who were now in their yards wondering what had just happened, it was once again a quiet residential neighborhood.

"Jacey, you're a natural," Marisa said.

"It was your idea, I just followed your lead," Jacey said.

"Actually it was James's idea," Marisa said. "He whispered to me, "give them something unexpected, like ice cream from a distant land, and they will feel special and report that as a newsworthy event. So I did."

"As clichéd as it sounds," James said, "I wondered what your brother would do in this situation, Marisa. He would have shared a good time with people just doing their job—even if it at first is inconvenient and frustrating. His abundance mentality is infectious. We don't have to lose for them to win, or vice versa. And I guarantee you they are going to do an internet search on Argentine ice cream before the day is done."

"It won't keep them away long," Mr. Nathaniels said. They got a story, but not THE story. That will sink in at any moment. Why don't the four of you run up to James's property and show it to Marisa. Mom and I will get back to our regular lives and give them nothing to report. Paco, I can't tell you what to do, but you could follow them, stay here, or go fishing."

"Fishing would be my choice, but my duty is to protect the Señorita Starhemberg. I will follow," Paco said shaking Mr. Nathaniels' hand. "I have no jurisdiction here, but I can still be your first line of defense. No offense, please, but I will feel better when we are gone from here. With anonymity we were safe. Now we are a worm on the line and the big fish could come anytime."

"Marisa, what is your plan now?" Mrs. Nathaniels asked. "Are we going to get to see you again before you leave?"

"To be honest I haven't thought this through beyond trying to get James back in my life," Marisa said. I don't need to leave until tomorrow afternoon, but I don't want to completely disrupt your world for my selfishness."

"Well, I am feeling sorry for Paco," Mr. Nathaniels said. "I've got a better idea. Here is what we do. I will go close out a few lose items at work—should take me about an hour. Sweetheart, you grab some clothes, essentials and go pick up some groceries for the next two days. Jessica, you take the rest of the family to James's place, but don't stay too long. Who knows what investigative reporter will discover the land and send a news crew there. Your land James is the opposite direction from the cabin, so if anyone sees you leave, they will be thinking north. I'm thinking we should rendezvous there in about two hours. There is only one way in and out, which might not be the greatest option for serious security, but the best to keep away news and paparazzi people. It will take some time for them to figure out we might be at our cabin and with some local police help we might be able to keep the access point controlled. And the best news is, the bass should be biting by this afternoon. What do you think Paco?"

"A better option than staying here," he said.

"I like it," James said. "I want Marisa to get as much time with all of you as possible."

"I'm in," Marisa said. "You won me over when you said, "Jessica, you take the rest of the family to James's place." I didn't catch much after that because I don't ever remember hearing those words or anything close to it in my whole life." That caused another round of hugs and then goodbyes.

The visit to James's property was inspiring for Marisa. She was used to beauty, growing up in Bariloche, but the independence of simply buying land and building on it with your own hands was outside of her life's expectation. "So this is what a family is like," Marisa said as she grabbed James's arm.

"Something I almost forgot," James said. "And our extended family is just as fun. More diverse and crazy, but just as fun."

They loaded up one more time and drove the hour south to the cabin. "This isn't Bariloche or even Calafate, Marisa, but we have had some wonderful times at this place," James said, trying to prepare her for the rustic place they called the cabin.

When Marisa first saw the Lake of the Ozarks as they pulled off the highway, it took her breath away. "It is so big and majestic. It is a different color blue than Nahuel Huapi Lake."

"It's fed by the Osage River and a bunch of creeks, not snow runoff," James said. "It has nearly 1,200 miles of shoreline, and we own our little peninsula—maybe 500 meters of that shoreline. My favorite boyhood memories were here."

"Are here," Marisa said. "Your memories always live in the present, not the future or the past. I had to learn that at an early age. Let's go make some new memories."

The stay at the lake cabin was glorious. It was like a new place for the Nathaniels because it was a first time for Marisa and for Paco who everyone automatically treated as one of the family. James's dad had a listening ear for his too often told fish stories, although the Nathaniels siblings pointed out that he often added new elements and bigger fish to the stories. So they were, in fact, new stories, but that was the only fact about them. The Nathaniels had a small boat for fishing and water skiing but hadn't brought it for fear that its absence might tip off someone really looking to their possible whereabouts. They still enjoyed the water, swimming, and fishing from the shore. They had a campfire and introduced Marisa to the epicurean delight of s'mores. They sang silly camp songs from their youth and Marisa sang an Andes folksong.

No one interrupted the 24 hours at the cabin, the *Cabin 24* as Marisa referenced it later. It was a brief interlude of peace, laughter, and family intimacy. Something James had forgotten. Something Marisa had never experienced. Something the Nathaniels had polished to a soft, warm glow.

"The thing about 24 hours," Marisa lamented on her last walk with Jacey and Jessica along the lake shore, "it's a full cycle. There's a beginning and an end. It's enough time to pack a lifetime into for a mayfly. So we shouldn't complain. But it's so short. It's 100,000 heartbeats, but only one day, one global pirouette. It's hardly a dance or a full performance. I've always felt a little melancholy when I've had to give up the day."

Jessica, in the lead on the narrow trail, turned and gave Marisa a hug. "You have helped us pack a lifetime into this day. James is the luckiest man alive, but we come in a close second in getting to know you and hoping to have many more heartbeats with you. I don't want to make any presumptions for you and James, but you are family, Marisa, our big sister. Whatever we can do, whenever, we are there."

"I honestly don't know what you see in, James," Jacey added. "Don't get me wrong, he is a pretty good big brother, but a saint, no way. But forget I said that because I want you to think he is the greatest guy alive so you will marry him and we can really be sisters."

Marisa saw Jacey's lower lip start to quiver and her struggle to keep her emotions in check. "How am I going to leave today?" Marisa asked them both. "That's another thing about a day. It is short enough that I always think it is a reasonable request for just one more. I will never take another day for granted, and I will pray for the day we can be together again. I won't make a promise as to when that day will come, but it will come."

"Make one promise for me," Jessica said looking into Marisa's eyes. "Take care of our big brother. He seems like he can take care of himself, but he can't. He can work really hard and accomplish a lot of things, but he is still so clueless about life. Far from stopping to smell the roses, he doesn't even know how to plant seeds and then help them to grow. You are making him into a gardener, and I never thought I would see that."

"I am no gardener myself," Marisa said. "We are learning together. We are learning from some master gardeners. Oh my goodness, the men you will let into your lives—they are the luckiest men alive. You keep me informed in that department! I will send Paco to interview them."

James had agreed to accompany Marisa back to Argentina, via Washington, D.C. They would sort things out along the way. He had turned his sprawling house project back over to his sisters and they in-turn had brought Marisa into their confidential plans and summarily banished James from any involvement except paying the bills. Everyone traveled to the airport, where they met up with Otto and Pepe Peralta Monti. Pepe made a special effort, probably at Otto's coaxing, to talk with Jessica about President Starhemberg's upcoming speech.

It is hard to hide a large aircraft, and as soon as the media had realized that there were celebrities in the local area, they had stationed a few cub reporters at the airport to warn of the guests' departure. More than one editor was pulling their hair out that these high profile visitors had just vanished. Within minutes of the Nathaniels' and Marisa's arrival, four news agencies and three television crews were threatening to commandeer the private goodbyes.

"May I suggest we retreat to the aircraft to say our final goodbyes?" Otto said. "I am sorry we will leave you with such a mess to clean up once we are gone."

They all began to follow Paco to a security door. Marisa stopped and said, "No, I am not leaving this way." She turned and marched into the crowd of frenzied media and others from the airport who were wondering what was going on. Jumping up onto the first seat of a row of plastic seats Marisa addressed the crowd. "I apologize for not bringing more ice cream to the party, but thank you for coming to see us off." The media crowd laughed, but only for a brief moment and then began shouting questions at her.

Marisa held up her hands and then started to talk again in a conversational voice. Everyone quieted to hear. "I have just spent an incredible 24 hours with dear friends. Thank you for allowing that to happen. I hope to return here many times, so I want to make a deal with you. I promise that if you are still interested in my visits in the future, you will all be invited for ice cream in the summer and Argentine hot chocolate if it is winter, and you can ask any questions you want. I promise open and honest answers. In turn, I would ask that you display the same constraint as you have during this visit. If we can work that out, then you will be seeing a lot of me and will probably quickly tire of me. If we can't work that out, then you will probably never see me again. I know you can't speak for everyone, especially the paparazzi, but you can do your best, and I promise to do my best. Now, do we have a deal?"

Marisa scanned the crowd as one reporter started yelling out questions. To everyone's surprise, another reporter turned to him and said, "It's time to listen. Shut up." This same person turned back to Marisa and said, "Deal, Señorita Starhemberg."

Marisa smiled at him and said, "You can call me Marisa. What's your name?"

"Um, Don," the stunned reporter replied.

"That means gift in Spanish," Marisa said. "You are a gift with your good manners, and so I will give you a gift in return. Ask me any question, and I will give you my honest answer."

"Thank you, Marisa," Don said, recovering his reporter composure. "I would love to ask you about why you are here, but I hope to see you again, and I am sure the answer to that question will become apparent. I am also married, so I won't pop that question." Everyone laughed and were enjoying this oddest of news conferences. "You are traveling with the President of Argentina's aircraft. Is that for your personal use or are you in the United States on business?"

"Tell your wife she is a lucky woman, Don," Marisa said. "Someone told me to never answer the unasked question to a reporter, but I want to do this differently as you can see. To answer that unasked question, I came here to be with my boyfriend and his family. I will let you connect the dots. I never use the property of Argentina for personal use. I am actually accompanying the Argentine National Security Advisor to the President, and our next stop is Washington, D.C. to meet with government officials. I am also here with a close family friend; Otto von Habsburg who as you know is also the Cambalache Confederation Administrator. He was family friends with Winston Churchill and had always wanted to visit Westminster College in Fulton of which Sir Churchill spoke so fondly. I would introduce you to Otto, but as you might have heard, there was a recent attempt on his life, and he is just a little camera shy right now."

"Just a minute, Marisa," a voice behind the crowd said.

Everyone turned to see who had spoken and interrupted the mood of the meeting. "You can't let me off the hook that easily. I am Otto, as Marisa explained. If Winston Churchill could travel here and share perhaps the most important post-World War Two speech in history, I can certainly offer my humble services to the good people of Jefferson City. I might also want to visit in the future and with security a constant challenge, I would like to know you have got my back, sort of speaking. If anyone would like to ask me a question, please do."

There was a brief pause, as no one was quite prepared for this turn of events. "Are you married?" a cute female reporter called out.

"Ah, the big question," Otto said. "Since we are all friends here, I will tell you that Marisa proposed to me when she was a young girl. I turned her down, considering our extreme age difference and preferring to be her unofficial uncle, but I have yet to find a woman to match her. I hold out hope still that this woman exists. Thank you for asking. Maybe this will help get the word out there that I am still looking."

"It sounds like your Camba-thing Confederation wants to take over the world and get rid of countries, countries like the United States. Is that your plan?" another reporter asked.

"Cambalache, just call it CamCon. I do," Otto replied. "Excellent question and the biggest misconception of our goals. CamCon is only a vehicle to bring order to and manage what will soon become as ubiquitous and free as the air we breathe. That is a beautiful thing, but it has its baggage. In less than two weeks, President Starhemberg will travel to London for the inauguration of CamCon and the grand opening of its new world headquarters. I learned long ago to never steal the thunder of a politician so I will be circumspect with my answer. The nations of the world have nothing to fear from CamCon. Indeed they will be bolstered by the organization I represent. I expect the President's speech to outline these aspects of the Confederation. Yet it is a confederation and will have the combined, but limited power of its members. CamCon will not have any standing military, only defensive security forces. CamCon will tax its members, but only for maintenance of electricity delivery. I don't' have all the answers of how CamCon will operate. That will primarily be in the hands of the Confederation members. In the short-term, I will be the chief administrator, but that role will probably shift to an elected position if the members so desire."

Otto bowed slightly and turned to the Nathaniels as if he was at a cocktail party and turned to a different circle of friends, having completed the conversation with the circle of other acquaintances. Marisa stepped down from the chair and shook hands with anyone who wished to and allowed them to take selfies with her. She then walked, unhampered to the Nathaniels. They all walked to the aircraft.

"That was crazy," James said. "I have never seen anything like that, and I have been to my share of media events."

"Ernesto's abundance perspective," Marisa said. "Just like you I asked, what would Ernesto do if he were in this situation? He would be authentic, make some friends, and invest in the future. I really do hope to visit here often. With or without you. Jacey has promised to teach me how to cook your favorite pie, although first I have to find out what Rhubarb is. The name doesn't sound very appetizing for a pie."

The Nathaniels got a quick tour of the Argentine President's aircraft and then steeled themselves for a different life then they had enjoyed just a day ago. "No turning back," Mr. Nathaniels announced as the family was escorted back to the airport terminal. The group hugs, a few tears, and more hugs and kisses were now events of the immediate past. The present felt formidable. The aircraft departed on schedule for Dulles International Airport. The terminal was empty of any media when the Nathaniels re-entered.

Like the new Americas Prelate, the BAJO operative unknown to the Prelate was at first shocked by the suddenness of the death of the old Guardian but then saw this change as the great opportunity long planned for. Time to put plans into action. "I could be the new Guardian within a month. First step, recruit the Buenos Aires JOAB, then find out who the new Guardian is. If all has gone according to plan, it is that incompetent milksop Rosado. That means there is also probably a new

Americas Prelate to deal with. First things first, a test of loyalties—get JOAB to frame Nathaniels.

BAJO CHAPTER 5

"**H**AVE YOU EVER READ THE novel *Waiting for Godot*?" the Guardian, now David Rosado's nom de protecteur de la société, asked the New Americas Prelate. They were meeting in Buenos Aires as the new Prelate had a "day job" that precluded travel to France at the moment. Responsibility and accountability was the topic. Rosado was hoping he was getting through to this new Prelate. Not only was he trying to help this new prelate think deeper about the BAJO mission, but also about the justifiable actions of a prelate. "Some say *Waiting for Godot*, others answer with the question *Who is John Galt?*" the Guardian said. "Both Galt and Godot are fictitious, even mythical characters, who are absent from the works they inspire, or almost absent. Their presence just offstage cast powerful shadows. In each case, the reader has to wait for Galt to reveal himself, or decide who Godot is. Galt is unflinching in his values and use of a rational mind. Godot is a ghost who apparently has no values or at least does not value showing up. In *Atlas Shrugged* there are four main characters, besides Galt. In *Waiting for Godot*, there are four main characters besides Godot. The four characters of each work could not be different. With all the hints at small similarities and obvious dissimilarities, they answer the same question. Who should govern? Free will vs. naturalism/ determinism… Dostoevsky vs. Tolstoy; in the case of these works, Rand vs. Beckett. Galt vs. Godot…

"I still don't see the connection to royalty and its right to rule," the new Prelate interjected.

"Ah, but you just answered your own question," the Guardian said. "Right to rule you said, not merely will to rule, or access to rule. Most of western society since the 18th century accepts one of the several forms of supernaturalism; that is, they believe that we have "free will" which causes events in the natural world. Of course, there are different forms of teleonaturalism that range from a hybrid form of determinism such as our more fatalistic Muslim brothers to the varying enlightenment thinkers such as Locke, Mills, Hobbs, and Rousseau. And most of us defend our "free will" without considering the consequences.

"The consequences of acting on free will?" the Prelate asked.

"Not exactly," the Guardian said. "The consequences of believing in free will. Where does that leave mankind?"

"Responsibility!" the Prelate said, suddenly understanding. "With free will comes responsibility. One cannot shift the culpability of their actions to someone else."

"Edmund Burke stated that we must adhere to the social and political institutions to find the "good," the Guardian explained. "If a society doesn't follow the natural order, it will decay. He was, of course, commenting on the chaos of the French Revolution and the overthrow of the Bourbon dynasty. He might have made a good JOAB. Burke believed in a natural aristocracy that defines and leads the nation. The aristocracy must do what is best for the people because they know what is best. If leaders don't follow their superior instincts, society will collapse. The reason corruption occurs is because aristocratic society itself is corrupt. Religion is crucial for public virtue, for the aristocracy and the masses. And then there is the sovereign.

"So, simply put," the Prelate summarized, "royalty exists, and will be called upon once again when the time is right, to take responsibility. Naturalism alone lets mankind off the hook. Free will on its own leads to chaos and anarchy."

"Exactly," the Guardian said. "Now enough of the philosophical side of our mission. What are your plans concerning the Starhemberg situation? I have not contacted the other JOAB that was working directly for the previous Guardian." In reality, David did not know who this other JOAB was. He hoped to solve this mystery soon. "Once I do I will pass that name on to you for your consideration." David was not at all happy that another JOAB was working in his previous prelature without his knowledge, but with his new expanded perspective, he was trying to understand and justify why such a thing could happen.

CHAPTER 23

Hacer Algo de Cayetano
Literal Translation: To do something
silently or without telling anyone

Marisa's Explanation: If you have the pleasure of visiting Argentina and a friend of yours asks you to do something "de cayetano," ¡Ojo! That doesn't mean you have to become the patron saint of work, gamblers and the unemployed San Cayetano. Nor do you have to march in the religious parade on August 7. **"De cayetano" means "silent" or "without telling anyone,"** like a gambler who might want to keep a secret. So, if you're Calle Florida and you find a Sarmiento banknote, about $50, pick it up, but "de cayetano…"

"**M**R. PRESIDENT," A MILITARY OFFICER said with some urgency in his voice, "may I speak with you for a moment?"

"Excuse me, Marisa," President Tony Marcasano said. James, Marisa, and Pepe Peralta Monti had spent the last half hour with the President of the United States. They had completed their meetings with the U.S. National Security Council staff and three officers assigned from J-7 of the Joint Staff across the Potomac River at the Pentagon. It had been a grueling three days, but support plans were in place and several assets already active. The three were planning on departing for Argentina that evening.

"Could the three of you follow me?" President Marcasano asked. "There is something you need to see." The President had turned from friendly politician to Commander-In-Chief. The group followed the President down a hallway to an elevator, and it descended to another brightly lit hallway. The sign on the door announced, "White House Situation Room." The group was instructed to leave their cell phones in a lead box and they were asked to take specific seats around a table.

Without preamble, the President said, "This is a live feed of one of our satellite assets over the Cambalache facilities."

All heads turned to the center screen, and a color picture came into focus. "There is a group of what appears to be 12 insurgents moving toward the Cambalache Project," a middle-aged woman in a blue Air Force uniform began without introduction. "They arrived on the island three minutes ago by fast Zodiac boats, coming from a direction opposite the town of Bariloche. We don't know who they are, or where they came from. We only started monitoring the island a few hours ago, after the agreement protocols were in place. They are armed and are carrying backpacks and other unidentified equipment."

"Have you contacted the security forces assigned at Cambalache?" Pepe Peralta Monti asked?

"Yes," the officer said. "We contacted them the same time we notified President Marcasano. Secure communications were immediately established and just like the only practice drill we've run, everything worked perfectly." The officer nodded to someone unseen to the group in the Situation Room, and voices were immediately heard in Spanish. "Take your perimeter position on the left flank and keep out of sight. Let's not spook them," someone on the ground whispered.

"Your security forces are receiving the same feed from our satellite at their headquarters on the island. We are also delivering this feed to your military command center in Buenos Aires," the officer said.

"Is my brother connected yet?" Marisa asked.

"If you are talking about President Starhemberg, we don't know mam," the officer replied. "We don't have insight into your local protocols or where your President would go to view this information. It appears the local commander on the island is running the defensive operation at this point."

The live video feed zoomed in on the group of insurgents. The picture was slightly grainy, but the tiny moving forms became people. James was amazed at the quality of the feed and even more surprised that he and two Argentines were being allowed to see this. President Marcasano was in quiet conversation with the military person that had interrupted the meeting upstairs. The conversation concluded, and the President turned to the group and said, "There are days when it's good to be the President,"

He walked back to the front of the room and continued, "The United States has an asset that will be overhead your Cambalache location within the next fifteen minutes. I won't say what or how, but I can allow you to view the fruits of this asset if you are willing to keep it completely confidential. That means you will not speak of this to anyone outside of this room. Are you willing to abide by that stipulation?"

"Not even to President Starhemberg?" Pepe Peralta Monti asked.

"He knows about it, but that has been between just the two of us," President Marcasano said. He will not actually get to see the system in action if it is deployed. We will black out the feed for the 30 to 45 seconds during the actual operation. You will be able to see it here, however."

Each agreed to the terms verbally, and James was again amazed, this time that no paperwork, like signing a nondisclosure agreement, was included. Everyone returned to watching the main screen. Suddenly, even to those watching this from the satellite's vantage point, there was an exchange of fire. The insurgents appeared surprised and retreated slightly, but didn't leave the fight. Presently there were only six Argentine Special Forces troops, commandos from the Rapid Deployment Force at Campo de Mayo in Buenos Aires that had been positioned only two weeks ago the group knew, defending a large area and a numerically superior force.

The insurgents reformed and attacked, using much stronger firepower. "Looks like they brought Carl-Gustaf with them," another man in the situation room said. "Anti-tank, anti-personnel weapon," he clarified for others in the chamber. "Serious firepower, six rounds a minute, 1,700-meter range."

The chatter on the radio increased and then went silent. The Argentine Commandos spread out even more, and the insurgents moved forward slowly.

"Asset in place," a person announced in the White House Situation Room. "Seven minutes earlier than expected. It happened to be already airborne and in the local area—flying a training sortie over the Caribbean."

"That's the local area?" Peralta Monti asked out loud.

"The asset is designed to be overhead any location on earth within one hour," President Marcasano said matter-of-factly. "Now comes the fun part."

On cue, individual insurgents glowed and fell, one after the other. "In the old days, a President would sit in this very room and watch the destruction of buildings in order to stop one bad guy. The asset was typically a Predator drone. So far, none of the insurgents we are monitoring here have died. Just tasered from the sky; temporarily incapacitated. Gone are the days of trying to kill a fly with a sledge hammer."

Mesmerized, Marisa called out, "Uh oh, watch out for that guy," pointing to the screen. One insurgent had broken the invisible commando perimeter line, and was moving toward the entrance for Cambalache. Without warning, the insurgent lit up and then fell to the ground.

"And sometimes it is not as fun to be the President," Marcasano said. "That man just died. Laser instead of taser. Sad whenever there is a loss of life."

"And the Lord's anger burned against Uzzah because of his irreverent act; therefore God struck him down, and he died there beside the ark of God," James said mostly to himself.

"Old Testament?" President Marcasano asked.

"Yes, sir," James said. "Sunday School lesson on the Ark of the Covenant."

"It does feel like this is just a movie sometimes," the President said. "I had never thought of it like that old Harrison Ford movie, but it fits today." After a pause, he continued, "And I guess the show is mostly over. You will probably know before we will who these people are and what their ultimate goal was. Just know that we've got your back."

On the flight back to Argentina James was amazed for the fourth time in less than 24 hours. The security guard on the flight arrested him and handcuffed him to his seat. He could see Marisa crying, but she was not allowed to come close to him. Pepe Peralta Monti was also angry, but he was also not allowed to communicate with James.

Upon arriving at Ezeiza Airport James was loaded into a windowless van and whisked away. Pepe and Marisa went straight to the Quinta de Olivos to see President Ernesto Starhemberg. It was nearly five in the morning when they entered the President's home. He was up and waiting for them.

"What is going on, Ernesto?" Marisa asked with fire in her eyes.

Some serious allegations have been made by Federal Police Intelligence," President Starhemberg said. "They have evidence that James has not been entirely honest with us. In fact, the recent attack on the Cambalache Project happened in part because of information he allegedly passed on to who knows who."

"What information?" Marisa asked. "What proof?"

"Contacts through IMF channels to Venezuela and Russia," President Starhemberg said. "Mostly emails and some written materials. I am as shocked and doubtful as you, Marisa. But it is pretty substantial evidence. I couldn't take any chances. Cambalache is bigger than any person or relationship."

"I want to see this so-called evidence," Marisa said.

"You are my sister, but I can't show you the evidence," President Starhemberg said. "It is still being analyzed, and we have to keep our personal feelings out of this. There is also the appearance of any favoritism we must avoid."

"But I do want to show favoritism," Marisa said with a raised voice. "He is innocent, and of all people, we need to stand by him."

"Of all people, I cannot stand by him, Marisa," President Starhemberg said. "I will stand by justice and truth. I will stand by the office I have been elected to uphold. I have faith in the system. If he is innocent, we will find out soon enough."

"Guilty until proven innocent?" Marisa asked, yelling now. "That sounds like the practice during the Dirty War, Ernesto. Shame on you!"

"If it were anyone else," President Starhemberg said. "But we have let this foreigner into the very core of our government."

"And I have let him into the very core of my heart," Marisa said. "That connection tells me he is innocent, Period."

"We will know soon enough," President Starhemberg said.

"In the meantime, our dear friend and supporter of Argentina and Cambalache, savior of Otto, rots in some jail cell, wondering where his friends are.

"And in the meantime," President Starhemberg said, turning to Pepe, "there have been riots in Nigeria and Venezuela, continued border skirmishes that have expanded in the Middle East—now with the United Arab Emirates, and we are getting word that the Saudi King may have been assassinated. Russia is rattling its saber. International media is tying all these events back to Cambalache." Looking at Marisa again he added, "On top of that I have preparations to make for the CamCon speech and my run for a second term. I have a lot on my plate right now, Marisa."

"Vangelina," Marisa said after she was out of the President's office, "I want to know what is going on with these ridiculous charges pointing to James Nathaniels as some kind of secret agent or something."

"I am on your security detail," Vangelina said. "I don't get involved in all of that and they wouldn't tell me a thing if I asked."

"Well, if you hear anything," Marisa said even more frustrated, "please let me know."

"This is going to sound harsh, Norisa," Vangelina said, using Marisa's nickname, "but these kinds of things are not issues to get involved in. It might harm the situation more than help it. It could look like you are tampering with an investigation. Besides, he is a foreigner, and I have never fully trusted him."

Marisa said nothing more about the matter to anyone connected with her brother. Using her well-known status as the President's sister, Marisa contacted a friend deeply involved with the Madres de la Plaza de Mayo. Historically, this organization had been an enemy of the government, and with good reason. Their goal was to find the children and grandchildren of parents who had "disappeared during the Dirty War. Since 2006, however, they had stopped their marches of resistance and worked to forge ties with the government. "I need some help on a very sensitive topic," Marisa explained. "Can you help me gather some information in strict confidence, both publicly and within the government?

"Sister, you have come to the right place," her friend said. "Let's meet, and you can explain your project to me and I will tell you what we can and can't do."

Marisa and her friend met at an office inside the Basílica de San Francisco, less than two blocks from the Casa Rosada. Marisa often used this Basilica office for non-governmental meetings for the various social programs she was involved with. "When you're not inventing cold fusion," her brother would add.

Marisa explained the situation, leaving out the romance but noting she had worked with him nearly every waking hour for the last two months. "I don't think he is involved in anything wrong and I need to prove it before those looking for promotion justifications can construct a case otherwise. There are forces against Cambalache or CamCon that are at work here."

"I have a close working relationship with an investigator who was active with the Secretariat of Intelligence before it was dissolved. He does part-time work for the Federal Intelligence Agency. They are used to him asking questions and not providing justification. He could check on this case and let's see what he comes up with. You can decide what to do after you have the same information the government has."

Marisa wanted to go visit James but knew that would only add to the complications and perhaps get her indirectly involved with someone following her every move. She kept up a small level of questioning and complaints to those who knew of her relationship. She didn't want to cause suspicions by totally dropping off the edge of the world either. The next morning she got a call from the friend. They met once again at the Basilica.

"He is being held because the Internal Security Services discovered several emails to unknown persons. The emails outline the President's travel plans to New York, his, James's dates and plans for his meetings with the U.S. President, and the location of the Cambalache Project," Marisa's friend outlined. Supposedly there were some international phone calls made also, but they were not recorded, and they were made from his office phone at the Casa Rosada. There is no conclusive proof he actually made the calls, and the numbers are now disconnected."

"How did they get into his laptop?" Marisa asked. "He has it with him all the time."

"The emails came from his office computer in the Casa Rosada," her friend explained. "Sorry, I forgot to mention that. My investigator friend asked if he could see the list of emails and he was turned down, but the officer he was talking to said it was odd because there were only about ten emails total registered leaving that computer."

"Did your contact get dates or subjects, any idea at all about the content?" Marisa asked feeling like she was grasping at straws.

"Here are the dates, but the FIA wouldn't release the content," her friend said, sliding a piece of paper over to Marisa. "Something about the court case and they didn't want to take the chance that this information falls into the wrong hands—read that as the defense attorney."

"Thank you," Marisa said. "I owe you."

"Invite me to the wedding," her friend said with a smile.

"Oh, we are just coworkers," Marisa said.

"Yeah, right," Her friend said. "I can see it in your eyes every time you talk about him."

Marisa tried to match the dates of the emails to James's calendar. Two of the five emails were sent when James was actually in the Casa Rosada, but the other three happened when she knew he had not been in the building. In fact, those three she was pretty sure she had been with him. Correlation with her own calendar confirmed this. "So who is trying to put you away,

Santi, or put you in front of a firing squad?" Marisa asked herself. "How are you doing? Are you holding up? Will you even want to stay in this crazy country once this is cleared up?" she asked the empty room.

Ernesto reported to Marisa and Pepe that James had not yet been visited by the U.S. Ambassador. "The ambassador knows of his arrest, but I have personally asked that the United States government not complicates this yet. I explained to the Ambassador that we have an internal problem that we are trying to uncover. If we don't solve it within two more days, we will support the full interest of the U.S. government to get involved. He is supportive to a point. If nothing substantive surfaces soon, I understand our government plans are to ship James off to Marcos Paz. I didn't share that with the Ambassador."

"Prison?" Marisa and Pepe said simultaneously. "How can that be? He hasn't even had a trial yet. Who is so bent on putting him away?" Marisa added.

"I am losing my patience with due process," Ernesto said. "Pepe, I give you permission to get involved up to the point of keeping him out of the prison system. Beyond that, I have never felt so helpless."

"So you don't feel betrayed?" Marisa asked.

"By what?" Ernesto asked. "The system or James?"

"Do you think he did it?" Marisa asked.

"No, I don't," I haven't said so because I don't want you taking things into your own hands, Marisa," Ernesto said.

"Patience is not one of my virtues, Ernesto," Marisa said. "I know for a fact he didn't do anything wrong. Someone is trying to frame him and take him out of the picture."

"What are you not telling me?" Ernesto asked his sister.

Something was obviously not going as planned. The attack on the Cambalache facility had failed once again. The defense force was small, I personally saw to that myself, but they easily defended against a much larger and more heavily armed attack force. Coordination with the Buenos Aires JOAB, who was also the new Americas Prelate had gone well. Nathaniels was in jail and slowing down Cambalache should have been an easy task. No matter, these are just means to an end, the side show. Rosado is digging his own grave and BAJO leadership will soon be open for the taking. The Americas Prelate is supportive, as were several JOABs that the previous Guardian had placed in key positions.

CHAPTER 24

Amores, Dolores y Dineros, No Pueden Estar Secretos

Literal Translation: Love, Pain, and
Money. They Can't be Secrets

<u>Marisa's Translation</u>: Argentine love to flaunt both their blessings and their curses. I think pain and money are easier to hide than love. **Some things are hard to hide.**

"LOVING ONE'S SPOUSE IS NATURAL, but why should love stop there? Loving one's offspring is natural, but why should one stop there? Loving one's extended family or even tribe is a natural thing, but why should one stop there? Does love stop at a border of blood, of culture, of geography, of values? Paradoxically, the broader one's scope, the less common identity, but the wider, deeper and more obvious the presence of what connects us all, the primitive cognates that tell us we are the same." James put down his pen and stood up to stretch. He had been incarcerated now for two, or was it three days? The interviews, as his visitors called these interrogations, were getting more and more serious. At first, they were almost friendly. When he continued denying their accusations of passing on information to some unknown person or group, they became more psychological and threatening.

He had asked at first to see Marisa or a representative of President Starhemberg. There answer hit hard. "You are here under the orders of President Starhemberg, so get it out of your traitorous heart that anyone in this country is going to help." He then asked to see someone from the U.S. Embassy. "That is not a right you have as a suspect of espionage. The sooner you begin to work with us, the sooner there will be light at the end of your very dark tunnel. You won't like what is at the other end of all this if you don't start talking."

James had not yet been physically abused, but he was trying to prepare himself mentally for it. He wondered where Marisa was in all this and whether the whole "come back to Argentina and help us," was just a ploy to get him back in the country so they could arrest him. "Could Marisa have also been play acting with her pledges of love?" James asked himself a hundred times. "No, that was real. Otto wouldn't have played that game either. But she was there when I was arrested. It's been days and no word from anyone. Maybe I really don't have a grasp of what is real. Maybe this is all a big game, and I am simply not a very good player.

James picked up his pen and continued writing. "Charles de Gaulle said something like, 'Patriotism is when you love your own people, and nationalism is when hate for people other than your own takes over.' It is so easy to give into hate or at least mistrust. Is this whole Cambalache Confederation idea so naïve that it is already dead and I am the only person who doesn't know it?" James asked himself out loud, knowing someone was probably listening. The cell was about eight feet by ten feet, with a ceiling much higher at about twelve feet. The walls were clean and appeared to have many coats of paint, the final coat being a drab yellow. There was a narrow bed with a thin mattress, one sheet, and one gray woolen blanket. A small metal sink and toilet were opposite the bed. At the foot of the bed was a small metal table, bolted to the floor just like the bed, that already had paper and a pen laying on top of the desk. The floor was cold cement painted with gray paint. He ate every meal at the table and had begun writing as there was little else to do. He had only left the cell for his interviews, which took place exactly 37 steps down the hall in a small room on the left. There were several doorways that he passed going to the interview room, but none were ever open. He heard no sounds in the hallway, although the heavy metal door to his cell could easily block out most noises. He knew there had to be a hidden camera and microphone in the ceiling or wall to monitor him, but he didn't try to look for it. What would he do if he found it?

That evening, with his dinner meal, which was delivered as it had been each evening at 8 P.M., he found a note slipped into his napkin. He had been searched when he was brought to this place, which he knew was somewhere in the south part of Buenos Aires, but they had let him stay in his clothes and had only taken his belt and shoes. The meals were excellent, and he received metal utensils, napkin, and even a handi-wipe. There was toilet paper on the floor by the toilet, but no towels and no soap. He had not showered in five days, counting the day he left the United States for Argentina and the long flight.

He opened the paper as he ate his bean soup. It was printed and had no salutation or closing. James read,

In 1938, a man on a Paris street stabbed the writer Samuel Beckett, perforating his lung, fortunately not at the fifth rib. A tennis acquaintance of Beckett's, a lady name Suzanne Dechevaux-Dumesnil, heard about the attack and started visiting him in the hospital during his two-week stay. He and Suzanne fell in love and were inseparable from then on. She died in July 1989, and he died a few months after his wife, in December 1989. Fifty-one years together, brought on by a freak accident and a sort of convalescent incarceration. They even fought together in the French Resistance during

World War Two. I know the similarities are a little stretched, but your arrest is just as bizarre as a stabbing on the street. It feels like a stabbing to me. My heart is aching for you. Don't give up hope. Don't give up on me, on Ernesto, on Argentina, or on our dreams. No matter how things appear, I am not a femme fatale.

The note was not signed, but the mention of the fifth rib was something only Marisa would say. This wasn't manufactured by his captors. He bowed his head in thanks, knowing that he had not been summarily thrown to the wolves and forgotten. He didn't know what the future held, but he had a new hope that the end of this tunnel was not what his captors had tried to get him to imagine. After finishing his meal, he folded up the note and put it in his pocket. What was the use of trying to hide it?

When the guard took the trey, he sat back down to write. His thoughts continued with the train of thought that had taunted him the night before. What if all this was either so naively ill-conceived or was, in fact, a scam? Was there really a way to govern such disparate interests as the world provided. Trust was so quickly thrown out the window. James had to admit that there were plenty of good reasons not to believe.

James read what he had written the night before. "Just like it says in the tango Cambalache, *Igual que en la vidriera irrespetuosa de los cambalaches se ha mezclao la vida,* Yes, just as in the junk-shop windows that show no respect for order, life is in confusion." He had been so mad at the whole Cambalache idea. Now he felt so different. He knew he wasn't a fickle person, but even he had lost faith after what was in a bigger picture a small setback. Yes, it could still alter or even take his life, but so could cancer or starvation, or being in the wrong place at the wrong time, like Beckett. How can Otto von Habsburg or Ernesto Starhemberg expect people to simply grasp their abundance mentality and jump into a confederation that offers little in the way of person or group protections? Now he saw a different perspective from this sad tango. *Siglo veinte, Cambalache problemático y febril,* Yes, our age is like a junk shop,

Hectic, without any rules... ¡Dale nomás! ¡Dale que va*!*, Go on and then go on some more! ¡Todo es igual! ¡nada es mejor! It's all the same, nothing is better. No rules, but as we press on, we discover an equality that is better perhaps than the more ordered past."

James suddenly added an insight that had tickled his thoughts before but now came with the clarity of a foghorn through the blinding mist. He wrote, "Yes, interdependency of economies can create dependencies and the subordinate nation can be enslaved or at least experience the involuntary reflex action in response to a dominant state tapping the patellar ligament for the desired knee jerk reaction. But interdependency by definition means the dominant needs the subordinate in some irreplaceable way. In that one way, the dominant becomes the subordinate. Inject into that equation something like free energy and the playing field become much leveler. Some measure of dominance and subordination dissolves." James wondered if this was possible or just aspirational, like his love for Marisa.

"An interdependent confederation of nations," James wrote, "requires equal access to essential resources, or an fair exchange of resources. Each nation could maintain its own culture and customs, laws and norms, but the ecosystem could only be maintained if the preeminent values of all parties were shared and aligned with universal principles. There would have to be both rewards and punishments to keep nations from going rogue or forming alliances within the ecosystem. Water and sunshine are the foundation catalysts of any physical ecosystems. What are the catalysts of societal ecosystems?"

"I suppose that brings us to meaning and love," James mused on the page. "Meaning flows like water connecting and nurturing. But without sunlight, love, the water can only do little. It is popular to say that love is a verb, not a noun. It can certainly be an action or a state of being. But one can express love without love. You can make love, but be void of love. Some of that is just semantics, differing definitions of the word. But there is even a bigger void. We can appear to love, but not really have love in our heart. Love starts as a noun catalyst, just like meaning. These two nouns provide the richest precipitates of life, joy, peace, understanding, truth. Love and the search for meaning are the two motives that define the rich life. Marisa described the Cambalache project as sunlight. I just described love as sunlight. Cambalache equals love, freely given? Is that enough of a catalyst to change human nature? Maybe." The door to James's cell opened. He had time to add, "and maybe not." He sat the pen down as the guard grabbed his arm and jerked him to his feet.

James would have been surprised to realize he was only blocks away from the Casa Rosada. He would have been more than surprised to know that Marisa Starhemberg was less than 500 feet from him. She was outside the building that the retired investigator suggested James was most likely held. She didn't want to make this a political event that could complicate James's case, nor use her brother's position to overturn this case without due process, but she wanted to help due process if she could. She hadn't admitted it to herself yet, but she also wanted to unravel who had set this set-up in motion. Her friend from the Madres de la Plaza de Mayo said she had talked to someone who was willing to get a note to James, as long as it didn't have any names, dates, or other direct identification. As she sat looking at the building, she was fairly certain the note had been delivered. That gave her the mental space and wits to consider her next move.

Pepe Peralta Monti had his own avenues of investigation. If James were innocent, that meant there was someone actively working against him. This opened up a host of concerns for the

President's National and International Security Advisor. That someone had access to internal working files. They were either someone in the government or an external actor that could gain access. Pepe's personal assistant had matched James's known schedule with the emails and noted he had not been in the Casa Rosada office from where the emails had been posted. He was not expert enough in computer forensics to rule out that anyone, including James, could have posted via that machine in proxy. Whatever the case, he agreed with President Starhemberg that James must be left in the system without any interference from the President's office for the time being. They didn't want to spook the perpetrator. He was concerned that the silence from the President's office might be interpreted as hands off acquiescence in the investigation by the Federal Intelligence Agency. The death of prosecutor Alberto Nisman six years ago still left Pepe still uncomfortable with the entire state intelligence apparatus. Nisman's body was found the night before he was due to appear in Congress and accuse the then President Cristina Fernández de Kirchner and other senior officials of trying to cover up the country's deadliest terrorist attack – the 1994 bombing of a Jewish community center in Buenos Aires that killed 85 people. Pepe also didn't want to appear covering up for the attacks on the Cambalache facilities, so he continued to keep his distance. He hoped James Nathaniels would forgive Argentina once this was over. "He might head home again, and we will never get him back," Pepe had told President Starhemberg.

"And Marisa might either lose him or follow him in which case I might lose her," President Starhemberg added. "Pepe, I need you to solve this and solve it fast."

"Not to change the subject, sir, but any thoughts on the Russia issue, the one you didn't mention to Marisa?" Pepe asked.

"Bringing back the Czar is a ridiculous notion, Pepe," President Starhemberg said in exasperation.

"You know back in 2015 President Putin invited the House of Romanov to return to Russia?" Pepe said. "This isn't a new idea. The problem with that was, there were at least three contenders for the thrown. It was a mess that even the Russians weren't willing to take on."

"So the plan is to elect one?" President Starhemberg asked. "That sounds like another catastrophe waiting to happen."

"Remember, when considering possible candidates to the Russian throne, the founder of the Romanov dynasty, Tsar Michael I, was elected by a national assembly of the day, the Zemsky Sobor ("Assembly of the Land") I think they called it. There is a precedent. Add to that the fact that Czar Nicholas II abdicated from the throne, willingly, under duress, so legally there is no basis for the Romanovs to demand the throne back. By far, however, Rostislav Romanov is the popular choice."

"Why go through all this?" President Starhemberg asked.

"I have been considering this, sir," Pepe said. "I think it serves several purposes for those who propose this. Otto von Habsburg and Rostislav Romanov are cousins, distant, but still related. Actually, you are a distant cousin as well. Is Russia building a bridge to Cambalache, or to the proposed confederation? Perhaps. And then there is Putin himself. He continues to contrive ways to stay in power. One of the more interesting is, the theory that Putin is a descendant of the Putyatin clan and thus of royal blood. This would mean that Vladimir Putin is related to nearly all the royal families of Europe. He could be setting himself up to become Czar. Coincidentally, the geography of the former Soviet Union, the sphere of ownership and influence Putin has been trying to recreate, is nearly identical to the former Romanov and Habsburg Empires."

"Doesn't the world have enough problems to deal with?" President Starhemberg asked his closest advisor. "We do nothing and ignore Czar Putin. Do you think the Russians were behind the attempted assassination of Otto, or the attack on the Cambalache facility?"

No, sir," Pepe said. The plan was clearly to kill Otto. If the Russians wanted that to happen, it would have happened. The same with Cambalache. That attack was more professional, but not the direct work of another state. I am not saying some state didn't hire mercenaries to shake things up. Perhaps Venezuela. The populist regime there has been on its death bed for six years. That they have lasted this long is a miracle. They only barely survive because of their oil revenues. With oil now down to $35 a barrel, they might think striking Cambalache would increase prices."

"Answers, Pepe, I need answers," President Starhemberg said. "Argentina needs to know if another nation attacked us on our soil, even if they hired mercenaries to do their dirty work. It is only a week until my speech in London. I have to answer to my country and the world."

Pepe left the President with his burdens and the clear marching orders to get to the bottom of these issues now, not tomorrow. The attack on the Cambalache facility was four days ago, and there were still no answers from the Federal Intelligence Agency. They were fast to jump on the James Nathaniels issue but so slow to provide any answers on an attack by foreign operatives on their own soil. The ridiculous reorganization of intelligence gathering under President Cristina Kirchner had severely hampered counterintelligence operations. It was time to reach out to some old associates if he were to make any headway.

Pepe's first stop was with a former Under Secretary of Intelligence, Osvaldo Martinez. Osvaldo and Pepe had attended the University of Buenos Aires at the same time. They hadn't been close friends then, but over the years, their common alumni status served to build a trusted friendship. Osvaldo had grown heavy set and didn't get out much, but Pepe knew he kept his ear to the ground and still knew more than anyone else he could turn to.

"Pepe," Osvaldo said in response to Pepe's direct questions, "I appreciate you coming to my home instead of meeting in public, but I don't have anything to offer."

"Yes, yes, dear friend, you will now tell me you have been out of the business for what, two years now?" Pepe said.

"Something like that," Osvaldo said with a quick smile.

"I really need some answers, and I need them fast," Pepe said with no smile on his face. "I consider Mr. Nathaniels a personal and trusted friend. He has done much to support Argentina and this whole arrest and investigation is a sham."

"Most moles enjoy the same reputations, Pepe," Osvaldo said. "I will see what I can come up with."

"And on the attacks of von Habsburg and the Cambalache Facility?" Pepe asked.

"I have heard some rumors, but you know me, I don't deal in rumors, just facts."

"I will settle for rumors at this point," Pepe said.

"The police are treating the Habsburg incident as a local criminal issue. I doubt anything will come of their investigation. Without finding the shooter, that is." Osvaldo took a drink of his agua con gas and cleared his throat. "As far as the attack on Huemul Island, there is extreme angst in the intel community that it happened right under their noses."

"As there should be," Pepe said with frustration in his voice.

"No room for emotions in this work," Osvaldo said. "You know that. The community is working on the premise that it was Venezuela. One of the shooters has been positively identified as Venezuelan."

"I take it from your tone that you think differently," Pepe said.

"Not exactly," Osvaldo said. "It was Venezuela, but not the state of Venezuela. It was orchestrated to look like it was Venezuela, but it was most definitely not the government of Venezuela that ordered this attack."

"Your reasoning?" Pepe asked. "They have the motivation with oil becoming cheaper than water."

"A good reason for someone else to use them as the fall guy," Osvaldo said as he stared into space and became very quiet. Pepe had seen this before and let him think. "Something occurs to me, Pepe. Your friend Nathaniels allegedly sent emails to Venezuela and Russia right?"

"Right, but not allegedly, Pepe said. "The emails were sent. I just question who sent them and who they were really sent to."

"And Nathaniels was present at the attempted hit on Habsburg, Right?" Osvaldo asked.

"Yes," Pepe confirmed. "You think he is actually involved?"

"No," Osvaldo said. "He was as much a target as was Habsburg. The hit attempt was not a complete failure. It pegged Nathaniels as being there and being the hero—not planned probably, but it makes him memorable. The Cambalache attack is being connected to Venezuela. The emails in question include dead end contacts in Venezuela. If Nathaniels was really talking with Venezuela there is a high chance some contact would still be active. He wasn't planning on being caught. But from my perspective, he was set up to be caught."

"But," Pepe said.

"But we don't have proof," Osvaldo said. "He could just be as dumb as this appears to make him."

"He is anything but dumb," Pepe said.

"Since we are grasping at straws," Osvaldo added, "I would say you have someone in the government that is involved in this. Any known or suspected enemies of Cambalache, or Nathaniels?"

"Plenty on Cambalache, only a handful of people even know Nathaniels even exists," Pepe said thinking. "I don't know of anyone that would go to these lengths to put him away."

"Go with the shorter list then. Put him away," Osvaldo said with that stare again. "If he were the primary target, he would be dead I think. He is a means to another end. Subterfuge. The only other common connection is Cambalache," Osvaldo said slowly, "Or Habsburg..."

"Ah, the Russians, they know how the game is played. I should reach out to them in my present capacity and leverage my Serbian ties, while also ensuring the support of BAJO's Russian Prelate.

CHAPTER 25

Pegar Un Tubazo
Literal Translation: To hit someone with a tube.

Marisa's Explanation: A Porteño might ask you to hit him with a tube. All he means by that is, "call me." Every once in a while hitting the guy with a tube would better serve humanity.

"IONCE DEMANDED THAT YOU NEEDED to feel more and know less. You chose, it seemed at the time, to know more and feel less." President Ernesto Starhemberg placed the letter on the desk and looked out the window of his office at the Casa Rosada. 'How many years had it been?' he asked himself, trying to calculate. His vision blurred, as did his calculations. 'Yesterday or an eternity ago. Both answers approximated the black hole, the frozen star, which had been a part of him since his former wife Gabriela had left him and annulled their marriage. He was over all this he had thought. But here was a letter from her. He picked up the perfumed handwritten pages again.

"I really believed that," Gabriela in her free-flowing cursive continued. Ernesto could see her soft tan hand forming the letters. "I was in good company. Fyodor Dostoyevsky said something similar to his brother Mikhail who he worried was becoming a hollow poet. The two, reason and free thought, live in the same soul, but we have to choose between them. As Dostoyevsky put it, "nature, the soul, love, and God, one recognizes through the heart, and not through the reason. Were we spirits, we could dwell in that region of ideas over which our souls hover, seeking the solution. But we are earth-born beings, and can only guess at the idea… Thought is born in the soul. Reason is a tool, a machine… When human reason…penetrates into the domain of knowledge, it works independently of the feeling, and consequently of the heart." I believed that, Ernesto. And I believed that you either did not or that reason only was your master."

Ernesto knew where this was going and wasn't sure he wanted to continue reading. The same argument they had the last weeks of their marriage. Gabriela felt that Viedma, the town that Ernesto had chosen to begin his political career, was a prison, a Plato's cave, where Ernesto's fellow politicians were just shadows and hollow poets. She didn't want to become one of the chained prisoners happily giving those shadows names and a reality. Ernesto knew her description was completely unfair and an excuse Gabriela used to escape to the big city and its shops, culture and fineries. "Everything important is in the city, not the rural country and its small towns. Why can't you start out in Buenos Aires at least?" she would ask almost hourly. After she arrived in Viedma and her fears were confirmed, she left. Ernesto resolutely picked up the letter to finish this once and for all.

"I was so wrong, Ernesto," Gabriela continued. "I have been wrong for a long time. I have attempted to make my decisions with a freedom that I thought I had, but actually never allowed myself to enjoy. I now know freedom comes from self-constraint. Some enticements we should obey, others avoid. We can't follow both and expect to thrive. Sound familiar? An echo of your own voice to me. Ironically, it was I who demanded we could not have a foot in both reason and free thought. I have grown to see we must have both. This letter is not to ask your forgiveness, I know I am long past the expiration date for that. I just wanted you to know that I am proud of you and your progress in the world. You wanted to make a difference, and I wanted to make a purchase. You wanted to be interested in life, and I wanted only to make life interesting. You wanted to have a meaningful life, I wanted to have a party. You wanted my love, I was content with its charlatan substitute. The theme here, in case you missed it is, "I now know." I know now what I didn't know then. It seems you always knew."

The letter was signed, Gabriela. As he began to fold it up, he noticed a P.S. on the other side of the last page. "I see you will be in London on the 21st. I will be there also. In fact that coincidence is what finally pushed me off the fence to write you. You don't have to see me, and I don't have any ulterior motives. Best wishes on your speech." She left her phone number and the address where she was planning to stay. There was no explanation why she would be there or how long.

"I know you have love life problems of your own," Ernesto said as he tossed the letter on Marisa's lap later that night. "I would be interested in what you think."

After reading it twice, Marisa said, "You dodged a bullet."

"Why do you think that?" her brother asked. "You think she is only contacting me because of my new celebrity status?"

"That might be part of it," Marisa said, "but you would have never become President with a wife who was fighting you all the way. It looks as if it took here all these many years to learn some pretty simple lessons. You didn't ask, but my thought is, don't contact her while you are in London. She dumped you, remember?"

Marisa had planned on talking to her brother about the information she had gathered on James's arrest and incarceration but decided not to. One look at Ernesto, and she knew he probably wouldn't even hear half the things she said. How could this ghost woman reincarnate right at the intersection of the Cambalache success and the launch of CamCon? Ernesto, James, and Marisa had considered the personal challenges that might come with Cambalache, but this had not come up even once. "What else did we miss?" Marisa asked herself after Ernesto left her room. "Russia getting a Czar, for one," her mind replied, followed by, "and James being arrested."

Marisa thought of the first day she had met James. It had been her idea to impress this North American with the high-tech security at the Casa Rosada. The passive NRFID with brain scan biometrics was a new security tool, and in truth, only a handful of people knew its full capabilities. During a briefing for Ernesto that Marisa had also attended, due to security's concern of potential kidnapping of the President's only family, she found out that the NRFID tag in the Casa Rosada ID cards could not only track a person within the building through constant electronic interrogation of the passive tags, but outside the building a person could be tracked as long as an electronic interrogator that could ping the chip was within 200 meters; far more than the 50 meters advertised within the building. As far as most tag holders knew, the tags did not emit a beacon for location unless interrogated and that interrogation could only happen within the Casa Rosada. Marisa smiled despite herself at the games she had played with James that first day. "Okay, I probably did want to kill him, or at least scare him away with that threat," she admitted to herself, "but he had persevered, just as Ernesto had predicted. "How could Ernesto read everyone so well, except for Gabriela?"

Suddenly, a new thought came to Marisa. "Reading people…" Marisa said out loud. "We can track just about everyone in the building in real time, but also there is a historical record." To her knowledge, that capability was not so much confidential, as just not announced. It was an afterthought statement by the contractor during the briefing to Ernesto and herself. This security measure was thought to be proactive and real-time. The historical record was mainly collected for data analysis of people movement and efficiencies, not security. Marisa went to bed with a plan.

Early the next day Marisa was in the Casa Rosada Security Office when the Chief of Presidential Security entered his office. "Señorita Starhemberg," he said not at all startled by her presence.

'Does anything surprise these people?' she wondered.

"What can I do for you?" he asked.

"As you know," she began, "the Federal Police have arrested James Nathaniels on concerns of possible espionage. He is a valued member of the President's team, and we believe him to be innocent, but have not wanted to get in the way of any investigation. On the other hand, something has come to my attention that suggests we could get to the bottom of this quickly."

"Are you proposing getting involved in the Federal investigation?" he asked.

Marisa was amused to see this had finally surprised him. "No, not at all. I really don't want to involve the Federal Police at all. I just want to run an in-house check on our systems. Can I use the contractor that briefed the President and myself on the use of the system?"

"I don't see any problems with that, as long as we keep this in-house," he said.

"And can we keep this between you and me for the time being?" Marisa asked.

"I don't keep anything from your brother, Señorita," he said. "Unless it is for his own good and security's sake," he added.

"Oh, no, of course, he can know," Marisa said. She wasn't sure he would approve, but she thought she could get to the bottom of this before Ernesto would find out; hopefully before he even got to his office. And she could always beg forgiveness if she had to. "I was just thinking of the political ramifications of the news of the Casa Rosada doing an investigation."

"This will be between you and me, Señorita," the Security Chief said.

Two hours later Marisa and the biometrics card contractor were looking at a computer screen full of data points. Using a data analysis application called Taction, they were looking at millions of data points in four dimensions, including color. The contractor was like a little boy with his first computer game.

"There is no way to move the computer located in that office you identified without us knowing it. Every machine has a built-in security tag that we can track. You would have to take the machine apart to get to the security tag. Not impossible, but highly improbable. The green colored pixels represent the person whose office this belongs to. We can see when he arrives and when he leaves. We can see when he uses the restroom or attends a meeting. I would say this person has set patterns and works too much. He even eats his lunch at the desk." The contractor didn't say it out loud, but he guessed that this must be the North American whose badge he had made quickly the morning the guy arrived in the building. No self-respecting Argentine would eat at his desk this time of year.

"So what about any people that come into that office?" Marisa asked. "Can you see who those people are and when they were there?"

"No problem," the contractor said, not taking his eyes off the screen. "I have coded the cleaning crew orange. For any other entries, the application assigns them a distinct color. It looks like only four people have been in that office, outside of the cleaning crew. Not a very popular person."

"Can you separate those who were in the office when the office's assigned occupant was there?" Marisa asked.

"Done," the contractor said. "It looks like we are down to two people. One of which was in and out only one time and was only there for 4.23 seconds. The other was there," he paused while hovering over the pixels to collect the pertinent information. "Okay, the other person entered three times for an average of ten minutes each visit."

"Who was that person?" Marisa asked.

"Interesting," the contractor said. "It must be someone the office person knew because this visitor also was in the office numerous times when the office was occupied. Suggests to me this person may just be using the office because information is there, on a white board, in open files, that kind of thing."

"That brings up another question," Marisa said. "Can you correlate those visits when the office computer is on?"

That is a different database, but yes I can do that," the contractor said. "For this little job, I will do it manually. If this is something you will want in the future, let me know, and I can build an interface to load that data as well. Then it will be another data point in Taction. I can get you your information in about five minutes."

"Great. Do it," Marisa said. "So who is the person?"

"ID number 2764P," the contractor said. "Hmm, security personnel," he said as he looked up the number in another file. "Security personnel IDs start with a 2. It is a Vangelina Pereira," he said.

Marisa was silent, shocked and not sure what to do with this information. She numbly asked the next question she had already asked herself. "Could a person log onto someone else's computer as if it were the computer's owner?"

"Normally I would say no," the contractor said. "In the old days, like just a couple years ago, it would have been possible to log in remotely or with a proxy account and make it look like the computer owner had logged in. Not possible today. But,"

"But?" Marisa echoed.

"But this is a security person with possible access to certain files," the contractor said, apparently thinking things out for himself.

"What certain files?" Marisa asked starting to feel sick.

"Like I said, it used to be that people could log into someone else's system. They did that by getting the person's password," the contractor said as he opened up another database on his screen. "That had its obvious weaknesses. As you know, our office computers now use your brain scan biometrics in your ID card for login. Every person's brain scan is unique and much more complex than even the best password."

"So, I don't understand what you are getting at," Marisa said. "Someone would have to have another person's brain scan to get into that machine?"

"Not exactly," the contractor said. "Any biometric, finger-prints, retinal scan, and brain scans have to be reduced to ones and zeros for use with a computer. That is all computers under-stand. Unlike traditional passwords, those ones and zeros are kept safe by the security department in this building. Not to get into other people's computers, but so those scans can be stored on a computer that authorizes access to the building for example."

"So we are back to where we were a few years ago?" Marisa asked.

"Not exactly," the contractor said. "Hmm, this is odd, but confirms my guess."

"What's that," Marisa asked, tiring of this mouse maze of information.

"We almost always set up office computers to know they are scanning an active ID card," the contractor said. "An additional security precaution is, if the computer scans an active ID card, that means the card is physically in the presence of the owner of that card. These cards only work in the NRFID chip is in alignment with the actual brain waves of the person holding the card. That's the real secret sauce of this card. It is real time biometrics without the problems of fingerprint or retinal scans."

"Last call for sanity here," Marisa said. "Where does that leave us?"

"Well, that function was either disabled on this computer or was never set up," the contractor said. "A person could just type in the brain scan code like a password and the computer wouldn't know the difference."

"Great, so we really can't say who might have gotten into his machine and made it look like the owner was operating it," Maris said, feeling like she had just wasted the last two hours.

"All is not lost," the contractor said. "Unfortunately the computer was vulnerable, but we can know after the fact what happened. Yes, here it is, the computer shows a manual login, and that correlates with this Ms. Pereira being in the office alone. No one else could have done it."

"Excellent," Marisa said, even though she didn't feel excellent. "Can you now correlate those times with these emails?" Marisa handed the contractor a hand-written list of the date/time groups of the emails that were sent out allegedly by James to Russian and Venezuelan contacts.

Within half a minute the contractor corroborated that in fact three of the emails corresponded with the last three times James's computer had been accessed by Vangelina. "Thank you for your time and excellent work. This is just between you and me as I explained up front. Are you still good with that?" Marisa asked.

"Yes mam," the contractor said. "Can I add one other thing?"

"Please, say what's on your mind," Marisa said, expecting a speech about the sterling attributes of the system or a lecture on security.

"Those emails that were sent out on the computer in question," the contractor began, "Only one of them went to a real recipient."

"What?" Marisa asked. "How do you know that?"

"They only went to two addresses," the contractor began to explain. "One is in Venezuela and that is a real address. The others look like they were sent to Russia, but they just went into the Internet ether. That address does not exist. I just checked it out. And before you ask, no, it was not an address that was closed. It has never existed. I just pinged it and got a 550 error. That comes with two possibilities. If that address never existed, the response will be: *The email account that you tried to reach does not exist.* If it ever existed, the response will be: *The email account that you tried to reach is disabled.* It would be virtually impossible to clean up the web and all the dark corners and inaccessible cupboards where that email address could hide forever."

"Wow, outstanding. Thanks," Marisa said. She walked out of the contractor's lair dialing her cell phone.

An hour later she was meeting with her Madre de la Plaza de Mayo contact and the retired investigator. Marisa explained what she had learned, but left out Vangelina's name. "So, what is the next step? Do I tell the President?"

"You've got a mole in the Casa Rosada," the investigator said. "You need to let the President know, but beyond that, you don't know who to trust. Even the most trusted must be verified. You only mentioned this one person, but that doesn't mean there aren't others involved. Almost anything you do will tip off those working against you."

"And in the meantime, as we sort that out, James rots in a cell, soon to be a federal prison?" Marisa said, so frustrated that she had gotten to the bottom of this and found her second mother implicated and no clear way to get James out of the due process clutches.

"I think I might have an idea to bring this to a close," the investigator said.

"I'm all ears," Marisa said.

Her Madre de la Plaza Mayor contact chuckled and said, "Señorita Marisa, even a blind man could see that is not so."

"I support your suggestion for the JOAB candidate you provided. He is already a known entity inside of BAJO. His connection with the previous Guardian and assessment by the former Americas Prelate, Rosado, make him an excellent candidate. That his loyalty is not with Rosado makes him the perfect choice. I will report my decision to Guardian Rosado. Not much he can do about it."

The new Americas Prelate was most pleased that Nathaniels was out of the picture. He was certainly not good enough for Marisa. Just enough input to the Starhembergs to plant seeds of doubt. Just a few emails and a failed attack on Cambalache to keep Nathaniels out of the picture for the foreseeable future. Von Habsburg crippled, and Marisa still protected from anyone who would break up our little family. You really can have your cake and eat it too.

CHAPTER 26

Me Cortaron las Piernas
Literal Translation: They've cut my legs off!

Marisa's Explanation: In 1994, Diego Maradona failed a drug test and was taken from the field in the middle of the World Cup in the USA. His fútbol career at an end and one of the saddest moments of Argentine sports, Diego said this memorable phrase that is still used to refer to **An Injustice**. You got dumped by your girlfriend? You would say, she cut off my legs!

"ERNESTO," MARISA SAID CHARGING INTO her brother's office. She had confirmed with his secretary that he had this time blocked to put the finishing touches on his speech for the opening of the CamCon Headquarters. "We need to go to the fish tank and have a talk." The fish tank, as Marisa called it, was a SCIF, a Sensitive Compartmentalized Information Facility. Officially it was called a Fondo de Información Compartimentada (FIC) in Spanish. Marisa called it the fish tank because the walls and ceiling were made of inch thick glass that had microscopic metal elements embedded to keep out electronic eavesdropping. The floor was ten inches of reinforced concrete, and there were copper foils built into each corner to prevent transmissions. Motion detectors, alarms, and a single distant camera that showed if anyone was in the room, made up the final security precautions. There was a single air conditioning vent with metal baffles supplied the place with fresh air, but no one wanted to spend too much time there. It was used for the most highly classified and sensitive briefings. The Cambalache team had used it several times, and that is how Marisa knew of its existence.

"Is that really necessary?" Ernesto asked.

"Yes, it is," Marisa said. "Now get off your presidential pompous and let's get going. I know you only have a few minutes of free time."

They traveled to the basement of the Casa Rosada and entered a large protected room. In the center of the chamber was the fish tank. It was not in use by any other government personnel, so they entered and shut the transparent door. "So what is on you mind that we have to come down here, Marisa?"

"James is on my mind," Marisa said. She explained all she had come up with and that it appeared Vangelina was involved in this somehow. As they had done since both were young, they put their heads together and came up with a plan.

James left the federal jail that evening for transfer to the Marcos Paz Prison. He never arrived, but the warden was not expecting him. James was instead transferred to a safe house in the Buenos Aires suburb of Palermo under the supervision of Pepe Peralta Monti and two of his most trusted staff. In the car, Pepe explained what had transpired since James's arrest.

"You have got to be kidding me," James said. Vangelina? Why?"

"I have no idea," Pepe said. "She hates you for coming between her and Marisa? I doubt it. She is working for a foreign government like Venezuela? Not likely, but possible. She is working for someone else that doesn't like Cambalache or CamCon? Again I give this a feeble maybe."

"How has Marisa taken this news?" James asked.

"She is the one who uncovered all this," Pepe said. "You would be getting all comfy in your new cell in the federal prison if it were not for her. In a very real way, she has sacrificed Vangelina for you."

"When can I see her?" James asked.

"She should be waiting for you at the safe house," Pepe explained. "She will explain the rest of our plans then."

The van that carried James and Pepe entered a garage, and no lights were illuminated, and no doors were opened until the garage door was completely closed. They entered the house from the attached garage. It smelled wonderful. The aroma of cooking food filled the air and was laced with Marisa's perfume. James could feel his heartbeat increase.

"Lucy, I'm home," James called out in English with a terrible Spanish accent

"Lucy? Who is Lucy?" Marisa asked exiting the kitchen. "A new prison buddy?"

"Just a joke, never mind," James said stopped in his tracks. Marisa's hair was up, but slightly falling. She had on an apron, but it did nothing to hide her beauty and the blouse and jeans that accentuated her exuberance. "You are beautiful," he said without thinking.

"That's what the ladies tell me all the time," Pepe said as he passed James in the hallway and gave Marisa a customary hug and a kiss on each cheek. "I will be out of your hair now unless you need something more from me. I need to get back to the office and take care of a few things before our travel."

"Thank you, Pepe," Marisa said. "I join your throng of admirers. You are beautiful. Now get out of here."

Pepe tipped his imaginary hat to James as he left with a big grin. One security guard went upstairs to check outside and to basically disappear. Marisa just stood there with a guarded smile on her face.

James stood there frozen. Marisa again broke the silence saying, "Dinner will be ready in just a few minutes. I moved some of your things to an upstairs room, so if you want you can freshen up. I, I am so sorry for everything," Marisa said as she allowed tears to quietly draw lines of light on her cheeks.

"It will be a great story to tell someday," James said smiling. He walked to her and wiped the tears from her face with his thumbs while framing her face with his hands. "I got some thinking and writing done while a guest of the state. It wasn't so bad."

"I want to ask you if you missed me, but that sounds so selfish. I was so afraid for you, for what they might do to you."

"Well, I doubt I will ever be able to have children," James said seriously.

"What?" Marisa asked with wide eyes.

"I'm kidding," James said. "They weren't friendly, but I was treated better than most alleged spies, I am sure. Pepe told me you would explain all this and plans for the future."

"After dinner," Marisa said. "For now there is just us, and I want to focus on you. Ernesto said he would make this up to you. He didn't come to meet you because as far as the world is concerned, you are still locked up. But more of that later. Are your really alright?"

"I am fine, really," James said touching her left ear with his right hand. Ears don't get much credit, but Marisa had two beautiful lobes that were screaming for a kiss. "May I kiss your ear?" James asked. "They do so much work, holding on to earrings, listening…"

"You may," Marisa whispered.

He gently touched his lips to the side of her face. He then breathed, "Touch elevates the senses, but listening, really hearing, elevates the mind. The mind makes meaning of it all. Thank you for hearing me in my childish retreat to Missouri and coming after me. Thank you for hearing me in my cell these past five days and again coming after me."

"Oh, Santi," Marisa said. "The most important listening is done with the heart, not the head. But I heard you just the same. What amazes me is that you could hear me through the noise of my defenses. 127."

"127?" James asked, wondering if he heard her right. He moved his head enough to look in her eyes.

"The number of hours you were incarcerated," Marisa said. "127 reasons to turn your back on this crazy country and never look back. I am so sorry, Santi. Can I make it up to you somehow, or will you be leaving for good this time?"

"Leaving?" James asked. "I just now fully arrived. 127 hours of anticipation is more like it. Maybe it was my heart not my mind that heard and never lost hope. I don't know. All I know is, over the past days I could see and smell, and touch, and taste this moment like it had already happened and I was just remembering it."

"I wish I had that ability," Marisa said. "I could hardly even remember the happy hours in Missouri that happened less than a week ago. I have been consumed by fear, not hope."

"It's fear when you run," James said with a soft grin. "I have never seen you run from anything. I saw this moment, and that kept me going. Hope was a fruit of that vision. You say you didn't see this, yet you kept going. You had to make your own hope, and that took more courage. And yes, you can make this up to me."

"And how might I do that?" Marisa asked with her own grin.

"In my darkest hours at the jail and when I thought I might be moving into a phase of questioning that might include physical pain, there is one thing that kept me going. One anticipation that never dimmed."

"And, what might that be?" Marisa asked now smiling ear to beautiful ear.

"Dulce de Leche ice cream bañado de chocolate."

"Not the exact answer I was anticipating," Marisa said. "To each his or her own anticipation I suppose. So sorry to disappoint you, but no ice cream tonight. You will have to make due with dulce de besos, sweet kisses. Definitely no chocolate bath." Marisa kissed his nose, then each cheek, then brushed his lips against hers and then broke away. "But first dinner. I have been slaving in the kitchen all afternoon to make your homecoming meal, and it is ready. Go wash your incarceration away and let's eat. Then we talk. Then we consider our options; both short-term and long-term."

"I don't know," James said. "I am still in my formative years, and I am discovering that I am becoming a dessert first kind of guy."

"You are the least "dessert first" person I have ever met," Marisa said.

"Maybe it's hope then," James said. "Remember, I saw all this before."

"And what exactly did you see?" Marisa asked, slightly blushing.

James was overcome with emotion and struggled to regain his composure. He couldn't keep up the half –joking ruse. "Honestly, Marisa, I saw a feeling, not a picture. I really did. It was more powerful than any picture, more tangible than touch. I will admit that some flashes of what I wanted to see broke into my isolation, but I painted over them because they weren't real. Those thoughts were counterfeit and corrosive and threatened to dissolve what I knew was irrefutably authentic. I was already back here with you the first hour after I was arrested. I can't explain it, but I knew it."

"Not de facto, but certain if we choose it to be so," Marisa said more to herself than to James. "I need to tell you a story about a girl on a bridge in Spain." Marisa had not shared her experience of facing the abyss of her life with anyone, not even Otto who had watched over her in those crazy years, or her brother who came to the rescue. Over dinner, she explained her fears and emptiness following her parents' death and her struggles. "I was too young to understand what I was suffering and just strong-willed enough to think I could handle it on my own. Of course, I found my own versions of self-medication; a few good, but mostly terrible. I had an emptiness in me, you know, like the empty quarter in Saudi Arabia, dry, blazing hot, mirages that tempted and then tormented, and I was so very much all alone."

James sat and listened, knowing any words of attempted comfort on his part would break the spell. Marisa needed to walk in this place one last time. He wanted to let her know she wasn't walking alone, though, so he reached across the table and took her hand.

"It was in this empty place that I struck oil," Marisa said. "I touched the water and it quenched my soul. I had been fleeing my center, but from that instant until this very moment I have been running to my center. I know those words don't make much sense, but I know our choices count. I know that nothing is guaranteed, but if we make the right choices, we can find what we desire most. I know now the journey isn't as scary and dangerous as it sounds. The counterfeits you mentioned, my mirages, might entice us to wander to our doom. But that is just it, we should be cautious of wandering. Serendipity is a wondrous thing. It led me to you, or you to me. But wandering without any map is futile. I know. I can't explain it any better than you, but thank God we can discern the irrefutably authentic."

"Thank you, Marisa," James said. "I couldn't have predicted it, but what you just shared and you sharing it, comes the closest to the feeling I saw, the vision I felt, I don't know, but it is what kept me sustained during my arrest."

"Well, speaking of that, James, we need to talk. I need to get back to the Quinta yet tonight, so I need to explain what is going on." Marisa explained what Pepe had already shared with James in the car. Then she shared the concern that Vangelina was not working alone. "You need to stay out of sight for now. I hope this prison is a little more comfortable."

"The warden is certainly cuter," James said.

"Hmm, and I think I like having a kept man," Marisa said. "We will visit that later. For now, we need to set a trap for the mouse. Also, if you are willing, Ernesto would like you to travel with us to London for his CamCon speech. Otto would also like to see you. I think he wants you to tell him it was his speech in Missouri that got us back together."

I would be honored to travel with you, and I am grateful for Otto's effort to go all the way to my parent's place to save us, but to paraphrase that Tom Cruise movie, you had me at Dulce de Leche ice cream."

"I don't think ice cream was in that movie," Marisa said.

"Their loss," James said.

Marisa explained the plans for luring Vangelina into contacting anyone that might be involved with her subterfuge and finally stood to leave. "I am afraid I am leaving you with the dirty dishes," Marisa said. "Part of my "kept man" scheme. I don't want to be gone any longer, though. Vangelina might get curious."

"Are you okay with this, Marisa?" James asked. "I mean, Vangelina has been at your side for a long time. I don't know if she is a best friend or a surrogate mom, or what, but this has to hurt."

"It hurts," Marisa said. "But hurting you hurts me too. I will sort out my feelings when we sort out all the facts. For now, let's press forward with getting to those facts."

"Will I get to see you tomorrow?" James asked not wanting her to go.

"I wish it would work out, but the next time I will probably see you is either on the plane going to London or in London if we have to travel separately. Traveling separately will only happen if we still haven't gotten to the bottom of the Vangelina issue."

"What I am supposed to do for the next two days?" James asked.

"I wish I had some meaningful work or something else for you to do," Marisa said sadly,"

"Since I might be traveling separately, would it be possible if I left tomorrow for London?" James suggested. "I could work with Otto and help prep for President Starhemberg's arrival."

"That's a great idea," Marisa said. "I will admit I want to have you close by, but since I probably won't even get to see you … yes, that is brilliant. I will talk to Ernesto tonight. Plan on it, and if it falls through for something we aren't thinking of, I will let you know by phone on the throwaway mobile Pepe gave you. We don't know for sure if your old cell phone is being tracked or not, so your old phone is actually in the warden's desk at the prison you were supposed to have been transferred to tonight."

"I really am starting to feel like a kept man, Marisa," James said. "All the demands and controls, but none of the perks."

"When things slow down, we can talk perks," Marisa said with a devious smile.

"I don't want things to slow down, Marisa," James said. "I don't think they will ever slow down. In fact, they will probably speed up. We need to figure out how we are going to get to the subject of us in the midst of all this."

"Do you know what "us" is yet James?" Marisa asked.

"Yes, I do," James said.

"It sounds like you just answered the question you need to ask," Marisa said. She kissed him on the cheek, fearful if she kissed his lips or lingered longer she would find this was all just another mirage. "In London, let's talk about us," she said and left.

"The transfer of James Nathaniels to federal prison opens the opportunity for an untimely death that could be easily arranged. Connecting his death to von Habsburg would be relatively easy. A few prisoners could say that Nathaniels told them that Habsburg was after him for his attempts to shut down the Cambalache project. Even if this didn't stand up in court, the seeds of doubt would be planted." JOAB

"Guardian, the message from our JOAB in Buenos Aires offers an extreme measure, but an excellent opportunity to taint Otto von Habsburg for life. I support moving forward with a planning phase for this action. Of course, the execution of the plan would need additional approval by you." Americas Prelate

CHAPTER 27

Buscarle la Quinta Pata al Gato

Literal Translation: To search for a cat's fifth leg

Marisa's Explanation: Even when we Argentines don't have anything to worry about or complain about, we look for it. We purchase with doubt, listen to people wondering if we should trust them, and see conflict where it doesn't exist. It's a national pastime searching for a cat's fifth leg and, from time to time, **We Discover a Real Conspiracy**.

JAMES DEPARTED THE NEXT MORNING by commercial flight to London Gatwick. He had entered the plane with the crew and was put in first class with the aisle seat empty. Otto met him in customs, and they departed by a private exit.

"You are a free man," Otto said beaming. "How was your flight?"

"Good, but I am still catching up on all the changes—time zones and otherwise. Less than two weeks ago I had decided to return to Missouri, then you and Marisa came after me. Following my rescue," James turned and smiled at Otto and then continued, "I returned with Marisa and a clear plan, but I was arrested. I tried to be really upset about that, but as strange as it sounds, it was almost calming after the first day. Like I knew things were going to work out. Then I was secreted to a safe house after nearly a week in jail. Now I am in London. I need to get off this merry-go-round."

"Stability is overrated. How are things with you and Marisa?" Otto asked.

"Wonderful," James said. "Thank you for all you have done in that department. I am overwhelmed you would travel to my parents' home in the midst of the CamCon stand-up. I am forever in your debt."

"You saved my life, James," Otto said. "I had a tiny part in getting yours back on track. You are hardly in my debt. The balance still tips heavily in your favor. Besides, I would do just about anything for Marisa."

"Then I have a thought on how you might fully repay the debt and tip the scale your way forever," James said with just a little tremor in his voice.

"Sounds intriguing," Otto said, letting go of the steering wheel with both hands and rubbing them together. "What do you have in mind?"

"You are as close to a father as Marisa has," James began. "In fact, from what Marisa tells me, you have been father and mentor to her. I love her, and so I thank you for everything you have done for her. I want to marry her and almost asked her yesterday. It was all I could think about while in jail. But I wanted to ask your permission first."

"Are you sure?" Otto asked. "Marisa has a fiery temper and is prone to pouting, she is brilliant which sometimes manifests itself as absent-mindedness, and she is dedicated to her brother who is on a fast track to becoming a world leader. She is all he has, you know."

"I am clueless about what lies ahead, but I am sure," James said. "I love her passion for life and believe it is the glue that will hold us together. She is brilliant, and I still don't know all she did with the Cambalache Project, but I want with every atom in every molecule in my body for her to be the mother of our brilliant children. And, her brother will not lose a sister, he will gain a dedicated and loyal brother-in-law. Marisa and I have both been putting our relationship on the shelf until things slow down. They are never going to slow down. I want to marry her as soon as possible."

"Good answers, James," Otto said gripping his arm. "You have my permission. Heaven help you." They talked briefly about Marisa and what life would be like with her and moved into CamCon and the upcoming grand opening of its headquarters. "Here we are, CamCon Central. Some of the administrative personnel have started calling it CCC or just C cubed. Not much to look at, but with a tiny budget to start a global operation, we didn't want to splurge on a fancier building in a more expensive neighborhood."

James looked out of the window of the car at York Gate, London. He could see the edge of Regents Park and a 19th Century Church at the end of the road. The three-story beige building was right on the street. A six-foot iron fence protected the building from pedestrian and vehicle traffic.

"It's a private street for permit holders only," Otto said. He turned onto a side street, wide enough for only one car and an electronic gate opened. "We took over the building from an international investment firm. All the security, communications, and electronics were already installed. It was an easy transition. We only have twelve offices filled, but that will grow as mega-city members come on board."

James followed Otto into the Chief Administrator's Office. "Easy access to the tube, the ubiquitous London taxi's, the A40 Trunk Road, plenty of places to eat, four and five-star hotels within blocks. Not bad for setting up shop in London. The Brexit jitters are long gone, and London is fast becoming an international hub to rival any in the world. We were really fortunate to find this location. Can I get you anything to drink?"

"Water would be great," James said. The offices were sparse, but the people were busy. It felt like a high-tech start-up company. Everyone he saw was in their late twenties early thirties. They were wearing everything from jeans and untucked shirts to ties and slacks. "So this is Rome," James said.

"More like the North German town of Lübeck," Otto said. "I have studied most of the world's confederations. The Toltecs in Mexico, the Aro in West Africa, the Swiss Cantons, even the Argentine Confederacy under Juan Manuel de Rosas. Perhaps the best example of what CamCon might become is the Hansa Confederation, or known at the time as the Hanseatic League. It was a commercial and defensive confederation of market towns mostly along the Baltic, which actually stretched from London to Novgorod. It had over 60 cities in the Confederation that were part of 32 kingdoms, duchies, principalities, and free cities. It operated for nearly 300 years and has enjoyed a resurrection of a sort in the last half century, although it is no longer a true confederation, just an organization to foster business links, tourism, and cultural exchange."

"I've read some about the Hansa House," James said. "I can see the similarities, but CamCon faces a significantly more complex world today. There were no mature nations, no nation-states in the 14th century. Kingdoms were much looser in governance of cities and subjects, with few real loyalties to win. Integration in a confederation was a relatively simpler exercise than what you are undertaking."

"I know where you are going with this I think. A nation, many nations at the same time, can be loyal to a single state," Otto replied. "There are Jewish Iranians. There are Jewish Iranian Americans. There are Jewish Iranian Americans that immigrate to Israel. They don't lose their complex identity with integration.

States are pretty good at integration. That is because integration is top-down and only requires a physical presence. States are notoriously terrible at assimilation, so I understand you concern, James. The thing is, the world isn't playing by those old rules anymore. CamCon exists because of that weakness. We are filling an underserved need. Assimilation is bottom-up and requires a psycho-social presence, more and more without a strict requirement of physical presence. It's happening without the nation-state, often despite the nation-state. These trends reflect the models of media, with traditional media being dictatorial, directed, and most often one to the many. New media, fueled by the Internet, is more democratic, participatory, and many to the many. CamCon is based on assimilation that is already taking place. True, assimilation requires a change in identity, but one does not have to give up all of who they are for something new. In our hyper-connected world, we are all going through this assimilation just connecting to the Internet, getting on an airplane, making a purchase."

"I have been concerned with those on the periphery of this assimilation," James said. "You and President Starhemberg have been intent on solely focusing on the mega-cities. What about the rural areas, the bread baskets of these cities?"

"We can't be everything to everyone on day one," Otto replied.

"You need to talk to everyone on day one," James said. "No one should feel left out, even if they are years away from full participation. No need to create an enemy that would happily be a patient supporter."

"We are already challenged with assimilation of the elements of diversity between and within the mega-cites. Bringing on the areas that are two standard deviations from the CamCon mean of the bell curve is asking for the kind of trouble my ancestors were faced with daily in the Austro-Hungarian Empire."

"Respect for each other's non-negotiables such as acceptance or rejection of alcohol, sex outside of marriage, dietary issues, and a hundred other matters will be CamCon's downfall unless its culture includes understanding and better, a celebration of differences," James said.

Assimilation is a give-and-take process as both the majority community, as well as minority communities get affected in the process and both become a part of the larger culture."

"I don't see the practicality of your perspective," Otto said. "I love it and want to believe it, but I am a realist, born of a family who faced this and tried to manage it on a day-to-day basis. It was impossible, and it eventually caused the downfall of their rule."

"The freedom and will to think and act according to your own dictates are compatible with the challenges of diversity," James said. "CamCon exists to manage and leverage a breakthrough technology. CamCon must lead the way to breakthrough understanding as well, or it will not survive."

"And when your think and act scenario leads a group, even demands their followers dictate or attack others?" Otto asked.

The root of your question lives in a zero-sum mentality," James said. "It is the final proof of an abundance mentality that your question does not even exist. At the highest levels of understanding, that is, judgment; and utility, that is justification, diversity thrives. If we leave the world to govern by knowledge and experience alone, decisions will be made by trial and error, emotion, ego, and habit. You are placing CamCon at the next level which I applaud, but it's not enough. The intersection of intelligence and a level of obedience that you see as the safe and secure route protects a community and nurtures identity and self as well as group meaning. The problem is this also creates independent and dependent actors and sews the seeds of dissent and frustration. There will always be a downtrodden minority."

"Keep going," Otto said. "I want to get to this breakthrough understanding you are talking about. I keep thinking of scenarios where everything eventually breaks down, not through. Maybe abundance is a goal, but never a reality we will reach. When there is a deep and wide chasm between moral or ethical issues, there should not be acceptance in the name of abundance. That acceptance will sow the seeds of long-term failure."

The abundance of energy is within reach, Otto," James said. "The abundance of thought and action are not far behind. There will still be opposition, just not zero-sum competition that tells us in order to win, someone else must lose; lose their power, lose their resources, lose their freedoms. As for breakthrough understanding, we will find that at the intersection of vision and wisdom. Those two words deserve defining. I am using vision to describe what we can see beyond ordinary sight. It is a developed competence in perception and discernment that comes from context and truly justified right reasons, not the lower reasons I have already mentioned and that we are really good at dressing in finer clothes. Wisdom is the highest level of accumulated and distributed meaning so that we can act with the highest level of practice and principle, not simply on unproven values. As you suggest, those values might not be aligned with principles. I have seen this work on smaller scales and it's the same principles at work here. If CamCon follows this road we will transform complexity into collaboration, chaos into opportunity; change into learning and growth, and friction into traction."

"Lofty, even idealistic," Otto said. "My father told me as a young boy I needed to learn to trim the sails of my idealism with the winds of reality."

"What if the wind is shifting and you still try to tack to port when it is blowing you directly there?" James asked. "You are the one who brought up traditional and new media as examples earlier. We all watched traditional newspapers, record labels, and book publishers try to tack their way to success when all they were really doing was wasting time and resources. Trial and error, habit, ego, intuition, tradition—that was their playbook. Like I said, knowledge and experience do not always provide the best course of action and are far away from breakthrough understanding. They could have let the wind carry them to their future and upon arrival have the energy and resources to dance at their success party."

"Unrepentant naiveté," Otto said with a smile.

"I prefer to call myself a Don Quixote," James said.

The first thing President Ernesto Starhemberg did after landing in England, after everyone else had departed for the Landmark Hotel just a few minutes down Marylebone Road from CamCon Headquarters, was make a call to Gabriela. He wanted this off his mind before he ushered in a new phase in his public life. No one answered, and he didn't leave a message. He sat in the aircraft trying to sort through his thoughts and emotions. He had told his sister and staff that he was going to work on his speech in the privacy of the aircraft and would join them for dinner, so he got out his speech to read one more time. His private cell phone rang.

"Hello," he answered, not sure he wanted to use his name. Only six people had this number, but he supposed he could get the odd wrong number. Half expecting a cockney accent of a man calling to brag to his wife about winning the dart tournament at the local pub, he was surprised to hear Gabriela's voice.

"Hello, I just got a call from this number," her voice said.

"Hello, Gabriela," Ernesto said. He was holding his breath and realized he had broken out into a sweat.

"Ernesto?" Gabriela asked. She too sounded apprehensive. "Where are you at?"

"In an airplane," Ernesto said, "parked at Heathrow."

"You are still waiting to deplane?" Gabriela asked.

"Well, no. I sent everyone to the hotel ahead of me," Ernesto said. "I told them I was going to work on my speech. My plan was to call you."

"You are sitting on a plane working on a speech?" Gabriela asked, and then realized. "Oh, right your airplane."

"The airplane the people of Argentina let me use," he said. "Are you close by? I could give you a tour."

"I'm not, but that sounds fun. Maybe another time," Gabriela said.

"Sure, of course," Ernesto said. "Obviously I got your letter. It was a surprise after all these years. Thank you. I am not sure if it brought closure or opened a new door."

"That's why I kept procrastinating writing it," Gabriela said. I didn't know how to open up a conversation and leave the past and future blank. Congratulations on your career. Even when my emotions wouldn't let me say it, I knew you were going to be successful. The minute we landed in Viedma that very first time it was like you were plugged into the electrical lines. You came alive in a way I had never seen. It kind of scared me."

"Ironic," Ernesto said. "It was an electricity that pulled us apart and an electricity that got us talking again. Both with origins in sleepy Rio Negro Provence."

"No, it was my immaturity that pulled us apart," Gabriela said.

"And my blindness," Ernesto said.

"I don't want to disagree again, Ernesto," Gabriela said with a quiet laugh. "It would sound too much like the past. I have come to think of you not as blind, but visionary, like Don Quixote. The mundane is simply lost from your view or transforms into dragons or princesses."

"And you, my Dulcinea," Ernesto said. "Who we never actually meet in the story do we? Only the imagination of her."

"As I remember," Gabriela said, "Cervantes describes her as having a bosom of marble. Perhaps he meant heart of stone."

"Not to bring up the past either," Ernesto said, "but I have an entirely different memory of your bosom."

"See, Don Quixote all the way!" Gabriela said now fully laughing. "So I know you are here for an important speech and opening of the Cambalache Confederation Headquarters. It has been in all the papers, in Mexico City and here in London. You are the talk of the town, and I am talking to you. I don't want to get in the way, and I am not trying to run back to you because you are now famous and labeled the most eligible bachelor in the world. I really just wanted to tell you I have grown up, a little, and wish you well."

Ernesto wanted to tell her of the months he had searched for her and the years of hoping she would contact him or at least pop up in the public realm so he would know she was alright. He had thought of this call all the way across the Atlantic. "I forgave you the moment you walked out the door, Gabriela. It took me years to forgive myself," he blurted out.

"Thank you, and I am so sorry, Ernesto, honestly," Gabriela said. Her voice was husky. "It took me a long time to get back to a normal life, whatever that means. I guess, just waking up each morning and not hurting so much that all I wanted to do is get back in bed. I tried dating, I tried not being social at all. It didn't matter except surviving to each sunrise and each sunset. I annulled the marriage not because I had stopped loving you or even that our love was a mistake, but that I was a mistake and I didn't want your political career burdened as a divorcee. It is amazing that the world has never discovered our brief union." Gabriela knew she was starting to ramble, but the words kept tumbling out of her with a freedom she was never able to achieve with the several therapists she had tried over the years.

"You weren't and are not a mistake," Ernesto said. "So you never remarried?"

"No," Gabriela said, not offering any further explanation.

"Me neither," Ernesto said. "Family trait I guess. Marisa hasn't either, but she is getting very interested in a man just recently. Do you still live in Mexico City?"

"Well, I know your life, at least what the magazines print," Gabriela said. I am happy for your sister. No, I moved out of the Distrito Federal some years ago. I live in San Miguel de Allende. I run an art gallery there where I am also a painter. I am starting to gain a clientele that likes my work. Maybe I am a Dulcinea— the simple peasant girl who only imagination has made her into something else."

"How big is San Miguel de Allende?" Ernesto asked, happy to get away from talking about him.

"It's in Guanajuato State and has about 140,000 people," Gabriela said.

"Not the big city for certain," Ernesto said. "Why there?"

"When I returned home I started painting again, as therapy I guess. I was deeply touched by the sacro-cubism work of Jorge Cocco Santangelo, an Argentine painter who taught in Puebla at the Universidad de las Americas, but has since moved back to Argentina. I planned to go paint in Querétaro for a month and dig deeper into Cocco's style. Early on I took a day trip up to San Miguel de Allende, and I never left."

"Wow, I am speechless," Ernesto said. "And now you are the champion of the small town? That is what your note sounded like."

"There you have it," Gabriela said, "The power of the rural to make a politician speechless. At least once a day it makes me speechless as well," she said growing quiet. "I forgot the rural, Ernesto. We all know it because that is where we all came from. I used to think that mankind had evolved from that ignorance and lack of something, I called it culture. I was wrong. Nothing against the city or your Cambalache mega-cities, Ernesto, but for all their diversity and vibrant collective of intellectual and artistic achievement, we all need a little Garden of Eden in us. That is where the Tree of Life and the Tree of Knowledge are planted. It is from the trees that not only the paper is made that holds our words of love and discovery, but it's from those trees that we breathe fresh air. Our skin touching the skin of the earth is more meaningful than any blockbuster movie or Paris fashion show. Knowledge under our fingernails is authentic culture. I still love the big city, but it isn't the entire picture I once thought it was. In my case I bit the apple, and was sent back to Eden."

"Guardian, request approval for execution of plans regarding James Nathaniels. False testimony prepared. JOAB Buenos Aires ready to move on this." Americas Prelate

JOAB CHAPTER 6

David Rosado heard the melancholy words of the French song for the second time today. The first time was on the radio at midday. The announcer had explained that today was the 16 April 1917 anniversary of a disastrous French offensive that led to the mutiny of over half of the French Army. The song took its name from the small village of Craonne, not more than eighty miles northeast of where David now lived. *Adieu la vie, adieu l'amour, Adieu toutes les femmes C'est pas fini, c'est pour toujours De cette guerre infâme C'est à Verdun, au fort de Vaux Qu'on a risqué sa peau* the song continued. "Goodbye to life, good-bye to love, goodbye to all the women, It's all over now, we've had it for good with this awful war. It's in Craonne up on the plateau that we're leaving our skins, 'cause we've all been sentenced to die. We're the ones that they're sacrificing." It was a warm spring day, but David felt a sudden chill run through him.

After hearing the song the first time, David had researched its origins which led him to the first Battle of Craonne, a French triumph of Napoleon over the Russians and Prussians in 1814. Over 10,000 men had died, about 5,000 on each side in that French victory. In World War One, when the song was actually written, the same states were at war again, and the battle for this same ground took the lives of 163,000 Germans and 187,000 French. A war that started with the assassination of a Habsburg and his wife and pushed by French royalists who wanted vengeance for the humiliating *defeat in the Franco-Prussian War led to the deaths of over 1.4 million and the debilitating injury of 4.3 million more. "Nearly 4,000 deaths or injuries per day for 1566 days; my God" David whispered to deity, "how could man do that to man?" And yet this anti-war song that David now heard on his afternoon walk had been prohibited in France until 1974. During those 57 years of its prohibition, an award of one million francs was offered for revealing the song's writer, but the author of the song remains unknown to this day.*

"How different the world looks from my new perch in France," David admitted to himself. "Exotic and lonely, more ordered than Lima, Peru, but so much more encumbered by the harsh realities of decisions. I used to think that in the battle for freedom versus stability, stability was preferable and the royalists, particularly the Bourbon royalists, stood on the side of stability so that these terrible things could never happen again. It was that very drive for stability which caused the stagnation of the European pond. Fewer living nutrients, little new life, decay and death."

Completing his walk, David ended his thoughts concerning a request from the new JOAB Buenos Aires and supported by the new Americas Prelate. He replied, "Your request concerning the North American Nathaniels is not only denied but seemingly lacking in your concern for ethical and moral consequence. We are not a Mafioso organization, nor do we let our personal feelings interfere with our mission. Bourbon ascendancy cannot, does not justify innocent death nor blatant disregard for unintended consequences. The world has had its share of both over the last century, and it will not happen on my watch."

He posted the communique over his secure internet channel and then began anew to search through records to uncover the recently discovered group of seven JOABs, on in each prelature that were managed directly by the former Guardian. He had uncovered only the Asian and African sub-continent operatives so far and closed down their activities and turned them over to the management of the appropriate prelate. BAJO was a house of cards and David knew he was fortunate that he took command when he did. Another year, perhaps another few months and he would have stepped into something he could not have salvaged.

CHAPTER 28

Hacer Fiaca
Literal Translation: To make the feeling or state of
being bored, idle, slothful or unmotivated

Marisa's Explanation: **To Bum Around** is another Argentine pastime and we do it with flair. This is a Lunfardo word that comes from the Italian word fiacca which means laziness.

ALBERTO GODOY WALKED BRISKLY DOWN the hallway of the CamCon headquarters building third floor. He had not initially supported the Cambalache project, thinking it a dangerous waste of tight funds. Its amazing success had not only won him over but captured his vision of this once side *what if* discussion that was now becoming a reality. The Cambalache Confederation was about to become a reality. He held the speech that would make it so. He entered the CamCon Administrator's office where President Ernesto Starhemberg and Otto von Habsburg sat. Otto seemed slightly nervous, but the President was relaxed and joking. He seemed to have an extra measure of lightness and confidence. Godoy could feel his heart fighting to escape his rib cage. He wondered again at his boss's ability to handle each new challenge like it was just another day.

"Your speech, sir," Godoy said. "Twenty minutes and you are expected in the first-floor conference room. Everything is ready."

"Thanks, Alberto," President Starhemberg said. "Perfect timing. I was just sharing with Otto a few tweaks to my words which I would like to make. Where are Marisa and James?"

"I haven't seen them, sir," Godoy said.

"Check the closets," Otto said with a snicker.

"Do you think we should become custodians in your new building, or are you suggesting something else?" Marisa said as she and James walked into the room.

"You have many talents, Marisa," Otto said, "but trusting you with a dustpan is not one of them."

"Here are those additional thoughts you wanted, Mr. President," James said.

Thanks, everyone," President Starhemberg said. "If you will now give me a few moments I want to go over this one last, first time. No teleprompter makes this more fun and more real, but I don't want to trip over my words."

Eighteen minutes later President Starhemberg and Otto von Habsburg walked into the conference room. It took up half of the building, seating about 200 people. There were flags of twelve mega-cities in the front, along with a Confederation flag in the center, just behind the podium. It was the sun on a blue background, with yellow rays stretching out to the four corners of the flag. Otto had released an explanation of the CamCon flag the week prior. The sun was both a slight nod to Argentina, the birthplace of the Cambalache project, but also the symbol of free energy now as a birthright of humanity. The rays reaching out to the flag's four corners demonstrates the delivery of energy to all four corners of the world and as a connection of all to all who join the Confederation.

The room had a polite buzz that rose slightly as the two leaders walked in. This was definitely London and not Buenos Aires or New York City. The wainscot paneling gave a feeling of safety and wisdom, but James noted it also amplified the quiet conversations. Every seat was filled, and at least fifty people were standing. In a glass booth at the rear of the hall and above the height of the standing crowd were seven media stations and twenty tiny translator booths. CamCon had its own web station, and they had the only roving camera in the room. James and Marisa sat in the one vacant translation booth to avoid attention. This was another Habsburg/Starhemberg show for history. Speculation as to who James was at the side of President Starhemberg's sister would be a distraction.

"Thank you for your attendance today," President Starhemberg said without preamble or introduction. "I have already shared with you, just weeks ago at the United Nations, the general outline of Cambalache. I won't waste your time on those details again. Instead, I would like to give you a brief update on our progress. Then I would like to turn the podium over to Administrator von Habsburg. As you know, I am an elected official of the people of Argentina. I can only speak for them up to a point. Some in my country want to nationalize Cambalache energy. That interest is understandable—the Argentine taxpayer paid for its development. The scientists and engineers who made this happen were and are 100 percent Argentine. In the words of the scientist who made the breakthroughs in cold fusion technology, "This is not an Argentine invention. This is not even a human invention. This is simply a discovery of what God gave us when the earth was born. For those who are uncomfortable with God, I say look, but I add, the absence of God in your equation is not a reason to take this gift from all of humanity. Whether it be of deity or nature, this energy existed long before we harnessed its power." This person has asked to remain anonymous for safety and humility reasons."

James wondered if he had met this scientist in his visits to the Cambalache Project. It seemed fitting to him that such a breakthrough should come from one who had the meekness to see what others had not seen all these years of research and nuclear developments. He assumed Marisa knew this person, but like President Starhemberg was describing, she too had honored his wish for anonymity.

"I report to the world today that Argentina has been paid in full plus interest for the development cost of the Cambalache project and the stand-up of the Cambalache Confederation. This bill has been paid by the first seven mega-city members of CamCon. As other cities join the Confederation, CamCon will ensure those founding members are partially reimbursed. These complex finances have also been audited by two international audit firms and Administrator von Habsburg will provide them for public review as well." President Starhemberg smiled at Otto, and he returned the smile and nodded.

"I will leave the topics of finances, security, and delivery, along with CamCon governance to the Administrator's remarks. I do have two additional points I need to touch on. I plan to run for President of Argentina for a second term. No matter how that goes, there is no danger to the future of Cambalache energy delivery to the world. I have been the project's early protectorate, but I turn that over to CamCon and able administration of Otto von Habsburg. The Argentine Congress has approved a draft bill that sets aside the Island on which Cambalache presently resides as an International trade free zone and under the jurisdiction of CamCon. Huemul Island will also become a sovereign free zone, not unlike zones established in Vienna after World War Two, the United Nations Headquarters in New York City, and the Channel Tunnel."

An increase of whispered words added to the surprise of what had just been said. A sovereign nation had just given up land to an international enterprise without any public protests or quid pro quo. President Starhemberg cleared his throat to get everyone's attention. "The second point I want to make is, as of today, I am removing myself from the direct decision-making loop of CamCon. I remain at the service of Otto von Habsburg and will continue to support the transition of Cambalache Energy from Argentina to CamCon control. As I said in my very first Cambalache announcement, Argentina will not shirk from its new duties. We will remain the first and most ardent supporter of the free energy Confederation, and we will hold the secrets of cold fusion until such a time as the world deems itself ready to manage this abundance. That will remain the responsibility of Argentina to determine that transition. I do ask that the Confederation consider an expansion to rural areas much faster than we had previously planned. A sage adviser recently enlightened me that megacities do not exist in their own bubbles. They are not the sole examples of the future of humanity. In fact, they could not survive individually without connection—connections of commerce, energy delivery, knowledge, and resources. I have mostly considered the idea of connection as to where it departs and where it arrives, for, without those two nodes, there is no coupling or association. But what of the space in between? The rural and smaller towns and cities is that space. They carry the burden of connection but also provide their own links. We are all aware that this is where 70 percent of the world's food is grown, where the fresh water lives, not just stored, but this is where humanity's seeds are planted. Please, do not allow humanity's heritage to be forgotten in a rush to support our concentrations of humanity." President Starhemberg stared into the audience and cameras and willed those in this room and around the world to not forget his words. He smiled in recognition that they would not forget and said, "Now, I turn the time over to the CamCon Administrator, and I thank him for letting me speak from his headquarters on these vital matters."

Questions were shouted to President Starhemberg, but they were ignored as Otto von Habsburg stepped to the podium. "It is indeed an honor to follow the example of one of the world's great leaders, President Ernesto Starhemberg. When he contacted me after the Cambalache Project became a reality and a viable source of nearly free energy, he explained he would be the initial lightning rod for the energy project and the Confederation stand-up. You have not heard much from me, and that is your good fortune as I do not share his talents for clear communications. His presence in front of the cameras has also allowed me the time to get the nuts and bolts of this grand endeavor in place. CamCon will soon begin the process of creating its own mission and vision, as well as governing values, values aligned with universal principles. If that were to just be a framed document on a wall, these words would have already been published. They will not be just words, but our governing focus owned by all. Thus they must be created by all."

Otto paused and looked at President Starhemberg and then the gathered audience and continued. "I can speak to one principle that will be non-negotiable—the only thing President Starhemberg has insisted upon. Complete transparency. Our financials will be published monthly and will be completely open to public scrutiny. Although we are a form of public enterprise, we will not be chasing after quarterly goals to meet Wall Street or London's Square Mile expectations. Energy delivery and plans for expansion, along with failures and obstacles will also be on the web in near real time. This will be the best way to provide the secure delivery and international cooperation of energy delivery. And speaking of security, just as the Vatican, another international island in the midst of a sovereign nation-state, is secured by Swiss Guards so Cambalache on Huemul Island will be secured by an international force trained and operated by CamCon. Now would anyone like to ask any questions? I will do my best to answer them."

The news conference lasted over an hour. The questions were quick and straightforward. Otto's answers were slow and complex. People trickled out throughout the hour, including President Starhemberg, Marisa, James, Godoy, and Peralta Monti, who had arrived just in time to hear the speeches. James had done his best to stay out of the camera's view, as he was supposed to still be in prison. Unknown to him, the one roving camera caught his profile through the translation booth window and Vangelina saw it as she watched the proceedings from the Casa Rosada. Something inside her turned out the last remaining light. The thought of him free and outside of Argentine justice enraged her, and she felt betrayed, even though she was the betrayer.

"That man is supposed to be in prison!" she bellowed at the computer screen. "I am done with subtlety, done with using the system to do the dirty work."

President Starhemberg, Marisa, Godoy, and Peralta Monti departed the next day for Buenos Aires. President Starhemberg asked James to stay in London, due to the ongoing sting operation against Vangelina and to support Otto. James was unsure who the owner of his contract was at this point, but knew he could sort that out with Otto in the coming days. It was the least of anyone's worries at this point. James was to be the house guest of Otto, who had recently purchased a flat not far from the CamCon building.

"I would like you to attend the first CamCon meeting, James," Otto said over dinner. "There is a long-term reason for this. I hope you will be available to facilitate a future string of meetings to develop our mission, vision, and values. My goal is not to take you away from Marisa, but I could really use you here for a month or so."

"You believe we can nail down a mission, vision, and values of an international organization, the first of its kind, in a month or so?" James asked.

"No, but the sooner we kick this effort off, the better chance we have to ingrain these guiding words into our culture and operations," Otto said.

"You can count on me," James said. "Sooner rather than later I am going to be of no use to you."

"Right words, wrong order," Otto said stifling a yawn. "It was a great day. A long day, however. I am going to go to bed early tonight. Tomorrow let's continue our conversation on the nation-state. I think you still owe me an answer on your question the first night we met. You said you believe there is something more important than national will. I have thought about that and have an answer, but not tonight."

"And you owe me answers to my question of the real reason the word Cambalache has been used in the energy project and this Confederation you now lead," James said. "We were also going to get to the bottom of the nation-state and its reason to exist."

James was asleep an hour after dinner. The jet lag, the busy days leading up to this day, and the lack of sleep during his incarceration had taken its toll. He never heard the door to his bedroom open at 5A.M. He woke to the sound of his name being called.

"James, wake up!" he heard Otto urgently calling out. "Help me. You were being attacked. Call the police. Now."

Fully conscious now, James saw Otto wrestling with someone in the dark room. Otto was a big man, but not a fighter. He tried to pull the person away from Otto.

"Be careful, she has a hypodermic needle in her left hand," Otto said. Call the police, 999!"

James found his phone and made the call. He sat the phone down after telling of the attack in progress and the address, with the police still on the line and yelled, "police on the way, Otto," hoping that would scare off the assailant.

Instead, the assailant turned to James with the needle and James froze. It was Vangelina. Just as she was about to shove the needle at him, Otto again attacked. Vangelina swung her hand backward, and the needle hit Otto's flesh just below the heart. Otto screamed and fell to the floor. Vangelina ran from the room.

James knelt by Otto, unsure what he should be doing. "Otto, are you alright?" James asked.

"Fifth rib, James," Otto mumbled clutching his side. "My answer, ironically," he mumbled, "is vulnerability. One thing more important than will." He coughed and felt freezing cold in James's arms.

"Stay with me, Otto," James said. He could hear the siren coming to a stop in front of the building. "That's a good answer, but there is more I think. You have to stay with me to know what I think the answer is."

Otto was still breathing when the police arrived, having an easier time of it than James. The police sent them both to the hospital in the same ambulance. They were separated when they arrived. The police were still in the process of taking James's statement and answers to their questions when a doctor walked in the room.

"Mr. Nathaniels?" the doctor asked.

"Yes, that's me," James said.

"Here are Mr. von Habsburg's personal effects," the Doctor continued. "He wanted you to have these and the words, 'carry on, here is the torch.'" James looked down at the items in the clear plastic bag. One was an electronic key to the CamCon Headquarters. His wallet and an "H" embroidered handkerchief were the only other items.

"Is he going to be okay?" James asked.

"Mr. von Habsburg passed away ten minutes ago," the doctor said. He was awake to the end, although struggling to stay conscious. He also instructed us to make a call to the Argentine Embassy, and someone in his family. His final words, before those I just shared with you, were to his lawyer. It lasted less than one minute. We thought we could overcome the effects of the drugs in the hypodermic, but it was too late. He was injected with a lethal dose of barbiturates. By the time we understood what we were dealing with, he was slipping into a coma. Our buprenorphine and naloxone emergency injection forestalled the coma, but not the resulting stoppage of the heart. I am very sorry." The overworked doctor exited without further explanation.

James continued to answer questions and attempt to breathe in five-second intervals. He didn't know what else to do but inhale, count, exhale, count. If he didn't count, he was confident he would forget to continue the cycle and pass out. 'Maybe that wasn't a bad idea,' he told himself. He was kept for observation until noon when the U.S. and Argentine Ambassadors entered his room together.

The U.S. Ambassador spoke first. "I was contacted by my colleague, Ambassador Rossi. I hope you don't mind my intrusion. He tells me you are a friend of the President of Argentina. I did my own research on you, and I understand you are also an acquaintance of the President of the United States. I am actually here at his personal request. I know none of that is of importance right now. I offer my personal condolences and my personal support if you need anything."

"Thank you, Mr. Ambassador, and please pass on my gratitude to President Marcasano. Is there any information on the assailant?"

"Nothing specific that I know," the U.S. Ambassador said. "Marcos, do you know anything ?" he asked turning to the Argentine Ambassador.

"I have been instructed by President Starhemberg to share any information I might have with you, but I caution that the investigation is still underway, so please do not share any of this with anyone." James nodded. The Ambassador continued, "We have confirmed that Vangelina Pereira did indeed travel to London yesterday. The hypodermic needle left on the floor of Mr. von Habsburg's apartment was traced to a known drug pusher in Hounslow. Traces of barbiturates were found on the needle. Although the alleged assailant is Argentine, Scotland Yard is not sharing any more information at this point."

"Nothing alleged about it," James said. "I fought with her. I personally know her. No mistake who it was."

"Do you have a place to stay?" the U.S. Ambassador asked. "I understand you are not to leave the country at this time and Mr. von Habsburg's flat is off limits for the investigation, at least until tomorrow.

"I can go back to the hotel I was staying at," James said. "No problems with that."

"We believe you are safe and that no further attempt on your life will be made, but the London authorities have offered to keep a security detail at whatever location you stay at, until the alleged, the assailant is captured," the U.S. Ambassador said.

"Attempt on my life?" James said starting to realize what had thus far escaped him.

"The police believe, from your statements, the location of the attack," the Argentine Ambassador said, "and the brief words of Mr. von Habsburg, that she was after you. It appears her goal was to apply a drug overdose to you and make it look like it was self-inflicted." He added, "President Starhemberg would like to speak with you by telephone at your earliest convenience, and he is sending several people to support you during this trying time. They should arrive first thing tomorrow morning."

"Thank you both for your personal visits," James said, suddenly exhausted again. "I know you have much more important things to do than be with me. Thank you."

"On the contrary," the U.S. Ambassador said. "Speaking for both of us, we are very happy to make your acquaintance. It is our job to know people and what is happening. That you up to this point have escaped any notice from anyone, anyone but two of the most powerful presidents in the world that is, is incredible. Your picture was on the front page of the *Times* and the *Guardian* this morning, however, so I am afraid your anonymity is gone. We will leave you to your own grieving. We are both here for you if you need our support in any way."

Minutes after the Ambassadors left James was released from the hospital. He had planned on taking a cab to the hotel but realized as he walked down the hall that everyone seemed to recognize him. He was about to take the police up on their offer for a ride when a lady approached him. Thinking she wanted to talk to him about what happened, he ducked his head and plowed forward.

"Mr. Nathaniels," the lady said. "I am a friend of Ernesto Starhemberg. I came to help you if I can."

"Otto von Habsburg dead and James Nathaniels still alive?" The Guardian had disapproved of any plan to kill Nathaniels. He thought it clear that no other deaths would even be considered. Something else was going on. Certainly, this has nothing to do with BAJO. "What a profound tragedy."

CHAPTER 29

No Hay Tu Tía
Literal Translation: There's no your aunt

Marisa's Explanation: "Atutía" was a substance derived from copper smelting. In the last century, it was used as medicine for certain eye diseases. "Atutía" sounds like "tu tía," which means "your aunt." "There's no atutía" was the original phrase to say that something had no remedy. Over time, distortions turned it into "there's no tu tía." When something has **No Solution**, you might hear an Argentine say, there's no your aunt.

"NOT THAT I DON'T BELIEVE you, but I am new to this um, non-anonymous status," James said. "Convince me before I get in the taxi. That is about twenty steps, I think."

"I was married to him," Gabriela said.

"You're Gabriela?" James asked.

"So Ernesto has told you about me?" Gabriela asked.

"Not exactly," James said. "I asked Marisa where President Starhemberg got the inspiration for the addition to his speech yesterday and she told me a little about you. Up until yesterday, I wasn't even sure if the rumors that he had once been married were even true. I didn't want to snoop."

"You are Marisa's boyfriend that Ernesto mentioned?" Gabriela asked. "So you are more than a confidant, you are practically family."

"Boyfriend, yes," James said. "Practically family, I don't know. I haven't asked that question yet. Listen, I count about ten people that are staring at us. Do you want to catch a cab with me? We can continue to talk if you like. I am alright, though. I'm not sure what you could do."

"I drove here. We can take my car. It's over there," Gabriela said, pointing to her left to a multi-story parking garage. She started walking faster, not giving James an easy way to decline politely. Gabriela was about Marisa's height, dark hair past her shoulders. Very pretty with a fuller figure than Marisa. Full eyebrows, but no resemblance to Frida Khalo. More like Julieta Venegas, James thought. The long dangling silver earrings matched with her colorful blouse and blue jeans. Even in multicultural London, she stood out.

"Thanks for the ride. I was going to check in at the Landmark off of Marylebone Road," James said.

"Is your stuff there?" Gabriela asked.

"No, it's still at Otto's, Otto von Habsburg's flat. The police told me I can retrieve my things from there tomorrow."

"Well, that makes things simple," Gabriela said. "I am so sorry for the loss of your colleague. A personal tragedy for many, I am sure, and a catastrophe for your Cambalache plans as well. I remember Ernesto mentioning Otto during our short time together, but I never got to meet him. When I saw the morning papers, which should have had only the great news of your headquarters opening, I just jumped in the car and came to find you. I waited in the lobby wondering if I should even get involved. Then I saw you and followed my feelings for a second time today."

She pulled into an underground parking entrance and parked the Mini Cooper in a parking spot labeled 4A. She jumped out, and James followed. She said nothing until she opened an apartment door. "I am flat sitting for an artist who I have featured in my gallery. He also teaches at the University of the Arts just down the street. I've been here a few weeks and have two weeks to go. Bloomsbury is a perfect location for a home base when exploring London, I have found."

The apartment was an open concept with twenty-foot ceilings. One wall was mostly glass. The rooms had walls that went up maybe eight or nine feet, but not all the way to the ceiling. "This is a beautiful place," James said. I love the openness. And the art is fantastic." All the walls in the apartment were white and only some modernistic wood beams interrupted the architectural mix of impertinent boldness.

"Do you know art?" Gabriela asked.

"No, not really," James said. "I buy what I love. That might be a $20 piece off of a street artist, or a much more expensive piece from a well-known artist. The problem is I basically live on the road or in places for a month or two, so most of my purchases sit in storage."

"Kind of like life," Gabriela said. "My life anyway. Not that many years ago all I wanted to do was go, buy, experience, and consume. I didn't have the time or patience to stop, look, listen, taste, touch, smell, and digest. Sorry, another time for my life story. There are two bedrooms, and each has a private bathroom. I was planning to meet up with some artists for dinner at a Tapa place nearby for dinner. You are welcome to come, or if you just need someone around, I can easily cancel, and we can talk."

"Thank you," James said. "Normally meeting some artists would be the top of my list, but honestly I have no interest tonight. Please go ahead, though. I am not sure I will be much of a conversationalist. I'm devastated at Otto's death, and I am still processing. It still doesn't feel real. I might try to call Marisa. I feel a little weird staying here. I mean you don't even know me. I could be an ax murderer."

"You could be, but that will be Marisa's problem," Gabriela said. "As soon as I understood who you were it felt right to bring you here instead of leaving you to some generic hotel room. Even though this isn't my place, it is someone's home and that, I hope, offers some comfort, or peace. Isn't it ironic that nothing is lonelier and more sterile than a big city when you need some human connection?"

"Cities can be brutal places," James said, feeling like crying for the first time since the attack.

"I'm sorry," Gabriela said. "I'm talking too much. One of my many faults. Still working on the listening and digesting. There's not much in the refrigerator. I will go get a few things and leave you a little space and some peace and quiet."

"I've enjoyed the talk," James said. "It is keeping me from the painful stopping and listening, and feeling that I know I have to face. I need to be strong for Marisa and her brother. Not only did they lose a father or sorts, but the person who did it was almost a mother, at least to Marisa. And, I think I was the target, the reason Otto is dead." James's eyes welled with tears, and he turned away embarrassed.

"It's alright, James," Gabriela said. "I don't know if you are religious. I wasn't but have grown more that direction over the years. Our first parents covered themselves out of shame, or embarrassment, but also in preparation for handling the harsh realities outside the garden. That is the lesson we learn very early in life, to protect ourselves from the harsh realities any way we can. By the time we become adults we are layered with all types of clothing that tell us we can't cry, we can't feel this emotion or that. Clothes provide protection from physical elements and a moral propriety that I have learned is a spiritual protection as well. Clothing also becomes a part of our identity. Removing clothing can be a step away from that physical and spiritual protection, but in some situations, it can be a step toward the spiritual. It all depends if we are walking toward or away from the Garden."

She paused and looked at James who clearly wasn't sure what she was saying. "Wow, there I go again," Gabriela said. "I never liked questions, but ever since leaving Ernesto, questions have been my constant companion. My answers are often my constant nemesis."

"Questions are the common heritage of mankind," James offered. "We all have them. And we all have our versions of the answers. It's the answers that differ with someone else that cause the problems."

"And brings the insights," Gabriela added. She walked to the wall of windows and asked, "What are your thoughts about this?" She pointed at a nearly completed oil painting of a young Latin woman in a village scene.

"It's amazing," James said. "Is it yours or your friend's?"

"Amazing is the answer I would get from an ignorant visitor to my gallery," Gabriela said. "I would double the price for that response. I am looking for questions and answers. Insight."

"Contemporary Impressionism with an exciting element of fantastic realism," James said. "I am guessing it is yours because it sings of Mexico or Central America. Your brushwork looks loose, but it is very controlled. Your use of color brings depth, but your emphasis of shadows makes me ask if you are lonely, or sad. The young woman in the picture seems almost secondary—something to catch the eye, but then I wander to the food on the table, only partially eaten and the table is at an odd angle, almost thrusting it at the viewer. Early afternoon? The time when one should be enjoying a siesta, but something is keeping this woman from peace."

"If the painting were mine, what should I do to complete it?" Gabriela asked.

"I am not an artist, just an observer," James said. "The question is what is your, the artist's, goal?"

"Build a bridge, maybe," Gabriela said, offering no further explanation.

James looked at Gabriela and then at the painting again. "I would improve your eyes and then send it to him."

"You think the young woman is me?" Gabriela asked.

"I think it is supposed to be, but you are too afraid to make it so," James said. "But I am in a very gloomy place, with Otto's passing and the woman I love an ocean away. I could be way off on everything I just said."

"Could be, but then, maybe the painting isn't mine to change," Gabriela said.

Vangelina walked up to the door of the Maison Decazes exhausted and scared. She had taken the train through the Chunnel to Paris and then local trains to the BAJO Headquarters. She remembered her initial training here, three Guardians and a lifetime ago. Not being a British or European citizen, she expected to be arrested several times, but somehow she was still ahead of the police. She knew James Nathaniels had recognized her and she was pretty sure the hypodermic needle had injected its poison into Otto von Habsburg. That probably meant she had killed him, although she was prepared to say that she had fought him to try to take away the needle and that she was trying to save his life, not kill him. In reality, she had broken into the flat to remove Nathaniels. That is not what she would tell the Guardian, however.

David Rosado had just completed a quiet lunch. Preparing for a conference call with the Prelate in Asia in 20 minutes, he was startled by the doorbell. He was still not used to a day butler that answered the door before he even left the library. He was even more surprised by the presence of Vangelina Pereira, the JOAB in Buenos Aires.

"Guardian," Vangelina began before he could welcome her, "I need your help. The police are almost certainly looking for me."

"Come into the library," he said, not wanting the butler to overhear the conversation. "What are you doing here?"

"I was in London as part of President Starhemberg's visit," she began. "An operation went bad. I am sure it will be in the evening papers here tonight. There is some good news, too."

"Please explain by what you mean when you say an operation went bad," David said. "Then assuage my concerns with the good news."

"I was in the midst of planting some illicit drugs in the apartment of Otto von Habsburg when James Nathaniels woke and saw me," Vangelina said. "He recognized me and woke von Habsburg. There was an altercation. Honestly, I had no idea Nathaniels was there. As you know from my last report, I framed him of leaking Cambalache secrets to foreign countries. He was supposed to be in prison."

"So, the police are after you for breaking and entering?" David asked.

"That and the possibility that von Habsburg was killed during the altercation," Vangelina said. "But that is the good news. One less Habsburg for any future throne."

"What authority, what permission, did you have to attempt to plant illicit drugs in the Habsburg home?" David asked. "For that matter, I don't remember approving your operation to frame Mr. Nathaniels. He is neither a Starhemberg nor a Habsburg."

"Tainting him was calculated to tarnish the reputation of those he worked for," Vangelina said. "That is my job as the Buenos Aires JOAB.

"Now you are on the run for a possible homicide," David said, "and you came here. You directed the police here. You have put the entire organization at risk. You are a fool, a dangerous fool."

"I am a loyal fool, Guardian," Vangelina said. "I did not expect to get caught and had nowhere else to turn. Please help me."

"You must leave now!" David said. "I can provide you with some cash, but I am not prepared to accomplish any more than that. We are not some special operations force. We are a diplomatic force dedicated to helping actual events along, not creating our own events. You will be safe if you can make it to the Asian Prelate. You can disappear there. Travel to the

Ukraine and purchase a flight to Dubai. Flights leave from there with little or no oversight of who the passengers are. Our JOAB there will facilitate your safe arrival and departure to Korea."

Only minutes after her arrival, Vangelina was again on the run. She would take local buses and train, Uber where it existed, and hopefully arrive in Lviv, Ukraine within 36 hours, where she would catch a flight to Seoul, Korea via Istanbul, Turkey.

The feel of Vangelina's clammy palms from their goodbye handshake lingered on David's skin. He washed his hands and wondered if he had done the right thing. He was an accessory to a probable murder. "An innocent man, perhaps a great man, had died," he told himself. "No matter his greatness or not, he was a human being. Now dead. And I just helped the misguided perpetrator escape. I have also jeopardized BAJO and its innocents." He dried his hands and walked back into the library. He sent a message postponing his conference call with the Asian Prelate. He had another call to make, which would change the conference call conversation.

Vangelina had provided him, during his tenure as the South American Prelate, with extraordinary intelligence. He had the phone number he needed and dialed it before he lost his nerve.

"Hello, is this Marisa Starhemberg?" David asked.

"Who is this and how did you get this number?" the female voice on the other end asked.

"We met once, several months ago," David began. "We met when you lost control of your bicycle while visiting the Bosque de Arrayanes National Park. I helped you up. My name is David."

"That doesn't answer how you got this number," the voice replied.

"I am calling about what I understand might be the death of your friend Otto von Habsburg," David said, not wishing to get lost in side issues. "I need to either meet with you or talk with you in a more secure and private electronic manner. Are you still in England?"

"I am en route to the airport now. I will be in England in twelve hours. What is it you want to say?"

"First ,my sincere condolences," David said. He took a deep breath and pushed on. "I also have information on the person who committed the crime. You know her, of course, but I also know her, and I know where she is."

"Why are you calling me?" Marisa asked. "That sounds like something you should pass on to the police."

"If that is what you want me to do, I will," David said. "It is actually more complicated, however, and I believe you will want to handle this more delicately."

"Can you meet me at the CamCon Headquarters, say at 4 A.M., London time tomorrow?" Marisa asked.

"A perfect time to meet," David said. "I will be there. Safe journey, young lady." David clicked the call off, removed the phone battery, smashed the phone, and added it to the burn bag that he would incinerate before leaving for London.

Marisa no more than hung up the call when her phone rang again. "Hello, Santi," she said.

"Marisa, I am so sorry," James said. "I wanted to call earlier, but I was in the hospital and then the police questioned me for hours. This is the first chance I had to call."

"You are getting a lot of practice talking to investigators," Marisa said. "I'm sorry. That wasn't funny. Are you alright?"

"Well, physically I am fine," James said. "I wish you were here."

"I will be soon. Late tonight," Marisa said. "I just got the strangest call. I will tell you about it when I get there. Where are you staying? Can you get me a room there, too?"

"I am so glad you are on your way," James said. "I think I have a bed for you. I will be sleeping on the couch. I, too, made an interesting connection. I will explain when you get here. Whoever might be traveling with you can stay at the Landmark.

I have a room reserved there under my name." He gave her the address to Gabriela's apartment and then hung up, hoping Gabriela wouldn't mind the additional guest.

CHAPTER 30

Por Si Las Moscas
Literal Translation: For if the flies

Marisa's Explanation: Flies are very annoying insects, especially in the neighborhoods of Buenos Aires. People needed to protect and cover the food so that the flies are kept away and could not spoil it. **Just In Case.**

"**M**R. PRESIDENT," ALBERTO GODOY SAID walking into Starhemberg's Casa Rosada office. "I need a few minutes if possible."

"What do you have for me?" Starhemberg asked. "News on the CamCon attack?" President Starhemberg was doing everything in his power to set the news of Otto's death on the overcrowded shelf in his mind where his parents' death and Gabriela's annulment sat.

"Not exactly, sir," Godoy said. "I have spoken with the von Habsburg family, and they are holding the funeral in Vienna next Thursday. The body will be moved as soon as the U.K. releases it. Apparently, the autopsy is going slower than expected. Their question was whether you would be attending the funeral."

"I want to go, Alberto, but I am President of Argentina. The time I have dedicated to CamCon has left me with little time for what I was elected to do. I just got back from Europe." President

Starhemberg took a breath. He was about to lose it. 'How could Vangelina have done this?' He felt more alone than ever in his life.

"We can't leave CamCon leaderless," Godoy said. "My personal opinion, of course, but it's not yet mature enough to allow a representative of one of the mega-cities to take the reins. That would send a shock wave through the entire organization. It would also set a precedent that assassination is the way to create beneficial change."

"What do you suggest?" Starhemberg asked, gaining control of his emotions again.

"I could do it in the short-term until you picked the right person," Godoy said. Changing weight to his other leg, he added, "Pepe could also do it. We have been with this project for four years. We know it better than just about anyone." He continued his thought to himself, 'Serve as an elected official in this quiet country at the end of the world, but crowning yourself king puts a Starhemberg on a throne and I can't let that happen.'

"I need you and Peralta Monti here," Starhemberg said. "Thanks for offering, but it's an election year, and many are not happy with me. I considered doing it myself, but I have a responsibility to serve through my term. I have been thinking about James Nathaniels. One of the reasons I went with von Habsburg was he was not an Argentine national." 'And a long ago promise made to my father,' Starhemberg thought but did not voice. "This needs to have an international flavor and a disconnection from us."

"He's an unknown and possibly tainted," Godoy said. "Sir, I am not saying this to get the job, but my job is to shoot straight with you. He was arrested here for possible espionage and then he shows up in London and his boss is killed with him in the room. It would appear to some like he was involved in von

Habsburg's murder to get the job. Talk about precedent. *Et tu, Brute* would become the new CamCon motto."

Good points, Alberto," Starhemberg said. "I won't be the king maker much longer, however, and I have to do what's best for everyone. He's known in the IMF community and within the financial markets in Europe. He was also the person who saved Otto in an earlier attack. The attacker this time will soon be caught, and from what our Ambassador in London says, James was the actual target. He might actually win some pity points when that hits the news."

"So they have identified the assailant?" Godoy asked.

Starhemberg stared at the wall beyond Godoy. He grimaced and said, "Alberto, the attacker was Vangelina Pereira. She was actually under surveillance for setting up James, although I was not aware of some of those details at first. I really need you here for damage control when that news comes out."

"Vangelina?" was all Godoy could muster in reply. "Whatever is best for the long-term." He nodded slightly and left the office. He walked back to his office, only twenty-three steps away and sat down. He opened his safe and pulled out a single sheet of paper. He should have burned it long ago, but he kept it to fortify himself. He retrieved a small box of matches from the safe. He lit a match and touched it to the corner of the paper. He read the note one last time as it was consumed by fire.

You have been selected by me and are only known to me. I have shared the identity of our JOAB in Buenos Aires with you and she knows of your existence but not your identity. If you need to use her, I leave that to your judgment. The traditional duty of BAJO is to politely nudge and assist the Bourbon Ascendency by increasing momentum and interest of royalty as the essential form of government. The companion duty of all BAJO members is to ensure the Bourbon Ascendency is the preferred resolution. You stand apart from these goals. Your duty is to follow in the footsteps of your ancestor Danilo Ilić, who masterminded the assassination of Archduke

Franz Ferdinand. His achievement helped end Habsburg rule and placed King Petar Karađorđević on the Serbian throne. As you know, King Petar, a Bourbon through marriage to Princess Zorka of Montenegro, daughter of King Nicholas I, was a key supporter of the Greek and Italian Bourbons and prepared the way for the Spanish Bourbon ascendency.

*Others share our vision, but not our will. Brock Adams, former Director UN Health Organization, outlined the path for non-nations-state rule with his statement, "To achieve a world government, it is necessary to remove from the minds of men their individualism, loyalty to family traditions, national patriotism, and religious dogmas." Man's only loyalty should be to royal rule. Add to that the words of the American historian Arthur Schlesinger Jr, "We are not going to achieve a New World Order without paying for it in blood as well as in words and money," and your duty becomes clear. BAJO will focus on the words and money. According to your **will**, you will, deal with the blood. Guardian*

Godoy crushed the ashes in his hand and then tossed them in the air. He reached into his safe a third time and his hand exited holding a Ruger SP101 revolver that he knew was loaded with five .38 Special bullets. He closed his safe and steadied himself. Killing Starhemberg had never been his intention. The Guardian and he had planned on using David Rosado to high-light the weak JOABs in BAJO and then have Rosado killed, and these JOABs removed—that was the reference to the blood in the letter Godoy knew. He had used Vangelina in his effort to get access to the Cambalache facilities on two separate occasions. When Vangelina had suggested the framing of James Nathaniels, he had provided the false email addresses and a contact in Venezuela for the mercenaries. He had reported all this to the former Guardian but had not made contact with the new Guardian, Rosado, of course. Vangelina did not hold the new Guardian in high esteem and felt he might not be trusted with these bold actions. He was not sure what had motivated Vangelina to take such drastic measures in London, but if she was still alive, her capture could be disastrous for BAJO and himself. He could not yet do anything to help her avoid arrest, nor ensure she would avoid talking. He had learned long ago as a political staffer, when faced with a game where it was almost certain you would lose, change the rules of the game. Godoy smiled as a new plan began to take shape in his mind.

"Now is not the time," Godoy said to himself, forcing his emotions back into their box. He opened up the safe and placed the gun back in. "I'm the funnel for all information about Vangelina's case. I will yet achieve my purpose."

Godoy reached for the phone and dialed James Nathaniel's number. 'What time was it in London anyway? Afternoon?' Godoy wondered and hoped he was waking James.

"Hello," James said.

"Nathaniels, this is Godoy in Buenos Aires. I didn't wake you did I?"

"No, Alberto," James said. "I am just getting ready to get an early dinner. What can I do for you?"

"Just left President Starhemberg," Godoy said. "We have a job for you if you are up for it. Be honest, we know you have been through a lot, so we understand if it is too much on your plate right now."

"Okay, what is it?" James asked.

"We need you to take on the interim leadership of CamCon," Godoy said. "President Starhemberg would make the announcement before close of business B.A. time. We don't want the Confederation getting the jitters as the word of Otto's passing hits the news around the globe. We will pass on your bio in the announcement."

"Why me?" James asked. "I mean, thank you for thinking I could do it, but you could do a better job than me, Alberto. You know the political side of this better than I ever will."

"I offered actually, but the President thinks I would be of more use here once the news of Vangelina leaks out. The President is spinning up for a run for a second term. Like you said, I know the politics."

"And Peralta Monti?" James asked. "I am not trying to run from this, but I am still sorting out 'why me?'"

"The President doesn't want an Argentine national," Godoy said, 'except maybe himself someday,' he thought. "Are you in or out?"

"I'm in," James said. "I will be in the office tomorrow, but I will do half days until I sort out living arrangements, and buy a few things."

"I can talk to the Cam Con Finance Officer for you to take on the lease of Otto's apartment unless you would rather not live there. I can also have your things moved from your rented house here to London. Too bad Marisa already left; she could have brought you some of your things."

"I will take Otto's flat for now," James said. "Do you have any idea how long this interim duty will run? That will help me decide what to do with my things in Buenos Aires."

"No specifics from the President, but he did say he was going to exit out of the king-making role soon," Godoy said. "Now, he may speak to you about this request in person, but I wanted to go through this with you now because he will want a direct answer and quickly. One last thing. I understand Vangelina was actually out to kill you. Terrible thought, especially that she's still at large. Probably long gone, though. She's not the type to act on her own. I don't know who could have ordered such a despicable act, but be cautious in who you consider as friend or foe. Like Otto's grandfather, or even President Starhemberg's grandfather would have told you, court intrigue is a deadly game. We don't even know we have stepped outside the lines of safety until we see chalk on our shoes and then it's too late."

James hung up the phone and shook his head. "I should have gone to dinner with Gabriela." He looked at his watch. Five more hours until Marisa lands. Instead of eating, he laid down and closed his eyes. Then he jumped up and smoothed out the bed. Marisa would be sleeping here tonight. He walked out to the couch in the living room and was about to lay down again when his phone rang.

"James, Ernesto here. Alberto said he has run the idea by you. Will you do the job?"

"Yes, sir," James said. "Any idea how long until an official Administrator is announced?"

"No time frame yet," President Starhemberg said. "You will be official, however. I will make the announcement within the hour. Any quote for the press release?"

"Oh wow, um," James stammered. "How about, CamCon is still an unknown, so what's more perfect than an unknown to lead it?"

"Not exactly a confidence-building statement," President Starhemberg said. "Try again."

"Right," James said, not sure if President Starhemberg knew he was joking. "Transparency, integrity, and loyalty to the ideal of CamCon will not only be my guiding principles but the measuring stick by which I invite the world to measure me. I am not a stranger to global affairs, but I don't know everything I need to know, so I will be in listening and learning mode. Together we will get this right."

"Okay, that's more like it," President Starhemberg said. "You have my full support. The same guy I hired for his values and brain less than half a year ago. Give Marisa a hug for me. This is tough on all of us, but I think this loss has hit her double hard. It is like losing our parents all over again. Both Otto and Vangelina. Unbelievable. I wish I could be there for the funeral. You and

Marisa will have to stand in for me. Call anytime. Let's for sure talk this weekend."

The President hung up the phone. James slumped on the couch feeling the weight of the moment. He was asleep before he could consider the full implications of Alberto Godoy's words which still rang in his ears.

"Santi, Santi," the voice said in James's dream. He felt a nudge and then he smelled an intoxicating aroma of cheese and burnt cinnamon? He had had this dream before, in Bariloche. He opened his eyes and nearly drown in the aqua blue eyes of Marisa Starhemberg that were only inches away.

"I've been here before," James said. "Are we in Bariloche, and if not, I can understand everything except the smell of cheese."

"Not Bariloche," Marisa said. "The only mountains outside are the London skyscrapers. As for the cheese, I grabbed a pizza on the way here from the airport." She leaned in closer and gave him a kiss. "You hungry?"

"Yes, but the pizza might get cold," James said smiling. He sat up and asked, "How did you get in?"

"Gabriela, let me in," Marisa said. "She was just entering the building when my taxi pulled up. She says she recognized me."

"You look the same as the pictures I saw of you," Gabriela said. "Well, a little filled out in places, but the same face. Plus your updated picture is just about everywhere."

"I am so sorry, Gabriela," James said. "I meant to tell you I invited Marisa to stay here. That's why I am on the couch, so she could have the bed."

"I can go to a hotel if it is a bother, Gabriela," Marisa said as she punched James in the arm and contorted her face at him.

"No way. It's an honor to have you here. I'm so sorry for your loss, Marisa," Gabriela said suddenly tearing up.

"Thank you, Gabriela," Marisa said. They hugged each other and then both started crying. James stood there not sure what was going on.

"Gabriela," Marisa said. "When Ernesto told me he had heard from you and asked my advice on contacting you, I said not to. I am so sorry. I am an overly protective sister and you are not who I remember."

"I would have said the same thing," Gabriela said, "even today. We never did meet up. He called me on the phone. Perhaps that is best. I am the one who found James. I saw his picture in the newspaper after the attack on Otto." They caught up on the last 24 hours, ate the pizza and then Gabriela announced, "Okay boys and girls, I am going to shower and go to bed. If you need anything, let me know."

"I will be leaving very early for a meeting tomorrow, well today, at 4A.M.," Marisa said. "Could I get a key, so I don't have to wake anyone, or will you come with me, James?"

"I won't let you out of my sight," James said.

"I am going to try to get a couple hours of sleep," Marisa said. "That might feel a little creepy you watching me."

"Ha, ha," James said. "I will be like your patron saint, always with you, but never there—when you are sleeping anyway."

"So you two aren't … ?" Gabriela asked without completing the sentence.

"No," Marisa and James said simultaneously. "Not that it hasn't crossed my mind," Marisa said, blushing at James, "but that is an inertia I choose not to entertain in my life right now. I will explain some other time."

"You don't have to," Gabriela said. "I am no angel, but I have done my own growing up since we last were in the same family. You know, maybe for some people this isn't something to brag about, but I have not been with a man since I left Ernesto. I am not sure I ever will again, but if I do, it will be on the other side of 'I do.'"

"Ahem," James said, clearing his throat loudly. "I am here, and maybe it's me who should go take a shower and let you ladies talk."

"That is very sweet, Gabriela," Marisa said, ignoring James. "I always felt like I was in the way, the spare tire when you were with Ernesto. I felt jealous, left out, and of course I blamed you, not who I thought was my perfect brother."

"He is a lot closer to perfect than me," Gabriela said. "You were the spare tire to me. I was so jealous of you and your relationship with Ernesto. Interdependencies scared me. I wanted to be independent and have my husband be dependent on me. I didn't know that at the time, but much self-analyzation has confirmed that I was a messed up little girl in a grown-up body."

"Ernesto saw more in you than your grown-up body, Gabriela," Marisa said. "You are selling yourself short. We all learn and grow. Some great things happen when we're young because we don't know any better."

"Some start their growth at a pretty low point," Gabriela said, "and sometimes some pretty disastrous things happen because of youthful ignorance." She got teary eyed again, and the two ladies leaned toward each other and hugged once more.

James was going to add something to the conversation about the danger of anyone comparing themselves to anyone else since we really don't know the other and are all too aware of our own faults and how that is a very rare trait of nations even if some people in those nations can do so, but decided not to say a word. He left and took a shower and shaved for the first time in two or three days. When he returned to the living room, both women were asleep leaning against each other on the couch. He grabbed a blanket from the guest bed and gently laid it on them. Since they were sleeping in his bed, the couch, he just sat there watching Marisa breathe, creepy or not.

CHAPTER 31

Estar Hasta las Manos
Literal Translation: To be up to one's hands

Marisa's Explanation: Sometimes, recognizing and accepting love is really hard, I know. Telling it to a friend, or especially to the one you love is even scarier. That's why, perhaps trying to mitigate the impact of the news, Argentines admit: "I think I'm up to my hands with this girl." But we also say we are up to our hands **When we are really busy, and we don't have enough time to do everything we have to do** (which can also be a consequence of being up to your hands in love).

"MARISA, MARISA, TIME TO WAKE up," James said. "I have no cheese or cinnamon to infiltrate your dreams, but I am pretty sure if you don't get up you will miss your 4 A.M. meeting. Hopefully, it is close by."

"What time is it?" Marisa asked trying to move away from Gabriela without waking her.

"Three," James said. "Is the meeting far from here?"

"Not that far," Marisa said. "I checked it out on the map when you gave me this address. It's at the CamCon headquarters, your new office. Ernesto called me after he talked to you."

"Oh, is this a CamCon meeting I should know about?" James said a little surprised.

"I really don't know," Marisa said. "I don't think it's related. Remember that older man who helped me when my bike slipped during our ride in the forest?"

"Yes, I remember when you lost control of your bike, and you crashed into that poor unsuspecting tourist, the older guy who nicely did not sue you for almost killing him," James said.

"Well, you have a terrible memory," Marisa said. "But that old gentleman, David Rosado, called me and wants to meet with me, as soon as possible. He says he has information on Otto's death and on Vangelina, although he didn't use her name."

"That is the same guy I thought I saw at the restaurant when Otto was attacked. Marisa, I am not sure I like the idea of you meeting with him alone. Did you let the authorities know?" James asked.

"Not yet," Marisa said.

"This could be some kind of trap," James said. "I am for sure going with you. "There will only be a single night watchman at CamCon, I think," James said, knowing he really didn't fully understand the security arrangements at the building.

"It's not a trap," Marisa said. "I can't explain why or how I know that. Rosado didn't even ask that I don't go to the police. He was happy that we were to meet so early."

"Talk about creepy," James said. "Okay, let's go. I trust your judgment."

"Do you need my help?" Gabriela asked from the couch, startling them.

"If we aren't back or don't call you by five, call the police," James said.

They both freshened up and left, catching a taxi looking for early morning commuters. They arrived with ten minutes to spare. David Rosado was watching them from some trees across the street at the Royal Academy of Music Museum. James and Marisa entered the building with his pass and were happy to see a night guard sitting at the reception counter. James explained that a visitor would be entering the building at four and to direct him to the Administrator's office. If he did not come alone, keep then at the Front Desk and call the Administrator's office immediately. David and Marisa went to the office.

"Marisa, I am going to go down to the first floor and wait by the elevators and watch for Rosado myself. If I see anything odd, I will give you a call and then call the police. Otherwise, I will escort him upstairs myself."

No sooner had James exited the elevator on the ground floor than he heard the door buzzer sound. He watched from a dark corner a man enter and approach the security guard. The guard directed the visitor to the elevators. He was alone and had on a raincoat that could easily conceal a weapon. James stepped out of the shadows and said in Spanish, "Hello, Mr. Rosado. I don't know if you remember me from our brief encounter in Bariloche. I am James Nathaniels."

"Yes, of course, I remember you," David said. "Thank you and Miss Starhemberg for coming alone. I assume she is upstairs waiting for us?"

James wanted to frisk the guy but decided to trust Marisa's judgment and just escort him upstairs. Neither man said anything until they reached the Administrator's office. Marisa rose from a seat at a small conference table in the room when they entered.

"Miss Starhemberg, I am so sorry for your loss," Rosado said not offering his hand. "I understand from my personal research that you were close to Otto von Habsburg. And a great loss to this extraordinary enterprise, as well," he said as he glanced at James.

"Thank you," Marisa said, suddenly so tired of the condolences that reminded her of her loss. "The event still doesn't feel real. Part of me still expects him to walk in at any moment. Please have a seat, Mr. Rosado."

The three sat at the round table and waited for the other to speak. James finally said, "Sir, you contacted Marisa with some surprising statements. We are all ears."

"When I met you at the National Forest near Bariloche it was not all by accident. Certainly, our actual meeting, our close encounter, was happenstance, but I was there to see you." He paused and then continued. "I have known of you, and much about you, but I felt I needed to see you for myself."

"So you are a Starhemberg groupie or some voyeur?" James asked suddenly on edge again.

"Of a sort, but not what you think, young man," Rosado said. "I work for an ancient organization. At the time I was, well let's say I was in middle management. I presently run the organization. We are based in France, but we have organizational members around the world. We are a small group, less than 100 people in all." David briefly outlined the history of BAJO and its structure.

"You have got to be joking," Marisa said. "You really do exist."

"You know of us?" Rosado asked surprised.

"My father used to scold me when I was very young and would not go to bed," Marisa explained. "He would threaten my brother and me with the ghost of Che Guevara or if we were particularly naughty, say, 'Be a good girl or BAJO will get you.' I thought it was entirely made up, like so many other fairy tales he would tell of the Starhembergs through the ages."

"I am afraid we are very much real," Rosado said. "I was recruited at a young age to join the organization because of my family history. For much of my adult life, it was a part-time paycheck that consisted mostly of intelligence work, watching, reporting, and not much more. When I met you, I was supervising other collectors, one of which was Vangelina Pereira. More about her in a moment. I very recently became the leader of this organization at the death of the previous leader. I am only now discovering the full extent of operations. In my experience, BAJO has been more than a passive organization. I wanted you to know up front that I have learned that the death of your grandmother, Nora Gregor Starhemberg, was at the hands of a long deceased BAJO operative. Your grandfather was very close to the Habsburgs and their potential ascendency before and immediately after the Second World War. He was also close to a Mr. Carl Richter, the fusion technology visionary. I knew some of this before I met you, but had assumed that the audacious rumors that BAJO was involved in the death of someone was just like your father's threats, a fairytale. I can now say that these were not fabrications, but sad fact."

Marisa sat there as tears welled up in her eyes. She said nothing, nor did Rosado. James could not believe what he was hearing. "Why did your organization do what you described?" he asked.

"My grandfather was going to use the discovery of fusion to help launch the bid of Otto's grandfather to reclaim the Habsburg throne," Marisa interjected before David could answer, tears running down her face. "Grandfather was very well known, and someone thought they could threaten him indirectly to deter him from following through on his plans. Attacking my grandmother could do that and keep the news and investigators off the trail of BAJO." Turning to Rosado, she said, "I still can't believe that story is real. Even my father had his doubts about that rumor."

"Yes, more or less that version of the facts is correct," Rosado said. "Although I understand from our records that the plan was only to threaten or at most injure your grandmother, not kill her. The operative was overzealous, however, and he set it up to look like a suicide. A tragedy and I am ashamed to be a part of that history even though it happened before I was born."

"It certainly achieved its goal," Marisa said. "It killed my grandfather's spirit." Marisa paused then asked, "So what does that history have to do with Otto's death exactly?"

"As I said, I am learning quite a bit about an organization I thought I knew well," Rosado said. "Our previous leader was a renegade and not who I thought he was. I received written reports from Vangelina and also believed I was the only person who knew her name and who she was. I now know she was also reporting to my boss, BAJO's leader. I now have all her correspondence. I do believe she loves you, Miss Starhemberg, and had respect for Mr. von Habsburg, but must have had something against you, Mr. Nathaniels. Without my permission, she orchestrated your framing and arrest. I never would have approved such a horrendous thing. She then traveled to London unknown to anyone in BAJO and says she was only trying to frame you as a drug user, but I believe she was lying to me with that explanation."

"Wait," James said. "You have spoken with her since the attack?"

"Yes," Rosado said. "She came to me for help. I put her into our system, and she is on her way to the Far East as we speak."

"What?" Marisa said. "You aided in her escape?" Her hands were balled into fists, and James thought she might tear Rosado's eyes out.

"Yes, but no," Rosado said. "What I hope I have done was put her on a leash, so I can find her again. I needed to understand what really happened, what is going on in the organization I am now supposed to be running. It was a delaying tactic."

"Still, allowing her to escape?" James said. "You should have delivered her to the police."

"It is a little more complicated than that," Rosado said. "There is another operative."

"What do you mean?" James asked. "You just told us there are a hundred people in BAJO."

"No, I mean an unknown operative in your inner circle," Rosado clarified. "And I believe this person is more dangerous than Vangelina. That is why I let Vangelina escape, but kept her willing to contact me again."

"You don't know who this person is?" James asked.

"I know this person exists, but was managed directly by our previous leader and mostly through verbal coordination, not our traditional BAJO written correspondence."

"So we have nothing to go on, and we aren't even sure what the threat is?" James asked.

"I will continue to research files, but I wanted to let you know of this additional possible threat. As for Vangelina, how would you like to handle this?"

"Does she know about this other person?" Marisa asked.

"I would have said 'no' a week ago," Rosado said. "Now that I know Vangelina was also taking orders from our previous leader, so I think it is possible she knows this other person."

"Then let's use her to get to this other person," James said. "Reach out to her and see what you can get from her. Surely there is some reason that would sound plausible. Once we have that additional information, is there a way to have her arrested, or brought to justice?"

"Absolutely," Rosado said. "I want to protect all the innocents in BAJO. I seriously think I will close the organization. It is an antiquated enterprise and has no business in today's world with such an 18th-century mindset."

"Tell me more about that," James asked.

"About what?" Rosado asked. "The mindset, the organization?"

"Your vision for what BAJO was and what it is," James replied.

"It was an organization created to work with the system of the day to help foster support for the House of Bourbon. There were only two options in that day. Royal governance or chaos. There were believers in the Bourbon over the Habsburgs and other royal houses. There are a few that still believe this today, but there are more options, better choices, and even untried possibilities, not to mention your ideas of confederation."

"Even through the centuries of royal households, the final say of power was bottom up. They justified power through bloodlines and God given rights, but there are numerous instances of middle class or peasant revolts that removed one house and put another in its stead. Today no government can exist for long without the consent of the people; even dictatorships can't last for long without tacit approval, or apathy."

"As I understand CamCon," Rosado said, "you are saying that the 'people' are not limited to a nation-state, but rather to some other community of interest or practice. It is interesting that BAJO was involved in the dissolution of the Holy Roman Empire, a Habsburg enterprise. That led to the rise of the Confederation of the Rhine."

"Interesting food for thought," James said. "Marisa will talk with her brother about your concerns and let's say we will make a decision on what to do with Vangelina by the funeral day for Otto. The goals being, uncover what we can, but bring her to justice within the week. In my book, ends do not justify the means. We can't let her go free just because she might know something about another threat."

"Basta Acendencia; Justicia y Orden, Enough with Royal Ascendancies, but Justice and Order prevail," David Rosado said. They traded personal phone numbers and Rosado departed.

"I still can't believe that BAJO is real," Marisa said as James sent an all okay text message to Gabriella. "I really need the world to stop turning so fast, I haven't even had time to mourn the loss of the person that was a father to me. He pulled me out of the fire at key intersections of my life. I wouldn't be here, or who I am without him. And it was me who brought Vangelina into the family. I feel so lost and broken. I only have you and Ernesto, and it sounds like you are both targets of some nut who thinks this is the 18th century."

"Let's take this a day, an hour, at a time, Marisa," James said taking her in his arms.

James's phone rang.

"Aren't you going to see who it is?" Marisa asked.

"It's probably somebody wanting to sell me a bridge," James said.

"I'm partial to bridges," Marisa said. "Buy me one."

James reluctantly looked at his phone and then answered. "Hi, mom." James explained that he was just fine and that the newspapers probably exaggerated the story. And, yes, he was now the CamCon Administrator, and he would be living in London for a while. "Marisa is just fine, in fact, she is right here." He handed the phone to Marisa who also switched to English without missing a word.

"I was just thinking the same thing," Marisa said. "Put them both on a plane tomorrow. I will have James wire the funds. Let me know the flight when you can. Here is my private phone number." They talked for a few minutes more, and Marisa hung up with tears in her eyes. I was wrong, I have more than you and Ernesto. I have a whole family worried about me. And you James Nathaniels, you had better start keeping your family in the loop, or I will finish what Vangelina started."

"I didn't think any of this would hit the news in Missouri until later today," James said. "I was going to call. What is that about 'both getting a flight?'"

"Your sisters are on their way to London," Marisa said. "They were afraid to ask and couldn't afford it anyway. It seems their employer who hired them to build him a house has not been paying them."

"Afraid to ask what?" James asked.

"Whether they could attend Otto's funeral. They were deeply touched that he would come all the way from Europe to plead my case with your family. They are also worried about you and wanted to see you. I think you should hire Jessica as a CamCon Intern and Jacey could pick up a few pointers on her art from Gabriela."

"My sister is an artist?" James asked.

"Yes," Marisa said. "I know more about your family in one visit than you know from your whole life. You better get it together and hold tight to what you have. I know what it's like to lose it all. You know, your parents are going to be pretty lonely with them gone. Why don't you send them on a cruise or something and then have them come visit."

The rest of the week leading up to Otto's funeral went by quicker than any seven days in James's life, even when compared with the worst days of his IMF contract. Both James and Marisa reveled in having his sisters in town, and Gabriela loved the company and the all night girl events. Two nights James actually slept at the CamCon building. On the day before the funeral, Marisa got a call from her brother.

"Marisa, I am going against my own better judgment, but Alberto seems to think it is a good idea. I am going to attend Otto's funeral. I am only coming as an official Argentine gesture to the person the country had entrusted with Cambalache. I understand from James that you are all staying with Gabriela. I have a personal favor to ask."

CHAPTER 32

Andar Como Turco en la Neblina
Literal Translation: To go like a Turk in the haze

Marisa's Explanation: The tango song says, "you're confused, and you don't know what trolley to follow," then that's because you go like a "Turk in the haze." Centuries ago pure wine (no water added) was called "Turkish," because it wasn't "baptized." One said, "to catch a Turk" when they got drunk. Today it is mostly used to describe that feeling of **Being Confused**.

MARISA, JAMES, AND HIS SISTERS departed for Vienna early in the morning the day of the funeral. They brought Gabriela along to watch over Jessica and Jacey, since both James and Marisa would have official duties to attend. "Nanny to two grown up and gorgeous girls," Gabriela said. "My primary job will be to beat away all these unfortunate European men who have been deprived of North American elegance and beauty—both Mexican and the United States."

David Rosado also traveled to Vienna to attend the funeral along with many other distant admirers. Vangelina was in a safe house in Seoul, Korea. It took five days to persuade her into admitting to David that the other BAJO operative in Buenos Aires was on President Starhemberg's personal staff. He had convinced her when he explained he was close to the truth on his own, having just discovered a copy of the letter the previous

Guardian had written explaining the task of this operative and his biological link to a former Serb assassin. David had also been in deep conversations with the seven prelates and most JOABs concerning the mission and actions of BAJO. He was certain it was not only time to change the organization, but he had a plan in place to accomplish his new vision. What David didn't see was the fast approaching freight train that could kill him.

Alberto Godoy had also been very busy. Through his own personal contacts in the government and BAJO, he was able to track down Vangelina. He was confident that if she were ever arrested, she would tell all and BAJO would be forced to disband or go so deep that it would not be able to resurface for a generation. He had no plans to let that happen. He and the previous Guardian had implemented a process that would eventually land him the Guardian's seat leading a much more aggressive organization. He would not be denied that opportunity.

Vienna, the most livable city in the world according to the Mercer International study and others, was just waking up when President Starhemberg's plane landed at Flughafen Wien-Schwechat. The people of Seoul, Korea were just getting back to work after a brief lunch break, if they stopped for lunch at all. Only 35 miles from the highly militarized Demilitarized Zone, Korea still operated on a warlike pace. Although the battles now were the occasional shots across the DMZ and lots of saber rattling from both sides, the city was still one of the most dangerous places in the world to be a pedestrian. Motorcycles on sidewalks and cars and trucks jockeying for position on the crowded streets made the city a kind of war zone for the unprepared foot traffic.

Vangelina exited the BAJO safe house in the Itaewon neighborhood of Seoul to do some shopping. She had left most of her clothing and personal items in Buenos Aires, and she wasn't sure when, if ever, she would be able to return. She stepped into the cross walk when the light turned and walked briskly across the road. A silver Hyundai sedan accelerated through the red light and hit Vangelina at high speed. She flew through the air and hit the metal traffic light pole with tremendous force. She died instantly, at least that is what the brief autopsy would report to sooth any family members that might receive the report. The sedan continued on, and a later investigation of the SPATIC traffic cameras would show the license plates covered with mud, rendering it untraceable.

President Starhemberg's security detail received the news of Vangelina's death shortly after the President arrived at his hotel. Vangelina had been carrying her Argentine Presidential security identification. The Seoul authorities were told she was in Korea on vacation. The Argentine Embassy in Seoul was directed to claim her remains. It would be several more hours before the BAJO Asian Prelate would communicate the details of her death to David Rosado.

"Mr. President," Alberto Godoy said, interrupting Ernesto's breakfast with the Argentine Ambassador to Austria. They were in a private room of a coffee shop on Kohlmarkt Street. Alberto leaned to the ear of the President and whispered, "Vangelina Pereira has been located in Seoul, Korea. She died in a hit and run car accident while walking on a public street."

"Seoul, Korea?" President Starhemberg asked. "How in the world did she get there?"

"I don't have any details, sir," Godoy said. "Our Embassy will take care of setting up the transport of the body."

"I am so sorry for her," President Starhemberg said. "She was duplicitous, an accidental murderer—at least that is what I will assume until I have conclusive proof otherwise, and she died without anyone she knew by her. Not a good way to end your battles."

Alberto Godoy suppressed a laugh. He thought the President too sentimental, trusting, and expecting good out of everyone which in his book equated to weakness. A president or any other type of ruler could not afford to be weak. "Would you like me to let your sister know?" Godoy asked.

"I will tell her, Alberto," President Starhemberg said. "I am meeting with her in, *mala leche,* I am going to be late. I have ten minutes to get to the Augustinerkirche, the Church of the Augustinian Friars. That is where the funeral will take place, in a couple hours but I have another meeting there, and I can't be late. I could walk there in five minutes, but I have to take a car to please our security people."

"You are the meeting, sir. You can't be late," Godoy said showing his smile this time. "It's just your sister, and heaven only knows how many times she has been late to one of your meetings."

"That is not the case this time," Starhemberg said. "Could you wrap things up with the Ambassador for me? It will take me five minutes to say goodbye. If I leave on an emergency errand, the Ambassador will understand."

"Certainly, sir," Godoy said. "I hope your emergency meeting goes well."

"Me, too," Starhemberg said running out the door to his waiting auto. Eight minutes later his limousine pulled up to the front of the private Habsburg church where Otto would be interred along with most of his ancestors dating back 400 years. He didn't wait for someone to open his door. He got out on his own, much to the surprise and frustration of his security detail. He wasn't sure where he was meeting Marisa but assumed if he entered the church someone would direct him. He didn't even notice the ornate gothic architecture or the woman sitting in the last pew by the door. She turned and stood.

"James Nathaniels was telling me that it was your ancestor, Ernst Rüdiger Graf Starhemberg, who was the city commander and hero during the Turkish Siege of the Habsburg Empire and the City of Vienna. He basically saved Europe from an Ottoman invasion."

"Hello, Gabriela," Ernesto said. "You look magnificent. Thank you for coming."

"I wouldn't have missed it for the world," Gabriela said. "You never told me you are an honorary citizen of Vienna and a Knight of the Order of the Golden Fleece, whatever that is."

"It's a 600-year-old men's club that allows us to wear a necklace," Ernesto said. The citizenship thing along with ten Euros will buy me a cup of Vienna coffee."

"I hear it's excellent. Wasn't there a war fought over it?" Gabriela asked as she left the pew and walked toward him. "Although I am an herbal tea drinker myself."

"The coffee beans left behind by the Turks were one of the spoils of war, but not the reason for the war," Ernesto said feeling his personal space pierced and Gabriela was still ten feet away. "There was a legal war fought over Vienna's chocolate cake. Ironic that I am talking to a Mexican who probably has some ancestral rights claim to chocolate and here we are across an ocean and a continent talking about ownership of a chocolate cake."

"Ironic, or merely a metaphor for our own legal reality?" Gabriela asked. "I was in the neighborhood but would have never thought to drop in had Marisa told me you requested me to meet with you. I thought I was here to help with the Nathaniels girls."

"Would you have come if I would have asked you?" Ernesto asked.

"I don't know," Gabriela said now standing within arm's length. "Maybe. I didn't contact you originally to try to get back together now that you are famous and powerful and running a country and saving the world with a free energy source and now being listed as the most eligible bachelor in the world," she said with a grin. "That would feel so two-faced, so deceitful."

"I didn't ask you to come here to ask you to be the president of my fan club," Ernesto said. "I'm still just Ernesto Starhemberg, trying hard, but often failing and remaining clueless."

"Why did you ask me to meet with you?" Gabriela asked.

"As you said, you were in the neighborhood," Ernesto said with his own smile. "I asked you to come here because I wanted one of two things, closure or hope of a new opening."

"Explain," Gabriela commanded.

Ernesto flung himself into the abyss of the unknown and took her hand in his. She didn't pull it away, but she didn't reciprocate his grip. "Closure. You left and disappeared out of my life in an instant. I tried to contact you but failed. I wanted so desperately to understand what happened. To put it to bed if I could, but I couldn't. It wasn't in my power to do so. Now maybe I can, with your help."

"I know now, and even then I could see through the fog of my own immaturity enough to realize that I had to sort things out on my own. I couldn't have given you any answers then. I hope our recent phone conversation covered my repentance and remorse. I don't know what I can do to help you with closure. Maybe this is as much restitution as I can offer."

"Married couples become stronger working things out together. Depending on and supporting each other is more powerful than anything one can do on their own." Ernesto took a breath and plunged forward. "Maybe the other option, a new start for us, is completely out of the question then," Ernesto said. "I have never stopped loving you, but I am afraid to say it on this first blind date for fear of scaring you away again."

"I hate to tell you this, but you just said it," Gabriela said.

"I know, but this is a church, and you can't hold what I say here against me, can you?" Ernesto said with a hopeful grin.

"I'm not a priest, and this isn't confession Ernesto," Gabriela said.

"You know, Gabriela," Ernesto said trying to fully smile but failing, "I have been a successful leader and politician in large part because I am pretty good at reading people. I am a miserable failure at reading you. I have no idea if you are playing with me if you are deadly serious, or simply don't care."

"Okay, here is 'Gabriela For Dummies,'" she said. "I wouldn't still be here at all if I didn't care. I am too independent for my own good, and so when I say things, it is often to protect what I really think, especially if it feels at all dependent. You can see around the corners of my independence curtain by my actions. I ran from you all those years ago because I was pretty sure I was going to ruin your life. If it had been that I just didn't love you, I might have hung around for the chance at being the wife of some powerful politician. Except I wouldn't have done that because I am not a leech—that would be dependent. Follow me? I wouldn't have sent the letter or taken your phone call if I was dead serious about staying away from you. I am dead serious about you understanding my motivations. I don't want the famous, powerful, irresistible, and very eligible Ernesto Starhemberg."

"You don't?" Ernesto asked almost to himself.

Gabriela continued, "I left Viedma because I thought I was going to lose my independence. I discovered I was frightened of being dependent in that small city. Requiring you for financial and emotional support. That is why I didn't respond to your contact efforts. I was an idiot. I didn't know what interdependence looked like. I discovered it in the ecosystems of the small town where I ended up living. That's Gabriela, in all my resplendent imperfection."

"Wait," Ernesto said, "somewhere back at the beginning of this you said something like, 'if it had been that I just didn't love you…' Does that mean you do love me, or did?"

"Of course I loved you then," Gabriela said. "I wouldn't have married you if I hadn't. I was immature and scared, but like I said, not a dishonest leech."

"And now?" Ernesto asked.

"I'm still sorting through that," Gabriela said. "I think I know, but first," she paused, stepped to him and kissed him gently, then more passionately. She enjoyed the shock she first felt from Ernesto and then the melting away of his fears and then the tremors of his passion. She broke away from him, surprised she was out of breath and said, "Yes, I do believe I still love you."

The funeral was a solemn affair, full of pomp and circumstance. Otto was well-loved, and so the Loreto Chapel of the Augustinian Church was full. The final ceremony, for family and select friends, including Ernesto, Marisa, Gabriela, James and his two sisters, was at the Herzgruft. Marisa explained to the group that the Hearts Crypt was a burial chamber of nearly 60 urns containing the hearts of members of the House of Habsburg dating back to 1654. Otto was in good company.

A member of the Habsburg family, who Ernesto obviously knew, had a brief conversation with Ernesto and then briefly with him and Marisa while the rest of the group waited. When they returned to the group, Ernesto explained, "There will be a special performance at the Spanish Riding School this afternoon for those who attended the funeral." He turned to Jessica and Jacey and said, "You might have heard of this school. It is where the Lipizzaner horses and their riders perform. The Vienna Boys Choir will also provide a brief performance in honor of Otto, whose ancestor Maximilian I founded the choir over 500 years ago. They will sing Wiener Sängerknaben by Mozart, who worked with the choir in his day. You are all invited."

"Will you be attending, Mr. President?" Jessica asked.

"I have been meaning to talk to you about something, Jessica. My name is Ernesto, and I am not your president. I am just a guy from Bariloche, and I would like to be your friend, so call me by my first name." Turning to Jacey, he added, "And sadly I must return this evening to Argentina, so again we will miss our dance." Turning to the whole group he said, "But Marisa is actually more familiar with Vienna and these kinds of things than I am. She went to school here and knows many of Otto's closer friends and relatives that will be attending."

"Sir, could I have a brief word with you, CamCon business, before you leave?" James asked.

"How about right now?" Ernesto suggested. "Let's take a walk through the courtyard. It's already secure for the funeral. I have something to mention to you as well." When they were away from the group Ernesto asked, "So I leave it up to you to sort out CamCon issues, but what can I help with?"

"It has nothing to do with CamCon." James said nervously. "I just said that for the group. I had already discussed this with Otto, but now it feels appropriate to talk to you. I would like your permission to ask Marisa to marry me."

"Ah, so that explains it," Ernesto said. "The person I was speaking with first talked to me privately at the behest of Otto, who fully expected to still be alive at this point." Ernesto's eye welled up, and he took a deep breath and continued. "He left a significant sum of money and a few pieces of artwork to Marisa as a dowry. I knew you two were getting serious, but this dowry business was the first I knew of how serious. If this is what it will take to get you to call me by my first name, then I give my permission, as did Otto before me." He hugged James and whispered, "I have lost a dear friend this day and gained a brother. Thank you, James, this gives me more strength to press on than you could imagine. Is this event to happen soon?"

"I plan to ask her before she returns to Argentina. I will leave the date of the marriage, assuming she says yes, up to her."

"Smart man," Ernesto said. "Now if you could do me a favor. I don't want to get tongues wagging, so would you escort Gabriela to the airport as if she were your date? I would like a few minutes alone with her before I depart. You will get back in time for the performance. I won't keep you both long."

James agreed and went immediately to Gabriela and invited her. He had worried that this might make Marisa jealous or upset, but she probably knew or guessed what was going on. Marisa's smile was as sparkling as the shimmer in Gabriela's eyes.

Marisa left with her brother. They talked about Otto and about the news Ernesto had on the death of Vangelina. Marisa brought up Gabriela to lighten the short time they had together. Ernesto brought up James and how wonderful his two sisters were. "Come home when you can, Marisa. Cambalache needs your oversight. But take what time you need to support James. I have asked him to fill some enormous shoes."

"And he will fill them, big brother," Marisa said. "Like you, he makes things look easy."

"Speaking of making things look easy," Ernesto said, "when are you going to tell him your actual role with Cambalache?"

"I don't know," Marisa said. "It will probably just come up sometime in conversation."

James's trip to the airport was not as somber. He knew the basic history of Gabriela and the President but didn't approach that subject. Indirectly he brought up the happy discoveries that had accompanied the ill-fated launch of CamCon and the tragic death of its first Administrator. "It's not that I think there is some sort of karma or universal balance that occurs," James offered, "but that nothing we experience fits perfectly into just one category. With every truth, there is a clever counterfeit. With every tragedy, there is a kernel of something heroic or fortuitous;

although we have to work with our constructive imagination to find those kernels sometimes."

"Thank you, James," Gabriel said turning to look out the window at the passing gray monotony of row houses near the Vienna airport that reminded her of the outskirts of London. Maybe this was a common European sight. "In every one of those houses is at least one life. Hopes, dreams, tragedies, successes, tragic and joyous events are protected within those walls. What puny edifices for such grand, awesome happenings. I almost didn't call out your name at the hospital because I didn't want to hope for something good in the midst of something so sad. Thank goodness I have grown enough to not have to justify being a friend or reaching out. For too long I was one of those bleak row houses, pretending no life was going on inside. The door is open, and the fresh air has rushed inside, and it is intoxicating."

"That's the danger of hypoxia. It's insidious. I was so focused on learning and grades in college. I was so focused on work and achievement for years after graduation. I missed out on the essence of simply living. Marisa has injected pure oxygen into my life, and I have never had clearer thoughts or brighter understanding."

"That must be a Starhemberg trait," Gabriela said. "No wonder the Habsburgs have depended on them century after century."

They arrived at the airport, and James escorted Gabriela through security while several people noticed and a few took pictures. Not until they boarded the Argentine President's aircraft did they see Ernesto Starhemberg. James said he wanted to see the cockpit and turned to the front of the plane. Gabriela followed Ernesto on a brief tour. They sat down next to each other on a small couch in the conference room.

"You know how to impress your ex," Gabriela said. "I wish you could stay longer. I really would like to get reacquainted."

"I wish I could," Ernesto said. "It sounds cliché, but I feel the expectations of 45 million Argentines on my shoulders. Is that blowing up any bridge we might have built over the past week?"

"No, but it is a pretty crowded bridge," Gabriela said. "I don't want to be the reason or excuse of failure to 45 million people. Go home, and we will work on a way to find each other in that crowd."

"I have already failed," Ernesto said, leaning his face down into his hands. "When I was young I promised my father that I would do what Starhembergs had done for centuries, support putting a Habsburg on the thrown of power. CamCon was not a kingdom, but it was the closest thing the world had to offer. Otto is gone. I have lost a dear friend and a promise."

Gabriela took Ernesto in her arms and held him as he silently cried. She stroked his hair and breathed deeply, hoping the rhythm would calm his heart. He eventually sat up and kissed her gently and then went to the small sink at the bar and washed his face. "That is the first time I have allowed myself to cry since my parents died. I am not sure I feel better, but I feel some of the burden lifted. Thank you."

They talked for a short time until Alberto Godoy and Pepe Peralta Monti arrived at the aircraft. Alberto opened his phone before ascending the stairs to the plane. He made a call and said, "Now is the time to execute. Loose ends have been tied up." The previous Guardian selected Rosado because he was soft and unwilling to do the hard things that must be done. He was to be the proverbial fall guy, the scapegoat. He has done most of the work for us. All the soft and unwilling have been identified. Now it is time to clean the BAJO house. He continued his conversation. "Your orders are clear. I will expect a report on your progress when I call you after I am home."

CHAPTER 33

Tirar los Galgos
Literal Translation: Release the greyhounds, or drop pickup lines

Marisa's Explanation: Argentina has notoriously beautiful women. In attempting to seduce them, Argentine men **improvise speeches, sometimes with success, other times not**. Obviously, this is not about hunting with dogs, (as is practiced in the Pampas and Patagonia where I grew up), but both ways of releasing Greyhounds may have something in common, right?

J AMES HELD A BRIEF PRESS conference exactly one week from the previous CamCon press conference. It was a much more modest affair and focused on his background and an opportunity for anyone in attendance or online to ask questions. The media in attendance quickly got bored as it was evident they were not going to trip him up or cause him to say anything incendiary, thus sensationally newsworthy. There were some great questions from individuals in the online community. Marisa stayed in the background helping him on some technical issues for his first week in his new role. Within the second week of CamCon opening its doors, twelve megacities from Europe, the Americas, and the Asian sub-continent were participating members.

"I need to return to Argentina soon," Marisa announced. "I need to check up on my associates at the Cambalache Project."

"I know," James said. "The London chocolates just don't match up to Bariloche confections."

"You see right through me, Santi," Marisa said.

"What are your travel plans?" James asked. "Soon as in tomorrow, or soon as in next month?"

"Those are my only options?" Marisa asked.

"Actually tomorrow is not an option. I told Jessica you might have time to go with her to the Paul McCartney concert. I think it might be his last one in London. I have the tickets, but I have to meet with the Mayor of Shanghai. That would be a great leap forward—pardon the Mao joke. It would be the first Chinese city to come on board. Jessica is having fun as an intern, but when Jacey left to go back to the States, it was a real shock for her. She now realizes, I am guessing, she has actually left home."

"That is already solved. Gabriela is leaving for home on Monday, and I offered your ticket to her. Her concept for the mural artwork in the CamCon lobby is going to be amazing by the way. Gabriela loves your sisters. She has talked about asking Jacey to come to Mexico for a visit, so she can work on her art."

"So that leaves you without a date on possibly your last Saturday in town?" James asked.

"Not quite," Marisa said. "I am meeting with David Rosado at his home in Paris. I leave in the morning. I will be back late tomorrow night."

"So neither of us was going to go to the concert?" James asked. "That cost me almost the same as your plane ticket to B.A."

"You are a good big brother, Santi," Marisa said giving him one of those smiles. "I am sure Jessica and Gabriela appreciate it."

"What are you and your new buddy meeting about?" James asked, trying to sound uninterested.

"Are you jealous, Santi?" Marisa asked, laughing at her discovery. "I have always liked older men. Otto would have made a great husband. David is certainly good-looking, cultured, and has layers of mystery."

"So does a pearl, Marisa," James said. "I can buy you a pearl. Be careful with that guy. He isn't a fully vetted contact, and it was his organization that has hurt your family, more than once."

"I will be careful, Santi," Marisa said more serious. "I don't exactly know what the subject of the meeting is, but it has to do with changes he is making to BAJO. Wow, just saying that name out loud still gives me the shivers."

"As it should," James said. "Maybe I should cancel my meeting and go with you."

"Then how would he make romantic advances to me?" Marisa asked.

"Okay, that's it, I'm going," James said, picking up the phone.

"No way, Santi," Marisa said. "This is something I am going to follow through on, and I don't need you there to make him feel uncomfortable. If he had wanted you there, he would have said so."

"Maybe, but will you do me a favor, no matter the time, would you stop by my place when you return? I wanted to go over something with you myself. I am sure Gabriela will also be out late with Jessica, so she won't mind you coming in late, or early morning, or whenever our meeting is over."

"So this is to be a meeting?" Marisa asked. "Oh boy, that sounds romantic. Can't wait. I am going to dinner with Gabriela and Jessica tonight, so I am afraid you are on your own. Pub food is good this time of year." She kissed him and departed.

James immediately started putting his own plans into motion. He actually really liked London pub food, the gravies and the deep dish berry pies that made him homesick for his mom's desserts. He was not at all sure that he would be able to answer all the Chinese mayor's questions and didn't understand how this mayor could even speak for her city in the strict single party system that ruled China. He did his homework and was prepared when he met with Ms. Xi Luan.

James knew Marisa was already gone the next morning when he got up. London just felt different without her somewhere in the city. His late afternoon meeting with the Chinese delegation included a dinner at the CamCon Headquarters. James was considering hiring an international chef as almost every serious meeting seemed to carry the expectation of dinner as a preamble. The dinner went well, and there was, of course, no mention of business. James understood the protocol, but it also irritated him. He hoped it didn't show. This night, in particular, he wanted to get home to prepare for Marisa's arrival.

"Thank you so much, Mr. Nathaniels for your excellent hospitality," Xi said. "I am also impressed with the quality of your Mandarin. I would like to talk seriously for a moment and will do so in English. You see, I have tickets to the Paul McCartney concert and do not want to be late."

"Of course," James said almost laughing. "I hope the information we provided answered your concerns. Please ask me any additional questions you might have."

"We actually have none," Xi said. "I have been authorized by the central government to enter into formal negotiations immediately. We will, of course, join, but we must preserve face and thus discuss for a time, our entry. My government sees this as a win-win for you and for the Chinese people. Your CamCon immediately interested us, but we had to wait. Our only requirement is that we be the 13th member."

"I see," James said because he didn't.

"We are well aware that 13 is not a lucky number in the western world. In China, however, it is considered very lucky. Our government is struggling with its own legitimacy and entering

CamCon will significantly improve that legitimacy. Also, being the 13th member is auspicious. We were unable to claim being the 8th member, so we had to wait until this moment. As you know, the number 1 in the second column sounds like the Mandarin word *shi*, which is translated as 'definite.' You also know that the digit 3 sounds closely to the word life, as in giving birth. Thus you see, the number 13, pronounced *shisan* could also mean 'definitely vibrant,' or 'assured growth.'"

James closed up the office at seven, wishing he still had a ticket to the concert. Thirteen mega-cities in the Confederation. Things were coming together. He no sooner left the CamCon building than he got a call from the personal line of President Starhemberg.

Are you still at the office, James?" he asked. "I have something I want to run by you, that is if you have a few minutes."

"I just finished up with the Mayor of Shanghai," James said, stepping back into the building. "They are coming on board. That opens up the possibility of several more Chinese cities within the next few months. I have a couple hours if you need me that long." He thought about mentioning Marisa's travel to the continent to meet with Rosado but decided to focus on the President's agenda only.

"I just got off the phone with President Marcasano," Starhemberg began. "Argentina's bid to become a permanent member of the United Nations Security Council has been denied. In fact, they even tabled our membership as an elected member. The traditional power brokers are feeling threatened."

"I am not surprised, sir," James said. "I don't think that is a major setback, however. We talked about this before your first Bariloche speech."

"I bow to your powers of prognostication," Starhemberg said. "I really thought they would want us closer, not push us away. They might not have seen us as an equal, but making us a member of the elite club would be a win for them and a perceived possibility for them to control us. They must have come to the conclusion that wouldn't have worked. So here we are, outside the game with the most important ball in town."

"To follow your metaphor," James said, "it's time to build the new stadium."

"I agree, although I am going to take a different path than any we had discussed previously."

"Okay," James said, arriving back at his desk and sitting down. "What do you have in mind?"

"I am going to propose that Argentina as a country become the first nation-state to join CamCon. I am confident I can garner the votes in Congress. Of course, this would have to go before the Argentine people for a final vote, but if it is pitched correctly, it could happen. We can still send an ambassador to the United Nations, but that organization will fast fall by the wayside. This is at least a six-month process, but it very well could happen that before my presidency is over, I could be working for you. Then I will call you 'sir.'"

"It will never happen, sir," James said. "The titles, that is."

"They said Brexit would never happen, but it did," Starhemberg said. "Now look at the UK, they are stronger than ever, soon to overtake Germany as the most robust and vibrant economy in Europe and in the top five in the world."

"I can see the power in that interdependent relationship for Argentina, but getting the people and the traditional power brokers in your country to see that is a tall order."

"That is my job, James," Starhemberg said. President Starhemberg discussed the particulars of the plan and how he would sell it. The discussions took about an hour. James was back at his flat at 8:30. He hoped to see Marisa by nine. She said she was planning on catching the 7:13 train so she would be at the London St. Pancras station by 8:40 and then a quick taxi ride to his flat.

Marisa was enjoying her meeting and early dinner with David Rosado. She had arrived at 3 P.M. to the address David had provided her. The Maison Decazes captured her imagination of another era. Its white stone three-story walls, the rounded guardrooms on each side of the mansion that began as appendages of the second story and stretched to the third story and the crystal windows sang of the glories of a past France. The interior was also richly finished, and the furniture must have been worth a fortune. Yet, David Rosado was humble, soft-spoken, and could have been the butler, rather than the *homme de la maison*. They enjoyed a simple lunch consisting of a mixed salad that David said came from the estate's garden, followed by a paté, a main course of poulet basquaise and some local cheeses and fruits for desert. Revisiting their initial happenstance meeting near Bariloche was the only conversation that hinted at business. After the meal, David escorted Marisa to the patio where they enjoyed a citron pressé drink, also from the lemon trees on the property.

"Thank you again for coming to my home, Ms. Starhemberg," David Rosado said. "Of course I didn't invite you here just to have a lunch companion."

"I told my boyfriend you were luring me here to make romantic advances. Thus he wasn't invited," Marisa said.

"Do I have a chance?" David asked, returning her smile.

"Not if you insist on calling me Ms. Starhemberg," Marisa said. "Please call me Marisa. May I call you David? We are both from South America, which makes us family."

"And alas, a family romance would be frowned upon," David said. "How is Mr. James Nathaniels? He has taken on a colossal project."

"He continues to thrive, no matter what is thrown his way," Marisa said. "He has yet to prove the Peter Principle, to rise to the level of incompetence."

"I fear I have," David said, suddenly serious. "This position came as a surprise and the longer I am here, the more I want to run from it."

"My brother would say, always run to something, not away from something," Marisa said.

"Precisely, Marisa," David said with enthusiasm. "I have a target idea I want your thoughts on."

"BAJO has a long history," David began.

"Yes, I know," Marisa said. "The name has been known to my family for generations."

"That history provides a pretty clear picture of the things we are good at, some things in which I would rate us as atrocious, and some things which are simply outdated," David began. "I am not saying we will never need to turn to the royal families for trusted governance again, but you and I both know that unfortunately totalitarian dictatorships are a much more probable form of oligarchy than the Royals. Organizations like BAJO can't really affect change toward a crown governance solution like they could a hundred years ago. We are terrible at any form of operational action. We have no training, procedures, checks and balances, or mitigation processes to play the very serious game of special operations."

"You mean like assassinations and attacks?" Marisa asked.

"Yes," David said. "And other less repugnant tactics such as arranging marriages, constructing alliances, and creating subterfuge. But we do have our strengths."

"And those are?" Marisa asked.

"We have a clandestine network that spans the globe," David said. "We are organized, self-funded, tested in intelligence collection, and for the most part we are passionate about making a difference."

"What are you suggesting?" Marisa asked, not sure where this conversation was headed.

"With a few minor adjustments and a name change to reflect our focus," David said holding Marisa's eyes with his, "we could become the CamCon clandestine intelligence arm. We would have some housecleaning to do. In fact, that has already started. We would have to prove our trustworthiness, of course."

"How would you propose you gain CamCon's trust?" Marisa asked. "You are starting out in a pretty deep hole. Someone I had trusted with my life and love was caught with one of your shovels. One of your people. And I wonder what else your organization has done. Was it BAJO that attacked the Cambalache project?"

"Yes, it was, under the old Guardian, the person who recently died and in whose chair I now sit," David said. "Additionally, I can tell you the other rogue BAJO operator is on your brother's presidential staff. At least that is what Vangelina told me. She was ready to give me the name but was killed in that suspect hit and run accident. I don't know who that is yet, but as soon as I find out, I will let you know." Marisa studied David and David let the silence continue. He then added, "We are not a bunch of old people who just want to pretend we are important. In information collection and operating quietly and independently we are professional and accomplished in this skill set."

"We will soon have the support of mega-city and national government collection assets," Marisa said.

"And those will be very valuable, especially the technical assets, satellites, signals and electronic intelligence, cryptology, and cyberops," David listed. "They will have their traditional zero-sum loyalties placed with their nation-state. The abundance mentality your boyfriend talks so much about will not happen overnight. It will evolve. Until then, what we can bring to your table is a human intelligence capability that is for your use only."

"So why did you want to talk to me and not my brother, or the new CamCon Administrator?" Marisa asked.

"I wanted the chance to make romantic advances," David said smiling. Then becoming somber, he added, "You have been most affected by our disgusting actions. I wanted the chance to convince you. If you could see the advantages of us on your team, then I think this will be a proposal that has some legs." David paused and then added, "BAJO can tell you many things about the leaders of nations and industries that no one else knows. I know for instance what your actual role has been with Cambalache. Our agents didn't know, but I was in a position to put one and one together. I respect your capacity to see beyond the known and see into the future. You alone may see the role BAJO can play in the changing roles of nation-states and the international governance systems."

"I think you will find I am quite myopic in comparison to James Nathaniels," Marisa said trying to regain her composure.

David smiled and thought momentarily about revealing what he had learned from his London JOAB just before Marisa's arrival, but opted to remain silent. Sometimes not sharing a secret reflects an even higher level of trustworthiness. "You have just missed your Chunnel train I am afraid," David said, looking at the wall clock. "There is another one in thirty minutes. I will drive you to the station to ensure you make it. You have an important meeting to get to yet tonight."

James wanted to call Marisa's cell phone, but decided not to. He was worried about her meeting with David Rosado and wished again that he had accompanied her. She was late, and he didn't know what that meant. 'Had something happened to her? Was she still in France? Had she forgotten to stop by his

flat? Did she know what he had planned and was avoiding him?'
Twenty minutes and an eternity later his phone rang.

"Santi," Marisa said. "I just arrived at the station, and I have
something exciting to share with you. Are you still awake?"

"Just barely," James said. "I was thinking about going to bed
since you hadn't shown. I figured you must have eloped with
Rosado."

"That topic came up," Marisa said. "I will see you in about
fifteen minutes."

Marisa buzzed James's apartment from the building entrance
eighteen minutes and twenty-two seconds later. "It's me and it's
raining," Marisa said. "Hurry and buzz me in."

James met her at the door with a warm towel and a hot cup
of cocoa. "I have some snack food if you are hungry," James said.

"I'm great," Marisa said. "This is perfect." She dried her hair
and took off her windbreaker. She plopped down on the couch
and propped her legs on the coffee table. She smiled at James
and said, "Wow, what a day. I can't wait to tell you what I learned."

James sat down beside her and asked "It sounds important.
I guess it can't wait?"

"No, I really need to run this by you before I call my brother
in the morning," Marisa said. She jumped right into the history
of BAJO and David Rosado, about the most recent events, and
that there is possibly still a mole on Ernesto's staff. "So here is
the part important to you. David has offered to put BAJO at
your disposal as the CamCon clandestine intelligence collection
service." Marisa looked at James expectantly. When he didn't
jump up or show the least bit of enthusiasm, she immediately
became frustrated.

James could see Marisa's lower lip begin to grow as that
pouty face that he loved so much started to take shape. Just
as spontaneous as her mood swings, James leaned to her and
kissed her lips. "You have had hours to think about this. I have

had less than a minute," James said. "Give me some more details and why you believe that this is such a good idea." James was thinking about his promise to the world and in particular the CamCon members that the organization would be completely transparent. After her longer explanation, James said, "That is unbelievable and a great opportunity. Remove an enemy and make them one of your most valuable assets. It's biblical." He still wasn't sure how this was going to align with the values he was trying to instill in CamCon, but he would set that aside until he could talk directly with David Rosado.

"Before the night gets too late, I did have one thing I wanted to bring up," James said, wondering if now was really the best time, but knowing there would be no better time. Without further explanation, he got up and walked into his library and return with something in his hand. He stood in front of her and could not get his mouth to move.

"What is it?" Marisa asked, sitting up straighter and obviously worried.

"Since the day I met you, your presence has been bigger than life," James began. "And like standing in front of the painted mountains and arches near La Quiaca that top those in North America, or floating in Devil's Throat at the Cataratas de Iguazu that is taller and twice as wide a Niagara Falls in the U.S. with three times the water flow, or looking up at Aconcagua, higher than any peak in North America and second only to Mount Everest, or catching the King Crabs in the waters off Ushuaia at the southern tip of the world that are nearly twice the size of any in Alaska, it has been an overwhelming experience. I could go on, but I know I'm sounding like a travel brochure. Most of those things I have yet to actually experience for myself. But from the day I arrived I have been humbled by the enormity of Argentina and how even it pales in comparison to my experience with you."

"Are you saying I am fat?" Marisa asked smiling.

"I am saying that I have felt small, Marisa," James answered. "But I have learned that just like the narcissist or egotist is diluted or depreciated by trying to appear bigger, my smallness has enlarged my essence. I have never felt more alive and capable than when I am with you." This was not going as he had planned.

CHAPTER 34

Ponerse la Gorra

Literal Translation: Put on the police cap

Marisa's Explanation: Argentines don't like authoritarian behavior...except our own! There is always somebody who, in moments of joy, prefers to get serious. That's why we immediately order them to "take the hat off. **Don't Be So Serious.**"

"WHAT I AM SAYING, MARISA," James paused and then lowered to one knee, "is I love you, and I want to marry you. I want to spend the rest of my life with you. I want to have a family with you. Will you marry me?" He presented the ring he had in his hand and looked into Marisa's eyes.

"Santi, where did you get that ring?" Marisa asked.

"I will tell you if you give me an answer," James said.

"No matter my answer, you will tell me?" Marisa asked, mixing her broad smile with tears.

"For a girl who has a quick answer to everything, you sure are stalling," James said.

"James Santi Nathaniels," Marisa said. "I have wanted to marry you since the moment you left the country, and I had to chase you down in Missouri. I loved you after our first few weeks together. You could have asked me over our first ice cream cone, and I would have probably said yes. Yes, yes, yes, I will marry you. I only wish my parents, Otto and my brother were here so I could tell them."

"I think your parents might somehow know and I did ask Otto's permission and then your brother if I could ask you," James said. "I mean, I would have asked you anyway, but I wanted to do this right and I wasn't sure what that meant, so I talked to Otto about it."

"So Otto knew?" Marisa said, starting to cry. James slipped the ring on her finger. She couldn't keep her eyes off of her hand with the ring on it. The center facet held a large ruby with alternate diamonds and green emeralds surrounding it.

"After I had asked Otto's permission, he gave it with one caveat, that he could provide the wedding ring," James said. "I didn't think much more about it until I spoke with your brother and mentioned it to him in passing when he mentioned a dowry that Otto had prepared in his will for you." James didn't want to dwell on the tragedy of Otto's death, so he simply said, "I was planning on buying a ring and wanted your brother's opinion on what style you would like. Of course, we could have gone ring shopping together, but I really wanted to surprise you. Ernesto contacted Otto's family on his own, and they knew about the ring, as Otto had mentioned it to his cousin. This ring was given to Marie Antoinette by your Starhemberg ancestor, and it has been in the Habsburg family since that time. Otto felt it was time for it to be on a Starhemberg hand again. Otto's cousin told me that when Count Starhemberg gave Marie Antoinette the ring, he had noted in his journal that day that the future Queen of France had impressed him with her perseverance, presence of mind, her ease and her grace. Otto felt the same about you, and that is what reminded him of the ring. In a very real sense, this is Otto's wedding present to you."

"I will treasure it with all my heart," Marisa said.

James stood and pulled another ring out of his pocket. He placed it in Marisa's hand. It was a simple band. "I had picked this out before Otto's family contacted me and sent me that ring. I was going to return this along with my matching one, but thought I would offer it to you also, either as a piece of jewelry or as a wedding band, since you probably won't be wearing the Starhemberg jewel every day." Marisa took off the jewel and tried on the band. In James's viewpoint, the band was just as beautiful. It was a titanium band with lapis lazuli stone inlay around the outside of the band. "The dark blue with the tiny lines and flecks of gold reminded me of that day at Habsburg Rock above Bariloche and the lake. You held my hand, and that is when I think I wanted to marry you. I was trying to concentrate on your brother, but all I thought about was you."

"We are a pair, Santi," Marisa said. "I remember holding back some tears. I wasn't worried what others would think because of the momentous event Ernesto was announcing. But the tears were really for you and my fear that you would complete your work and return to your life in the United States."

"Ah, going home," James said now moving to sit beside her. "I don't even know where home is anymore, except that it is wherever you are. I have been so worried about you today, your trip to France to meet an unknown potential danger alone. Home is a precious thing, but it also defines a vulnerability I have come to face for the first time in my life. Home is a place, thus an internal domain and external surroundings. The internal is safe and secure. The external suddenly feels filled with threats and I, we, feel vulnerable. Otto told me recently that vulnerability is greater than will. He said will without vulnerability is prideful independence and that can be a dangerous thing, for people and for countries. Vulnerability without will is even worse. That creates a dependency. Together, will and vulnerability create a healthy interdependence that can face the hardest challenges together."

"Leave it to you and Otto to make the international political system sound romantic," Marisa said, kissing him on the cheek. "I want to be interdependent with you. Can we get married this afternoon?"

"That works for me," James said kissing her. "What about your brother and my family? They will want to be a part of a wedding, right?"

"And Gabriela, I think," Marisa added. "There is another factor as well. Ernesto is up for reelection. I am not a political expert, but a wedding of his sister would be a big event if we did it in Argentina, a plus for his campaign."

"Look who is making politics romantic," James said laughing.

"Would you be willing to wait?" Marisa said. "It would be at least a month to put a wedding together. It should take four months."

"Willing? Yes," James said. "Now that this is official my bias is for action. I struggle with patience when the goal is right in front of me."

"Santi, the goal is doing the right thing for the right reasons," Marisa said soothingly.

"You have many strengths and virtues, Marisa, but I am coming to see that volition is maybe at the top of your list and attributes."

"What exactly is volition?" Marisa asked. "My brother says I am volatile and he is probably right. I never saw that as a good attribute."

"You wear volatile better than anyone I know, Marisa, but volition is completely different," James said laughing again. "In fact, Otto and I were having this very conversation. I told him I thought there was something more important than will. His answer was vulnerability. I think it's volition."

"You are both crazy," Marisa said.

James almost pointed out that she said that as if Otto were still alive. Instead, he said, "Maybe it's just semantics, but it is important. Will, or willingness goes back to what we were just talking about. Will suggests a sense of absolute, autonomous, unbridled freedom to act. Volition is more important than will because to me it implies the power of choice. It is knowing that we can't do whatever we want and expect a successful result. Volition suggests an interdependency, whereas will is strictly independent. Will forces our values on principles. Principles are immoveable, and thus we often set ourselves up for failure. Volition is the practice of values to help us discover universal principles and eventually align our actions with those principles. It is being teachable so that in the long-run we can adjust our values with those unbending principles and not be tempted by a quick win that leads to long-term failures. Like you said, doing the right thing for the right reasons. That goes for you and me, CamCon, states, the world."

"Like your country training the Mujahidin to fight the Soviets in Afghanistan and then having Al Qaida bite the hand that nurtured them? Or allowing that little splinter group calling themselves the Islamic State to thrive because they are fighting against the Syrian Regime? It sounds a lot like taking a leap off a bridge and hoping to grow wings before hitting the river and rocks," Marisa said, thinking back to lessons in her own life.

"There are probably always unintended consequences, but yeah. Anyone can squeeze a short-term win out of a situation, but long-term success is the province of principles. Hey, speaking of bridges," James added, "I was going to tell you this later, but since you brought up bridges, as a wedding present I bought you a bridge."

"What?" Marisa asked, sure she misunderstood.

"Come to find out, in the United States, the Department of General Services sells old bridges. I mentioned to my sister Jessica that you love bridges. She told me about this program. The local state park bought one. It was in the news. So I checked into it, and I bought you a covered wooden bridge that was deemed unsafe and too narrow for automobile traffic. It is being installed on our land in Missouri, by the house."

"Say that again," Marisa said suddenly.

"Say what, that I bought a bridge?" James asked.

"No, Santi, where is the bridge being installed?" Marisa asked.

"Oh, on *our* land in Missouri," James said. "Our land. I am already thinking interdependently.

"That deserves another kiss," Marisa said. "Actually, one kiss for the bridge, and another kiss for the 'our.'"

Marisa's phone began to ring, and they both tried to ignore it.

The ring was insistent, and Marisa finally broke away and looked at the caller ID. "It's David Rosado," she said. "Do you want me to take it?"

"I am trying to like this guy," James said, "but he keeps giving me reasons to dislike him."

Marisa put the phone on speaker and clicked receive. "Hello, David," Marisa said. "I am with James and I have you on speaker."

"I am so sorry to bother you both so late at night," David said. "After you left my home I did some more research on the other JOAB, the operative that I was certain was in Argentina. I finally made a connection. The letter I have mentions this person has a Serbian ancestor. It took me several days to build a reliable gene-alogy of Danilo Ilić. Only tonight was I able to cross reference that list with any names in historical BAJO correspondence. Our files appeared completely void of any connections, except for an invoice I found for travel. The corresponding name checks out with a staff member on President Starhemberg's staff. Do either of you know Alberto Godoy?"

"We both know him," James said. "You are saying he is one of your spies?"

"I am not entirely certain what his directives were with the last Guardian, the last leader of BAJO, but a letter in my possession suggests he is more than just a clandestine information collector. He could be very dangerous."

"Are you absolutely sure about this?" Marisa asked. "Could this be a coincidence or pure supposition?"

"I am certain," Rosado said. "I am not certain what his mission is, but I fear President Starhemberg might be at risk. That is supposition, but I thought I should call you immediately to be on the safe side."

"Thank you, David," Marisa said. "I will call my brother and let him know right away."

"I will be at your service," David Rosado said, and the line went dead.

Alberto Godoy also just hung up his phone 7,000 miles and four time zones away. Gregor had botched the killing of Otto von Habsburg, and the smelly brute owed him one. "He had better get it right this time," Godoy told the phone. "If he does what he claims he can do, I will fill the vacancy in the Argentine presidency with the upcoming election, as well as seize leadership of BAJO and possibly the top spot at CamCon. Over time I can adjust that position from Administrator to Leader for Life, or Czar, like that wild Russian Putin just did in Moscow.

Gregor, a distant Serbian relative of Godoy, was mad. Angry at himself for failing with his first assignment, livid at the lucky punch American who foiled the easy hit, and mad at Godoy for pushing him around like he was a Croat. He would finish this assignment and then either leave the country or finish off Godoy. He lit another Murad cigarette, the only thing Turkish he allowed himself to enjoy and began planning the how and where of this task. Godoy had promised some vital information to make this as easy as possible.

"He had better deliver, or he will be the one feeling the might of Gregor," the angry and bored Serb mumbled.

Gregor had escaped his first attempt with the Hungarian quite easily. "Security in this country is not a problem," he told himself. That the Hungarian had been a Habsburg made the job a duty more than just a money-making event. Godoy had told him a woman had finished the job where he couldn't. This new target was supposedly some kind of historical royal with ties to the hated Habsburgs. That was good enough for him. 'Redemption of a sort,' he told himself. He could return home with some bragging rights and a wad of Euros.

That the target was the President of Argentina complicated matters, but it was an election year, so that opened up numerous possibilities. Gregor smiled as he thought of the still talked about assassination of the Habsburg Archduke. Just as the names of the Archduke assassins, Danilo Ilić and Gavrilo Princip, were still mentioned with pride in certain Serbian patriotic circles, so would the name of Gregor Jovanović.

Alberto Godoy did not trust Gregor with this mission. He was happy to pocket the BAJO funds the previous Guardian had sent him for the original plan by telling Gregor he had failed in his first assignment and would do this one for free. Gregor was incompetent, but also, untrustworthy. If he were caught, he would surely talk, and Godoy would most probably be implicated. Thus, Godoy planned to have a front row seat at the assassination, where he could close Gregor's mouth forever and become a hero at the same time.

CHAPTER 35

Ir a Llorarle/Cobrarle a Magoya
Literal Translation: To go crying to
(or get your money from) Magoya.

Marisa's Explanation: Magoya is the first name of a person whose origin, history, location, and other biographical data are totally unknown. But there is one thing we do know well: Magoya will never be there when we search for him. **Magoya represents an indubitable void that we all experience from time to time. We have never seen him and we never will.** We just know that if someone warns us: "Do not sell that thing to Fulano, because he never pays his bills," we do it under our responsibility. And if finally, Fulano fails to pay what he owes, our knowing friend will laugh and tell us to charge Magoya, who probably lives at the same place as Godot, get it? A little cross-cultural humor.

MARISA HUNG UP THE PHONE. "Ernesto is crushed. First Vangelina, now Alberto. He doesn't know who to trust or even if all his work is really worth it. I wish I were there to comfort him. He has no one there close to him."

"Any plans?" James asked. "Just arrest Godoy?"

"He wants to wait," Marisa said. "He is going to sleep on it and intends to talk with us in the morning. There really isn't any concrete evidence to go one. Just David's word. It's late, and I am not thinking very well."

"I hope he doesn't wait too long," James said. "We know there is a wolf in the henhouse and sooner or later something bad is going to happen."

"He wants to handle this delicately," Marisa said, rolling her eyes. "He doesn't want to pull the media's primary attention away from all the great things his administration has accomplished. I wonder sometimes, even with all the good he has accomplished, if it has been worth it. I mean, he has sacrificed his life, his love, everything for his country. Now he is talking about sacrificing that for a greater good embodied in CamCon, which still needs to be burped after eating."

"There is an extra bedroom here, with a lock on the door, if you want to sleep here tonight," James said, exhausted himself.

"Would I need the lock?" Marisa asked.

"No," James said. "But that was the room where," he began and stopped.

"Oh right, no way," Marisa said. "Walk me to a taxi, and I will go back to the hotel. I really miss Gabriela's place."

"And Gabriela, any chance for your brother and her?" James asked as he grabbed his apartment keys.

"I don't know," Marisa said. "It's obvious they still love each other, but they live in different worlds."

"Kind of like us?" James asked.

"Do we?" Marisa asked, not looking at him. "I know we have never talked about that, but maybe we should."

"The way I see it is, we need to leave both our worlds and build one together," James said opening the apartment door. ""It's not about what we give up, but what we want to build, together. Those celebrity couples who live on separate coasts in the U.S., or across an ocean, they aren't as interested in their 'us' as they are in their individual 'me.'"

"That's not fair, Santi," Marisa said. "Sometimes couples have to sacrifice for survival, or for a greater good, like a military person who has to serve remotely, or an economic refugee who has to live somewhere else, so his family won't starve, or to give their children a chance at a better life. There are hundreds of other reasons for being apart until being together can happen."

"True enough, but those are all choices," James said. "Some separations are required for survival, and that is a tragic category that all humankind should fight, but most are for something the couple is willing to strive for and sacrifice for. So what does sacrifice really mean? Giving up something for something you want more, I think. At some point, so many of these justifiable sacrifices stop becoming the temporary thing and the final goal. I never want that to happen to us. There is nothing I want more than us."

"I have never really experienced, or at least I don't remember an 'us' in my life," Marisa said. "I've had my brother, but that has not been the ultimate 'us' of a family in the full sense of the word. I want that more than anything else too."

"Do you think nations will ever have that goal, an interdependent 'us' rather than an independent 'me'?" James asked. "I know I always go back to the nation-state system, but for the moment, that is what I am sacrificing our 'us' for, and I wonder, as you do about your brother's efforts, if it is all worth it. I wish you didn't have to leave so soon."

"Being together, Santi," Marisa said, "is not always being physically in the same space. Presence is more than geography. Place, over the long–run is important, but we can be together in other ways. In purpose, in love, in identity, in a manner that keeps us together even when we are apart in other ways. We will figure this all out, and we will be together soon. For now, I need to return and help my brother sort things out. There is no reason we can't sort things out at the same time."

"Take good care of your brother," James said. "He is an example to the world and the world needs good examples more than ever. He has so many talents that touch so many lives. I suppose if we discover our talents as he has, our chief purpose would be to give of them freely." They said their goodbyes and shared a long embrace, then a black London taxi whisked Marisa away to her hotel. James was able to see her one last time, taking her to the airport for her flight to Buenos Aires, but they talked only of surface things. She departed, and James jumped back into CamCon with all his energy. He did take time the evening after Marisa left to send an email of support to President Starhemberg, hoping it would also reach Marisa's ear through him.

President Ernesto Starhemberg was struggling in the public polls. He had used up every favor and political debt to get the votes needed to pass his CamCon membership through Congress. It would be on the general election ballot, along with his presidency. He found himself spending more time defending CamCon and the loss of Cambalache as a purely Argentine resource of energy, profit, and power than any other issue while on the campaign trail. His past successes in domestic issues were rarely noted, and it seemed the public's memory of the achievements of the past four years had been forgotten. Marisa was an enthusiastic and steadfast support for her brother and often garnered more media coverage than Ernesto on any given day.

"I got this magnificent email from the love of your life," Ernesto shared with Marisa when they found themselves at the Quinta on the same night.

"You are the love of my life, big brother," Marisa said, seeing how exhausted he was.

"Yeah, right," Ernesto said. "I haven't gotten an email, text, or phone call from you the entire week since you have been home. How many times have you talked or written James? Maybe fifty times?"

"The number is insignificant, dear brother," Marisa said, her back suddenly extra straight. "It's the quality of the communications that matter. We are talking now, and that is what's important."

"I don't buy the quality over quantity argument," Ernesto said. "It takes both, but no complaints on my part. It somehow strengthens me that you and James have found each other. His email was also a strength to me. I almost didn't read the email because he started it by calling me a genius. I think the content is more applicable to you, my genius sister than me, but I enjoyed it just the same."

"And what did it say?" Marisa asked. James had not mentioned it to her in any of the over 100 times they had talked or texted. She would never admit that to Ernesto.

"It was about opposition," Ernesto said. "He ran down a list of significant changes or disruptions in world progress highlighting the author of the new and the challenge to that author. Like two sides of the same coin. Edison and Tesla, Bill Gates and Steve Jobs, Mozart and Salieri, Michelangelo and Leonardo da Vinci, Gould and Dawkins, Cope and Marsh. It was a fascinating romp through history. He told me he collected accounts of historic rivalries, partly because with every great discovery there is always a rivalry. His questions to me was, if there is a principle here, what is the Cambalache rivalry? What is the principal opposition to CamCon? He didn't answer the questions, but it has really had me thinking."

"You think Godoy or BAJO itself is the opposition?" Marisa asked. "I don't place BAJO in a rival category of opposition genius."

"You have to admit it has been odd that Cambalache has pretty much sailed through invention and deployment without significant direct challenge."

"And that has you spooked?" Marisa asked. "How about the Richter history of cold fusion and its ignominious failure as compared with Robert Oppenheimer's successes with fission?"

"Maybe, but I keep asking myself where these projects are going to hit a wall?" Ernesto said.

"My advice," Marisa said, "don't worry about it. Like you have done all your life, be the bigger person, in meekness and giving. I told you not to contact Gabriela, but I was wrong. I have learned it is best to error on the side of leniency. Tesla basically invented AC electricity and wanted to give it to the world for free. He had a vicious rivalry with Edison that is famous. But you never hear about the rivalry between Tesla and Einstein. Tesla disagreed with Einstein on relativity and took every opportunity to discredit it. Yet, when someone asked Einstein how it felt to be the smartest man alive, he purportedly said, "I don't know, you should ask Tesla." Now was that a sarcastic remark? I don't think so. That wasn't Einstein's style. He had a quick wit but was never into tearing down another person. Theories, indeed, but never people. He was the bigger person and thus any rivalry was diminished. I don't know about the rivalries James listed, but I will bet they could have been avoided with more of an abundance mentality."

"I wonder what Tesla or Einstein would have thought about you?" Ernesto asked. "You are certainly a peer, and yet the world is oblivious."

"Ha, Einstein was a ladies man and unfaithful to his first wife, but he had respect for intelligence, whether it was in a male or female body. He would have appreciated my work, but he would have made a pass at me. Tesla is an enigma on this subject. He never married, and I don't know if he had a romantic life. He respected women greatly but thought they should stay in their place. I would present my work to him with only my first initial and last name and then shock him when I actually met him."

"It is time for the world to know you, Marisa," Ernesto said.

"It's not important, Ernesto," Marisa said. "When you bring it up it always feels like pride motivating you. I don't need the notoriety."

"The most eligible bachelorette has bit the dust, and that will soon be in the news," Ernesto said. "Get used to it, Marisa, you will always be a media magnet."

The next day, almost as if Ernesto had prophesied it, the La Nación newspaper headline read: "Argentine Einstein, the Brains Behind Cambalache and the Starhemberg Presidency." The article outlined Marisa's brilliant leaps of insight in making Cambalache actually work and her theoretical physics research that built provable bridges between General Relativity and Quantum Physics.

"You need to get it over with," Ernesto said smiling. "I don't know who leaked this information, and I will try to get to the bottom of it, but you need to stop the vicious rumors attacking you, or I will. I can't sit here and listen to the ignorance of people saying you are an idiot in a beautiful body."

"And what about being the brains in your presidency?" Marisa asked. Can I talk about that? I couldn't politic my way into winning a spot on a local school board."

"Don't do this to explain my faults as their president," Ernesto said. "Do it to protect your character and good name."

"Fine, set up a meeting with the press," Marisa said. "I will do it if you are there with me."

A press conference was set up for that afternoon. Marisa tried to call James to talk with him about this, but he was tied up in meetings. She was afraid what her new notoriety would do to their relationship. She had not explained to him her actual impact in the Cambalache project. It simply never seemed necessary. The impromptu press conference was standing room only and was finally shifted to an outdoor venue, but securely within the courtyard at the Casa Rosada. Microphones were set up on both the ground floor and the floor above that surrounded the Moorish designed courtyard. Marisa wore a very feminine blouse and skirt and didn't look anything like a stuffy scientist or nerdy nuclear engineer. That was her plan, to simply be herself and not cater to anyone's expectations.

Her brief opening statement set the tone. "Many of you have attacked my possible inputs to cold fusion development because I am a woman. According to my fiancé, a beautiful woman." She figured she might as well announce her engagement, but tried to treat it like it was old news. "I am here to tell you that all men and women are equal, but we are not the same. I am not claiming to be a woman in a man's world, just a person in our world. I don't apologize for inheriting some of the beauty from both of my parents, or some of their mental capacity either. And I certainly don't apologize for my hard work at university. I do apologize to my understanding professors for my late work and late nights trying to find myself instead of focusing on my studies. I don't know what makes someone smarter than someone else, but I will tell you now, I won't be answering any questions if they include anything to do with comparing me with anyone else. It's my brilliant brother who is in politics, and he loves competition and elections, and since I have the podium at the moment, I will tell you he is the most selfless and inspired leader I have ever known. Argentina is blessed to have him at the helm of our ship. Now if you still want to talk about the boiler down in the engine room of that ship, ask away."

The questions were provoking, but Marisa never took the bait. She had nothing to prove, but she did admit that it was her breakthroughs that led to Cambalache's reality. She highlighted the work of others who also achieved new insights and that it was a team who harnessed cold fusion, not her individually. Many of her answers were a variant of "It's important to me that you know that I am an honest and caring person. I support my brother's vision for Cambalache and CamCon. I am engaged to the new, amazing in his own right, Administrator of CamCon and the previous Administrator was an important father figure in my life. And, I really don't care whether you know my part in this project or not."

There were a few questions about her relationship with James Nathaniels, and Marisa was afraid that she had just complicated his life. The press conference was coming to a close when a reporter from the newspaper Clarín directed a question to Marisa's brother. "President Starhemberg, do you feel threatened by your sister's brilliance?"

"I have basked in the brilliance of her life since I was a boy," Ernesto began.

As the President opened his mouth to elaborate, he fell backward as if he had been pushed by an invisible assailant. Before he hit the ground, the courtyard echoed with the sound of a muffled explosion. By the time the President crumpled to the floor, everyone knew he had been shot. Before the screaming and pandemonium began, a second shot was heard, but no one knew what the intended target was, as the President was behind the podium and two security agents were covering him. Many looked at Marisa, expecting her to be the other target. She had jumped to Ernesto but was being directed away by security. The screaming and crash of bodies attempting to find safety almost muffled the sound of a third shot that increased the turmoil to stampede levels.

Over the past day or two Alberto Godoy had noticed the very slightest of discomfort toward himself from the President and had deduced that there was a possibility the President knew Godoy was planning something. He had to act quickly. He made the anonymous tip to the newspaper about Marisa Starhemberg's starring role in Cambalache to create this opportunity. He had allowed Gregor entrance, along with late arriving members of the press, into the second-floor venue. Getting Gregor here on time for access to the conference was a major accomplishment. Godoy kept a close eye on Gregor, maintaining his distance but also a clear line-of-sight path to him. The moment Gregor made his shot, and Godoy saw the President go down, Godoy maneuvered to shoot Gregor. Gregor turned, either to escape or to look for Godoy. All Godoy knew was, when Gregor turned and saw Godoy, he broke into a broad yellow-toothed smiled and raised his weapon. Godoy shot first, hitting Gregor in the chest. Gregor continued to smile as if the bullet had bounced off him and fired at Godoy. Both hit the ground at the same time. People tripped over both bodies in their rush to escape an unknown danger. Godoy's subclavian artery had been nicked, and it took security nearly seven minutes to clear the second-floor balcony and arrive at his body. He appeared to have bled to death. He had no measurable pulse. He was declared dead on the way to the hospital. Gregor was dead before he landed on the marble floor, the single bullet puncturing his heart.

The status of President Starhemberg was unknown. Various eyewitnesses stated he had been killed. One cell phone picture by the Administrative Vice President of the Buenos Aires City Legislature showed the entire chest of the President soaked in blood. Others said they had seen his eyelids move as security whisked him away. The Country's Vice President, who had been in Comodoro Rivadavia giving an election speech, was rushed back to Buenos Aires. That night national news announced that the President was in a coma and the Vice President was managing governmental affairs for the time being. One radio station reported that the President had actually died, but the government was sorting through the implications of his death before officially declaring him gone. Some who wanted Cambalache to be owned, operated and leveraged for profit and power by Argentina took to the streets. Marisa had become invisible.

CHAPTER 36

A Grandes Males, Grandes Remedios
Literal Translation: Desperate Diseases, Desperate Remedies

Marisa's Explanation: **Drastic action is called for and is justified when you find yourself in a particularly difficult situation** and as long as that justification is moral and ethical. Few know this better than those of us who witness La Guerra Sucia, the Dirty War, when moral justification took a tragic and terrible wrong turn.

"PRESIDENT ERNESTO STARHEMBERG HAS RESIGNED the presidency. He has lived and nearly died by his openness and accountability," the newscaster reported on the third day after the assassination attempt. "Those who know him well, and that could be the claim of our entire nation, said his willingness to be open and without pretense or guile were the seeds of his meekness and his ability to truly listen to and connect with the people. His openness and close touch with those he served also almost led to his demise. Vice President Hugo Bullrich was sworn in this morning to serve the remaining three months of the four-year term. President Starhemberg's sister, Marisa Starhemberg and her North American fiancé were in attendance. President Starhemberg was not allowed to attend due to doctors' orders."

"If it is good enough for a sitting Pope and the King of Spain, it is okay for a sitting president to resign," Ernesto Starhemberg said.

"But you are needed badly," Pepe Peralta Monti said. "The people of Argentina need you, and the world needs your example. Cambalache and CamCon are nascent projects, not mature fixtures in the world's energy ecosystem. You said it yourself during your speech announcing Cambalache, never again will we turn our back on our destiny."

"The destiny of this country, Pepe," Ernesto said while grimacing to find a more comfortable position. "Not my destiny." His left shoulder was in a cast, and he was still on a pain IV. The single bullet that was meant for his heart had missed its mark but had shattered his clavicle. Pieces of bone had severed his brachiocephalic vein in his left shoulder, miraculously missing the adjacent artery, and caused some damage to the thoracic nerve and surrounding muscle. He still almost bled to death, but Pepe, accompanying the ambulance to the Sanatorio Otamendi Clinic, was able to control the blood loss.

"At least don't make a final decision until you are out of the hospital and feel better," Pepe suggested.

"My mind is working fine, Pepe," Ernesto said. "It's my shoulder that's broken, not my head. In fact, your passion suggests to me something I have thought about several times over the last year," Ernesto paused while studying Peralta Monti and then said, "Yes, that is exactly what I am going to do. He pushed a button near his bed, and a nurse ran into the room. Could you please gather whatever medical staff, patients that can walk, and visitors to the area around the nurses' station? I need to make a statement, and I want as many witnesses as possible."

"Yes, sir, right now?" the nurse asked.

"Right now," Ernesto said. Ernesto got up from his bed slowly, had Pepe switch his IV from the station connected to the bed, to the mobile one he used when visiting the restroom. He walked out into the hall three minutes later and was surprised at the crowd. Over 50 people were crammed into the open area and the four hallways that ran from the station. Several were recording him with their phones.

"Thank you for supporting one last wish," President Ernesto Starhemberg said, deeply moved. "I love you all, and there is nothing I will treasure more than to have served you. I practically had to break Hugo Bullrich's arm to run as my Vice President almost four years ago. He has told me he is not interested in running for President. Our opposition sees an opportunity here, but they are wrong. A better man than me will be our next president. I am announcing today that I endorse José Pepe Peralta Monti to be the next President of Argentina. He doesn't want the job either, but that is one reason he is the right man for this stewardship. Please pass the word to your friends and family and ask them to do the same. We need trusted leadership, and this is the person who I trust, with my life. It is a great thing to be passionate about the people, but an even greater thing to be passionate and extremely competent. Pepe is both."

Pepe was speechless. With everyone looking at him for his acceptance of President Starhemberg's endorsement he knew he needed to turn this down now or say something to support the President he loved. He took a deep breath and hoped his wife would understand. "I have never been comfortable with uncertainty, risk, or personal emotional exposure, but I have learned from President Starhemberg that keeping those doors open, despite my fears, leaves room for unimaginable opportunities. I am not perfect, neither is our President, but his outward confident and caring smile and inward brave and compassionate heart have taught me that imperfection has its bounds and that facing the unknown with the sparkle of enthusiasm makes all the difference. I love my country, and I am honored to follow in the footsteps of President Starhemberg if you will let me."

Pepe stared at his boss and chuckled, and then began to shake everyone's hands. James and Marisa wondered what was happening when they entered the supposedly private hall where Ernesto was recuperating. "So this is convalescing, Argentine style," James said with a soft guffaw.

Pepe shook their hands as they walked by and only said, "Ask Ernesto." Then he noticed James's huge smile and asked, "So did you know he was planning this?"

"Planning what?" Marisa asked. "What's going on? It looks like you just had a baby and you should be passing out bubble-gum cigars."

"Oh, well, I plead the Fifth," Pepe said. "Isn't that what you North Americans say? So why the huge grin. What's going on?"

"May I interrupt your party for an announcement?" James asked Pepe.

"No, Santi, not here," Marisa said, with a quiver in her voice.

"Might as well get it over with in front of a small group of strangers than in some other more formal fashion," James said.

"Okay, then, but make it simple and fast," Marisa said. "We came here just to tell Ernesto, remember."

"Everyone, may I have your attention," Pepe said. "James Nathaniels, fiancé to Marisa Starhemberg, has another surprise announcement. I have no idea what he is going to say, but it will be good. I have never seen him with such a broad smile."

"Marisa and I were coming here to share some news with President Starhemberg before it becomes public in an official announcement this evening," James began. "As you know, I am engaged to this magnificent woman, and I think the world of her. It appears that a group of Scandinavians also adore her. Marisa was informed about an hour ago that she is to be awarded the Nobel Prize in Physics for her work on Cold Fusion."

Everyone began to applaud and take pictures of Marisa with their phones. James held up his hand for everyone to quiet. "I have an additional announcement. Only one woman has been award two Nobel prizes, Marie Curie, for physics and chemistry. Only one other person has ever received the Nobel Prize in a science or literature and also the Peace Prize, which was Linus Pauling. His prizes were eight years apart." The room was buzzing with anticipation of the obvious announcement, but they were to be surprised once more.

"Not surprising, five Argentines have received the Nobel Prize in the past but," James paused for effect, "no brother-sister team, Argentine or otherwise, have ever been awarded a Nobel Prize in any category, until today. Ernesto Starhemberg and his sister, Marisa Starhemberg, are to be awarded the Nobel Peace Prize for their work in successfully making CamCon a reality."

The room erupted as if Argentina had just won the World Cup again. "Talk about going out on top," Pepe shouted in Ernesto's ear.

"You deserve a big chunk of that gold coin, Pepe," Ernesto said and then became silent. He smiled and shook people's hands, but if one looked closely, he was only in the room in body, not spirit.

The party went on until the nurse shift change. Ernesto was exhausted and only wanted to sleep. His upper torso was throbbing with pain. Despite the fatigue and discomfort he hugged his sister, whispered something in her ear, and even began to cry. "It's the painkillers. They make me emotional," Ernesto said.

Marisa and James were also exhausted. The shock of the attack, the constant recognition of both of them and now the additional notoriety was too much. President Bullrich had told both Starhembergs to stay at the Quinta de Olivos through the end of the presidential term. He had no interest in moving for just a few months and with the need for security until the attack was sorted out, privacy, and convalescing, the Quinta would offer just the right amount of safety and solitude. James had taken his old room, and it felt like his first few weeks getting to know the Starhembergs. Now he was practically family.

"What's the next step, Santi?" Marisa asked.

"How about get married and live happily ever after?" James said.

"Works for me," Marisa said, "but what I meant was, what about CamCon? Any thoughts on using BAJO, or whatever name they decide to call themselves? I owe David Rosado a call. He has been in the dark for days while his rogue operative has been running amuck in the Southern Cone."

"How's this for a name," James said. "HALO, Human Ascendency Liberty, and Order?"

"I will run it by him," Marisa said holding his arm as they walked the Quinta grounds. "Does that mean you are willing to take them up on their offer to become the CamCon clandestine intelligence service?"

"The world, starting with CamCon, needs to reboot when it comes to their stance on secrecy over transparency. Legitimacy and credibility of a government or organization often need to lean on plausible deniability and subterfuge for the protection of secrets. That is not my style, and it will not be the operating practice of CamCon, at least while I am in the leadership seat."

"So everything is to be completely open?" Marisa asked. "I am not sure Cambalache would be a reality today had it not been protected by a shroud of secrecy."

"You are right, it wouldn't be what it is, but it still could have happened. Except for your brilliance, it might not have happened at all. With many brilliant minds together, it could have happened, maybe, without you. The cloak of invisibility is a great trick, you should invent it, but there are other ways, abundance ways, to get things done. Secrecy is an important tool in a zero-sum game. I certainly don't advocate breaking the rules of secrecy to achieve transparency, but I do believe in making new rules if one has the chance. The way the world works now, one country wants something that other countries don't have. That gives them leverage in the big game. I get it, if everyone is playing by zero-sum rules, it's dangerous and nearly impossible to have an abundance mentality. CamCon has the opportunity to make new rules, however, so why not try?"

"CamCon can only try because it has the leverage of Cambalache, which is a zero-sum leverage point," Marisa countered. "That feels a little hypocritical to me."

"I know," James said. "But I was handed the plate with the food already on it. It's a conversation I want to have with Pepe and your brother soon. I am sure they stepped through this conundrum already. I am guessing that they felt they had to maintain leverage in one world while trying to create another."

"Could be," Marisa said, sounding appeased. "I was never brought into those conversations. I was so focused on hydrogen nuclei and nuclear binding energy curves that I probably wouldn't have been much help even if they had involved me in those conversations. What about privacy?" Marisa asked as the thought came to her.

"A person should be able to go to the bathroom without the world watching, but you can't have clandestine meetings, or secret intelligence collection and claim a privacy clause or non-disclosure agreement to keep it hidden. Medical records, personnel files, electronic passwords, and safe combinations, should still be guarded of course. An abundance perspective should not make us stupid or naively trusting that there are no criminals or people that would take advantage of transparency. In fact, transparency only works with trust that professionalism is also respected."

"So 'no' is the answer I pass on to David?" Marisa asked.

James was quiet for a brief moment and then said, "I want to talk with him, but here is what I think: If all information is available, there is no need for secret collection. The problems are, that is not the situation in the world today—maybe tomorrow, and the information must also be freely given, not coercively taken and by coercive I include clandestine collection. But here is where I think Rosado and his group might fit. Anonymity is not subterfuge. BAJO, or HALO, or whatever they call themselves could be anonymous, but not a secret collector; declared, but not identified. Loyal to the information, not to CamCon, or any other country or organization. They could collect, analyze and provide in an open forum the data, knowledge, and intelligence they produce. Unbiased information and thought are rare things in the world. Of course, people will still use it for their own purposes, but the perturbations of bias will be dampened with additional credible reporting."

"I lost you with that last statement," Marisa said. "I am not sure who should be getting a Nobel Prize in this relationship."

"Prizes are not given for common sense," James said. "That's all this is. In fact, common sense is often the first idea run out of town with threatening pitchforks and tar. There was a time not long ago in the United States when there was such a division between the political parties that if one side had an idea, it was automatically lampooned by the other side, no matter the merits of the issue. If one leader did something or didn't do something, the opposition highlighted it as a terrible weakness or flaw, even if the same or similar action had been taken by the accusing party only months or a few years prior. It was ridiculous. That has slowed somewhat with the Marcasano Presidency, and now the general populous rejects that type of childish attack. It just took one person to say, we aren't going to play that game."

"He seems like a good person, Marcasano," Marisa said. "But honestly, I am having trouble trusting anyone right now."

"I'm with you," James said. "That is where governments are now. No one trusts them. They self-servingly leak something about a covert action by an "unnamed source who cannot officially report because they have not been authorized," James said as he made comma marks with his fingers in the air. "At the same time, they still keep the program or events officially secret from their citizens, who might actually want to add their wisdom and even debate the appropriateness, morality, and efficacy of that issue. Maybe I am the naive one in my transparency approach, but I don't want to operate as we have in the past."

"Speaking of scary government actions," Marisa said, "Ernesto told me when we were embracing that Alberto Godoy's body has disappeared. No one knows who took it or why. He said to stay vigilant. There may be other operatives who have a vendetta or sick plan to carry out."

"Wow, shades of Evita Peron," James said. "Disappearing bodies is an Argentine tradition."

"How about we disappear, Santi," Marisa suggested.

EPILOGUE

Al Fin es Debido el Honor
Literal Translation: At Last is Due the Honor

Marisa's Explanation: Problems and misfortunes along the way can be forgotten as long as the end is satisfactory. This doesn't mean the ends justify the means—Argentina has danced to that tune and found it tragic. It does mean that **all the hardship if the right thing is done for the right reasons, is worth it**.

JAMES AND MARISA WERE MARRIED in a quiet ceremony by Archbishop Poli at the Quinta de Olivos in late November on a perfect summer day. James's entire family was in attendance. Marisa requested the ceremony take place in English so her new family would feel at home. None of the Nathaniels felt at home, and they loved it. Ernesto attended, but Marisa could tell he was not fully there. James seemed at peace, even happy, with Ernesto's attitude. Something about a painting he had received in the mail from Gabriela. Pepe Peralta Monti took time out from his campaigning to be there. He was twenty points ahead in every poll with the election only two days away. The most watched couple in the world, according to People Magazine, left on their honeymoon with planned visits to Morocco, Italy, Austria, and culminating in Scandinavia where Marisa would represent herself and her brother in accepting their Nobel Prizes.

On 10 December, Marisa was awarded her Nobel Prize and delivered her acceptance lecture. That same day, in Buenos Aires, José Pepe Peralta Monti gave his inaugural address as the newly elected President of Argentina.

James and Marisa were officially scheduled to travel to London where they would take up residence so James could continue his duties as the Administrator, no longer the interim placeholder, of the Cambalache Confederation. Instead, they disappeared from public view. They flew to San Miguel de Allende, Mexico to deliver Ernesto's Nobel Prize to him. He and Gabriela were married in a quiet ceremony with just the four of them, plus Jacey Nathaniels who was also living there as artist protégé to Gabriela.

On their last day in Mexico, Marisa asked Ernesto to take a walk with her. "How are you doing big brother? I have been worried about you."

"I am doing better," Ernesto said. "Much better."

"What happened, or do you know?" Marisa asked.

"What are you asking about?" Ernesto asked. "About Vangelina, Otto, Alberto, me?"

"You Ernesto," Marisa said. "You. It's like you were defeated. You checked out of life."

"No, I hadn't checked out, Marisa," Ernesto said. "I checked in. I lost Gabriela once, I was willing to sacrifice whatever it took to not lose her a second time. Let the world think I was running away, that I was a coward, or that I was defeated as you said. It's not that important. I knew I couldn't come here and have the life Gabriela and I wanted if I resettled in San Miguel de Allende while still seen as the kingmaker and power behind some world events—none of which I really ever was, but the world wouldn't believe it. The things I wanted to accomplish are going strong. Argentina is in great hands, as are Cambalache and CamCon. That's what's important, not my reputation or public status. You had to come here almost incognito. I can walk the streets without anyone caring who I am or what I can or can't do for them."

"So your loss of the old Ernesto spark was an act?" Marisa asked.

"No act," Ernesto said. "Our Grandmother's death was part of someone's tragic agenda. I don't really know whether our parent's death was an accident or something else. Vangelina's betrayal hurt, Otto's resulting death was a meaningless tragedy, and Alberto Godoy's duplicitousness seared my core. I am just good at keeping everything inside." They walked in silence, feeling the sun and hearing the coarse dirt on the trail behind the art gallery crunch under their feet. They watched a lizard cross their path, and Ernesto said, "There are millions of people that have it much worse than you and me, so I don't want to complain or whine. Yet, everyone's challenges, and we all have them, are relative. That is, I don't think we should ever compare one with another. They are all tailored made, just for us. Mine led me here, so in a way I am grateful. I only wish Otto could come for a visit now and then. I will be alright sis. Gabriela is the best medicine in the world. Don't you and James be strangers, though."

James also had a parting conversation with Ernesto. It seemed Ernesto was sharing his wisdom one last time before setting his world leader hat on the shelf. "So can you bring yourself to call me Ernesto?"

"With effort," James said. "You will always be the consummate leader to me. And you know, Gabriela still has the mural to complete at the CamCon Headquarters. You could accompany her. I would always appreciate your advice."

"Here is my best and last advice, James," Ernesto said with a tired smile. "Wake up each morning to the new gift that it is. Celebrate its surprises, and make sure you are present for the wisdom it has to share so you understand what must be done.

And by all means within you make sure you are standing tall to do it. Don't be encumbered by yesterday or fearful of tomorrow."

"You can have my job anytime," James said, "if you get tired of the quiet life."

"What you are really saying is," Ernesto said chuckling, "you want me to play Mexican tag team Lucha Libre wrestling so you can live the quiet life. I don't know if I want to put on a mask and a pair of leotards."

"Ha," James said. "There is a famous luchador named El Hijo del Santo. Your masked wrestling name could be Hermano de Santi," James offered.

"I'll think about it," Ernesto said. "Now one last thought that I hammered out with Pepe, Otto, and Alberto a few years ago that I wanted to pass on to you. What makes a great nation-state is not always what makes a great world, or even a great global organization, like CamCon. Don't follow the old rules. Of course, alignment of values and principles always applies, but the issue is in the definition and measure of great. Nation-states usually measure that in election cycles or annual GDP, or some other short-term measure. CamCon needs to always think of the long-term."

"And the definition of great?" James asked.

"Significantly above the normal or average," Ernesto said. "But you see, that is a comparison, designed to keep everyone thinking the same way. Don't follow the old rules. Power, influence, wealth—those are the old rules. Service to the greater good, sustainability, meaning making—might provide insight to potential new rules. You know, Otto talked to me about the conversation he had with you on the most important thing a nation-state needed. I guess my answer got you two started when I mentioned will. He told me his idea was vulnerability, and I understand from Marisa your response is volition. Can I have a second chance at a reply, an answer I never fully gave in the first place?"

"I believe in second chances," James said.

"I like your triumvirate of will, vulnerability, and volition, but none of those concepts are safe in the hands of a nation-state or other governing organization, without a system or process of moral meekness to provide boundaries for the practice of those words. The Bible, and the God who gave us its words, were not mistaken in the wise council that the meek will inherit the earth. Only the meek will be teachable enough to learn from your definition of volition. Only the meek will employ raw will with compassion instead of oppression. The vulnerable will be crushed without the power of meekness."

"Meekness is almost synonymous with weakness, isn't it?" James asked.

"Meekness is anything but being weak," Ernesto said. "In open learning mode, a person or a governing body is emotionally driven to provocation but is more patiently accommodating. Self-mastery defines the meek because they are those who learn from their follies. Moral courage, doing the right thing for the right reasons—my direction to you not too many weeks ago, and trust by others because the meek are not pushed here and there by the winds of fashion or unjust pressures."

"The world really needs you and that kind of wisdom, Ernesto," James said.

"Yes!" Ernesto said raising his arms in the air.

"So you are willing to return to some public leadership role?" James asked.

"No way," Ernesto said. "I'm just grateful I finally got you to call me by my first name. Now off with you. Take good care of my sister, and we will see each other soon enough."

Marisa and James traveled to Missouri while still under the radar. They enjoyed the anonymity provided them by the locals and returned the favor with an authentic and growing relationship that made everyone feel unique and special, especially Marisa.

"I could live here and feel at home," Marisa said on their last day there as they sat in the shade of their very own covered bridge.

"We would have to invest in an ice cream start-up because I don't think I could live without dulce de leche ice cream," James said. "How about we live in London while CamCon gets its feet on the ground, but very soon set up residence in Bariloche and here?"

"With visits to Mexico?" Marisa asked.

"It's the perfect waypoint traveling both north and south," James said.

They were interrupted by James's dad who thought he knew where to find them. "You have a visitor up at your house," he said out of breath.

"It's our last few hours here," James said. "Who wants to see us? If it is the media, we promise to talk to them next trip."

"It's President Marcasano," James's dad said.

"We'll be right there," James said with a questioning look.

"I'll head back to your house and tell him you are on your way. I voted for the guy. I can't wait to actually meet him."

After James's dad was far enough away, Marisa said, "Let's make him wait." She offered a sensual smile and explained, "I had planned to seduce you and see if we could start our family right here on our bridge. I love the metaphor."

"Hmm, I love the, um, metaphor too," James said kissing her.

"I know," Marisa said standing up trying to sound defeated and frustrated. "We have to go see the most powerful man on the globe, but I am going to hold you to this metaphor, Mr. Nathaniels.

They arrived at the house minutes later. "Mr. President, I am surprised and delighted that you have dropped in for a visit," James said, not sure what would be appropriate.

"I am told by your father that it was a fifty-fifty shot that you would even come up to the house to meet me," President Marcasano said. "I am glad you did. Thank you."

"How did you know we were here?" Marisa asked.

"I am the President of the United States," President Marcasano said. "Actually I picked up the phone and called James's dad. It ends up your dad voted for me, and we have become good friends. I wanted to give you a wedding present, and I didn't know when you would be able to drop by my house, so I thought I would stop by yours." He nodded at a Secret Service Agent who brought a framed painting to the President.

"This is by my favorite artist," the President said. "He coincidentally is Argentine," he added, looking at Marisa.

"Raul Alonso," Marisa said. "Where did you find this? His works are hard to come by."

"I am the President of the United States," President Marcasano said again trying to keep a straight face. "Actually I picked up the phone and called President Peralta Monti. It ends up he knows some Argentines that know some Argentines that were willing to sell this particular work, knowing it was going to you two.

The work was a large pastel drawing entitled Espiral II. Deep browns and tans with hints of other colors framed a broken ribbon spiraling around itself. It looked like a person, but then a journey, or maybe a goal achieved, but not without sacrifice.

"This work reminded me of the two of you, and I am honored to give it to you," President Marcasano said. "It's a personal gift, not a gift from the United States. I wanted my wife to be here also, but schedules did not allow it. I just wanted you both to know I value your friendship and your wisdom. There will be no media coverage of this visit. I don't want you to think I am trying to be seen with the most interesting couple in the world, but if you ever want to stop through Washington, DC, I would love a photo op with you," he added with a smile.

"So two other quick items if you have time?" President Marcasano asked.

"Absolutely, sir, James said. "We were just going to sort out a metaphor, but we have time."

Marisa punched James in the arm. President Marcasano didn't ask what that was about. He said, "First, I want to know, some other time, how you and this community have such a trusting and open relationship. I am the President of the United States; okay, that joke is getting old. Sorry, my wife usually keeps me in line. What I mean is, my security team asked a few directions, and no one wanted to tell us where you might be. It's like you are family and they didn't care who was looking for you."

"Transparency and ice cream," James said. "I will explain some other time."

"I would love to live in a place like this," President Marcasano said. "These people humble me as I realize this is real America and I get to represent them. Cheesy, but the truth."

"The second thing?" Marisa asked, hoping to get off the subject of her speech the day she first arrived here.

"Right," the President said. "When I called President Peralta Monti, he asked me to tell you something that will become public knowledge next week. It seems you had some conversations with the British government since you have been in London, James. Your efforts have come to bear fruit."

Marisa looked at James and said, "What is he talking about Santi?"

"Your husband simply pointed out to the British government that Argentina had freely given away a very valuable island, Huemul where I understand Cambalache is housed, to the world. It was time Great Britain gave away freely an island to Argentina. It seems they saw the logic in his full proposal and the Falklands will become the Malvinas very shortly."

"There was a little more to it than my involvement, sir," James said. "It didn't hurt that one of the reasons they were holding onto the islands were the potential petroleum reserves in the area, made nearly irrelevant with Cambalache's free power. The big thing was really President Peralta Monti's strategy to downplay the imperialism and nationalism that defined the Islands' past and authentically want to support the Islander's themselves. Win the people, not the island, then the people will give you the island."

"Yes, President Peralta Monti told me where that idea came from," President Marcasano said. "When you get CamCon on its feet, would you like to take a look at the Israeli-Palestinian situation and see if you have any ideas?"

"Oh, I have some ideas, Mr. President that I think might work," James said.

"Does it also involve ice cream?" President Marcasano asked.

"I hadn't thought of that, but it could," James said smiling.

The President departed, and James and Marisa had time to visit their bridge one last time before saying goodbyes and departing for London. On the plane, they received word from HALO's David Rosado that Alberto Godoy had been spotted alive in Serbia. It seems he was found to be barely alive and was taken from the morgue by the new and now former JOAB in Buenos Aires. He was hidden while he regained strength and then escaped, supported by a significant amount of cash taken from BAJO coffers he and this misguided previous JOAB made their way to the Balkans. Godoy is purportedly plotting to reinstate the Serbian monarchy, with the help of Czar Putin of Russia.

Additional works on sale by this author:
(recent works available at Amazon.com)

Transitions from Military Rule in South America: The Obligational Legitimacy Hypothesis
Published by Naval Postgraduate School Press, 1987,
210 pages; Approved for public release.

Long-term Success: A New Paradigm for Personal and Enterprise Achievement
Published by Byblos Press, June 2003; 40 pages;
ISBN 0-9746003-1-8

The Seeds He Planted
Published by Byblos Press, December 2007
ISBN 978-0-9746003-2-1

Nahum's Story
Published by Byblos Press, December 2007
ISBN 978-0-9746003-3-8

Media in the 21st Century: Meet-Up or Meltdown in the Meaning Marketplace
Published by Byblos Media, June 2010; 583 pages
ISBN 978-0-9746003-6-9

Conversations Among Butterflies
Published by Byblos Media, August 2015; 393 pages;
ISBN 978-0-9746003-7-6

Kitab Kabbani
Published by Byblos Media, November 2015; 407 pages;
ISBN 978-0-9746003-8-3

Chinese Circus
Published by Byblos Media, 2016, 437 pages;
ISBN13 978-0-9746003-9-0

Upcoming Fiction and Non-Fiction works by this author:
see www.mike-mitchell.com

For more information:
www.mike-mitchell.com

Sign up for the author's mailing list at:
www.eepurl.com/bviacf

Or scan the QR code